The Taste of Lies

The Halcyon Universe

Mindi Briar

MINDI BRIAR
Hopeful, Inclusive Futures

Mindi Briar

Contents

Author's Note

In my ideal future, there is space for everyone to find their happy ending. As part of my commitment to promoting diversity, I want to take the opportunity to uplift diverse voices when I can. Please check out the recommendations list in the acknowledgements section for a reading list that spotlights M/M romance by men and transmasc authors.

This book is intended for adults and may contain themes that are not suitable for younger readers. Below I've written a spoiler-free overview of some of the potentially disturbing themes. I encourage everyone to make informed choices about the books they read and to feel empowered to put this book down if it's not right for them.

- Domestic abuse (implied, off-page, and/or threatened)

- Sexual assault (implied, off-page, and/or threatened)

- Discussion of (past) suicide

- Acts of terrorism

- Child endangerment & kidnapping

- Strong language

- Violence and character death

- Non-graphic depiction of sex work

- There are no on-page sex scenes included in this book.

I dedicate this book to the state of American politics in the years 2023-2025.

Thanks for all the inspiration.

Part One

DAYONE

Year 3750 DE, Week 45

Chapter 1

CONCERT HALL, THE IMPERIAL MOON PALACE

JED

The concert hall is an ocean of ecstatic screams and brilliant light. All I can do is surf it. When I'm onstage, nothing makes sense but the guitar strings under my fingers. I focus on building the music to a fever pitch to match the energy the audience is pouring onto us.

They're nothing but shrieking darkness in front of me. The stage lighting dazzles my eyes and blurs their faces. Flashing them a smirk and a wink, I bask in the answering swell of sound.

Andi, our keyboardist, trained me well. She's the one who knows how to work the crowd with an expression, a gesture, a perfectly executed body roll or shake of the ass. When we were thrown together as a band, training our undercover personas to infiltrate the Imperial Moon Palace, I had zero charisma, stiff as an uncracked glowstick. Andi made me pull faces in the mirror for hours on end until those muscles learned the art of flirtation.

The things I fuckin' do for this mission.

I let the guitar's notes linger as the song ends. Then I hear a soft, deep voice murmuring in my earpiece: "Target in sight. Middle hoverpod. The plan is a go."

I can't respond because I'm mic'd up. But I know the other four people onstage are hearing the same voice, and though we're bowing and throwing kisses and bantering with the crowd, we've all gone as tense as the strings under my fingertips.

The next song passes in a blur. My body knows what to do when my mind is elsewhere. Coax the right sounds out of the instrument in my hands. Smile and stick my tongue out. Roll my hips and toss my ginger hair around like I'm the hottest shit this galaxy has ever seen.

And the whole time, I'm plotting murder.

Chapter 2

CONCERT HALL, THE IMPERIAL MOON PALACE

SARAY

This concert blows. I can't believe Her Grace insisted on *using* the tickets she bought months ago to see this mediocre rock band.

I'm pretty sure she only bought them in the first place because she found out I'd slept with one of the members and got curious. But that's *long* over now, and it's uncharacteristic of Her Grace to put up with ear-grating "music" just to inspect one of my exes. She's the sort of person who exclusively listens to calming nature sounds at home.

Maybe it's just that she can't sense what I can. My unique cocktail of genetic modification allows me to taste and smell the intent behind people's words. And every song by Tarantula, the inexplicably popular band taking the Imperial Moon Palace by storm, is redolent of cinnamon. The taste of lies.

Our hoverpod floats high above the crowd on the dance floor. Only three concert-goers are VIP enough to warrant their own private pods at tonight's performance. The other two are Prince Alvin and Prince Jinan, high-ranked sons of the Emperor. And then there's our lady: Her Grace Geneva Milagro, primary consort of the Emperor.

Nuala, one of my fellow ladies-in-waiting, steers the hoverpod back and forth to give us a dynamic, unobstructed view of the stage. Her Grace sits in front, flanked by her two bodyguards. I and the other four ladies-in-waiting are seated behind her. We're here to attend to her every need and, if necessary, to shield her from dangers that might be lurking in the crowd.

Because, as the Emperor's current favorite among his scores of wives, Her Grace might as well have a target painted on her exquisitely embroidered overrobe.

The only person on this moon who has more jealous eyes aimed at him, more assassination attempts thrown in his path, is the Crown Prince Jinan, the man Emperor Soren is said to be grooming as his heir. With close to a hundred children vying for their place in the succession—a place determined by how much the Emperor likes them, not necessarily by birth order—the Imperial princexes will do nearly anything to claw their way up another rung.

Ironically, the Emperor himself remains in little danger. He rarely shows himself in public, and when he does, he's so well protected that no one would dare assault him. The penalty for one of his consorts taking out a rival or a princex murdering one of their siblings would be a slap on the wrist compared to the fire and brimstone that would rain down if someone attempted to kill His Imperial Majesty. Death would be a blessing and a relief after the torture that poor unfortunate would endure.

The band below wraps up their latest blast of noise they call a "song," taking bows and working the crowd with winks, smiles, and arms flung around each other's shoulders. It's a smoke screen cleverly designed to make their audience forget that their music sucks. I lean back in my seat, mentally rolling my eyes as I idly scan the crowd below.

My stomach lurches as I lock eyes with someone staring up at us. The dark room, hazy with fake smoke, obscures their features. All I get is a flash impression of dark hair and an intense gaze behind a sparkling veil that drapes across their nose and mouth. Then Nuala steers the hoverpod to the side to avoid another hovering royalty-filled private box, and I lose sight of them again.

I lean forward and tap Autumn, one of Her Grace's guards, on the shoulder. "Noticed someone watching us in the crowd," I murmur. "Be on the lookout."

She nods, bracing herself on the edge of the pod to scan the room.

Without taking her eyes from the stage, Geneva says, "People always watch the nobles in their hovering boxes." I catch a whiff of lemongrass from her words. She's trying to soothe us, but she's anxious, too.

"Can't be too cautious, Your Grace," Autumn says. "Destra, you double-checked the blast shield on this thing?"

The other bodyguard nods. "Twice. If anyone shoots at us, it'll bounce right off."

And probably hit some hapless bystander in the crowd. I wince. For the sake of everyone in this concert hall, I hope none of our enemies are quarkbrained enough to try anything.

The band leaves the stage for a break, leaving only one of their backup singers, a woman with a dark-blue bob. Her voice is quite good. Accompanied by her own soft keyboard notes, she sounds much better when she's not fighting to be heard over the male singer's rough growl and the other band members mangling their instruments.

Below us, the audience lifts their hands to display the glow-bracelets distributed by the band. It's a luminescent sea, surging against the stage like waves on the shore. The keyboardist's voice is a hypnotic siren song. I've had earplugs in since the beginning of the concert, and only now am I tempted to remove them.

But I can't let myself relax when I still smell cinnamon.

The other members return to the stage, carrying long, flat oval boards under their arms. They've changed costumes from dark, gothic-inspired leather pants and tops made of chains. Now they're in skintight bodysuits with neon slashes down the side. They launch into another punishingly upbeat number. I wedge my earplugs deeper in.

As the song ramps up, the band members mount the hoverboards they brought onstage and zip across the crowd. The keyboardist stays behind—I guess her instrument wouldn't fit on a board—but the drummer abandons his drumset to do daring loop tricks. The crowd roars.

The rest of the band aren't quite as daring, but they do a creditable job of playing guitars or singing while zipping a few meters above the crowd. One of the guitarists skims close to Geneva's box, trailing his fingers across Nuala's outstretched hand. He flashes me a smirk, tossing shoulder-length ginger hair.

Jedrek Blaze. The man I mistook for a courtesan a couple of months ago. The man who pretended he wanted more from me, when all his kisses tasted like deception.

I meet his shocking blue eyes for an instant, and my heart thumps in spite of myself. He's committing treason against the concept of music, but the man is handsome enough to make up for it. His trimmed pale stubble of a beard, sexily smudged eyeliner, and the artfully ripped, unnecessarily tight pants he favors are all part of selling the lie.

I jerk my eyes away from his, tossing my hair and pointedly looking at one of his bandmates instead.

That's when the hoverpod just a few meters behind us explodes in a fiery *BOOM*.

I shriek and duck. Jagged pieces of metal hurtle toward us in my periphery. I dive toward the center of the pod to cover Geneva with my body, ending up in a heap with the other ladies doing the same. Our pod's force shield activates, deflecting the shrapnel. Below, joyous screams turn to panicked ones.

Jed drops away, fleeing back to the stage. Nuala takes control of our hoverpod, speeding toward the upper-level dock. I fight the acceleration force to turn and stare at the billow of smoke behind us, clinging to the seat for stability.

With its hover mechanism knocked out, the wreckage of the other pod is plummeting. The crowd surges toward the exit, creating a bottleneck.

As Nuala guides Geneva's pod safely into its dock, the damaged one crashes to the ground. My stomach gives a sick lurch. There's no way the people on board the pod survived—let alone anyone the pod landed on.

"Come on, come on!" Destra yells. "Move it, Saray! We gotta go!"

I tear my eyes from the crash site, climb out of the pod, and sprint after Her Grace as Autumn hustles her down the corridor.

Just as we reach the zip-lift, a figure in a dark red robe pushes in front of us. Destra throws herself in the person's path, but Geneva puts a quelling hand on her shoulder. "It's all right," she murmurs. "They're a friend."

With a jolt, I recognize the sparkling veil hiding the interloper's face. This is the person I saw staring up at us from the audience.

"For you." Their voice is a husky whisper as they pass Geneva a folded piece of paper. I catch my breath. To send and receive offline messages indicates the parties have something to hide.

For that matter, so does the veil. Geneva might recognize this stranger, but the rest of us don't—and apparently Geneva prefers it that way.

I want to question them, to taste more of their words, but they disappear into the growing crowd. Autumn and Destra hustle us toward the zip-lift, shamelessly using Her Grace's status to cut the line.

Geneva's already tucked the note away. When I ask, "Who was that?" she pretends she didn't hear me.

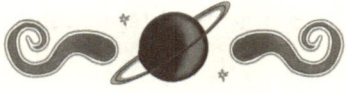

"I t was Prince Alvin's pod," Nuala reports later, after Destra and Autumn see us safely back to Geneva's suite of private rooms. "He and a couple of governors' daughters were in that box. All three confirmed dead."

Pearl and Yumiko gasp nearly in unison. Yumiko looks like she might cast up. I'm surprised she even came to the concert tonight—she's a bit of an agoraphobe. I doubt we'll be able to convince her to leave the suite for months thanks to this incident.

"What about the people in the audience?" I ask. "Did anyone get hurt when the pod crashed?"

Nuala flicks her finger across her scroll-tablet. "They're still counting the injuries. They think at least six other people died, but they haven't released names yet."

Fuck. I know I'm supposed to be more torn up about the Emperor losing yet another son to an assassination, but Prince Alvin was a glitch to me the one and only time I talked to him at a party. (He referred to me as "the help" and then handed me his empty cocktail glass like I was a serving bot.) I feel worse for the poor souls who just wanted to listen to some mediocre music and lost their lives as collateral damage.

But I'm not allowed to say that. Unspoken rule of the Moon Palace. We all have to live in silent agreement that some lives are worth more than others, whether or not they deserve to be.

"Do they know who did it?" Kina asks.

Nuala shakes her head. "Had to be one of the other princexes, though, right? Who else would—" She bites off the end of the sentence, but we all know what she was about to say. *Who else would give a shit about Prince Alvin?* He wasn't even in the top ten for succession. Top twenty, maybe. He'd only have hit the top ten if we were ranking the Imperial princexes by narcissistic assholery. He hadn't even (as far as I know) flared off anybody important recently.

"The person wearing the veil," I say quietly. Nuala raises an eyebrow at me. "They were staring at us right before it happened. Then they accosted Geneva afterward. Do you think they could have had something to do with...?"

"Oh, probably not, honey." Pearl consoles me with a pat on the shoulder. "Even if they did, we couldn't have done anything."

To save Alvin? No. Doubtful that I would've, even if I could—though I'd have liked to save those poor girls and the audience members they crash-landed on.

But what if the target had been Geneva? What if it was our box that had gone up in flames?

What if it was supposed to be?

We're all dancing around saying it out loud, but we all know that Alvin was the lowest-value target for an assassination attempt at the concert tonight. Geneva and Prince Jinan are both in coveted positions of power. Plenty of people, both princexes and Imperial consorts, would kill to take their place.

What if the assassin hit the wrong pod? What if it was Geneva who was supposed to die tonight?

I approach the corner sofa where Geneva is lying, a cold cloth over her eyes. "Your Grace," I say quietly. "Who was that stranger who slipped you that note?"

My lady lifts the cloth from her eyes and pushes herself upright. "If you know what's good for you, you'll forget you saw that," she says sharply. "It was careless of both of us."

"I don't think Alvin was meant to die tonight," I murmur.

"Perhaps not. But Princex Somin is not an assassin, I can assure you."

I raise my eyebrows. This is the first hint I've heard that Geneva is still in contact with the exiled princex. They haven't shown their face in Moon Palace society since their mother, Lady Haneul, the Emperor's former favorite, passed away under mysterious circumstances.

That was five years ago, right before I was hired as Geneva's newest attendant, following her sudden promotion to the coveted status that Lady Haneul had just vacated.

Somin fell hard from the Emperor's favor after Lady Haneul's death, and they haven't bothered to climb back up. In the succession line, they hover around ninetieth. Any lower, and they'd be competing with Prince Devon, who's in prison for treason against his father, and Princess Cilla, who's been in a medical coma for the last ten years after a nearly-successful assassination attempt.

I bow and back away, my mind whirling. Why would Somin reappear now, slipping notes to Her Grace? Was it mere coincidence that Alvin's pod was attacked tonight?

And why did every song by Jed's band sting my nose and throat with the scent of cinnamon?

Part Two

DAYTWO

Chapter 3

SEQUIN ROW, THE IMPERIAL MOON PALACE

JED

"I need you to walk me through exactly what happened from the moment you flew out into the crowd on that hoverboard."

Authority General Davan Ajax stares at me across the table, impassive. I'm not under arrest—none of the band is, not yet—but we were in the air when that pod exploded. Of course we're suspects.

This is it. I trained a full year to withstand interrogation for this moment right here. The moment when I lie to the Authority General's face, knowing he's monitoring my heart rate and facial expressions to catch any sign of deceit.

My heart's already thudding against my ribs so fast, I don't know how he'll tell the difference.

I try not to think about my bandmates in other rooms down the hall, facing the same questions. We had just enough time to get our story straight before the Authorities arrived. They all had the same training I did. They'll be fine.

And I especially try not to think about how I'm looking into the eyes of the evil glitch who sanctioned the attack on my hometown fifteen years ago, resulting in my father's death.

I slip deeper into the character of Jedrek Blaze, galactically famous rock-star, and drape an arm over the back of my chair before I begin.

When they finally release us, it's already the next morning. We lug our equipment back to our lodgings, Kyle quietly complaining that the Authorities damaged his drum set during their search. Nobody else says anything. We're all coming down from the shock of the crash, exhaustion setting in. We let ourselves in through the alleyway side door, stow our instruments, and collapse.

Before anyone says a word, Forrest runs our usual bug check. Sure enough, the Authorities placed a couple of devices inside the instrument cases. Forrest detaches the tiny machines and carefully places them in a soundproof lockbox our hacker Simon gave us. When we give it to him later, he'll set them up with a feed of nonsense background noise that'll keep the Authority surveillance team busy.

Once Forrest does one final sweep, then nods that we're clear, we all collectively let out a sigh of relief.

"Well, that couldn't have gone worse," Andi groans, slumping back against a threadbare, formerly-crimson, currently-pinkish fainting couch.

You'd think a group of mega-popular rockstars could afford a decent suite while they're in residence on the literal Moon Palace, but nope. Since *everybody's* rich on the Moon Palace, allocation of resources comes down to how much political power someone has. Or how much the Emperor personally likes them. We, as low-born entertainers, are just about at the bottom of the barrel, barely outranking serving bots. We're lodged in the basement of a courtesan house, in one huge room populated with furniture too battered to be seen by their clients. Old-fashioned folding screens partition off private spaces for each of the six of us. Some of the band managed to dibs stuff like the fainting couch; Kyle, the lucky asshole, found a deflated waterbed stuffed in a storage cupboard. The rest of us poor bastards get stained mattresses on the floor, with faded silk curtains or hole-riddled sheets to cover us.

I mean, it's not the worst place I've ever slept. But it's not what I pictured when I was told we'd be performing on the Moon Palace. On the bright side, it does make it easy to get laid. You live in a courtesan house, people assume you're a courtesan.

Including, in my experience, the part where they don't want to stick around afterward. Not that I'm dwelling on it.

"This is all my fault. I threw the gas bomb at the wrong pod." Nigel, a tall, gray-furred feline-humanoid Paotherrian, slouches morosely against a clothes chest.

"Look on the bright side," I say. "At least that bastard Prince Alvin is exed."

"So are ten other people!" Andi snaps. "And Crown Prince Jinan got away without a scratch. That's not what I'd call a success."

Forrest holds up a finger to correct her. "Seven. Those folks in critical condition might pull through."

"I was counting those poor noble girls on the pod with Alvin," says Andi frostily.

"Well, still only nine, then," Forrest says. "And honestly, given that those girls' parents are some of the worst planetary governors I've ever seen…"

"So we should blow up their dads, then! Not some seventeen-year-olds whose only crime was being groomed by a man in his thirties."

"One of them was nineteen," Forrest mutters.

Andi throws an embroidered cushion at him. It biffs him in the side of the head. "Shut up, Arbor."

"Jar." Forrest points to the blown-glass vase that sits on a two-and-a-half-legged side table propped up by a box of sewing patterns.

It's not labeled, but we all know what it's for: every time one of us slips up and uses our real names, they owe a credit to the jar.

"Fuck," Andi groans. She taps on her keycuff to transfer a credit to the jar's virtual account, which we dip into every now and then to buy snacks for the team. "Sorry, *Forrest*."

"Don't mention it." He bows graciously, like a feudal lord accepting his serf's fealty.

She sticks her tongue out at him. "Stars, you're annoying."

"If only the fans knew," I say dryly. The Tarantula fangroup on the uniweb is good for a laugh every now and then. They're under the impression that Forrest, our lead singer, is a smoldering, deep-poetry-writing, soulful hottie. They'd be super disappointed to find out he's the galaxy's most annoyingly literal-minded pedant. If he wasn't aroace as fuck, he'd probably correct the grammar of his partners' moans during sex.

"Aaaanyway." Andi flicks the sapphire-blue fringe of hair out of her eyes. "The point is, I seem to remember warning you all that planning that attack at our own concert was a huge mistake. But *you said*—" she points at Forrest—"that it'd be easy. We toss a gas bomb, Jinan drops dead of unexplained causes, no suspicion on us. Yet here we are, an explosion, a crash, and a ton of collateral damage later. So I'm putting my foot down: no more concert assassinations."

"I agree," Kyle puts in. He's curled up on his waterbed in the corner with his scroll-tablet open next to him. Probably typing a love letter to his sweetie back on her middle-of-nowhere colony planet. Of the five of us, the skinny, head-shaven drummer is the only one who's in a stable relationship. Feels pretty fucking unfair, but dating's tricky when you're undercover.

I would know.

"It would've worked fine if Alvin didn't look creepily similar to Jinan from behind," Nigel says. "And if he hadn't lit up a bliss pipe right when I threw the bomb."

Kyle shakes his head. "Andi's right. There was way too much room for error. What if the gas bomb fell into the crowd instead? I know the gas is supposed to dissipate fast, but that concert hall was packed. It could have taken out twenty, thirty people, maybe more. We got off easy with just nine."

Nigel chews on one of his long, sharp fingernails, looking nauseated.

"What do we want to try next, then?" I ask, hoping to take some of the heat off him. "Jinan's schedule is practically impossible for even Simon to dig up. The fact that he bought a ticket to our concert was a random stroke of luck. Waiting for another chance like that might take months." My foot taps a nervous rhythm as I resist the urge to get up and pace. "Do we want to give up on him and aim for a lesser target? Someone like Alvin, less dangerous but just as hateable?"

There's a short silence, then Andi says, "Why aim low? We could go for the Emperor instead."

Kyle and Nigel both laugh. When Andi's face doesn't crack from its grave expression, they trail off and look at each other in confusion. "Is she serious?" Kyle whispers. "I can't tell."

"I'm not joking." Andi crosses her arms. "Why not at least pursue it? We could ask Simon to make a timeline of the Emperor's appearances. Maybe there's a pattern, something he does every week at the same time where we can lie in wait for him."

I lift an eyebrow. "If we get caught, it wouldn't be anything like taking potshots at Jinan. We'd be tortured to death. Slowly. On a live broadcast."

Andi says, "This is our fucking mission, guys. We've been here for a whole year, but we've only managed to take out four of the vile fascists in line for the throne. That includes Alvin, who was way too incompetent to ever be a threat." She glares at each of us. "We're here to remove dangerous people from power. Not to play rock shows and flex our abs onstage."

"Wait, we're not?" Nigel asks, fake-innocent.

Andi snorts and reaches for another pillow to throw at him.

Just then, there's a knock at the basement door. We all tense up, eyes darting around the room.

Nigel gets up to answer, guitar still in hand. He peers out through a tiny crack, then breathes a sigh of relief and slides it the rest of the way open.

"Simon!" Andi says, as soon as the door shuts behind our guest. "You scared the living shit out of us. What are you doing here?"

We haven't seen our surveillance expert in person in weeks. He's not an undercover Greenjacket spy like the rest of us; he's lived on the Moon Palace all his life. But he's just as motivated as we are to see this monument to Imperial corruption torn down.

Simon Kim was one of our first contacts when this mission was still in the planning stage, and I'm not exaggerating when I say we would've crashed and burned without his help. He knows *everything* that happens on the Moon Palace. Before tonight's mission went sideways, he helped us carry out three political assassinations without a hitch and not a single scrap of suspicion placed on us.

I'm so used to hearing his soft, smooth voice in my earpiece, directing me through a mission with unshakeable calm, that it's almost jarring to see him in person again. Every time I do, I'm reminded afresh that under the scruffy beard and bland outfit that he wears to deflect attention from himself, he's surprisingly fine. Long-lashed brown eyes, a runner's sleek muscular form, and a kissable mouth that almost never smiles. He rarely reveals anything about his life outside of helping us, to my eternal disappointment. Fuck if I don't dream of being the one who unravels his secrets.

"I would've sent a message," he says now, sinking onto the couch next to Andi, "but the Authorities are on high alert over the concert incident. Anything we send over the uniweb could potentially be intercepted."

"I thought you encrypted all your transmissions," I say.

He looks at me, and my heart skips a beat without my permission. "I do. But I can only get away with so much, especially when the Authorities have an eye out."

"Speaking of which"—Forrest hands him the soundproof box with our brand-new bug devices inside—"we got you a present. From the Authorities."

Simon takes the box gingerly. "Good catch. I'll take care of them for you."

"You weren't hurt when the pod crashed, were you?" Kyle asks.

Simon's shoulders tense up. "You saw me in the audience?"

"Well, yeah," says Kyle. "Nice disguise, by the way. Almost didn't recognize you."

"You were in the audience tonight?" Andi bursts out. "Simon, that's not safe!"

It's also a shock, at least to me. I was under the impression that Simon rarely leaves his home base. Wherever that is. He still hasn't told us.

He ducks his head. "It would've been, if the pod hadn't crashed."

"Uh, no, it wouldn't!" Andi braces her fingertips against her forehead, clearly furious at Simon's nonchalance. "You were literally talking us through planting a gas bomb on Jinan's pod. What if someone overheard you?"

"They couldn't. It was too loud."

Andi looks like she might spontaneously combust. I keep my mouth shut, but I kinda agree with her. I already felt terrible when I saw my ex, Saray, in one of the hoverpods. Knowing Simon was also in danger tonight might have convinced me to call the whole thing off.

Also, it would've given me a shit-ton of stage fright.

"Listen, I know how to assess risk," says Simon into the awkward silence. "I, uh, may have been a little off this time, but..."

"But *fuck!*" I burst out. "We were just saying we can't have any more of these attempts linked to our concerts. That means *you* can't be linked to any of the crime scenes, either."

Simon frowns. "I'm not going to give you away to the Authorities, even if I get caught. Which I won't. Because I'm careful."

I groan, frustrated. Why can't he see I'm not worried about *us?* I want *him* safe.

That veers too close to a squishy space in the back of my brain that I can't pay attention to, not when we're discussing the mission. *Maybe not ever.* Because why would someone so smart and capable be interested in a guy like me?

I let Kyle steer us back to a debrief, and sit with my feelings in silence.

Chapter 4

GENEVA MILAGRO'S SUITE, THE IMPERIAL MOON PALACE

SARAY

I'*m dreaming I'm back in Haven.*

The hidden community of rebels, housed in an unassuming apartment complex in the cheaper outskirts of Hepburn City, Monroe, was my home ever since I left Halcyon at eighteen with sky-high ambitions of becoming a fashion designer. A decade later, I was still working in a boutique selling other people's designs, but that was only my day job. At night, I came home to these cozy apartments full of anti-Imperialist scientists and strategists who schemed over home-cooked meals.

Plus my siblings and me.

I sense them on either side of me as we stare at the wallscreen, jaws dropped at the newsies' delightedly scandalized announcement.

"Lady Haneul was found dead in her bedchamber on Daysix, allegedly after taking more than the recommended dose of sleep patches. Moon Palace officials have ruled it a suicide. However, an anonymous source claims that the Emperor had been displeased with Her Grace, and speculates that the death may be a sign that the Emperor is not above fatal retaliation when his wives rebel."

My sister, Clara, is the first to react. "So, he definitely killed her, right?"

"They can't come out and say that," says Miri.

In real life, she wasn't there when the news broke—she'd already left Haven for a quiet life on some nowhere planet, scared away by the ethical implications of her own power. In my dream, she's still with us. Twenty of my siblings, by upbringing if not blood, survived the genetic modification experiments run by Drs. Melanie and Oberon Ediya. As adults, only a handful of us chose to embrace the abilities that came with having partially alien DNA.

"What would happen if someone called him on it?" my dream-self surprises me by asking. "If the newsies accused him, rather than dancing around it with anonymous sources. If there was public outcry and demand for him to protect the women in his power, what would happen then?"

"He'd kill the rest of us, too," Clara murmurs, a cynical twist to her mouth. "Men never give up power once they have it."

"What if one of us killed him first?"

Clara frowns at my words, treasonous if I were to say them while awake. "Saray, be careful—"

The on-call alert wakes me early. The Emperor has requested Geneva's attendance, and we have to make her ready.

A flurry of bathing, makeup, and wardrobe swallows up the first hour of my morning. When our lady has been cleansed, scented, painted, and decorated to perfection, we stand in a somber line and bow as she taps her keycuff to the panel hidden behind an abstract painting on the wall. The hidden door slides open, and Geneva climbs through into the private zip-lift in her chamber. It only has one other stop: the Emperor's private suite, forbidden unless he issues an invitation. Entering without one is a death sentence.

Even having access to this private lift is a sign of the Emperor's special regard. Most Imperial wives, when summoned, have to run down the hall to the public lifts, dressed in scanty garments for everyone to gawk at. Geneva hasn't had to do that since I entered her employ, but she makes no secret that she found it humiliating. Dangerous, too, as it left her wide open for attackers to lay in wait.

When the zip-lift door closes, the five of us straighten and look at each other grimly. Sending Her Grace into the Emperor's presence is supposed to be a joyous occasion—an honor—but we've all worked for her too long to be that naïve.

"He asked her and a few other wives to dance for some guests," Yumiko says, her voice trembling. "She won't be alone with him. It should be a good day."

The words are a transparent attempt to convince herself, but I hope she's right. Yumiko worries the most about Her Grace because she's the one who performs the medical scans afterward. She hunts down the bruises Geneva hides. She administers fast-heal nanites to return our lady to her natural flawless beauty so that the Emperor never has to see the touch of his cruel hands painted onto her skin.

Each lady-in-waiting has a "job," a specialty that we use to assist Her Grace. Yumiko is the medic, Pearl is her makeup artist, Kina is her wardrobe expert, and Nuala organizes Her Grace's schedule. I am Geneva's informant, the one who weaves through crowds at parties and gathers whispers that I can bring back to my lady. Even information that has nothing to do with her—who's dating whom, which Imperial consort is pregnant again, a rumored assassination attempt against another princex—helps Her Grace navigate the complicated political landscape of the Moon Palace.

Geneva doesn't know the truth of *how* I get my information. She knows nothing of my past except that I was recommended to this position by my adopted father, Alan Lake, a respected planetary ambassador. I've taken care to keep it that way. All anyone needs to know is that I'm a very perceptive judge of character.

If someone were to discover who I really am—and that truth-telling is the least of my abilities—the Emperor would have me in a cage at his feet before Dayseven. And not just him. Any number of people on this moon would love to use me against their enemies.

But I'm here for Geneva Milagro. Because Haven deems her important enough to keep an eye on…and to protect, insofar as I'm able.

I wish I didn't feel so helpless to guard her against her husband.

When Her Grace is with the Emperor, none of us can relax. We never know when his unpredictable moods will leave her with broken bones or bloody gashes. The first time I saw it happen, I was sick for the whole night afterward. This is the kind of man who rules us: a man with untouchable power, who gets away with hurting his wives, knowing there's not a thing they can do to escape him.

I've gotten used to it. But that doesn't mean I accept it as normal and right.

That doesn't mean I wouldn't, given a chance, put a blaster shot through His Esteemed Majesty's head.

Geneva is gone for two hours. We ladies-in-waiting have to remain on call while she's in the Emperor's presence, which means we're stuck in the suite, growing increasingly antsy.

I'm keeping myself busy by deleting hate comments from Geneva's uniweb profile, but I'm wound so tight that.I nearly jump out of my skin when my scroll-tablet flashes a call request.

<Alan Lake: Got a moment to spare for your old dad?>

I snort. *"Old,"* my ass. Alan's barely fifteen years my senior.

I excuse myself to the other ladies and return to my private room to take the call. I turn on my hologram projector, allowing Alan to materialize in my room as if he were standing right in front of me.

"Saray." My adoptive father, the planetary ambassador from Halcyon, offers me a tight smile. His robe, chestnut brown embroidered with a scattering of autumn leaves, drapes across wide shoulders. He keeps his dark brown hair cut unfashionably short, just enough to part it on the side and slick it back with pomade. Tortoiseshell spex perch on his nose despite the fact that his stipend would easily afford him vision-corrective surgery. Compared to the stylish elite here on the Moon Palace, he looks like a university student borrowing clothes from donation bins. He's always been the type to spend more time reading than looking in the mirror.

Even though I pretend to be exasperated with his lack of fashion sense, it's secretly one of the things I love about him.

"I assume you're calling because of the concert crash," I say without preamble. "Don't worry, none of us got hurt."

Alan nods. "Your name wasn't on the list of victims they released this morning. Were you there to see it happen? I wouldn't have guessed you'd be a Tarantula fan."

I wrinkle my nose. "I'm not."

My father chuckles. "Well, I'm glad you're safe, but that actually wasn't why I called. I've heard from Adina."

"Oh?"

My biological mother is even more distant than Alan these days. It's not necessarily her preference. She's a member of Haven, the underground scientific collective that funded my genetic modification as an embryo.

When I left Haven to take the lady-in-waiting position on the Moon Palace, she told me we'd have to be careful with our communication. Alan made sure my ties to them were thoroughly erased from record, but with the Authorities monitoring all my messages, I can't afford to send or receive a single line that might link me to Adina and Haven.

Instead, I pass the occasional update to Alan, and he, in turn, makes sure it finds its way to Adina. I don't often hear messages in return beyond "I love you" and "stay safe."

Alan pours himself a glass of wine and takes a sip. "She was cautious, as usual. She couldn't spell out what she was warning me about, exactly. But I gathered that she knows something that's about to happen here on the Moon Palace. She said you're in danger, and she all but demanded I send you home to her."

I scoff. Neither he nor Adina have the right to tell me what to do anymore. I'm thirty-three years old, and while Alan's position as an ambassador *is* what got me my job, I've held it for five years based on my own merit. I'm not about to throw away my entire life just because my mother heard a rumor and got worried.

"I told her you wouldn't go for it," says Alan wryly. "But you should be careful, Saray. Please."

"Am I ever not?" I say lightly, hoping to put him at ease. "Thank you for the heads-up, though. Last night's 'accident' was too close for comfort. If Geneva was the real target, that could be the danger Adina was worried about. But I'll find out who's trying to hurt her before they get the chance."

Alan's forehead creases. "Don't dig too deep and find yourself in a hole."

"I'll be careful," I promise.

Yet I have to admit he's right. That's one thing I've had to learn the hard way here on the Moon Palace. The truth isn't always safe. Sometimes it's a jewel in my hands, an item of value to be bartered, and sometimes it's a grenade. A threat. A reason to attack.

The trick is knowing where, when, and to whom to hand it off. And paying attention so that I know to stop digging when the canary keels over.

After ending the call with Alan, I return to my scroll-tablet with renewed purpose. It's time I talk to Jed again. I dumped him because I knew he was lying to me about something. This time, I'm not going to let him off the hook until I know what's flavoring his band's songs with cinnamon.

They don't have another public appearance until Daysix, and I'm not interested in waiting that long. Obviously, their address on the Moon Palace isn't public knowledge—wouldn't want them to be overrun with fans begging the band to sign their asscheeks—but the few times I met Jed, it was always in the Entertainment Sector. Specifically, Sequin Row, which is why I mistook him for a courtesan. As I comb through their uniweb fanpages, I note a handful of pics from different days of individual band members picking up food at vendors near the courtesan houses.

Renting a room in a courtesan house is a genius idea, really. The general-population housing in Entertainment Sector is all long corridors with nowhere to hide if fans mob them. Pleasure houses have strict security, and being seen coming in and out of one is easy enough to explain away as "just getting their kicks," without anyone assuming they *live* there. Plus, I've talked to enough courtesans to know that they're a fiercely loyal sorority (in the gender-neutral sense) and would definitely cover for a resident who wanted privacy.

It should take me an hour, tops, to wander Sequin Row and find out which courtesans smell like deceit when I ask them if they know where the Tarantula members live.

With a solidified plan, it's nearly unbearable to lounge around in Geneva's sitting room, waiting for the Emperor to be done with her. At least the other ladies are as tense as I am. Yumiko's sipping tea and paging through a novel on her tablet, but she keeps looking up every five seconds to stare at the on-call alert panel next to the door. It's currently at solid red; when it flashes and chimes, we'll know Geneva's on her way back.

Pearl's fished a gold stylus out of her voluminous updo and is using it to sketch makeup designs on a model of Geneva's face. She leans sideways to show Kina. "What do you think of—"

A rippling chime sounds, making us all jump. Yumiko spills her tea.

"Blast it," she whispers, rushing to mop it up.

"Hey, Miko, don't worry about it," Nuala says. "Go to Her Grace. I'll clean up."

Yumiko seizes her healer's kit and disappears into Geneva's bedroom. Pearl and Kina put away their scrolls, Pearl stowing her stylus in her hairdo once again. I close the tab in my scroll that's full of pics of Tarantula, braced for any reaction from Yumiko. If it's bad, she'll call us in immediately.

But minutes go by as Yumiko performs her routine medical examination, and my shoulders begin to relax. She's fine. She's returned to us safe and whole.

At last, Yumiko calls, "You can come in," and the rest of us step through the sliding door, practically on tiptoes as we assess Geneva's mood.

Her Grace sits on the edge of a purple-cushioned daybed, dressed in a fluttery dancing costume in shades of sunset orange and pink. Beads of sweat dew her temples and neck, but there are no cuts or bruises visible on the light brown skin of her bare arms. Her long, dark hair straggles out of the half-up, half-down style Pearl twisted it into this morning.

It's not hard to guess why Her Grace captured the Emperor's interest. Even sweaty and disheveled, she's the loveliest woman I've ever seen. It seems obvious in the perfect symmetry of her features that she was born to a wealthy family that embraces cosmetic gene modification, but I can't know for sure because she never talks about any biological relatives.

Still, I don't think I'm alone in feeling almost motherly toward this woman who's probably ten, fifteen years my senior. (She tells people she's thirty-eight—five years older than me—but that's cinnamon-flavored. More likely she's had anti-aging treatment to *look* thirty-eight.) I can see it mirrored in the other ladies' faces as we gather around her bedside.

"These slippers are horrible," Her Grace announces, toeing them off as she flops back against the abundant pillows on her bed. "Whose idea was it to bring back pointed toes? I know that wasn't one of yours, Kina. Your designs are always comfortable."

"How did it go?" Pearl asks tentatively.

Geneva smiles, rolling to the side to prop her chin on one hand. "His Majesty, my adored husband, is in a good mood. If I'm lucky, it may last all week." She pushes herself upright again and gestures to Pearl. "Bring me my robe, would you? The soft green one. I'd like to run a bath. And, Nuala, will you send for some food, please? I'm hungry."

Nuala hurries out the door. Kina's already gone to brew more tea. Yumiko kneels by Geneva's feet, rubbing them, careful of the red spots where blisters are forming.

"Shall I go start the bath, Your Grace?" I ask.

"No, no," says Geneva. "Yumiko will do it. She knows which bath powder to use. I want you to go get Miles for me. I need to see him."

"Of course." I bow and head for the door. I'm surprised Geneva's asking for her son today. Usually, she calls for him when she's had a bad few days with the Emperor, when depression threatens to drown her, when she's caught in the throes of nightmares. The Emperor limits how often she's allowed to see her five-year-old child, so she parcels out her time with him as a reward to herself for being strong. As a reminder of what she lives for.

Well, who am I to judge? Even today, a day with no bruises, can't have been easy for her. I don't envy the life she lives, always holding her breath, always walking on tiptoes and keeping herself small. I can only imagine what it must feel like to go back to the Emperor again and again, never knowing whether she faces affection or cruelty.

Or one disguised as the other.

Chapter 5

THE IMPERIAL MOON PALACE

SARAY

P rince Miles is just finishing up his piano lesson when I catch up with his nanny, Megs. She stands just inside the door of the piano master's studio, observing as Miles plinks out a tune. He's no prodigy, but there's something endearing about the intense concentration scrunching his little nose.

He's very much his mother's child; her beauty is reflected in the shape of his face, and her poise in his posture. His eyes are the only feature in which I can see his father, the Emperor. In that man's face, they're ice-cold. In Miles's face, they're wide ocean blue, innocent yet confident. I hope to the deities of times long past that this child doesn't grow to be anything like the man who helped conceive him.

"He's doing well," I whisper.

Megs nods, proud eyes locked on her charge. There are streaks of gray in her brown hair, sweeping from her temples to the tight knot at the back of her head. She wears the plain black trousers and shirt of a servant unconnected to nobility, an outfit designed to make her and others of her class disappear into the background.

Servants like Megs are everywhere. Because they're treated as if they're invisible, they see and hear things no one else is privy to. I make it a point to know as many of their names and positions as I can. Partly because servants are my best informants and partly because...well, need I explain it? They're fucking human beings and deserve a kind word every now and then.

That's how I know that Megs is a former tutor for the governor of Esperanza's six children. She supported herself through an education degree while working as a creche-minder in a Gila City factory complex. She's got a near-photographic memory for historical dates and textbook factoids, and she can pick up nearly anything, from violin playing to origami folding, within an hour of watching a master perform. These talents landed her increasingly higher-paid positions until she found herself here, minding Prince Miles. He must be one of her easiest charges ever, and yet, the pressure has never been so intense for her to keep a child safe.

Because Miles isn't just any prince. As Geneva's son, and thus favored by the Emperor, he's risen close to the top twenty in the ever-fluctuating order of succession. It changes near-daily with the Emperor's moods—but it also steadily shortens year after year, despite a handful of new babies each season. It's the palace's worst-kept secret that Imperial princexes make a sport out of weeding away their competition. The second an Imperial baby is born onto this gods-forsaken moon, it's thrown into a fight for its life against a bunch of wily adults with more ambition than heart.

Guardbots and vigilant nannies employed by the royal mothers manage to keep enough of the poor things alive. But I've never been so glad to be a commoner as when I heard Megs recount the assassination attempts she's helped thwart. It breaks my heart to think of Miles growing up with that fear hanging over him.

Miles jumps up from the piano bench and comes over to stand in front of us. He studies me with hands behind his back, already well-trained in royal composure.

"Am I going to see Mama?" he asks. I don't miss the plaintive hope in his voice.

I glance at Megs. "She's requested him."

"Just a quick visit," Megs relents. "Miles has social time with some of his friends in an hour."

"I want to see Mama," Miles says firmly.

So much about his bearing already shows the leader he's being groomed to be. Shoulders straight, chin lifted, he strides out in front of us, leading the way to the zip-lift. Megs and I walk directly behind him, while Miles's four guardbots flank our group. They're state-of-the-art models, no jerkiness in the joints; their humanoid legs walk in a fluid, gliding motion. They have a dozen gun-arms ready to deploy in any direction, sensors scanning the hallway around us. Their chests are blaster-proof metal plating, and they're programmed to throw themselves in front of Miles to shield him.

There are two lord-attendants waiting in line for the zip-lift, but they step aside when they see Miles. Even for Geneva, that kind of thing rarely happens. She's *only* a royal wife. But her son is a prince close to the top of the succession line. Even as young as he is, people already defer to him.

At least, they bow to him in public. In private, I've no doubt there are already several bounties offered discreetly to intrepid assassins who are willing to risk death to remove a five-year-old from the succession line.

So far, the closest call was the venomous snake left coiled under a pillow in Miles's sleep pod, detected by one of the guardbots an instant before Megs lifted him in. Second closest was a breach of the atmo-grav dome during an educational outing with his social group. His class all carried their oxygen masks and were well-trained on breach protocol, so no one was hurt. The Authorities ruled that one an accident, but I smelled cinnamon during their report to Geneva. They were covering for someone—likely one of the other royal wives.

I feel sorry for Miles having to keep his guard up at such a young age. It's not fair to raise a kid in fear for his life, no matter who his parents happen to be.

When we arrive at Geneva's suite, my fellow ladies-in-waiting have obviously been busy. Her Grace is freshly bathed, hair still coiling damply at her temples and ears, but dressed casually in a well-worn green silk outer robe and soft brown leggings underneath. Her feet are bare, even though Kina trails behind with a pair of soft, flat-soled slippers dangling from her fingers.

Geneva opens her arms to Miles, enveloping the child in a cloud of lavender bath oil and soft fabric. "My miracle," she greets him as always.

"Hi, Mama!" Miles comes alive with his mother's attention on him, bubbling over with stories about his day.

Megs backs out of the room, taking her place just outside the door to give them privacy. Geneva doesn't like to be disturbed when she's with her son.

"Don't forget, we still have to get ready for the ball tonight," Kina reminds Her Grace. "We'll need to start in an hour."

"Yes, yes." Geneva waves us away.

Kina follows me down the hall, closing the door behind her. We join the rest of the ladies-in-waiting in the kitchenette, where Yumiko is making something that smells gingery and garlicky.

"Broth," she says when I peer into the pot. "It's good for weight loss."

I frown. "His Majesty doesn't demand that she loses *more* weight, surely? She's thinner than any of us."

"She asked, not His Majesty." Yumiko sighs. "She is afraid she may lose his favor."

"Why would she?" I plop down at the small table, my elbow jostling Pearl's drawing tablet. "He still asks for her at least once a week. And he has how many wives? Some of them don't hear from him for months at a time. *Years*, even."

Yumiko shrugs. "I didn't say it was a rational fear."

I unroll my scroll-tablet and open a book, but I can't focus on the words. I stare at the page, seeing Geneva's face instead. The worry doesn't line her face, due to constant youth treatments, but still shines out of her eyes. Every move she's made since I've met her—clothing and makeup choices, which parties to attend, who to befriend and who to snub—it's all been calculated for one purpose: keeping the Emperor enthralled with her, playing the part demanded of her, a desirable and tempting woman who's nevertheless utterly submitted to the Emperor's every cruel whim. I've seen glimpses, little more, of the woman she must have been before the Emperor took her into his bed and effectively imprisoned her for life.

Under Soren's rule, a reigning monarch doesn't require consent to bind someone in marriage, and his consorts have no right to request a divorce. The best they can do is play the petty game of vying for royal favor—because disgrace tends to end in an "accidental" death.

If he was to tire of her... If it was all for nothing...

Maybe that's why she asked to see Miles today, of all days. Because she does it all for him. The same as most of the Emperor's wives, I'd venture a guess. They all suffer whatever abuse they must, scheming and manipulating everyone around them toward one goal: making their child the Emperor's successor.

Because that's the thing. If the Emperor dies, only one of those children can take his place. And the rest of his wives and children...the moment an heir is crowned, they all become superfluous.

For royal wives like Geneva, the choice is this: place her child next in line for the throne or know that someday she will have to watch him die.

You know what? Fuck this. Hanging around here moping isn't going to help Geneva.

"Yumiko, I'm going out," I say, snapping my scroll shut. "Be back in an hour."

The zip-lift to the Pleasure Sector drops me at the entrance to the Tranquility Garden. Even though I have somewhere to be, I can't resist lingering for a moment.

The garden sprawls across a few kilometers of the moon's surface. Through the transparent atmo-grav dome, the orange-red Jovian planet Satang blots out the blackness of space. This is one of the best views on the Moon Palace. There's a storm building on the surface of the planet, marbling the gas clouds into vibrant swirls.

Under the dome, floating lights scatter like fireflies across a crystal-clear river. The trees and flowers come from all across the galaxy, selected for exquisite beauty and tantalizing scents. A gentle hum of chirping song arises from thousands of bright-winged insects and exotic avians kept here as pets. It's an explosion of pinks, reds, deep violets, and bright yellows, with a perfume that, replicated and bottled, sells for thousands of credits in designer shops.

It's all excruciatingly expensive to maintain. All of these fancy flowers need individualized care and, despite the gardeners' best efforts, they die and have to be replaced, like, once a week. The bots cleaning the walkways, trimming and weeding the growth beds, and filtering the river suck up enough energy every day to warm a poor farming community through several cold winters.

If the galaxy had such wealth to spare for all its citizens, I wouldn't mind spending a little of it to create this beauty. But I know all too well how many of the worlds ruled by this glittering little moon live in poverty, going without as their labors fuel our luxury.

I turn my back on it all and step onto the steep escalator that leads into the underground levels. As I approach Sequin Row, my stomach growls at the smells from the food court: chocolate crepes, synthmeat skewers in peanut sauce, cups of scalding-hot kimchi soup, and waffle cones swirled full of ice cream. I tell myself I can stop to get something later. I'm on a mission, and I can't be distracted—not even by the lovely courtesans lying in wait along both sides of the corridor. Some have arranged themselves in front of their houses in an artful display, draped in exquisite robes and winking at anyone who'll meet their eye. Some lean out of upper-story windows, blowing bubbles or singing.

My first couple of years on the Moon Palace, I went to the courtesan house more often than I do now. I liked the no-strings companionship, the ease and simplicity of not bringing feelings into the equation. My romantic history has been somewhat rocky. While I'm physically attracted to lots of people, I've found it next to impossible to translate desire into an emotional bond. As a result, I get accused of being aloof and cold. Jed's not the first to say that to me, and he probably won't be the last.

After Jed, I haven't been back. That situation got too messy. I'm better off alone.

As I approach a noodle vendor, I notice a courtesan waiting for her lunch in an awful stained robe and unbrushed wig. My instinct is to ask her if she needs help. But then I spy the red-gold beard under the veil covering the lower half of "her" face, and I grin to myself.

He'll have to do better than that disguise.

Chapter 6

SEQUIN ROW, THE IMPERIAL MOON PALACE

JED

"Your turn to go out for food, Jed," I mimic in a high-pitched voice, rolling my eyes.

The emergency-exit stairs that lead to a side alley door onto Sequin Row are narrow and smell like piss, even though Miz Crystal swears she cleaned up the "accident" one of their patrons had there two years ago.

It actually *is* my turn to brave the crowds, but the way Forrest said it flared me off. Can't the guy say "please" once in a blue moon? Eleven months in close proximity has cured me of any desire to have a roommate ever again.

At least Forrest, Andi, Nigel, and Kyle knew each other before this. They were all teammates on some planet's peacekeeper force before they defected to join the Greenjackets. I'm a stranger to them, recruited into the Greenjackets at age sixteen. The Imperials seized the farming colony I grew up in and repossessed our homesteads, forcing the inhabitants into indenture contracts. What was an angry teenager to do but run off and join the rebel army?

I don't know what that fired-up idealist kid expected, but it definitely wasn't that I'd be a rockstar living on the Moon Palace ten years later. I thought my life would be military uniforms and starship battles, not taking sniper shots at asshole royals while wearing full makeup and dressed in a shirt made of chains. Definitely not living in a pleasure-house basement and having to throw on a wig and a dress to go out and buy dinner in case I get mobbed by fans.

The alley door slides open. I peer out, making sure no one will see me exit before pushing it shut behind me. Thank stars the team all agreed on noodles today, so I'll only have to visit one vendor, loiter for fifteen minutes, then make my escape. I gather up the train of the sheer pink feminine robe I found in the courtesans' storage cupboard. It's got oily stains all over it—I don't even want to know what from—but I'm hoping that, along with the blond wig frizzing out of a lady's towering updo, might trick the casual onlooker's eye into seeing a courtesan instead of a rockstar.

Quentin at the noodle stand recognizes me, of course, but he didn't get to be a neighborhood favorite without learning some discretion. "Five noodle bowls coming up," he says with a wink. Behind him, his assistant is already ladling steaming broth into to-go containers.

I step off to the side and pretend to read the menu painted on the side of the stand. If I just keep my head down, nobody will...

"That wig doesn't suit you, Jed."

Fuck.

I reluctantly turn to face the woman who, for a couple of recent weeks, I thought I was dating.

Saray has her arms folded, staring up at me with those weird, pale-gold eyes that give away her modified genetics. My stomach flips in half appreciation and half dread. With her warm brown complexion and upswept dark hair that gleams red where the light hits it, she's a stunning woman. But if looks could kill, I'd have a knife at my throat at the very least.

"Want a fashion tip?" She huffs, a sound that's one part amusement to three parts disdain. "Next time, use a veil that's not so sheer. I can still see your beard. And restyle that wig."

"What do you want?"

"I think you know why I'm here."

"Not really," I lie. Then I gesture at the noodle stand. "I'm kind of busy right now. Can we do this another time?" *Like never?*

"No. I have some questions," Saray says firmly. "About the concert last night."

I look over my shoulder. No one's paying attention to us yet, but... "Let's take this somewhere else."

"Five orders of noodles, toppings on the side, to go," Quentin calls. He's hanging out the front of the cart, head turned to peer at us, eyebrows furrowed. "Hey, JB, is this lady bothering you? Want me to call the Authorities?"

"No, no, no." I stride over to pick up the to-go bags. "It's fine, Q." I lower my voice. "Just a fan who saw through my disguise."

"Gotcha." Quentin wrinkles his nose. "What's a guy gotta do, wear a bag over his head?"

"Kinda feels like it." A bag might be less itchy and heavy than this blasted wig, too. "Thanks, Q. See you next time."

I heft the bags and lug them toward the alley. Saray trails behind me. I can feel her hawkish gaze on my shoulder blades.

She saw something, I just know it. I thought I'd managed to distract her while Nigel planted the gas bomb, but stars, it's like the woman has eyes in the back of her head. Or a sixth sense for when I'm bullshitting.

I drop the food off just inside the door, not wanting to let it go cold, and message the team that I'm getting rid of a persistent fan before I come in myself. I never got around to telling them about Saray; they'd only have told me she was a bad idea.

I'm starting to see why.

"Say what you came to say," I tell her.

She scans the ceiling and walls around us, looking for cambots. The alley is empty but for a trash chute set in the back wall, and Simon rerouted the

Sequin Row security cams so that they never patrol our alley. All we have to worry about now is drunk nobility stumbling in by accident and peeing on our stairs.

"It's as private as it gets back here," I say. "So? Out with it."

Saray nods once, decisively. Then she steps forward, putting her hands on my shoulders. I flinch, half expecting her to go in for some weirdly timed make-up kiss. But instead, she just stares into my eyes.

"Tell me the truth." The intensity in her golden irises clashes with her calm, even tone. It's like her voice reverberates inside my head, shaking down my carefully constructed walls. "The attack at the concert. Do you know anything about what happened?"

My mouth moves without me intending it to. "The crash was a mistake. We meant to gas Jinan in his pod with no other casualties." I nearly swallow my tongue in an effort to cut off the words. What the blazes am I saying? "The light was down too low, and Nigel threw the gas bomb at Alvin instead. He was smoking a pipe and ignited the gas."

Saray takes a step backward. She seems just as shocked as I am. "*You* killed Alvin?"

"The band," I babble. "We came here undercover to assassinate problematic royals." I clamp my hand over my mouth, hoping to muffle any further verbal diarrhea spilling out.

"Interesting." She narrows her eyes. "Last question. Is Lady Geneva in any danger? Do you intend to target her?"

"No," I mumble into my palm. "Far as we know, she's never done anything to deserve it."

It comes out a muffled garble, but Saray seems to understand the gist. "Thanks," she says. "You can go." And she turns on her heel, the emerald robe swishing behind her.

Oh, fuck no. My hand shoots out and I grab her by the collar, dragging her back in front of me none too gently. "What the blazing fuck did you just do to me?" I hiss. "Making me say that shit out loud, in the street—do you have *any idea?* You could have just signed my execution order. *What did you do to me?*"

Saray grasps my wrist, digging a pointed nail in just the right spot to force me to release her with a yelp of pain. "You finally decided to be honest with me," she says, cool and blank. Her eyes are still narrowed and her jaw set, belying her controlled voice. "You said it yourself, it's private enough here. No one heard."

"See, this is your whole problem," I snarl. "You never tell me *anything*. Nothing about your life, your past, and now not even whatever weird hypnosis thing you just did on me. Yet you accused *me* of lying to you when I never—"

"You were an *undercover assassin* the entire time we dated, and said nothing? That constitutes lying." Saray curls her lip. "You're lucky I didn't force it out of you sooner. Imagine that—I felt bad. Wanted to *respect your privacy.*"

Fury zips along my nerves, flushing me hot. "Guess it was my fault for assuming you were *capable* of trust. You've never cared about anyone a day in your life, let alone trusted them."

Saray folds her arms around herself, a defensive gesture, even though her eyes are spitting fire. "Well, now that it's all out on the table, rest assured I won't blab your secret. I'm here to find out if Geneva's in danger, nothing else." She gives me a severe look. "You should quit while you still can. Get off this forsaken rock and go back to whatever rebel group sent you. It's only a matter of time before someone else comes asking, someone who isn't on your side."

"Oh, you're on my side now?" I growl. "After mind-controlling me to spill my guts?"

"Believe it or not, yes," she says, her voice low and serious. "Prince Alvin was an asshole, and Jinan's just as bad. As long as you stay away from Geneva, I have no reason to interfere." Her golden eyes bore into mine. "I mean it. Leave her alone."

Then, without warning, she vanishes in front of me.

I stagger back, cursing. The glitch teleported! She was so quick about it, I didn't even see the dragon appear.

I'm surprised she could do it right in the middle of an argument. Dragons, wispy alien life forms who've formed a symbiotic relationship with humankind, are picky little assholes and won't usually teleport people if they're experiencing any emotion other than blissful calm. Most of the galaxy has to rely on mind-alts to achieve the right state.

Rattled, I scan my keycuff at the alley door again and take refuge inside the basement stairwell, wondering what the blazes I'm going to tell my team—or if I should tell them anything. They deserve to be warned if we're about to have our cover blown, but they might flay me alive once they find out that I just fuckin' *told her everything*. Still can't figure out how she did it. Some fancy new mind control tech? Hypnosis? Maybe she's a witch.

I wasn't lying when I said Geneva wasn't on our hit list. She keeps her name clean, and her kid is too young to be a player in the ongoing power struggle between princexes.

But if her lady-in-waiting is going around magicking secrets out of people, that might just make her dangerous enough to catch our attention.

Chapter 7

THE IMPERIAL MOON PALACE

SARAY

I shouldn't have teleported in broad daylight. What was I thinking? It's pure luck that there weren't any cambots to witness me exiting a public washroom I never walked into. It's also lucky there wasn't anyone in the stall when I appeared out of nowhere. Explaining *that* would have been tricky. A dragon would never 'port someone into a private space—it's against their ethical code.

My hands shake as I make my way to the zip-lift station. Using my abilities so much feels dangerous as blazes. Jed accused me of not trusting him, but by using my powers on him, I handed him knowledge that could ruin me. I just have to hope he's either too honorable, or too quarkbrained, to use it.

Worse, I'm not even sure this was all worth it. Plenty of things still don't add up. The fact that Tarantula is a band of undercover spies may explain their cinnamon songs and the concert attack, but not the warning from Adina and not Geneva's mysterious correspondence with Princex Somin. In fact, what I thought was a promising lead is little better than a dead end.

Blast it.

When I get back to Geneva's suite, Miles is already gone. I find the whole team in Geneva's washroom, doing each other's makeup while Geneva reclines on her couch with a cooling pack over her eyes.

"Hey, Saray!" Nuala chirps. "Nice break?"

I smirk at her, then fetch my makeup case and join in the preparations. Geneva's engagement calendar is always crammed with events. Whether or not her rivals actually like her is moot because her presence at their events is seen as a way to curry favor with the Emperor.

Tonight's ball will celebrate Princess Iris's twentieth birthday. It's a milestone because half of all royal-blood births are assassinated before that age. So a twentieth party is just as much a "congratulations on your against-the-odds survival" party as it is a thinly veiled courting opportunity.

Prepping for each event is a monumental team effort. Imperial wives don't just have to be pretty and poised themselves; they have to walk the line of having the most lovely and popular attendants without any of those attendants outshining them. Certainly not to the extent that they might tempt the Emperor's eye. Plenty of royal wives started out as court ladies. Plenty of ladies-in-waiting would kill for the chance to elevate themselves.

Geneva has been extra careful in choosing her attendants. None of us harbor secret ambitions to be an Imperial consort; I'd be able to taste it in my fellow ladies' words if they envied Her Grace. It's become ever more abhorrent to imagine taking her place as we watch the way she's forced to live. As the most skilled spotter of bullshit in this household, I'm confident in saying we'd all rather jump out an airlock than become Geneva's competition.

That's top of my mind whenever I begin the process of decorating myself for a social event. Geneva's planning to wear violet tonight, so I have to coordinate my own outfit. I decide on a fawn-colored slip dress paired with a sparkly sheer overdress under a lilac robe. Floor-length, open-front garments have been a fixture of Imperial fashion for decades, and it's not hard to guess why. They're silky and comfortable, not terribly warm but forgiving in shape. With the long expanse of fabric trailing on the floor at the back, they give ample opportunity for artistic expression. Kina lets us go wild with her embroidery machines whenever she's not working on a project for Geneva, and I've had fun building myself a wardrobe with subtle personality, one that includes almost every color of the rainbow. This robe is embroidered in silver floral patterns, vaguely shaped like lilacs. It reminds me of the smell of desire: bright, fresh, alluringly sweet.

I caught a hint of it in Jed's words earlier. But that was before I forced him to incriminate himself. I flush, feeling unaccountably ashamed. The desperation in his eyes—it was cruel of me to pull his secret out of his lips without consent. I violated his trust...after accusing him of violating mine.

You've never cared about anyone a day in your life, let alone trusted them.

His words sting because they feel true. Alan, Geneva, my mother and siblings back in Haven—they all know parts of me, but not everything. I've kept it that way on purpose. It feels safer, somehow, keeping myself aloof. No one can betray me if I don't hand them the ammo.

But no one can love me, either.

Maybe that's just the price I have to pay.

Chapter 8

THE IMPERIAL MOON PALACE

SARAY

We enter the ballroom an hour late. Pearl firmly believes that someone as important as Geneva should never arrive on time.

Princess Iris and her mother have outdone themselves. The ballroom has been decorated to look like a forest glade. There's a huge lawn for dancing, bordered with trees obscuring the tables where guests who aren't dancing can sit and chat in dimly lit privacy. A stage built from mossy boulders takes up one side of the lawn. Above my head, there's nothing but the translucent dome between me and the hulking, fiery shape of the planet Satang.

A fleet of kitchbots circulate the room, distributing cocktails and party patches. In another half-hour, everyone will be at their preferred level of intoxication, and the music will kick up louder and more frantic. Until then, it's a soft croon with piano accompaniment. I lift up on my tiptoes to see if I recognize the singer. I think I've seen her in music vids from that popular holo-drama. *Angelique Azalea, that's her name.*

Geneva leads the way, nodding and smiling as we dive deeper into the crush of courtiers. Pearl and Kina really outdid themselves this time. The deep purple fabric of Geneva's robe is woven so fine, it floats behind her as she walks. Diamonds twinkle throughout the sheer fabric. The dress she wears beneath it is silver, fitted, and floor-length with beaded off-the-shoulder straps, a plunging neckline, and a cutout back. She's sexy and ethereal at the same time, an elegant, untouchable swan in a crowd of posturing peacocks.

Autumn and Destra walk on either side of her, dressed in the formal black of on-duty guards. I spot the telltale shimmer of shield generators on both of their wrists. Geneva's also wearing one, disguised among her bracelets. Parties like this are supposed to be weapons-free zones, but that doesn't mean it's safe here.

Geneva accepts a dance with a member of the Emperor's advisory council, an old man known to have wandering hands. Her Grace is one of the few women in the room who can safely come within arm's length of the old pervert. He knows he can't take liberties with the Emperor's favorite.

Now that our lady has accepted a dance, her ladies-in-waiting are free to do the same. The others fan out and begin to mingle, but I skirt the edges of conversations. These parties are fertile ground for gossip and rumors, and people aren't terribly careful about what they say in loud crowds.

"I heard that Lady Penelope stopped Prince Ervin from marrying a very unsuitable man, and that's why he..." A whiff of vinegar hits my nose. Malicious rumor. A grain of truth in it, maybe, but spun to its teller's purpose. I move on.

"Have you met that brain surgeon who saved Prince Nico's life? That's them over there. Yeah, with the long blond hair. Tai Valik. My stars, I'd love to—"

Cloyingly floral lust. I suppress a smirk. The gossiper is bound for disappointment; I read a newsie story about Dr. Tai Valik last week. A celebrated brain surgeon who specializes in repairing cybernetic neural enhancements, they're in an exclusive partnership with noted historian Dr. Athena Valik, who's waiting for them back home at Halcyon University. The surgeon is enjoying the hospitality of the Moon Palace as a personal thank-you from the Emperor after they saved a young prince from injuries incurred during a flyball mishap caused by a malfunctioning grav-sim.

I suspect it was less "accidental" than the newsies painted it, and it was a relief that the twelve-year-old prince survived. I'd like to strangle whoever's responsible myself. But the Emperor won't bother looking into it. He never does.

Jed's earlier confession drifts across my mind. He claimed that his band only attempts to kill people who deserve it, but who decides what crimes merit a death penalty? To some, simply being born royal is enough. I planned to keep Tarantula's secret, but now I'm not so sure I should. If I get the faintest inkling they're hurting royal kids, I'll turn them in myself.

Through the cacophony of competing scents, I catch the citrusy tang of hatred, carried on the words, "Alvin deserved it."

Jinan. The bastard is bragging about his survival at his brother's expense. My lip curls. I suppose I don't have a leg to stand on, considering I also think Alvin deserved it, but Jinan's gloating rubs me the wrong way. Well-intentioned as Jed and his band may be, they're basically doing Jinan's dirty work for him by removing his competition.

I rearrange my face into blank serenity. Maybe next time the band will take out the intended target, and the Crown Prince slot will go to someone marginally less of a sociopath.

The next scent I catch is powerful, almost overwhelming jasmine—despair, the strongest I've ever tasted—as a low voice murmurs, "You look beautiful tonight."

My ears and nose instantly alert, I look for the source. It's a tall man I haven't seen before. His robe is a blood-orange shade with bronze accents, cut in the masculine style: boxy rather than flowy, fabric ending at the heels of his boots instead of trailing on the ground behind him. A tall hat, intricately painted, crowns his head. His makeup, in bright sunset colors, is interrupted by the presence of a waxed and curled mustache.

I follow his gaze. Who could be the source of such desperation?

My breath catches as I see Geneva reaching out to take his hand.

Then they're dancing, weaving in and out of the crowd, and I no longer have a clear line of sight. I have to get back within earshot. What is he saying to her? Are Destra and Autumn watching?

I push my way toward the edge of the crowd, skirting the dance floor and dodging waiter-bots, tracking them across the dance floor until they retire to a tree-shaded corner. As I fight to get closer, I see Autumn and Destra standing close, guarding the table where Her Grace now sits. There's a tiny bliss-liquor glass in front of her, empty.

Given that she typically doses her night's anxiety medication before a party and refuses mind-altering substances that Yumiko did not directly prescribe, the sight of her drinking—even small amounts—makes me stop short.

The strange man sits across from her, speaking quickly, the words lost to the noise of the party. I try to read his lips, but that cursed mustache keeps throwing me off.

I weave closer, staying out of sight behind the tree at Geneva's back, and manage to catch the very end of the conversation. "—must do it now, Lady Milagro, or the consequences will be worse than either of us imagine. Once she gets her claws in—"

"Your Grace!" The interruption comes from my adoptive father, Alan Lake. I'm shocked to see him at a formal event like this—and even more surprised that he actually dressed for it in silver-trimmed midnight blue. I edge further behind the pillar, hoping he hasn't noticed me.

Mustache stands, tosses back the rest of his drink, and strides away. His red robe is quickly lost to the vibrant crowd.

Alan bows to Her Grace and says, "I trust I wasn't interrupting?"

"Not at all. Our friend was just filling me in on some news I had missed." The tremble in Geneva's voice is unmistakable, as is the smell of cinnamon. "I imagine you've come to tell me the same thing."

"I'm afraid I just learned it myself," Alan says grimly.

There's a burst of noise as a new band starts up, and I miss Alan's next words. I tune back in just as he says, "—out while we still can. I tried, but she is...stubborn. Perhaps you can do something."

"I'll begin making arrangements tonight." Geneva sighs deeply. I smell green tea and chocolate, weaving together in her words. Fear and sorrow. "Thank you, Alan."

He reaches across the table, and for a brief and forbidden moment, their hands touch. I suck in a breath. Alan is a fool to risk touching the Emperor's consort. If anyone saw and took it the wrong way...

My father gets up to leave and finally makes eye contact with me behind the pillar. He sighs and says, "Careful who catches you listening," before making his way toward the exit.

I come out from behind the tree and drop into the chair he vacated. "What was that?" I demand. "Who was the man in orange?"

Geneva looks up at me. Worry flashes in her eyes, the briefest flicker before her calm mask settles back into place. "An old acquaintance," she says evenly.

"He was acting suspicious."

"It's just the mustache," Geneva says. Under the sweet spice of her lie, I hear the shake in her voice she's trying to hide. "If it's an attempt to start a trend, I doubt it'll catch on."

"Your Grace..." I hesitate, weighing my words carefully. "If there is anything I can do to help..."

"Thank you, Saray, but I'm fine." Geneva puts on a small smile. "Go enjoy yourself. I find I'm rather tired from this morning."

"Yes, Your Grace." I bow, but as I turn away, discomfort gnaws at me. Something big is happening, something Geneva wants to keep from me, and I can't see how the pieces fit together.

I won't force Geneva to tell me the truth. That's a line I can't cross. But how can I help her if she won't open up to me?

Despite my best efforts, the rest of the night is a complete wash. Mustache appears to have vanished into the void.

When Geneva finally flags and calls it a night, Autumn and Destra bundle our whole group into a zip-pod. Nuala and Pearl are drunker than the rest of us, pink-cheeked and giggly. Kina looks like she would have liked to have been asleep three hours ago. Yumiko already bailed and went back to the suite by herself; she can really only stand, like, two minutes in a crowded room.

Makeup hides Geneva's dark circles, but her exhaustion is evident in the slump of her shoulders. She stares blankly into the middle distance as Nuala and Pearl catch each other up on the night's best gossip. She looks so adrift that I have the urge to hug her—but that would be inappropriate.

Maybe that's the problem. There's no one she's allowed to hug besides Miles and the Emperor—and the latter is a soulless abuser.

I wonder if she'll try to ask for Miles again tomorrow.

The lift lets us off in Geneva's home corridor. A few other courtiers linger in the hallway, chatting before they return to their various suites. One of the princes' men-at-arms turns to us and says as we pass, "Your nursemaid came by a second ago, Lady Milagro. She's waiting in your suite."

"Miles," Geneva says, almost a sigh of relief, and quickens her steps.

But when we step into the sitting room, Miles isn't there. Only Megs, sobbing on the couch, with Yumiko next to her, speaking softly and rubbing her arm.

"Your Grace!" they both exclaim as Geneva sweeps in.

Megs jumps to her feet but then collapses. It takes me a second to realize she's kneeling, hands reaching out in supplication.

"I am so sorry," Megs sobs, her voice raspy and broken.

Geneva goes very still. "Wh—what—" Her lips move, but the words catch in her throat.

"Your Grace, I swear, I tried my best, but he—it was too fast, and I couldn't—"

"What. Happened?"

At first, I don't recognize the cold, hard voice that speaks the words. Then I realize they came from me. I crouch next to Megs, gripping her chin, forcing her to look at me.

"What happened?" I ask again, my own words tasting of bitter dark-chocolate fear.

Megs meets my eyes and recoils, falling back as she tries to scramble away. "You," she gasps, throwing out a hand to ward me off. "Not you."

"Fucking *tell us!*" I shout, ready to strangle her. "Where is Prince Miles?"

She turns her attention back to Geneva, and words tumble out of her, quick and pleading. "I was—it was almost bedtime, and he wanted to take a walk. We sometimes do that, walk up and down the hallway to get his energy out at night. He likes to splash in the waterfall features. I was holding his hand. His guardbots were right behind us; we were taking every precaution—but it happened so fast. We looked up, and there he was. Threatened me with a gun. Snatched Miles's hand right out of mine. I should have fought, I should have—"

Geneva emits a small whimper, pressing her hand to her mouth. Yumiko and Destra catch her as she begins to crumple.

"Who was it?" I insist, not ready to let Megs off the hook. "Who took Miles? Did you see his face? What did he look like?"

"Of course I saw his face!" Megs spits. "It was Ambassador Lake. Your *father*, Lady Saray. He kidnapped Miles."

Part Three

DAYTHREE

Chapter 9

GENEVA MILAGRO'S SUITE, THE IMPERIAL MOON PALACE

SARAY

I've *never* seen Geneva break down. She's kept her cool through whispers from glitchy rival wives, through assassination attempts, through bloody lips and black eyes inflicted by her husband. If anything, she'll weep silently when she thinks we can't see.

But, stars, the scream she lets out when it finally sinks in that Miles has been taken... I thought nothing could be more heart-wrenching than to see her tortured by the one man none of us can stand up to. I was wrong. It's this, right here, this moment when the one thing Geneva truly cares about is ripped away from her. The way she falls to her knees, screaming as if she's letting loose all the pent-up fury from five years of abuse. Yumiko rushes to her side, readying a calming patch, but Geneva pushes her away.

"*Don't,*" she growls, teeth clenched, eyes streaming.

"Your Grace," Yumiko whispers. "This will make you feel better—"

"*I don't want it.*"

Autumn steps forward, like she intends to hold Geneva down so Yumiko can administer the patch to her. I throw out an arm to bar her way. "Not right now," I say firmly. "She doesn't need to be quieted. She needs to feel this."

I can taste it in her screams—raw, burning hot-pepper pain. It's not my sense of taste or smell that tells me what she needs, though. It's being Geneva's lady for five years. Prince Miles is what Geneva Milagro lives for. Full stop. Everything else—the Emperor, parties, politics, her ladies and friends—it's all flat like stage scenery. None of it means anything. Miles is her whole world, and she can't risk muting the pain of his loss, not without flattening him into an object in her orbit like the rest of us.

If he matters, then she has to let herself hurt for him.

Autumn kneels at Geneva's side and bows her head. "We won't sedate you, if that's your wish," she says. "But would Your Grace prefer I remove Ambassador Lake's daughter?"

"What?" Outrage shrills my tone.

"You could be a part of his plot," Autumn says matter-of-factly. "It's probably best if you leave."

"There's no plot," I insist, my voice rising. "My father has no reason to take Miles. Obviously, Megs was mistaken about who she saw."

"I wasn't!" Megs cries.

Geneva takes a huge, gasping breath and says, "Stop it."

All of us immediately turn to her.

"Whatever happened outside of these walls, I'm confident in Saray's loyalty," says Geneva. "She stays."

Warmth fills me. "Thank you, Your Grace," I murmur, kneeling and bowing in a mirror of Autumn's posture.

Then I excuse myself to the next room to call Alan. Surely, I'll find him having a late-night coffee or whiskey in his suite, and this misunderstanding will be quickly cleared up.

But the call won't even connect. A cool automated voice states that the recipient's keycuff is powered off, and invites me to leave a message.

Dread pools in my stomach. *It can't be true. It can't.*

I don't know what Megs saw, but clearly something *did* happen to Alan tonight.

I close my eyes and send up a prayer to the dragons who barely acknowledge me anymore. ::*Find my father. Watch over him and Miles. Keep them safe until I can get to them.*::

A faint shimmer in the air tells me my request has been acknowledged. Whether or not they'll follow through is anyone's guess. The dragons always do whatever the blazes they want, and I've been a piss-poor devotee since leaving Halcyon and embracing my powers. Powers the dragons heartily disapprove of.

But I'm not leaving it solely up to them. I'm going to find Alan and Miles, even if I have to drag the truth out of every liar on this moon.

Chapter 10

SEQUIN ROW, THE IMPERIAL MOON PALACE

JED

The guilt's been eating me up all morning.

Andi, Nigel, and Forrest have their heads together, trying to plan another attack on Prince Jinan, while Kyle is scrolling through newsie feeds planting rumors about the concert disaster that point to anyone but us. We're set to practice later, but I can't concentrate on anything unless I come clean. I already tossed and turned all night. Every time I closed my eyes to dream, I saw Authorities breaking our door down and shouting that Saray had told them everything.

She wouldn't, not really.

I don't think.

But the team deserves to know that she knows, and more importantly, *how*. This might be a new weapon we're dealing with, some kind of interrogation device. We should all be prepared to fight it.

"I have something I need to tell you," I finally force out.

Kyle looks up at me, pale eyebrows raised. "What's up, Jed?"

"Yesterday, when I went to get noodles—" No. That's not the start of it. I owe them the full truth. "Right, actually, back up. A few months ago, I started seeing someone."

Andi drops her stylus. "Are you *engaged*?"

I make a face. "Far from it. Just let me tell the story, yeah?"

She makes a zipping motion across her mouth.

Deep breath. "It was the day after we played that absolute flop of a concert for Princex Owin's eighteenth birthday. Remember, the one where some kid jumped up on stage and tried to smash my guitar?" The only reason I didn't give that little asshat a black eye is because he ducked when I threw the punch.

We'd agreed to take a day off so that we could collectively recover from that shitshow. Kyle and Nigel went off to a virtual gaming room to play hoverbike jousting. I guess Forrest found a digital library to borrow some "light reading" (history of war strategy). Andi...well, who knows what Andi does with her off time. I don't ask questions I don't want the answer to.

I didn't tell the team what I was planning, either. Because I actually didn't have any plans. Pathetic, right? The undercover soldier gets some free time and realizes he's forgotten how to have fun.

I thought about messaging Simon and asking him if he wanted to hang out. But as my fingers hovered over his call code, I imagined him saying, "That's so sweet, Jed. I'm flattered. But this is strictly a business relationship." My heart constricted, heat burning my cheeks, and I chickened out.

The courtesans upstairs had given us a standing invitation to come hang out in their front lounge. If we wanted their back-room services, we had to be paying customers like anyone else, Miz Crystal had informed us, but the public areas—where courtesans played games, flirted, and drank with potential clients—were open to us anytime.

It was a kind offer, but for the most part, it was safer for us to keep to ourselves downstairs. The chances of a fan recognizing and accosting us grew with every concert. On that day, though, I decided to take my chances.

"While you all were out, I went upstairs to Miz Crystal's lounge," I tell my team, who are all at the edge of their seats. "And that's where I met...a lady."

I'd been finishing up a humbling game of chess with a courtesan named Velour (ve was trouncing me) when I glanced up at the bar, contemplating another drink, and locked eyes with Saray.

She'd been staring at me, and I did a little staring in return, flashing her a subtler version of my stage smirk. With a tilt of her head, she invited me to sit at the bar.

She bought me my next drink, then another. I thought at first that she must know me from the band, but when I brought it up, her blank expression told me I was wrong. She seemed fascinated, though, and asked me questions about musician life that kept us talking for hours.

She was the one who kissed me first. Then she suggested retiring into one of the back rooms.

"I won't kiss and tell, but let's just say I gave her my call code at the end of the night," is how I decide to sum up our encounter.

The guys on my team are grinning. Nigel mutters, "Nice!" and flashes me a thumbs-up. Andi rolls her eyes.

I don't tell them the part I'm most embarrassed about. Like a quark-brain, I assumed the money Saray left in an envelope on the bedside table was a tip for the house for letting us use their room.

"We saw each other for about two weeks," I tell them. "We only ever met up in Miz Crystal's lounge. She seemed really weird about talking about herself, but I just brushed it off. Then we...uh...broke up."

It was my fault, I suppose, for trying to deepen what wasn't there for her.

I'd asked her to go on a walk in the garden instead of staying in the lounge. As we walked, I asked about her family, her childhood, her job, her dreams. She got uncomfortable, then angry.

She told me I had no right to ask invasive questions. I said that was what boyfriends do. When she laughed, it stung more than I'd like to admit.

It came out that she thought I was a courtesan the whole time. She thought my band was a side gig while I worked at Miz Crystal's to pay bills. Insulted and more than a little hurt, I accused her of leading me on and acting the heartless siren. She retaliated by calling me a liar and a scammer.

People in the park were starting to stare, so I suggested we talk about this somewhere more private. Instead, Saray stormed away and blocked my call code.

"That was the last I saw of her," I say, "until yesterday." Then I recount the events of my ill-fated noodle run.

When I'm done, the team sort of just stares at me for a solid minute. I sweat through the silence, bracing myself for the impact.

"Let me get this straight," Forrest says slowly. "She dumped you—"

"*I* dumped *her!*"

"—and then she turned up yesterday and used some kind of hypnosis on you to get you to confess to killing Alvin?"

"Oh, worse than that," Andi butts in. "He told her we *meant* to kill Jinan. And threw in our entire mission statement, for funsies."

Nigel rubs his neck fur. "Jed, I honestly never thought you'd be the stupid one in this team. That's obviously Leo."

Andi jabs a finger at him. "*Jar!*"

"Sorry. That's obviously *Kyle*." Nigel transfers a credit to the jar.

"Hey, rude," says Kyle, crossing his arms. "So, Jed, do you think this woman is going to tell on us?"

I bite my lip. "Truthfully? No."

"You literally just said you know nothing about her," Andi points out.

"Yeah, I know. You're not wrong. It's a risk, and that's why I was so flared off when she did it." I sigh. "But...I don't know. She seems to only care about the lady she's serving. She just wanted to know we weren't trying to attack Lady Geneva."

"It is a risk," says Forrest, "and one that I'd have wanted to kick you off the team for, if you told her all that shit willingly. But if you're right, this lady-in-waiting has some kind of tech, poison, or mind-control method that we've never seen before. I don't know about you all, but it sounds pretty blazing useful to me. We should look into what she did and how to acquire it ourselves."

"Or, wild idea," I say, "we *stay the fuck away from her*."

Nigel says, "I like that idea better."

"I think Forrest has a point," says Andi.

I heave a sigh, rubbing my forehead. It feels like this argument's just getting started.

Chapter 11

GENEVA MILAGRO'S SUITE, THE IMPERIAL MOON PALACE

SARAY

I t takes hours for Her Grace's tears to stop. We keep vigil with her, our plans for a restful night's sleep forgotten as we wrap her in blankets, hand her absorbent cloths, and offer endless cups of tea. Every hour, Destra calls the Authorities demanding an update on their investigation, and every hour, the Authorities snap back that they can't disclose any information.

I try to call Alan at least as often, but his keycuff remains powered down. That, more than Megs's accusation, has me worried. He's never gone dark before. He might dash off a quick message—*<Can't talk, council meeting,>* or, *<I'm not alone, call you back later>*—but he'll never leave me hanging.

The rest of the ladies keep their distance from me, clumping together on the other side of the room. Geneva might be willing to put her trust in me, but it seems they aren't. Even though anger smolders in my chest at how quickly they abandoned me, I have to admit, I'd be similarly reluctant if the same accusation was leveled at any of them.

Stars, I might even be showing *myself* out...if I didn't believe with one hundred percent certainty that Megs is wrong. It couldn't have been my father. He would never do this.

I'm not naïve enough to think that I know all of Alan's secrets. But I know Alan himself—the kind of man he is. There's a reason he was chosen to represent Halcyon as their ambassador. The kind of unshakable moral fortitude it takes to represent a planet of socialist communes who worship dragons in the court of a power-hungry Emperor who hates every part of that phrase...he doesn't lack backbone. His mission is keeping the peace, and he believes in it with every fiber of his being.

Often more than I do.

There is absolutely no reason I can think of—literally not one—that would make him kidnap *any* child, let alone Geneva's son. He was literally urging her to send someone (me?) to safety mere hours ago. He could've easily *asked* Geneva if she wanted him to arrange to hide Miles away, and Geneva might've said yes.

It just doesn't make sense. Why would he put his (and my) job at risk? For what? He and Geneva are cordial with one other, so it's certainly not personal. And he's not great friends with any of her enemies, either.

Maybe, *maybe*, if he found out Prince Miles's life was in more immediate danger than he thought...but he wouldn't threaten Megs and disappear with the kid, if that was the case. He'd go straight to Geneva, knowing she and her guards would keep the boy safe.

My mind churns, trying to fit the facts into new shapes, like a kid pushing spinach around on their plate in hopes it'll turn into cake.

Eventually, morning arrives, signaled only by the gradual brightening of the nightlights into daylights, and by Yumiko offering everyone some oatmeal.

Autumn clears her throat to announce her presence in the doorway. "Your Grace," she says, addressing the Geneva-shaped blanket lump on the divan, "the Authorities wish to speak with you and your ladies."

Geneva sits up at once. "Is there news?"

"They wouldn't say, my lady."

"Let me make you presentable first, Your Grace," Pearl butts in.

Geneva puts a hand to her hair, tangled from a night of burrowing. Her makeup is long gone, half of it cried off, the rest of it removed somewhere in the middle of the night before Yumiko brought cold cloths for her swollen eyes. Nothing can disguise her natural beauty, but normally she'd be too proud to allow anyone but us to see her in this state.

But today, she brushes Pearl aside. "I won't make them wait."

Kina drapes Geneva's dressing gown over our lady's shoulders as she sheds her blanket nest. Pearl flutters behind them, picking pins out of Geneva's hair so that the snarled knot of last night's updo uncoils down her back. Now she looks like she's been wandering desolate moors barefoot, a tragically beautiful figure holo-drama viewers would sigh for. It sells a certain narrative. Maybe she's hoping to garner their pity and convince them to prioritize this case.

Destra and Autumn usher the Authorities in. There are three of them, all men, clad in the blood-red jacket of the Imperial soldier force. To my surprise, I recognize the man in the middle as Authority General Ajax. His square jaw and silver buzzcut are a staple on the Moon Palace's nightly newscast, due to their ever-popular Crime Corner segment. It's jarring to see him unframed by a screen. His legs seem way too skinny for his broad shoulders.

"General, sir," Geneva says, with just the right amount of breathy entreaty. Ah, yes, she's *definitely* going for the heartstring tug. "Please tell me you've found my son safe."

"Not yet, ma'am."

Pearl sucks in a breath at the General's refusal to use Geneva's honorific. But I don't think Geneva even notices.

"I don't want to bother you during this difficult time," Ajax says. "We're here to take statements from two of your ladies: Miz Megan Kittredge and Miz Saray Lake."

I can't say it's unexpected. If my father is their main suspect, of *course* they'll want to talk to me. I have nothing to worry about. I'm confident that he's innocent. Even so, a wave of adrenaline crests, quickening my heartbeat, as I lead the Authorities into my room for privacy. One of the soldiers splits off to usher Megs into a side room; General Ajax and the second soldier come with me.

"I apologize for the lack of seating," I say as the door closes behind us. "I don't usually entertain guests here."

General Ajax spares my room an uninterested glance. "I prefer to stand anyway."

He nods to the other soldier, who opens the case he's carrying to free a floating cambot. It's the kind newsies use, capable of capturing a 3D recreation of the surrounding two meters or so. It will record my expressions and body language, no doubt to be analyzed in detail later. I'll have to be doubly cautious about what I say.

"Miz Lake, I'll get right down to it. When was the last time you saw Alan Lake?"

I fold my hands in front of me, hoping they won't betray me by shaking. "Yesterday evening, at the party."

"Did you speak to him?"

"No. The last time we talked was on a vid-call earlier that day."

"What did you speak about?"

"He had news from home. Wanted to pass along some greetings from old friends. I told him about the incident at the Tarantula concert."

"Did you notice anything off about him?"

I shake my head. "He was concerned when I told him about the attack, but otherwise he seemed normal. Relaxed."

I don't want to tell them about my mother's warning. *She all but demanded I send you home to her.* It seems extremely relevant, but if I bring it up, it'll send the Authorities hunting after Adina.

Is this what Adina was trying to warn us about? If she knew Alan was going to be framed for a kidnapping, why didn't she just say that? Why tell him to get *me* off the Moon Palace?

Then again, I can't swear it would've made a difference. Alan might've chosen to stay anyway. And *I* certainly would've, because I want to know which lying bastard is dragging my father's name through the dirt. They aren't going to get away with this. I'm going to make sure they don't.

"Did he say or do anything odd? Anything that indicated his plans for that night?"

I shake my head. "General, sir, I would swear on my life that Alan didn't do this. I can't think of any motive that would make him act against Her Grace in such a cruel way."

"I thought you might say that," says the General with a hard, thin smile. "Which is why I brought a recording of the security vid."

I take an involuntary step forward. Solid evidence! I'll be able to show them proof that they've got the wrong man.

The General taps on his scroll, then holds the unfurled tablet flat on his palms, showing me the 3D capture of a nondescript hallway.

The people in the image are barely the size of my thumb, but it's easy to tell that's Prince Miles in the vid. He walks into the frame holding Megs's hand, with a retinue of guardbots behind him. There's no sound, but it's clear from their movements that Miles is chatting away to Megs. She nods along encouragingly, though her eyes are constantly scanning the hallway ahead, her hand firmly gripping her young charge's. Such vigilance would be suspicious if I didn't already know this is how Megs acts while she's on duty.

And she's by no means bad at her job. Which makes it all the more shocking when the first of the guardbots goes down, sparks flying as it seemingly overloads for no reason.

Megs whirls, pushing Miles behind her as she dives for the concealed blaster in her boot. Another guardbot spits sparks and falls onto its side, proving the first was no accident. The rest fall in a domino line, and only then does the attacker drop into the frame, apparently out of the ceiling.

He *looks* like Alan: roughly the same height and build, same aquiline nose, same outdated spex because the man refuses to get his eyesight corrected. He holds some kind of short-range pulse weapon, which must be what he used to overload the guardbots. I don't know where Alan would get hold of one. It's definitely outlawed here on the Moon Palace (anything that could interfere with the function of life support tech is strictly prohibited), but it's just as illegal on Halcyon, where nearly all projectile and blast weapons are forbidden. Maybe Alan has some black-market connections I don't know about...but I still can't imagine *why* he'd do any of this.

Interestingly, the attacker doesn't bother to shoot and disable the cambot. Another reason it can't be Alan. If he *were* going to do something illegal, he'd definitely have shot the cambot first. Such a huge oversight in an otherwise meticulously planned attack says to me that the attacker wanted this recorded—wanted the Authorities to believe Alan had done it.

I squint at the figure, trying to figure out how they managed to fake his appearance so convincingly. They've even got his mannerisms, down to favoring his left leg (his knee's been acting up, but he stubbornly refuses to see a healer) and adjusting his spex with his middle finger. If I didn't know my father, I might be doubting, too.

He holsters the pulse weapon and exchanges it for a laser pistol, which he aims at Megs. The practiced ease of that motion breaks my illusion. This can't be Alan, an avowed pacifist who, to my knowledge, has never touched a gun in his life. Whoever this is, they've got no problem threatening someone's life.

The fake Alan's lips move as he and Megs face off, each pointing a gun at the other. Miles clings to Megs's trouser legs, eyes wide with fear.

Megs fires off a shot, but not-Alan dodges it with impressive agility. He fires back, clipping her shoulder. She fumbles and drops the gun.

As she bends to retrieve it, not-Alan surges forward and swings a hard blow at the back of her head. I wince as it connects, but it doesn't totally knock Megs unconscious. She's still groping for her pistol when not-Alan sweeps an arm around Prince Miles, hoists the boy onto his hip, and disappears into the ceiling. This time I see the cable he has attached to his belt, allowing him to reel himself back up. The vid ends there.

"I assume you already checked the ventilation ducts," I say calmly.

"Of course. And the bot access tunnels. He may have used them to get around unseen, but he didn't remain inside them for long."

"And you haven't found where he came out?"

"Not yet. We're checking, but..."

I nod. "I imagine he chose a place with no cambots. Curious, then, that he chose to stage the attack in full view of one, though he had the tech to disable it easily. Doesn't that strike you as suspicious?"

"It's common for criminals to flaunt their skill," says the General dismissively.

"In a way that could get them caught immediately?" I shake my head. "I think someone went out of their way to frame my father for this. I don't know how they faked him so well, but that can't be him. He's being set up."

"Perhaps you don't know your father as well as you think you do," the General suggests. "I know this must be hard for you to accept, but the evidence is clear."

It's certainly hard to argue with. A nasty little voice in the back of my mind whispers that maybe he's right. Maybe Alan's been lying to me this whole time. Maybe I only know a single facet of my father's complex self.

I might be more inclined to believe that if my father had ever given off the barest whiff of cinnamon. But no one's that good. No one can avoid telling a single lie while living a constant one.

"He's not a kidnapper," I say firmly. "I'm going to prove it to you. I don't know how, but I'll find him and prove it."

At that, the second officer looks up from his scroll and levels a stern glare at me. "Miz Lake, any information you have on your father's whereabouts is to be immediately reported to the Authorities. You are not to try to contact him on your own. If you hide something from us—if you obstruct our work in any way—be warned that you could face the same penalty as your father does."

"Which is?"

"Immediate execution when we catch him. By order of the Emperor himself."

My pulse beats thickly against the high collar of my robe. Execution. *Oh, Alan.* But they haven't caught him yet; there's hope. If I can find him before they do, maybe I can help him escape the Moon Palace. If he makes it back to Halcyon, he'll be safe from arrest while I work to prove his innocence.

Until they come for me, too.

"I won't get in your way," I promise General Ajax, tasting cinnamon.

I'm half shocked the Authorities leave without arresting me. But they do, leaving Megs a sobbing mess and Geneva confined to bed with a stress migraine.

None of my fellow ladies-in-waiting seem interested in speaking to me, whether or not the Authorities think I'm guilty. So I lock myself in my private room, claiming a headache of my own.

But there's absolutely no way I'm staying here. Not when I can teleport and have a perfectly good lead on a group of undercover rebels who've been attacking royals. Jedrek Blaze's words were grassy truth when he said he wasn't targeting Geneva. What if it was a clever dodge, hiding his real intent: kidnapping her child?

I don't know how the glitch could've lied to me, but I'm about to go find out.

Chapter 12

SEQUIN ROW, THE IMPERIAL MOON PALACE

JED

The wrong chord resonates under my fingertips, and I curse, thrown off. The rest of the band dribbles to a halt. Forrest shoots me a glare as he's forced to stop singing midline.

"Sorry, sorry," I mutter. "Fucked up. Let's go again."

Kyle sighs, twirling one of his drumsticks. "From the top?"

This might be our worst rehearsal since the very beginning, when the Greenjackets threw together five soldiers who didn't know how to play musical instruments and told us we were going undercover as a band.

Except this time, it's my fault.

The group's been at each other's throats all morning. Team "Jed is a dumbass who fell for a honey trap" (Andi and Nigel) and Team "Lady Geneva has access to cutting-edge interrogation tech that we need" (Kyle and Forrest) can't seem to agree on what to do next.

Andi's yelled at me about four separate times for "thinking with my southern brain," which feels undeserved. This moon is almost exclusively populated with folks who can afford a shit-ton of cosmetic surgery and expensive makeup. It's not like I haven't seen pretty people all day, every day, for the last several months. If that was all it took to get me to spill my guts, I'd have been arrested on day one of the mission.

I'm not gonna lie and say that Saray isn't attractive. But there's hot, and then there's, "I literally can't control myself when she speaks," and trust me—I say this as a flagrant pansexual—no one in the galaxy is *that* hot.

Personally, I'm with Forrest and Kyle here. We need to get to the bottom of what interrogation tech Lady Geneva is giving her subordinates, and I can't think of a better person to help us than Simon. Only one problem: Simon's only helping us with the understanding that we'll keep his involvement a complete secret. If he thinks we've compromised our mission, he might ghost us. Without him, we'd be completely vortexed.

Not to mention that telling him will shrivel me into a pathetic little sun-dried tomato of humiliation.

I take a deep breath and try to focus on the music. If I let my brain wander, my fingers will, too.

"Fuck!" A discordant twang throws off the song yet again. I toss my guitar onto my mattress. "Sorry, guys, I need a break," I mutter, storming toward the stairs to the back-alley exit.

I slam the door shut behind me and lean against the wall, watching a cleanerbot polishing the tiled floor. The air isn't exactly fresher out here; smells from the food vendors battle for dominance against the noise of a busy corridor just meters away. I let my head fall back and try to relieve my feelings by cursing emphatically.

It doesn't really work.

What does happen is this: a whirl of turmeric-yellow robe, dark auburn hair, and snarling maroon lipstick appears out of nowhere and fists the front of my shirt.

At first, I think it's a courtesan mistaking me for someone with a strangulation kink. But as soon as she speaks, my brain connects the dots, and I recognize Saray.

"Tell me it wasn't you," she growls. "Tell me quickly, and I won't wring your neck."

"What wasn't me?" is all I'm able to stammer out, my hands instinctively coming up to pull hers from my collar. She refuses to let go.

I drop my hands and start fiddling with my keycuff instead. Here's hoping I remember how to type our emergency code without looking. The intense fury radiating from her face has me nervous that I'm about to be strangled to death.

"You said you weren't planning to hurt Geneva," Saray grits out. "Does that include her child?"

"I...uh...yes?" I was only vaguely aware that Geneva Milagro *has* a child. *A toddler, isn't he?* Too young to be responsible for anything resembling a crime.

Her fingers loosen enough for me to pry them off my shirt. "You're telling the truth," she says, her shoulders slumping. "Blast it."

And then, to my horror, her eyes go glassy with tears.

"Whoa. Right. I'm lost. What the fuck's going on with you?" I take a judicious step backward, but tilt my head to try to catch her gaze. "What was that about Geneva and her kid?"

"Check the newsies," she says tightly..

I reach for my scroll in its belt holster and scan the highlight page of local news. I don't have to look far. The top article reads, <*Prince Miles Milagro, age five, kidnapped by Ambassador Alan Lake near Moon Palace residence. Any information leading to the arrest of the perpetrator or the child's safe return will be rewarded generously.*>

"Oh, shit," I mutter. "Geneva's kid got kidnapped?"

"And they're framing my father for it." Saray's voice wavers. "I *know* he didn't do it. But the evidence the Authorities have is...convincing. Someone's gone to a lot of trouble to make it look like he did it."

I frown. "So, you came here because...you thought *we* did it?" Her guilty expression tells me I'm right. "Stars, Lady. Why would you think we'd kidnap a kid? Not to mention frame the Halcyon ambassador? He's supposed to be one of the good guys."

She shrugs, her golden eyes defiant. "Was it such a huge leap?"

Well, now I'm *really* offended. "We don't hurt babies," I snap. "And you don't even have to hypnotize me to get me to say that."

Saray groans. "I'm sorry, for what it's worth." She runs her thumbs across the ridge of her eye sockets, as if to relieve a headache. "I didn't think you were going to tell me all that. I just knew I sensed something *off* about your band. I thought I was going to have to chase down a dozen leads to get to the bottom of it. But I couldn't wait to act if Her Grace was in danger."

"What made you think she was in danger?"

My anger is fading into curiosity. This woman is a loaded blaster, but I'm starting to get the feeling she's more of a hazard to herself than to me at the moment.

Her eyes rove over my face, and I wonder if she might be thinking along the same lines. Obviously, she needs an ally right now.

Finally she says, "The last time I spoke to my father before the—the kidnapping happened, he warned me. One of his contacts had heard there was some kind of plot. He told me to leave the Moon Palace for my safety." A dramatic eyeroll. "I decided to investigate instead. You were supposed to be my starting point."

I snort. "Incredibly lucky starting point." I glance toward the busy corridor, barely a stone's throw away. "Nobody followed you here, did they? If your father is the suspect in a kidnapping, the Authorities are almost certainly watching you—"

"I'm not a complete quarkbrain," Saray says. "They questioned me this morning. I knew they'd have me followed if I went out the usual way. So, I teleported. No one knows I'm here. Geneva's ladies still think I'm sulking in my room."

I raise my eyebrows, impressed. "How come you can call a dragon without getting too blissed to talk in complete sentences?"

"I was raised Halcyonite," she says, as if that's an explanation. When I still look confused, she says, "You know, the planetary religion that's all about communicating with dragons?"

I gotta be honest, I don't know much, despite my bandmates being former Halcyonites. Kyle's made a couple of offhand references to Halcyon's religious order, which teaches everybody from childhood how to meditate and/or suppress their feelings to appease the dragons. That's a "no thanks" from me, even though being able to disappear at will would be useful. Pretty sure Kyle and Andi have already leveraged their dragon pals a couple of times to avoid the Authorities.

That gives me an idea. "Hey, you should meet my bandmates! They're Halcyonite expats, too." Also, she needs to do some 'splaining about how the fuck she yanked my secrets out of my mouth, so the band can stop hating me for being a blab.

She takes a step back. "I...I don't know if that's..." Her body language is screaming discomfort.

Too bad, Lady. I slide open the basement door. "This way."

When she doesn't move, I grab a handful of her sleeve and pull her along with me.

"Excuse you, this robe is designer—"

"Hey, team!" I yell. "We have a visitor." To Saray, out of the corner of my mouth, I say, "Don't you dare teleport."

As we reach the bottom of the stairs, there's a loud crash. Kyle has just jumped up, knocking over his stool and half his drum set. "*Saray?*"

I glance back and forth between them. "Hang on, I didn't tell you her name. You two know each other?"

Saray's staring at Kyle, eyes narrowed. "Do we? You look kinda familiar, but..."

Kyle steps over his stool, almost trips, then catches himself on the paper screen that partitions his "room," putting a catastrophic rip right through the intricate painting that decorates it.

"Ohhhh. Wait." Saray points a finger at him, a smile tugging at her mouth. "You shaved your head. Blond hair, right? Miri's boyfriend. What's-your-name. *Leo.*"

"Jar," says Forrest loudly. Everyone else is too busy shushing Saray in panicked unison.

"Can't use real names on the Moon Palace, in case there's anybody listening," I explain. "He's *Kyle* while he's here. So, Kyle, want to explain how you know her?"

Kyle's too busy stammering in shock. Saray answers for him. "He's dating my little sister. Or he *was*, five years ago."

"Still am." Kyle's face is on fire now. "Well, this explains a lot." He gestures at me and our bandmates. "We all thought you had some kind of top-secret interrogation tech. But you're an Ediya Experiment."

"Ohhhh," chorus Andi, Nigel, and Forrest.

Then Andi says, "Hey, sorry, Jed. I really thought you were just a quark-brain."

"Wow, fuck you, too," I mutter. "So who wants to explain what a Dia Experiment means, exactly? Because I seem to be the only one who doesn't know."

"You're gonna want to be sitting down," says Nigel. "Here, Saray, pull up a seat."

He drags over a storage trunk from the pile of junk against the wall. Saray swishes her yellow robe to the side and perches on the lid, crossing her ankles and folding her hands like a princess holding court.

I drop onto the pink fainting couch next to Andi, staring at each of my teammates like it's the first time I'm seeing them. I've only known these people going on three years. Why did I assume they'd never done anything worth keeping secret before they met me?

My keycuff buzzes against my wrist. A message from Simon: *<Got a weird message just now. Are you safe?>*

Oops. I forgot about my panicked attempt at sending our emergency code when Saray had me by the throat. I check my outgoing messages and cringe. It's a garbled mess, and it didn't even go to anyone but Simon.

I type back, <*Yes. But come over anyway if you can. There's been a...development.*>

<*I'm on my way.*>

I should probably tell him to wait until after we're done here, but selfishly, I want him to witness my vindication.

"Saray, you'd better be the one to explain," Kyle says.

Saray gives me a narrow-eyed look. "Swear you'll never tell anyone else what I'm about to tell you," she demands.

My instinct is to argue that I have no idea what secret I'd be swearing to keep, but I catch Andi's glare and swallow my protests. "Yeah. I won't tell."

Saray takes a long, slow breath in through her nose. Then she says, "The Ediya Experiments started when Drs. Melanie, Oberon, and Gaela Ediya ran unapproved genetic modification tests on twenty embryos. They wove alien DNA into our cells, with the goal to create humans who had the same abilities as the dragons." She smiles grimly at the way my jaw drops. "They succeeded."

"You—"

She holds up a finger to stop me from interrupting. "Yes. All of us have unusual abilities: reading minds, healing, turning invisible, that kind of thing. They kept us hidden on an uncharted space station for years. I was thirteen when we were rescued by our sister, Amy, who underwent the same gen-modding but was raised on Halcyon. She brought all twenty of us to her home planet, where we were adopted out to random homes. No one except Amy ever knew about our gen-mods. We were told to keep them secret, so we did." She gives a thin-lipped smile. "The end."

I press my fist to my mouth, blinking fast as I try to process. A single cogent thought, *No wonder she never wanted to talk about her family,* wanders across my mind. The rest of my mind is scrambled eggs, because *gen-modded dragon powers? Surely this can't be real life.*

"Not quite the end," Kyle butts in. "What about the part where Haven—"

"Not relevant," Saray snaps, cutting him off. "I've told Jed what he needs to know. I'm gen-modded with abilities that some would consider inhuman. One of them is forcing the truth out of someone who's lying to me. That's what I used on you the other day. I'm sorry that it put you in a bad position, but I'm not sorry that I did it. If I hadn't, you'd still be on my suspect list for Prince Miles's kidnapper."

"Oh stars! I just saw that newsie alert!" Andi taps on her scroll, pulling it up again. "Alan Lake...that's the Halcyonite ambassador!"

"And my adoptive father." Saray's voice wavers. "He's being set up. Someone wanted to hurt Geneva by taking Miles. I can't help but wonder if they also wanted to hurt me by framing Alan. I need to clear his name before the Authorities find him. They've as good as told me they plan to execute him on the spot."

There's a hush as my teammates take in her words. For once, even Andi and Forrest don't have anything to say.

An insistent knocking on the basement door breaks the silence. The team glances at each other, panicked.

"It's probably just Simon," I say. "I called him."

Nigel climbs the stairs, holding a guitar over his shoulder like he's ready to use it as a battle-axe. His tail swishes, the fur standing on end to make him look fluffier.

"In case it's not Simon, you should hide," Kyle whispers to Saray.

But then we hear, "Oh! Sorry. You scared us, coming in the back way. Come on down," and we all relax a tad.

Simon descends the stairs ahead of Nigel, a wild look in his eyes. "Is Jed in here? Are you all safe?"

"We're fine," I say, jumping up.

His eyes meet mine, then scan the room for any sign of danger, then snap to my face again. His shoulders sag in relief. "You are," he says, a smile touching the corner of his mouth. "Good."

"Um, we have some information for you, though. Or...someone to introduce you to." I turn to Saray. "Meet the final member of the Tarantula team, Simon Kim."

Chapter 13

ENTERTAINMENT SECTOR, THE IMPERIAL MOON PALACE

SARAY

When the knock came at the door, my instinct was to teleport away—and I'm still considering it.

Talking about my past always makes me feel like a little kid again, like everything I've fought for and achieved is ripped away, leaving me unmoored and alone.

Never tell anyone about our gen-mod abilities: the directive was impressed on us young. Even when I joined Haven and began to exercise my powers, the need for secrecy was held above all else. If the wrong person discovers how to manipulate us, the whole of human society would suffer.

But if I'm going to trust anyone, it might as well be Leo Galway (or Kyle, as he's calling himself now). Most of my siblings keep their past hidden from their various romantic partners. My sister, who is a very good judge of character—given that she literally sees people's energy like an aura of colors—not only trusted him enough to tell him everything, but has remained in a relationship with him for five years. That says something about the guy. If he vouches for his bandmates, I'm willing to give them a chance. Even Jed.

And whoever the blazes they just let into their basement.

I'd put him in his mid-twenties. Looks like he just rolled out of bed. His dark hair is rumpled, there's a shadow of stubble on his cheeks, and his black robe falls open to reveal only a pair of loose trousers underneath. He apparently rushed over here so fast, he forgot to put on a shirt.

I cough awkwardly, tearing my eyes from his chest. "Uh...hello." *Would it be rude to say, "Who are you?"*

I glance over at Jed and see that he's still staring at the stranger with hungry eyes. *Ahhh, so it's like that, huh?*

The man steps forward and holds out a polite hand. "Simon Kim, audio-visual tech specialist."

"Saray Lake, lady-in-waiting."

"I know," he says, bowing over our clasped hands with a prince's manners.

I glance at Jed, who jumps in with, "Simon knows just about everything that happens on the Moon Palace. He's been a great asset to our team."

"Saray," Kyle/Leo asks tentatively, "is it all right if we tell him about..."

I want to say no, but it doesn't make strategic sense to leave a lone member of their team in the dark. Slumping down onto the couch, I mumble, "You might as well just search it on the uniweb. The newsie articles are all still out there."

My heart thuds as Leo types "Ediya Experiments" into a private uniweb browser. Leo turns the scroll toward Simon. The tech specialist's eyes flick back and forth across the article that fills his screen. "I remember hearing about this," he says. "Kids rescued from an illegal laboratory...and you were one of them?"

I point at the photo of me and my siblings, lined up on a beach, our eyes wide and curious and a little shell-shocked. "That one," I say. "That one is me."

Simon and Jed both examine the photo. I was thirteen when it was taken. My hair, auburn-touched dark brown, is tied back in a simple braid, my face bare of makeup. It doesn't look anything like me, and yet those are my features: my strong nose, sharp cheekbones, and bow-shaped lips. Those are my eyes, bright gold and fierce. Those gold eyes are the only feature all of the Ediya Experiments share.

The eyes, and the potential to become a dangerous weapon in the wrong hands.

Simon looks at me, head tilted to the side, and asks, "Why reveal yourself now?"

I hesitate, then tell him the truth. "Desperation."

Silently, Jed navigates to the newsie alert about Miles. Simon skim-reads it quickly.

"I see," he murmurs.

Something about him rings a bell, something I can't quite put my finger on. I search his face, wondering if we've met before. Maybe it's just that the grassy, honest scent of his soft voice puts me at ease.

Jed fills him in on the accusations that brought me here. Simon takes a moment to digest it all, then says, "Trust me, Lady Saray, I would never let this team target Geneva Milagro. Not on my life."

"Or her child?" I ask, eyebrows raised.

"Or her child," Simon confirms.

It smells like the truth.

He adds, "She was my mother's best friend. I still owe her for...well, I owe her. Which means I want to catch this kidnapper just as much as you do."

Interesting. I've never heard Geneva mention this guy before. I wonder if she'd tell me what she did to buy his loyalty.

"So, we're on the same page, then," I say. "Convenient."

"Yes," he says, without sarcasm. "I want to invite you to my control center. Your knowledge of your father and of Geneva's intimate circle, combined with my surveillance tech, might have a chance at pinpointing the real criminal before it's too late for Miles."

Audio-visual tech and surveillance... The light goes on in my brain. Simon has access to spy-tech that's almost definitely illegal for non-Authorities to use.

He's a hacker. That's...exactly what I need.

"Can you check if a cambot recording has been tampered with or faked?" I ask, trying not to sound too eager.

"I can certainly try."

B eing seen in public is a risk right now, so I call a dragon to teleport myself, Jed, and Simon to Simon's lair. Dragons typically refuse to teleport directly inside someone's residence—it's a privacy and consent issue—so this one drops us off in the corridor outside.

I've gotten accustomed to the sparkling luxury suites that royalty and their attendants reside in. It's a bit of a culture shock to see how dingy this residential hallway has been allowed to get. I scan the doors in front of us. People have tried to make these bleak apartments homey. Handpainted decorations, welcome mats, bells, and banners lend personality to each portal, saving this hallway from looking like a prison. And yet there's one door that's blank, without even a nameplate. My eyes bounce right past it, assuming it's a vacancy.

But Simon heads straight there, scanning his keycuff to unlock the door. "Quick," he whispers. "A cambot's coming around the corner in thirty seconds."

Jed and I stumble into each other in our rush. I wish I knew how Jed talked his way into coming with me. Of the Tarantula members, he's still the one I trust the least. But he seems to have the best rapport with Simon—if that's what they're calling it these days.

Once the door shuts behind us, Simon beckons us into the room. "Have a seat. We can speak freely here. I perform daily security scans."

The layout of his apartment reminds me of my room in Geneva's suite. There's a recently vacated sleep-pod with the lid hanging open, a partitioned-off waste receptacle and cleansing unit, a small mini-kitch, and a wallscreen across from a cozy, blanket-draped brown couch. Not much room for anything else.

Jed lowers himself onto the couch, his eyes eating up the room in a way that makes me suspect this is his first time here, too.

"I assume this is the recording you want to check?" Simon asks.

He flexes his hand into the wallscreen control gauntlet, sliding the network of silvery sensor rings over his fingers in a smooth, precise motion, then gestures with it to wake up his screen. Splashed across the wall, larger than life, I see the recording that shattered my world this morning.

I stare. "How'd you get access to this? The Authorities haven't released it publicly, have they?"

"No," says Simon. "I told you, I specialize in surveillance. That includes keeping track of the Authorities and their active investigations."

Yup. Definitely a hacker.

He begins flipping nonchalantly through classified Authority files that he shouldn't have the clearance to access. At least, *I've* never managed to get into the Head of Security's private digital archive, and believe me, I've tried.

"So far, they haven't been able to track the perpetrator beyond the recording of the incident," Simon muses. "It seems to me that this person knows how to avoid cambots when they want to. They wanted the kidnapping to be recorded. They were sending a message of some kind."

"I thought so too. A message that frames Alan as a kidnapper." I cross my arms, sinking onto the sofa next to Jed. "I've been trying to contact him nonstop, but I can't connect. Has he been found yet?"

"No. And that does make it difficult to believe Ambassador Lake is innocent," Simon points out. "If he didn't do this, why has he disappeared?"

I've been thinking about that, actually. "Two possibilities. Either he fled the planet right after the ball—but I didn't get the sense that he would—or the person who kidnapped Miles also kidnapped Alan." I don't want to say, *Or murdered him,* but that's also possible.

"Hmm. So if the Authorities find Miles and Alan in the same place, they'll take that as proof of his guilt." Simon taps his chin with his non-gauntleted hand. "You need to find them before the Authorities do."

He flips back to the recording of the incident, and we watch it again in silence. Simon turns up the sound so that we can hear the faint outlines of words spoken.

"Alan's voice is deeper than that," I murmur. "It can't be him. They've dressed up just like him, but..." I squint at the features. "Stars, whoever did it, they're good. Are you sure this isn't faked?"

Simon replays it again, squinting at the figures, blowing the size up until they're blurry and huge. Then he shakes his head. "This is the raw footage from the cambot," he says. "I can't see any evidence of an edit."

"Then how did they fake him so well?" I lean forward on the couch, hands steepled under my chin. "It looks *so much* like him. Only the voice and some of the movements are off."

Simon walks in a meandering circle around the holo outline of the impostor's face, still blown up larger than life in the middle of the room. "If I had to guess...makeup and prosthetics. Maybe even surgery. Whoever made this disguise is an expert."

"Of course," I mutter to myself.

Megs wouldn't have recognized the kidnapper as my father if it hadn't looked like him. Unless Megs was in on the plot, which would be a serious accusation to throw at the woman Geneva spent months vetting and interviewing exhaustively.

Then an idea sparks. "A makeup expert, professionally trained, would probably be a member of the artists' guild." I jump to my feet. "Pearl!"

Jed blinks. "Who?"

"Another lady-in-waiting. She's a makeup artist and a guild member." I pull out my scroll, then decide it'd be better to ask Pearl in person. I can't taste lies over a message.

"And you don't suspect her...why?" Jed prompts.

I sit back down. It's a fair question, but... "She couldn't have been involved. I was with her almost that whole day. We were at Princess Iris's party together, and we all got ready together."

"I was at Iris's ball too," says Simon. "I remember seeing Lady Pearl. I can trace her movements, if you'd like to be certain."

Jed lifts his eyebrows. "How'd you get invited to a princess's birthday party?"

"I didn't," Simon replies mildly. "But surveillance via cambot isn't always practical. Sometimes, I need boots on the ground."

"Yeah, but..." Jed frowns. "I dunno, I just never pictured you cozying up with the enemy."

"*Cozying* isn't the right word." Simon's eyes flick to me. "I'm sure Lady Saray will back me up. What goes on at those parties is much closer to warfare."

He's right, but I bristle. Has he been watching us? Why have I never seen him before?

Or have I, and didn't know it?

Simon's already turned back to his screen, pulling up footage of the ball. Pearl is clearly visible in several shots throughout the night, dancing with a different person for every song. "She has an alibi," he confirms. "Still, be cautious what you say to her."

Another idea occurs to me as Simon flips through cambot recordings as easily as book pages. "Could you find the footage of the hallway outside Alan's quarters?" Obviously, this would've occurred to the Authorities, too, so it must be a dead end, but...I want to know where he went on his last outing before he disappeared. What he took with him.

"Sure. What's his address?"

Moments later, Simon has three different angles on the hallway outside my father's suite. I'm impressed and a tad appalled at how quickly he's able to start spying on almost anywhere in the entire palace. I wouldn't want to be on this man's bad side.

Simon fast-forwards through the day of the kidnapping, but Alan only appears once: when he leaves to go to Princess Iris's ball. According to the security cams, he never came back. We watch as, hours after the kidnapping, the Authorities override his door code and force their way in to search his apartment, coming up empty.

"Something happened at the ball," I murmur. "Or right after. Either he found out something and ran, or..."

Or. Sickness churns my stomach as my brain supplies gory images that I don't want to see. *Stars, please let Alan be alive.*

I still can't believe he was involved in Miles's disappearance, whatever anyone says. I'll just have to speak to Pearl and find out who's capable of such a convincing transformation.

"I have to get back to Geneva's suite," I say. "Thank you for your help, Simon."

"Tread lightly," Simon warns. He holds out his wrist, offering his key-cuff. "Would you give me your call code? I'd like to stay in touch. If you find yourself in danger, feel free to teleport back here. Just make sure no one tracks you."

I lift my wrist, cupping my own gold-filigree keycuff thoughtfully. "Why are you so willing to help me?"

His words had the scent of truth, but I still find it hard to trust this man who watches everyone in the palace like a spider in a web made of cambots. Is he an Authority? Is he a Greenjacket like Jed? What's his angle?

Simon pauses for a long time before he responds. "My mother loved Geneva Milagro," he says softly. "Before she died, they were inseparable."

That piques my interest. Geneva doesn't have many friends, certainly none that close. I would expect her to have mentioned Simon's mother at some point.

"Mom would've realigned the planets bare-handed to get Geneva's kid back for her," he continues. "Since she's not here to do it, my bots and I are at your service."

"What was your mom's name?" I dare to ask.

Simon's brown eyes search my face. "Haneul," he says finally. "Kim Haneul."

Princex Somin's mother. Geneva's closest friend, dead for five years.

And that's when it clicks. I've seen his arresting eyes before, hidden behind a veil.

No wonder nobody's seen Princex Somin in years. They've been Simon all along.

Seeing the recognition light up my face, Simon turns away, expression closing off as he strips the control gauntlet from his hand. "You should go."

"It's all right," I say quickly. "I won't tell anyone."

Over his shoulder, I see Jed sitting forward on the couch, listening intently. Has Simon not even told *him* yet?

"Geneva knows," Simon mutters. "She's the only one. No one else. Especially not my father."

The Emperor. Shit. Not only is he keeping a secret from the man the Authorities' spies report to, he's actively hacking into those spies' databases. Simon Kim is bold as fuck.

"You've been passing notes for her," I accuse. "Why? Who are they from?"

He hesitates for a long moment before saying, "Your father."

My eyebrows shoot up. "From Alan?"

He nods. "After my mother died and Geneva helped me go underground, I told her I would repay her in any way she wished. This was her only request. Once in awhile, Alan would have a message for her, one that was too secret to send in a traceable message. I was not to read the papers, just get them to her in some unobtrusive way. I'm very good at disguising myself."

That he is. If I hadn't already tasted the truth in his statement that he would never come for Geneva or her child, I'd be wondering if *he* was the false Alan.

"I think..." Simon presses his lips together. "I don't know for certain. But they seemed like lovers' notes to me."

Geneva? Take a lover? I can't imagine where she'd find the time or the privacy. Yet my heart drops as I remember that stolen moment at the ball, Alan's hand pressing into hers. From anyone else, it would be nothing more than a friendly gesture, but given the risk of touching the Emperor's favorite at all, I wonder...

Stars above, Geneva is so far out of Alan's orbit, she might as well be in another galaxy. But is it so impossible for a woman starved of love to seek it in an unexpected place?

Simon watches the confusion play on my face and says, "Forget I said anything. I've already violated her trust by telling you. I'm sorry."

I smile in what I hope is a reassuring way. "Don't be. I appreciate your honesty. I'll keep your secret as safe as hers. Oh, and..." I glance at Jed again and drop my voice to a whisper. "Do you prefer *he* or *they*—?"

"Either is fine," says Simon with a small smile, "but mostly *he*. Somin is dress-up for me now. Simon is who I am."

Nodding, I hold out my wrist, allowing him to tap his keycuff against mine, adding each other's call codes.

My anxiety at revealing my identity earlier has faded into relief. If Simon is someone Geneva trusts to pass top-secret information for her, then I know I can trust him, too.

For once in my life, getting someone's call code doesn't feel like a flirtation, or even like setting up an informational contact. It feels like making a friend.

As I reach out with my mind to call a dragon, preparing to teleport back to my room, I pause one more time to look at both Simon and Jed. "Thank you," I repeat, my voice thick in my throat.

Jed is the one who says, "Don't make us regret this." Simon just nods solemnly, throat moving as he swallows.

We're all taking risks here. I hope I don't regret it, either.

Chapter 14

ENTERTAINMENT SECTOR, THE IMPERIAL MOON PALACE

JED

As soon as Saray disappears, Simon turns to me with a stricken look. He obviously didn't want me to overhear what he just told Saray. That stings—we've been working together for months, and he's known her all of five minutes, yet *she's* the one he opens up to?

Yeah, fine, I'm jealous. Shut up.

"So, now you know the truth," he says, fiddling with the metallic rings of the wallscreen gauntlet he's still wearing. "I was born Kim Somin. A...princex." He grimaces, like he's bracing himself for me to shoot him.

I search Simon's face for evidence of the Emperor's features, but I just can't picture him as a prince. I wonder if he had facial surgery to erase the resemblance, or if he always took after his mother.

I almost don't believe it could be true. But he has no reason to make up something like this.

Princex Somin's always been low on our list of royal targets. I barely know anything about them. When we first arrived on the Moon Palace, Simon briefed us on every living Imperial scion, complete with dossiers on each one's political stance and relationship with the Emperor. Somin's file was sparse: just a recap of Lady Haneul's death by poisoning and the princex's disappearance into exile. Simon assured us that the princex was probably dead by now and posed no threat.

It hurts that he lied to us. But I guess I understand why.

"I won't tell the rest of the team if you don't want me to," I promise. "It doesn't change anything, right? You're still on our side."

I let that dangle as a question. He nods, deflating a little as the tension leaves his shoulders. "I am. I swear to you, I am."

There's too much pain in his eyes. Unable to bear it, I default to a joke to lighten the mood. "Just don't make me call you *Your Highness.*"

Simon jabs a gentle punch at my shoulder. "I'll kick your ass if you do." But at least he cracks a smile. His arms fold across his chest, though, as if to protect himself. "Sorry for dragging you into this, Jed. I won't let it jeopardize your mission. I do plan to help her, but I'll keep your team out of it."

I hesitate. It would be smart to accept these terms, or at least run this by my team before I promise my help. All eyes are on Saray now that her father is plastered across the Palace News. Distancing ourselves would be wise. Not to mention I shouldn't be digging myself in deeper with a man who I now know to be a son of the Emperor—the very bloodline we've been sent here to pick off.

And yet.

Whoever took Geneva Milagro's child and is trying to frame Saray's dad, I can't walk away until I know *why.* My instincts are telling me this could be huge—and if we play our cards right, the Greenjackets could take advantage of it.

Plus, there's the lure of spending more time with Simon. I'd like to say that's not my primary reason, but...he's hot, and I'm a dumbass.

"Let me help?" I ask. "I'm invested. We gotta find Ambassador Lake and that poor kid before something worse happens."

Simon's smile widens, and my heart stutters.

Blast me, I'm so fuckin' vortexed.

Chapter 15

GENEVA MILAGRO'S SUITE, THE IMPERIAL MOON PALACE

SARAY

I take a chance and don't use a dragon when I teleport, knowing that dragons would object to 'porting me into a private space without an explicit invitation. My return to Geneva's suite is fortunately timed. I barely have a moment to orient myself to the return of gravity before a fist is pounding on my door.

My heart jumps into my throat. I glance in the mirror, assessing my appearance. There's nothing out of place to signal that I've been running around the Pleasure Sector. I just have to pray they haven't been knocking for long.

Just in case they have... *Act like you've been sulking in your room ignoring everyone for hours.* Wrenching the door aside, I snap, "What do you want?"

It's Nuala. "Her Grace has been asking for you," she snarks back, lip curling. "I wouldn't keep her waiting much longer if I were you. You're lucky to still have a position here."

I sweep past her, slamming the door shut behind me. Hopefully that wasn't playing up the sulking too much.

When I make my way into the sitting room, cold expressions greet me from all angles. Kina wordlessly points me in the direction of Geneva's bedroom, but none of the other ladies say a word to me. Not even Yumiko.

They all believe Alan's guilty, and they think I'm guilty by association. That I'd allow someone to hit Geneva where it hurts the most. It rankles, knowing I'm the only one of us who's actually working to track down the real culprit.

But if the roles were reversed, would I trust them? I have to admit I might not. Even though we spend our days serving the same mistress, I barely know them outside of work. Have I let a single person see my true self since I came to this moon? No—not until Jed and his band pried it out of me. And I certainly haven't looked for someone else's.

With everyone against me, I'm starting to wonder if that might have been a mistake.

My chest feels frozen solid as I tap the entry-request button on Geneva's door. The door slides aside with a gentle chime, and I let it close behind me, cutting off the chilly gazes on my back.

"Saray. Come here, please."

Geneva's body looks so small and fragile in the curtain-draped, pillow-festooned expanse of the bed. I take slow steps forward, nervous despite Geneva's defense of me earlier. What she has to say in public and in private are not always the same.

She lifts the cold pack resting across her eyes, laying it on a cushion beside her. "It's all right. I'm not angry. You may approach."

The words don't smell of citrus or vinegar, so I pull up a short stool and perch on it, leaning on the edge of the mattress. I keep my mouth shut, waiting for Geneva to tell me what she wants.

Presently she rolls to her side, cheek pressed to the pillow, and examines me with those piercing violet eyes. Sometimes, I'm gripped with an irrational fear that Geneva can read my mind—which is ridiculous, since I have nothing to hide from her.

Well. Nothing *much*.

"You don't believe your father did this," Geneva says at length.

I shake my head. "No, Your Grace, I truly don't."

She nods slowly. "I don't, either."

The words smell of fresh-cut grass. *Truth.* My shoulders relax ever so slightly. "Thank you," I murmur. Even if the Authorities don't believe me, it means the world that Geneva does.

"Alan and I talked right before he disappeared," Geneva admits softly. "He told me that he warned you of danger. He said he knows you would never leave me voluntarily. He requested that, if it came to it, I should dismiss you and rescind your approval to live on the Moon Palace—if it was the only way to keep you out of danger."

My jaw drops. "Alan asked you to fire me?"

"Naturally, I didn't tell the Authorities about it." Geneva folds a corner of the blanket between her fingers, absently rubbing the seam with her thumb. "I'm certain they would take it as an admission of guilt. They would say that he knew what he intended to do and wanted to keep you from facing the backlash. However, I don't believe Alan Lake had any motive to kidnap Miles."

I digest that for a moment. The question is on the the tip of my tongue: *Why are you and Alan exchanging secret messages?* But now that I'm looking her in the eye, I don't dare make the accusation.

I'm afraid I won't like the answer.

"Why did you call me here?" I venture instead.

The answer is what I feared the most. "Because I am dismissing you."

To my horror, tears spring to my eyes. I'd been half expecting this, and yet it still blindsides me. "I want to stay," I force out, my throat closing around the words. "This isn't just a job for me, Your Grace. I care about you. I want to help you catch who did this."

"I already know."

The words hit me like a punch to the throat. I jump to my feet. "Who? Did you tell the Authorities?"

"No, I haven't." Geneva sits up slowly, covers and nightrobe puddling around her. Her hair falls in tangles across her shoulder. "The Authorities are not on our side, Saray. They're on *his*."

My breath catches. She almost never refers to the Emperor as anything but her "adored husband." We all know the affection is a lie, but it's a lie she must tell or risk death. Even hinting that she might oppose him is dangerous.

"Are you saying that you think..." I scarcely dare to say it out loud. "His Majesty is involved in Miles's disappearance?"

"No."

Grass. I breathe a sigh of relief.

"But he will not help, either," Geneva says. "This is a problem I alone must solve. And just like your father, I want to protect you from the fallout. That's why I'm sending you away. I should have done so immediately when Megs brought us the news...but, selfishly, I wanted your support for just a little longer." She sighs. "We both need to be strong now."

I sink back down onto the stool next to her bed. "Please don't do this." My voice is almost plaintive. I hate how pathetic my words taste. Chamomile heartbreak.

"I wish I didn't have to," says Geneva, reaching out to place her hand on my wrist. "You have served me well, Saray. Your loyalty has not gone unnoticed. I pray that one day we'll see each other again."

The way she says it makes me go cold. It sounds like the goodbye a person gives right before they're about to die.

"Your Grace," I choke, standing to make a deep bow. "It has been my honor."

And I'm not going to stop serving you just because you're letting me go.

When I storm out into the sitting room, the false sympathy in the other ladies' eyes tells me everything. They knew I was about to get kicked out, and they're relieved to see me go.

Impotent fury bubbles up in my chest. I very nearly unleash it on them. But I can't burn bridges yet.

"Her Grace has asked me to leave," I announce, my voice tight. "I will need assistance packing. Pearl, Kina, can you come help me?"

Pearl raises her eyebrows. "Of course." I'm sure she's wondering why I'd want her help. Kina is an expert at packing clothes for minimal wrinkling, but Pearl's room always looks like a hurricane ripped through it.

But I'm determined to continue this blasted investigation until it kills me.

I've kept my space neat; there's not much to pack beyond layering my wardrobe into two hover-trunks. Pearl takes the robes from their hangers, Kina folds them, and I transfer them into my luggage. Nobody talks for the first several minutes, though I know the two of them are dying to know what Geneva said to me.

"Pearl," I say casually, "if I wanted to train as a makeup artist, which masters are the best to learn from?"

"Here?" Pearl asks sweetly. "Are you sure you don't want to go back to Monroe for a little while?"

"I'm not ready to leave the Moon Palace yet," I say. *I refuse to let people think I'm running away.*

"Well, there's a great cosmetology school in Hepburn City, of course..." Pearl lets that sentence dangle for a long moment before she sighs and says, "It wouldn't do any good to give you a list of the masters on the Moon Palace. They're too busy to take students. If you're determined, you could apply to apprentice with the Pavilion Theater. Their new director is supposed to be a master at costume and makeup design. But I warn you, the competition is cutthroat."

The word "costume" gets my attention. "Oh? Would I have seen their work in anything recent?"

"Yeah, that play we went to, like, two months ago? *Rosalina?* Director Quell oversaw the costuming and makeup for that one."

I do remember being impressed at how much the main character resembled the actress who played the same character in a recorded holo-drama two hundred and fifty years ago. At the time, I assumed they simply cast a similar-looking actress, but...

An actor would have all the skills necessary to pull off a convincing impersonation. It's blindingly obvious now that the thought occurs to me. Why didn't I start my search at the theater in the first place? Because I was too distracted by Jedrek Blaze on his hoverboard?

Embarrassing.

I swallow my excitement. "Maybe you're right," I muse, tasting cinnamon. "Maybe I should just try Monroe. I don't know if I want to get involved with the theater."

"That might be for the best," says Pearl, patting me on the shoulder. "Now, honey, do you want to wrap your toiletries before you pack them?"

With all my belongings stuffed into hover-trunks, I perform the walk of shame through Geneva's suite. The other ladies have gathered to watch me go; they paste on sad faces, but I'm sure they're relieved. If I were them, I'd be eager to get rid of anyone who brought the slightest whiff of scandal or danger into Geneva's private space.

The guards, Autumn and Destra, both hug me before helping me float my trunks out the door.

"I'm so sorry about all this," Destra whispers. "We don't think you had anything to do with it."

"Hopefully your father will be caught and brought to justice. Then you can come back," says Autumn.

I know she means well, but I can't help but wince. Even my supporters can't believe that Alan is innocent.

"Thank you," I choke out. "Tell Geneva...tell her..."

No. Geneva and I have said all we need to say. I let the sentence trail unfinished, turn my back, and leave.

My slow procession down the corridor, trunks trailing behind me, heart breaking in my chest, becomes even more humiliating when a newsie cambot zooms up to follow me. Then all of Geneva's neighbors tumble out of their front doors to watch. Ladies-in-waiting line the hall, tittering, while no doubt the Imperial wives they serve are having a good laugh watching me on their newsie feed.

As I wait for the zip-lift, I feel something hit me between the shoulder blades. I turn, incensed as I realize it was a thrown slipper. Rage boils in my throat, and I want to scream in their hideous, beautiful faces. But I swallow it, straighten my shoulders, and lift my chin. More shoes pelt me, but I ignore them.

The zip-lift dings, the door sliding open. I shove my trunks inside and mash the close-door button, struggling to strap the luggage down as shoes continue flying at me through the slowly closing door.

Only when the zip-lift begins to move do I allow the tears to come.

Chapter 16

ENTERTAINMENT SECTOR, THE IMPERIAL MOON PALACE

JED

Although I still have some unresolved hurt feelings about the way Saray's treated me, it doesn't feel good to see her in disgrace on a trashy newsie site, having stuff thrown at her in the corridor.

Simon's face is impassive as he continues flicking through his network of cambots, looking for any sign of Alan Lake. He keeps the Saray feed open in a corner of the wallscreen, his eyes straying to it every minute or so.

"Should somebody go help her?" I mutter, knowing I can't volunteer.

"She can handle it," says Simon calmly.

"*Fuck*." I run my hands down my face. "What if someone in that crowd has a gun?"

"They don't need to shoot her." Simon pauses the vid he's watching and turns to look at me. "She's been socially ruined. In their eyes, she's already dead."

"You know by experience?"

"I grew up in the women's wing of the palace." Simon's tone is flat. "I know their world, their rules. Saray was in more danger from the other ladies when she still held a coveted position of power next to Lady Geneva. She's no threat now."

His voice resonates with suppressed emotion. Stars, I spent all that time wishing he'd let me get to know him, but seeing him sad short-circuits my brain. I'd do anything to take that hurt away. But I barely know how to deal with my *own* shit.

Ugh, why am I like this? Don't people in holo-dramas, like, hug each other when they're sad? Do that, then, dumbass.

I'm not quite brave enough to go for an embrace. Tentatively, I reach out and put a hand on his arm, hoping he won't notice how my fingers tremble with the electricity of touching him.

He leans into it slightly. My heartbeat stutters.

As we watch the feed, the moment between us lengthens, brittle and sweet as spun sugar. I breathe a sigh of relief when the zip-lift closes on Saray's blank expression, cutting her off from the barrage of jeers and slippers—and watching eyes, including ours.

"Do you really think she's going to leave the Moon Palace?" I murmur.

Simon tenses, as if the sound of my voice reminded him how close we are. He plays it casual as he pulls away, though I can hear the shake in his exhaled breath. "What do *you* think?"

"If I were her, I'd be even more determined to prove them all wrong."

"Me, too," says Simon, very softly, as he turns back to the screen.

Suddenly, a "BREAKING NEWS" animation flashes across the newsie feed, interrupting their slow-motion replay of Saray's descent into exile.

Simon and I listen to the update in growing horror, glancing at each other as if to reassure ourselves we're hearing it right.

"Shit," I hiss when it begins to replay. "This changes everything. She's in danger."

Simon's already tapping her recently added call code to send her a message. "Get back here," he murmurs, his voice low and gruff. I feel a tiny bit guilty about how much that voice turns me on. *Now's not the time, Jed.*

Not five minutes later, Simon's door chimes with a request for entry. She's teleported again. Maybe I *should* get the team to teach me how they communicate with dragons. It's a seriously enviable talent.

She's breathless, like she's been running. "Would've been here sooner," she explains, "but I had to stow my trunks in a locker by the docks. I tried to make it look like I was really leaving. Maybe the newsies'll leave me the fuck alone now."

The sharp bitterness in her tone and the redness in her eyes make me regret what we're about to tell her. She's already barely holding it together—but this news can't be put off.

"You, uh, might want to be sitting down," Simon tells her apologetically.

He's been recording the feed, and now he loops it back to the beginning for Saray to see.

"Breaking news: Suspected kidnapper Alan Lake has been caught."

Chapter 17

ENTERTAINMENT SECTOR, THE IMPERIAL MOON PALACE

SARAY

I suck in a sharp breath. "How long ago was this?"

"Minutes," Jed murmurs. "Just listen."

"Ambassador Alan Lake, yesterday accused of kidnapping Prince Miles, has been apprehended. Lake, a Halcyon citizen, was found inside a shipping crate in an apparent attempt to smuggle himself onto a cargo vessel. He has been imprisoned pending execution, which will be carried out as soon as Authorities determine the location of the young prince. A thorough search of the docks is in process, but the prince has not been found."

"Saray?"

It's Simon calling my name. Both men are giving me concerned looks. I feel very far away, my vision growing spotty, as if I might faint. What is my face doing right now? Most of the time it's easy enough to arrange it into a pleasant mask. At the moment, I'm so lost in the thundering of my pulse that my features might as well be someone else's.

I put my head between my knees and breathe deep. As I focus on not passing out, a tentative hand begins to stroke my back. Then a second one from the other side. I keep my head down, hiding the tears that well up.

I wish they'd stop being so kind to me. It makes this blasted situation so much worse.

"I'm fine," I mutter into the folds of my skirt. "It's all right. Alan's not dead yet."

But he might as well be. The only reason the Authorities are keeping him alive is so they can torture Prince Miles's location out of him. Which, if I'm right, he doesn't even know. He's about to face the worst imaginable pain for no reason.

I look up at the screen again. The newsreaders can barely hide their smirks as they discuss this development. I'm sure they've been pantomiming their horror and sorrow at the kidnapping all night. Now it's their favorite part of the story arc: the evil perpetrator getting his just deserts.

Simon skips forward to a live feed again, just in time for one of the talking heads to make another announcement.

"And now, we have the extraordinary honor to host a message from His Imperial Majesty, the Emperor of the United Galaxy. We just received His Majesty's recorded statement in response to this atrocious act against one of his blood children. Silence as our Emperor speaks."

Jed hisses between his teeth as the array of newsie heads is replaced by the larger-than-life head and shoulders of our illustrious ruler.

His Majesty is at least ninety years old at this point, but with access to the finest anti-aging treatments and genetic modifications that stolen money can buy, he's managed to stay looking like he's in his late forties. If I hadn't been seeing this face on newsie vids my whole life, I'd say he's no more remarkable than any random guy you'd meet on the street. He has a well-structured face, square jaw, strong cheekbones, and pale skin that only shows his age if you look too close at how tightly it's stretched. His hair is black, combed in a sideways swoop—it's almost definitely a wig, but people have gotten arrested for saying so on public message boards. He wears strong winged eyeliner in a signature design that makeup artists across the galaxy have been forbidden to copy on pain of treason, with thick, pointed red and gold lines curving up the sides of his cheeks in a nod to the red Imperial flag with its gold rampant dragon. His robe, what I can see of it from the tight frame, is plain black with more dragons embroidered along the collar. They aren't the peaceful alien dragons we know today; they're the mythic ones from ancient Earth, toothy and ferocious, breathing fire and destroying anyone who stands against them.

But under the trappings, he's nothing above average. It's just the eyes—pale blue, strangely wide, cold and flat as a predator's—that hint at what kind of man he is. The kind to abuse the women he has under his power. The kind to have indiscriminate numbers of children and then encourage them to murder each other for a chance at his throne. The kind who sees nothing wrong with a system that enriches him and his cronies while impoverishing millions of people on the planets he exploits.

Seeing that face makes my stomach lurch.

"It has come to our attention," the Emperor says, *"that Ambassador Alan Lake has kidnapped our child, the son of our most favored consort. Ambassador Lake was invited here as a representative of Halcyon, with the express purpose of fostering peaceful relations between our Empire and their rebellious society. As such, we cannot but see this kidnapping as an act of war."*

Oh, stars. I might actually cast up.

"If Lake does not return our child unharmed by tomorrow, we will dispatch a hundred warships to attack Halcyon," the Emperor continues. *"You Halcyonites may think that your dragons can protect you, but you are wrong. By sending this man to harm our family, you have signed your death warrants. Even if our son is returned, we expect your surrender and assimilation as a vassal of our Empire before our wrath will be appeased. Whether it is done willingly in peace or violently with your demise hinges on your ambassador's cooperation."*

Jed, Simon, and I stare at each other in stunned silence.

"Well," says Simon finally, "I think we found the motive for framing Ambassador Lake. It's an excuse to start a war."

"But how are they planning to get around the dragons' blockade of Halcyon?" Jed asks. "No dragon will ever teleport their ships there, and it'd take way longer than a human lifetime to travel there without teleporting, even at lightspeed."

The sick churning in my stomach intensifies. "It's possible," I say.

Possible because of me and my siblings, who can teleport without dragons. We have power equal to the dragons...and fallible human minds that can be twisted and controlled.

Does this mean the Emperor has one of my siblings in thrall? But how? And, for stars' sake, *who?*

Simon narrows his eyes. "What do you know that we don't?"

"It's not what I know," I say, throat tight. "It's what I can do. Me and all my siblings. Truth-telling isn't my only skill." I swallow hard. "I'm gen-modded with dragon DNA. I can teleport."

Jed lifts an eyebrow. "Yeah, we know..."

But Simon's eyes pierce me. "You're not talking about dragon-aided teleporting, are you?"

"No. I don't need a dragon," I whisper. "No one is supposed to know. My siblings and I aren't bound by dragon rules, either. We can 'port into people's private residences. We can teleport someone who's sick or dying. And..."

Jed's face falls as he understands. "You could teleport a warship to Halcyon against the dragons' will."

"Theoretically. It's why we've kept our powers so secret for so long. For this exact reason. If the Emperor's willing to make this threat public, that must mean..." I rub a hand across my mouth, trying to tamp down the nausea. "He found out what my siblings can do. I'm guessing he has one of them captive. Or worse—willing to help him."

There's a long beat of silence. Then Simon says, "Or..."

I glance at him sharply. "Or?"

"Or he's about to come for *you.*"

Chapter 18

ENTERTAINMENT SECTOR, THE IMPERIAL MOON PALACE

JED

Saray looks like she's going to be sick. I kinda feel like I might follow suit.

I came to the Moon Palace to commit treason, but somehow, I didn't picture interplanetary war breaking out. Especially not against a famously pacifist planet and, by extension, the dragons who control it.

On the one hand, the Greenjackets are going to *love* this. If the Empire's entire armada is out in force, it'll be a prime target for guerilla attacks.

On the other hand, if the Emperor has a way to teleport without dragons, Halcyon and its Knights don't stand a chance. The rest of us are in trouble, too. If the galactic rules have changed—if the Empire doesn't need to contend with the limits of dragon travel anymore—then there's about to be chaos.

Saray looks at Simon. "How much security footage of the Emperor do you have access to?"

Simon is already tapping into a new window on his holo screen. "Not as much as I'd like. There isn't any cambot footage of the Emperor's private suite, and he stays in there most of the time. He only comes out for council meetings and the occasional social event."

"I want to see whatever you can dig up for the last couple of weeks."

Simon brings up a series of cam feeds, swiping through them slowly. Several long, boring recordings of meetings with planetary governors reporting their revenue. A brief hallway shot of the Emperor striding along, a retinue of guards and lords-in-waiting behind him.

"Looks like he was visiting the Crown Prince," Simon comments as the Emperor sweeps out of view and the vid cuts off.

"How can you tell?" Saray asks.

"That's the hallway where Prince Jinan lives. I went to a few parties there, before Mom..." Simon trails off, wincing. "Here's another one. His Majesty inspecting the Authority troops last week."

The holo displays a long line of redjackets, standing at attention shoulder to shoulder. Loathing kicks my heartbeat faster and heats up my cheeks. It's hard to see the army I've spent my whole life fighting without a visceral reaction. The atrocities I've seen these bastards commit—enslaving people, starving them, ignoring whole colonies as disease and natural disaster ravage them—makes me want to leap through the screen and cut all their throats.

And here comes the Emperor with his retinue. The man who gives them their orders.

I'm not about to give the foot soldiers a pass. "Just following orders" is no excuse. But this man is far more monstrous than any of the redjackets he surveys. A cold smile plays on his mouth as he nods to General Ajax.

"What is it, Saray?" Simon murmurs.

I tear my eyes from the screen to look over at her. Her fingers are pressed to her mouth, eyes wide with—*fear?* What the fuck? I didn't think anything could freak her out.

"She's supposed to be in prison." Saray's voice trembles.

Simon is already zooming in on the Emperor's attendants, pausing on a dark-skinned lady in her sixties. Tiny silver braids cascade down her shoulders. Paired with a white outer robe and eye makeup sparkling with rhinestones, her look reminds me of an elf from ancient fantasy tales. What surprises me most is that her face shows lines of aging. Almost no one on the Moon Palace gets to age fifty without some type of rejuvenating beauty treatment.

"Wait," says Simon. "That's not..." He pulls up that same article about the Ediya Experiments and scrolls past the picture of the children to the mugshots of the two accused of the crime.

The woman's face stares defiantly back, makeup-free, decades younger, but almost certainly the same person.

Saray whispers, "That's Dr. Melanie Ediya. The scientist who created me. If she's talking to the Emperor, he knows *everything*. We're all vortexed."

Chapter 19

ENTERTAINMENT SECTOR, THE IMPERIAL MOON PALACE

SARAY

T he last time I saw Dr. Melanie Ediya in the flesh, I was thirteen years old.

My whole life, as far back as I could remember, was organized by Arrow Station's strict routine. Wake up in my sleep pod. Clean my teeth next to a row of mostly younger siblings. Sometimes I'd help the nannybots teach them to wipe their butts and comb their hair. We'd troop to the dining hall for breakfast and then the day's activities would begin.

The nannybots called it "school," but looking back, it was obvious we were being trained more than educated. In addition to reading, writing, and numbers—which were almost an afterthought—we were given several hours of physical education every day, burning off our youthful energy on running, climbing, and a variety of sports. Then there were the mental exercises, where we'd be put alone inside a room and told we could have extra dessert that night if we managed to move an object without touching it. Or that everyone else was playing a fun game in the gym, and we could go join them, but we couldn't go through the door.

Half the time, they were impossible tasks that set us up to fail. I'd find my little siblings sobbing after these sessions, and futile anger burned me up inside. But what could I do? The Drs. Ediya were not parents to us—not safe people we could ask for help with our problems. They were like gods, cold and untouchable presences that observed us from afar, doling out punishments and rewards according to obscure requirements only they fully understood.

Once a week, we were required to enter their lab for a physical exam. We were told this was for our health. Often these physicals required samples of blood, which I loathed.

That last time, I remember asking Melanie Ediya, "Do you really have to take blood this time? Isn't last week's good enough? What's it for, anyway?" Normally, asking questions was met with swift punishment, but I was feeling surly and rebellious.

Melanie's answer had been something like, "Children grow very fast, and illnesses can come on suddenly." I remember noticing that it tasted like cinnamon, as her words often did. I hadn't put together what it meant. I thought maybe different people tasted like different things, like how my older brother Raoul always smelled citrusy, or how the little ones gave off a scent like chamomile tea when they cried.

I gave the blood sample, went back to the dormitory, and changed into my nightsuit. And the next thing I knew, Raoul was waking us all up, and we were running to a spaceship that would take us to an entirely new life as the station exploded into tiny pieces behind us.

Our rescuers told us that the Drs. Ediya had been captured and jailed. Some of my siblings even visited them in prison. I could never bring myself to do the same, not after the slow-dawning horror of realizing that I had been a victim, a lab rat, created to be a weapon rather than a person.

I thought I'd forgiven and forgotten after meeting Haven, the group that Dr. Ediya had splintered from. They didn't *hate* the dragons, as she did, hoping to use us to defeat them like an enemy. The founders of Haven simply wanted humans to be independent, to take our place in the universe as equals. They taught me and my siblings to use our power not as a weapon, but to survive. Their sights were always on bringing down the Empire, creating a world that valued all human life equally.

Seeing Melanie now—dripping with jewels, a white robe trailing from her shoulders like some kind of angelic figure—I'm hit with a sudden surge of rage. The fact that she could twist Haven's agenda so horribly that she'd work *with* the Emperor, that sadistic son of a glitch, to attack the dragons' homeworld of Halcyon... My teeth grit with the urge to draw *her* blood for a change.

"Pause it," I demand. "Zoom in on her."

Simon does so. Melanie's face enlarges to life-size in front of us. I look into her unblinking brown eyes like she might be able to look back at me and explain how the fuck she got here. Is it my imagination, or does she look smug as blazes?

"She's been in prison for the last twenty years," I say. "Or that's what we all *thought*. I'm guessing she offered the Emperor information on us in exchange for her release. Which begs the question...if she told him all our names..."

"How many of your siblings does he already have captive?" Jed finishes.

Simon swipes away the old picture and begins typing. "I'm doing an image search," he says. "Going to see if I can track when she arrived here."

It's not too long before he finds cambot footage, about three weeks ago, of Melanie disembarking from a taxi shuttle. She's dressed in a faded jumpsuit, graying curls held back with a simple headband. The Authorities escort her to a zip-lift, and Simon's facial recognition search does not note her again for several days.

When it does, I gasp.

Melanie is dressed royally now, her hair in fresh braids and makeup smoothing her age lines. She stands with the Authorities, not as a prisoner, but front and center, as if she's their leader. And she blocks the path of a couple who are floating hover-trunks toward the docks.

"I know her!" I exclaim, pointing. "That's my sister Clara."

Jed lifts an eyebrow, but Simon simply pulls up the photo of the Ediya Experiments from that long-ago article, comparing the paused cambot footage. "Front middle?" he asks, tapping the display with his gauntleted hand.

I nod. Clara Seranath and I don't look like siblings. She's white, with platinum-blond hair and a round, doll-like face. But it's not blood that binds us. It's our childhood, trapped together on Arrow Station, having the same experiments done to us.

We reconnected at Haven as adults, but in the five years since I left for the Moon Palace, I've had to let go of knowing what my siblings are up to. Clara is just another family member I can't contact too frequently for fear of drawing Authority attention.

Seeing her here, mere weeks ago, on the same moon as me, is nevertheless a strange disappointment. Why didn't she tell me she was here?

Maybe she didn't have a chance before she was caught in Melanie's snare.

At Clara's side, there's an older person with a shaved head, wearing a gorgeous purple robe that manages to toe the line between masculine and feminine. Clara steps out in front of them, her arm out to hold them back, as if protecting them. As if offering herself up in their place.

"Who's that?" Jed asks. "They look weirdly familiar."

"That's the new resident theater director over at the Pavilion," says Simon. "Rodan Quell. You might recognize em from all eir casting-call billboards."

Director Quell again. It can't be a coincidence that e was the next lead I was about to investigate.

Simon rolls through the rest of the scene, which ends in Clara being escorted away with Dr. Ediya, and Director Quell being marched to the ship with eir trunks. E's not gone long. The ship doesn't even weigh anchor before a person who must be Quell steals down the ramp again. E changed clothes and donned a wig, but who else would be disembarking the ship right before takeoff?

"They tried to get rid of em, but it looks like e's still here," says Simon.

I quickly explain what Pearl told me about the director being a master of makeup and costuming, then say, "This seals it. We have to investigate."

Simon nods. "I agree. But you'll need to be careful, Saray. It's dangerous for you to be seen in public right now."

"I'll go with her," Jed jumps in. "If this Dr. Ediya lady is as bad as Saray says, then she just might have jumped herself to the top of Tarantula's hit list. We gotta find out what Director Quell knows about her."

My instinct is to protest that I don't need a babysitter, that I can look after myself. But I swallow the words back and look at each of them in turn: Jed's warm blue eyes, full of mischief in his band posters but dead serious in person, and Simon's sharp, calculating gaze that misses nothing, yet somehow doesn't judge at all.

Tonight, they were here for me at my lowest. My fellow ladies-in-waiting, people I've worked with for five years, threw me out the airlock at the first chance. But these men—near-strangers—believe I'm not a traitor. They hid me, helped me when no one else would, and even committed espionage for me.

Also, I can't save Alan or Clara on my own. I'm going to need their help. *Thank you* sticks in my throat, so I just say, "Fine. Come on, then."

The Pavilion Theater is a jewel in the entertainment sector's crown. It's a transporting, fantastical experience, which starts as soon as I step onto the garden path before the entrance. Tiny bug-drones swarm around me, flashing twinkly lights like this is an Old Earth period drama.

The ticket-checking bots are designed to look like a pair of lions lounging in front of the door. One of them speaks in a deep baritone. "There is no show tonight. Do you wish to purchase one for the next show on Daysix?"

"I don't want to go to a show," I say. "I want to speak to Rodan Quell. Where is eir office?"

The lion stands still for so long that I start to worry I've made it glitch out. Then it says, "An usher will be here to assist you shortly."

The usher, when it arrives, is a bot made to resemble a cute little monkey wearing a vest. "This way," it says. "Follow me."

We step inside the Pavilion's gold double doors, engraved with scenes from dozens of famous plays. Behind them, the hallway is dim and full of vaguely frightening organic shapes. I've been here on a show night when it's lit up for guests, so I know those shapes are faux tree branches and hanging vines that come alive with shimmering firefly lights. The slowly curving ramp, carpeted with fake grass, breaks the illusion of a forest wonderland with its golden banister and walls of signed, framed actor portraits. I've climbed the ramp and entered the main theater, which is built to resemble the ancient Roman Colosseum, an enormous ring of tiered plush seats with a circular stage in the middle. It's wildly impressive even before the galaxy's best actors set foot onstage.

But today, the usher-monkey leads us to a hidden side door where stairs spiral down instead of up. It swings along tiny handholds in the wall, staying just ahead of us.

We only go one floor down, exiting into a curving hallway lined with doors. Down here, they didn't bother with the elaborate décor—it's just gray carpet and white walls.

"This is the backstage area," the bot says helpfully. "These are dressing rooms for the actors, and over there is prop storage. Lighting and hologram control are—"

"Save it," Jed says. "We don't need the tour. Just find Mx Quell for us."

In our ears, Simon whispers, "I thought it was kind of interesting."

Jed immediately looks ashamed of himself. We agreed to let Simon hack into our audio feed so he can listen in on us and send help if needed. But Jed gets all weird every time he hears Simon's voice.

I don't even have to smell the florals every time he talks to know he's crushing *bad*. Makes me feel slightly less awful about the way things ended with us. I was never going to be the partner Jed wanted, but maybe Simon…

"Director Quell's office is just ahead on the left," says the monkeybot. "Shall I announce your arrival?"

"No," Jed says, and then adds, "thanks," clearing his throat.

Good call. I don't want Director Quell to know we're coming. I want to see what eir honest reaction is, without giving em a moment to compose emself.

The monkey taps on the office door. There's a faint, "Who is it?" from inside.

I slide the door open and barge in, ignoring the monkeybot's squeak of protest.

The walls of Mx Quell's office are lined with squishy, old-fashioned synthetic leather armchairs, and e sits in one of them with eir head in eir hands, bowed almost to eir knees. From the sound of eir muffled sobs, e's in the middle of a certified breakdown.

Well, this is awkward.

Eir head jerks up, red-rimmed blue eyes meeting mine. I'd hazard a guess e's in eir fifties, but that's assuming e hasn't had any of the youth treatments that are popular among performers. Eir head is shaved bald, and e's not wearing any makeup, which is probably good, considering even the sturdiest makeup would probably be getting a little smeary around eir eyes right now.

"Who are you?" Director Quell demands.

I draw myself upright, determined not to show pity just because of a few tears in the eyes of a seasoned actor. "My name is Saray Lake. I am…"

"Clara's sister," supplies Director Quell softly.

"Um...yes." E's thrown me off guard. "How do you know her?"

"She's one of my principal actors," says Director Quell. "And my...partner."

When I left Monroe, Clara was still taking classes at an acting school. Apparently, her career is going well. I'm a little surprised she's dating someone so much older, but Clara's type has always been anybody she "vibes with" regardless of the body they're in.

"We don't exactly...look alike," I probe. "How did you recognize me?"

Director Quell lowers eir voice. "I may not be associated with Haven anymore, but I'm familiar with their...experiments."

I freeze. "Don't say that name here," I hiss. "You don't know who's listening."

"I'm fairly sure I do," says Director Quell dryly. "They can't get more dirt on me than they already have. Melanie Ediya has seen to that."

Jed touches his earpiece and murmurs, "Can you check this room for bugs remotely?" to Simon.

A pause, then, "There are no cambots anywhere near you. That's about all I can guarantee. If the director is recording on eir personal devices, I can't do anything about that either."

"Have a seat." Quell makes it sound more like an order than an invitation. "I know it won't mean much, but you have my word that I will not turn you in to the Authorities. Do I have yours in return?"

"That remains to be seen." I level a glare at em. "I came to ask if you know anything about the master-level makeup and acting job that framed my father for kidnapping." I fold my arms. "And you'd better talk fast, because he's being tortured for information as we speak."

"I know." Quell winces. "I never meant for that to happen. This has all gotten so—so out of control, when all I wanted was—" E presses eir mouth flat.

"Was?" I prompt.

"To keep Clara safe." Quell bites eir lip. "I left Haven for a reason, you know. The Ediya debacle was the last straw. I couldn't agree with their methods, using kids like lab rats. I thought once Melanie was in prison, I'd be free to live my life. But she's slippery, that one."

I sink into one of the armchairs. This feels like it's going to be a long story. "Tell us what you know."

Chapter 20

THE IMPERIAL MOON PALACE

Rodan

1 *Week Ago*

The call came at third hour in the morning. My audio earring chimed over and over, dragging me into wakefulness and also flaring me off.

Clara was sleeping. Her ice-blond hair sprawled across her pillow and tickled my arm. I slid out from under the sheet as slowly as I dared and grabbed my scroll-tablet, which was silently blinking its orange call alert.

I carried the scroll to the next room and, once the door closed behind me, clicked into the call without bothering to check the ID. "What?" I snapped. "It's the middle of the ni—"

My words died in my throat when I saw Glenna Ediya's face.

Thank stars, Clara was still asleep. Since she found out her brother was messing with her memories five years ago, reminders of her past can trigger panic attacks. She barely even talks to her siblings anymore.

I'm careful not to mention my own history with Haven, either. She's forgiven me for my part in what happened to her, but the situation was messy.

I'd been raised in the beginnings of Haven's colony. As an idealist teenager, I was honored when Glenna had asked me to ferry a shipment of samples to the lab where Melanie, Oberon, and Gaela Ediya—her adult children—were doing experiments "for the good of humanity." What I saw in that lab changed everything. Disgusted by their lack of respect for the lives they were creating, I wrote an article exposing them—which got me kicked out of Haven and sent the Ediyas on the run.

After I separated from Haven, Melanie found a way to contact me from prison. She blackmailed me into passing her information on Haven's activities. In that capacity, I unwittingly helped her develop a plot with Raoul, the oldest Experiment—and as part of that, I gave him access to torment Clara.

When I found out Raoul was mind-controlling his sister and planning genocide, I told Melanie I was done. I changed my call code and moved to another theater on the other side of the planet. Eventually, the job on the Moon Palace opened up, and I jumped to take it.

Melanie never contacted me again, though that might have had something to do with me calling the Imperial prison warden in charge of Hawking Penitentiary anonymously to let them know which employees were helping Melanie get messages out.

The Emperor, I'm happy to take down, but I draw the line at hurting children. Or blowing up a bunch of quaint little temples on a pacifist colony just because they worship dragons. Call me when they start using the dragons' power to oppress people, but until then, I couldn't care less.

Glenna hasn't contacted me again, either. I sort of figured she could still find me if she wanted to. She just hadn't wanted to...until now.

Haven's leader hadn't changed much in five years. Her coily white hair and smile-lined dark eyes were still just as disarming.

"Hello, Rodan," said Glenna, calm as the sea before a storm. "I have some bad news."

"Clearly," I said. "If you're bothering to contact me, you must be out of options."

She gave a small, wry smile. "You were one of the last known people that my daughter contacted from prison. I feel it's fair to warn you that she has been released."

"Released, not escaped?" A chill ran down my arms as I did some quick mental math. It had been twenty-two years since the Ediya Experiment scandal. Was that long enough for Melanie to complete her sentence? It didn't feel like long enough.

"My sources suggest that she managed to appeal directly to Emperor Soren," Glenna said. "Who knows what information she used to barter her release."

Her words were neutral, but the warning was clear. Melanie could be whispering dangerous truths about both of us directly into His Majesty's ear. By tomorrow, I could be on "Wanted" bulletins instead of playbills.

I glanced at the door to the bedroom, where Clara still slept, oblivious. Whatever the Emperor could do to me, the things he could do *using* her were far worse. "We have to send C into hiding," I said softly. I didn't even dare speak her name on a vid-call, knowing our correspondence might be monitored.

Glenna raised one eyebrow. "So it's true. You *are* dating her. I'd heard the rumor, but truly, I expected better from you. A student, Rodan?"

Curse it. It shouldn't have been so easy for her to make me blush. "Clara is—not that it's any of your business, but Clara hasn't been my student in three years. She graduated and took a job with another acting company. I would never behave inappropriately with someone under my care."

I'm aware that Clara and I are an odd mix. When she first came to my academy, I'm certain she saw me as ancient. At the time, I remember liking her flamboyant spirit and charming personality, but as a proud teacher, not a suitor. It was only after she left, and a few years had passed, that we reconnected. At first, meeting in that little downtown Monroe lounge, she'd wanted to confront me about my association with Melanie. Her acting company was about to partner with mine, and she insisted we clear the air.

Once I reassured her that I was no longer under Dr. Ediya's control, she'd relaxed and begun reminiscing about her student days. And then we'd just *talked*, our shared love of theater building the foundation of a friendship that lasted another six months before blooming into romance.

We were fortunate that her director approved a staff trade to allow Clara to accompany me when I took the job on the Moon Palace. Or so we thought. I got the sense that our luck was quickly running out.

"Your business is none of mine," Glenna said. "I agree, she should be sent into hiding. I'm also in the process of relocating. I can't give you any more information than that, but I will tell you this. If you hire a taxi and tell the pilot to take you to the Waystation, you'll end up on a seedy little asteroid pit stop. Go into the café called Grandma & Grandma's and tell them you're a friend of Prince. They'll help you get to safety."

"A friend of—which prince?" It was a struggle to think of a single princex on this entire moon who would spit on me if I was on fire.

"Privileged info," Glenna said. "Go. Don't wait until morning. I have more calls to make."

She clicked off the call, leaving me to break the news to Clara.

The good thing about a girlfriend who can read minds is that you don't have to waste a ton of time explaining things. The bad thing about it is that she often reads subtext that I wouldn't have said out loud. Like the fact that I was planning to follow Glenna's instructions to send Clara to safety, but that I personally wasn't interested in trusting my life to Haven anymore.

We wasted too much time arguing as we packed. Clara kept trying to convince me to swallow my pride and accept Haven's help. "Why isn't Glenna's offer good enough for you if it's good enough for me?" et cetera. By the time we headed to the docks in the low-lit corridors of fifth hour, avoiding main thoroughfares where late-night revelers still stumbled along in unsteady clusters, we were deeply flared off at each other.

So maybe we were both too busy silently fuming to see Melanie and the Authorities until they had us cornered.

They paid me no mind at all once they'd taken her. Just shoved me on an outbound ship and told me not to come back. It was Clara they wanted.

I never again want to feel as helpless as I did watching the redjackets drag my partner away, while they kept me pinned so I couldn't lift a finger to stop them. Stars, it broke my heart. I couldn't just leave her like that, or I'd never be able to meet my own eyes in the mirror again.

So I bribed the pilot to let me off before departure. I disguised myself with what little makeup and supplies I had in my go-bag and stepped back onto the docks with the confidence of a tourist. But I had no idea what to do from there. I tried contacting Glenna again, but she had gone silent. Probably dropped her old call code to avoid being traced.

I only knew one other person from Haven who still lived on the Moon Palace. A long time ago, Haven went to a lot of effort to install a sleeper agent among the Emperor's consorts. The idea was to get someone close enough to His Majesty to carry out an assassination attempt. But when the opportunity came to strike, the agent choked. She had just seen her best friend killed during a similar attempt, and she was pregnant, fearing for the life of her child. So, she refused to act, and Glenna withdrew support once she found out.

I knew it was a long shot, but this woman had access to the Emperor's high-security suite, where Clara was being held captive. She'd been trained, however long ago, for stealth operations. She was my only remaining hope for rescuing Clara.

I went to a party where I knew she was scheduled to make an appearance. A mustache, a wig, a bit of extra bulk under my clothes—theater costumes can do wonders to disguise one's true visage. Ah, I see you recognize me now. Yes, that night, I was there to accost Geneva Milagro, to beg her to use her access to the Emperor's chambers to rescue Clara.

It was a shock to recognize Saray among Geneva's ladies. Fearing you were in danger of sharing Clara's fate, I pleaded with her to help me for *your* sake.

But Geneva feared retaliation too greatly to help me. Though she sympathized with my plight, she refused to access the Emperor's sanctum to break Clara free. The backlash for such a betrayal could cost more than her life, she said. She would not put the lives of those who depended on her in such danger—especially not her son.

Once Alan Lake approached her, I realized I could kill two birds with one stone: ensure that you, Saray, were exiled, while also removing Geneva's greatest barrier to action.

I swear I didn't intend it to come to war.

That night, I pickpocketed a pulse blaster from a careless bodyguard's belt. Then I lay in wait outside the ballroom. When Alan left, I lured him into a supply closet and slapped a deep-sleep patch onto his neck. Then I stole his clothes and adjusted my disguise before climbing into the ventilation duct and making my way to the nursery wing.

The cambots were the easiest to take care of. I allowed one to remain—I needed Geneva to know what I'd done. Even very well-made guardbots can still be stunned with a pulse blast, if only for a few seconds.

It was enough.

I took Geneva's child.

Part Four

DAYFOUR

YEAR 3750 DE, WEEK 45

Chapter 21

THE IMPERIAL MOON PALACE

SARAY

"You *fucking evil glitch.*"

My voice sounds foreign to my own ears, low and fierce. The rage coursing through my veins makes it hard for me to think straight. If Jed didn't have his hand on my forearm, I'd already be lunging for Director Quell. Maybe to strangle em. Maybe just to punch em. I haven't decided yet.

"Simon, are you getting this?" Jed mutters. "E just admitted it, straight out."

I can only choke out one question past the tightness in my throat. "Where's Miles?"

Quell shakes eir head. "That's the problem. I don't know. I put him in that shipping crate with Alan and paid the pilot a boatload of credits to take them both to the Waystation Glenna mentioned." E scrubs a hand over eir face. "When I saw the news that they caught Alan but hadn't found Miles... I've been panicking trying to figure out what went wrong. All I know is that the kid's still out there somewhere, but now there's nobody to protect him. You must believe me, that wasn't my intention."

"Oh, you took a child from his loving mother who would do anything to keep him safe, but you didn't intend him to be unprotected?" I let the sarcasm flood my mouth, peppery and sour. "Without a guard, Miles is as good as dead. Do you know how many people have already tried to kill him before he's even old enough to start Gen Ed?"

Quell hangs eir head. "Believe me, I'm aware."

"The Emperor is holding eir partner hostage," Simon whispers in my ear. "No need to rub it in."

I take a deep breath, trying to get a handle on my emotions. As angry as I am for what Quell has done, I understand why e did it. If it had been Geneva in danger, and some random princex I needed to screw over to save her, I can't swear I wouldn't've done the same.

"Have you been able to communicate with Clara at all?" I ask. "Do you know for sure that she's being held in his private suite?"

Quell shakes eir head. "All my messages are blocked. Nothing goes through. But I did hear one of the Authorities tell her that she was going to be an *'honored guest'* in the Emperor's house." E spits out the words. I taste an echo of bitterness on my tongue.

Well, that complicates things. Not even the Emperor's wives are allowed to stay in his private rooms longer than a few hours, or a day at most. If Clara has been there almost a week, she's a prisoner. And one with no protection against her monstrous captor.

Someone has to go rescue her. Someone with access to the Emperor's inner sanctum. I don't want it to have to be Geneva, but if not her, then...

An idea hits me with the force of a subtrain. "We're going to need your help, Director."

Jed gives me a strange look. "What for?"

Grinning, I say, "Something super illegal."

It's around fourth hour in the morning when I teleport back into Geneva's suite.

My old room is dark and cold, emptied of my possessions. I already changed into borrowed clothes in Simon's apartment: plain black leggings and a tunic, plus a black scarf to cover my hair. I open the medicine cabinet and find the emergency patch kit I chose not to pack. I slap an energy booster on my forearm, sighing as the fog of exhaustion clears away like the sun coming out. I tuck a second one into my pocket. The patches don't last long, and I can't afford the crash in the middle of a stealth operation.

I quickly dodge out of my room, my bare feet silent as I hurry toward Geneva's room. At this hour, the only people who should be awake are Geneva's night guards, and they typically remain in the front hall. I slip through the sitting room, holding my breath as I pass the glow from the kitch where Yumiko's slight figure sits at the table, sipping chamomile tea to calm her anxiety.

Geneva's room is dark and still. I hold my breath, approaching her bed on tiptoe. Is she asleep? If she's awake and catches me, I'm not sure even her forgiving nature will save me.

I hear nothing. No breathing, no rustle of movement within bedsheets. I reach for the dimmer switch and turn up the lights just a tiny bit, just enough to make out Geneva's shape in the bed.

It's not there.

Her bed is neatly made with just a few dimples on the edge where she must have sat. I run a hand over the butt-print. It's still warm.

That's when I hear a faint ding from the huge ugly painting against the wall.

That's the sound of the zip-lift returning...without a passenger.

I suck in a breath. I'm too late. Geneva has gone to the Emperor. And in the middle of the night, with no one else awake, it's unlikely she went there at his call.

I have to stop her before she gets hurt.

The borrowed keycuff on my wrist is unfamiliar, a little too tight, tarnished from disuse. Its mechanism hasn't been updated in a few years. But the panel behind the painting still recognizes its authority and allows me to enter the zip-lift without sounding an intruder alarm.

Inside, the pod is like any other zip-lift I've ridden. I suppose I expected gold-plated walls or seats cushioned with fur from extinct animals. But it's the usual utilitarian lift interior: egg-shaped, dull metallic walls, padded maroon seat cushions, safety straps that whir across chest and lap as soon as I sit.

The only difference is that, where most zip-lifts on the Moon Palace have an extensive list of locations a rider can request to stop, this one has only two options. *Home* and *Inner Palace*.

As the lift smoothly accelerates, I imagine what it must be like for Geneva to take this trip, often multiple times per week. Does her heart pound like mine is right now? Does she swallow nausea at the thought of what awaits her in the Emperor's sanctum?

Residual fury blazes to life in my veins as I picture how it must feel to put herself through that, only for Director Quell to snatch away the only person that makes her life worth living. I wonder if she's been planning to do this ever since she sent me away. Was that the moment she decided she had nothing left to lose?

The journey isn't short. Minutes feel like hours as fear swells in my ribcage, but I count at least thirty minutes on my keycuff. It's impossible to gauge which direction I'm going, but I have a suspicion. There've always been rumors about the location of the Emperor's secret living quarters. No one knows for sure, because only wives and very privileged councilors ever get an invite, but the general assumption is that the Emperor lives somewhere deep, deep underground. This makes the most logical sense, people say; after all, if there was ever an attack on the Moon Palace, the surface regions would be first to take fire. Safety lies far below, where an attacking force would need to search, dig, or bomb their way through thousands of other citizens before cornering the Emperor.

But it's a double-edged sword. Hidden deep, with few avenues of escape, the Emperor could easily find himself trapped.

As the lift plummets ever deeper, I become aware of a faint sensation of wrongness, akin to nausea, but higher in my chest. I recognize it as the sensation of entering a dragon-repelling field. The emitting devices are most commonly used to stop people from teleporting out of prison, but wealthy people deploy them in any high-security area. The fact that dragons would refuse to teleport a stranger into a private residence is immaterial.

Though the average human can't sense the repellent fields at all, my siblings and I are somewhat sensitive to them. It wouldn't stop me (or Clara) from teleporting, but it does slightly mess with my concentration.

The zip-lift slows to a stop, chiming its arrival. I unstrap myself and take a deep breath as the pulse pounds in my neck. I could be about to get myself shot by a security drone the moment I step out of the pod. Geneva's always been tight-lipped about what the Emperor's private spaces look like. For all I know, I could be walking directly into His Majesty's bedchamber.

Fuck it. This isn't just about one or two individual people anymore. I have to get Clara back—if I don't, it's not just my father's life on the line, it's the entire planetary population of Halcyon. We, the former Ediya Experiments, have hidden ourselves all our lives, not only to keep ourselves safe but to protect others from us, too. The Emperor *cannot* be allowed to exploit our power. More than half of us still live on Halcyon. If Clara can be coerced to get his army onto the planet, he'll have a dozen more super-powered people in his clutches. A few of my siblings even have *children*.

I open the pod door, tensed and ready for anything.

The smell of water hits me before my eyes adjust to the dim lighting. Wood creaks under my feet. Reddish light filters between cracks in the walls. The pod swishes closed behind me, leaving me standing alone in a long, narrow structure.

One side of the floor is a boardwalk; the other side is water, dark and restless, lapping at the sides of the...boathouse? I've never seen a boathouse in real life, but that must be what this is, because as I advance down the boardwalk, the light spilling from the opening at the end reveals a flattish, iridescent-white boat that reminds me of an ancient Venetian gondola. It's full of cushions and draped with a gauzy fabric suspended from a flimsy mast. There are no oars or sails anywhere around it. I kneel to examine it and realize it's shaped from an enormous seashell.

"What is your name?"

I startle hard. A tiger-bot, cousin to the lion-bots I saw at the theater, lies in the shadows just beyond the boat. It licks its paw casually, but its cold green eyes are fixed on me. If I answer wrong, I'm dead.

"Kim Haneul," I lie. *Cinnamon.* I hold out my arm to present the silver keycuff that Simon reluctantly allowed me to borrow, the one that once belonged to his mother. If I'm very, very lucky, the Emperor doesn't think to remove his wives' entry privileges after they're dead.

The tiger cocks its head to the side. I barely dare to breathe. In this low light, will Director Quell's hasty costume makeup be enough to convince the bot that I'm Lady Haneul?

"The Emperor has not called for you, Your Grace," the tiger says solemnly. "He is entertaining another. Return to your room."

Blast it. I was afraid of this. Even if I'm not about to get shot on sight, the bot will let me go no further. And the way to get to the Emperor is clearly by taking this boat...

Another idea occurs to me. But it's foolish beyond belief. Even if I do have my emergency breather mask with me, as all citizens of the moon do in case of atmo breach...it would definitely be a bad idea...

I do it anyway.

"My mistake," I say to the tiger, backing toward the zip-lift. "I'll just go then." I push the call button and wait, slowly tugging the breather out of my back pocket and pulling it out of its pouch.

As the door to the pod swishes open, I shout, "Who's that?" and point to the open mouth of the boathouse. As soon as the tiger's head turns, I pull the mask on, crouch, and slide into the water.

I was worried it would be freezing, but the water's actually not bad—I'd call it lukewarm. The bottom of this artificial lake is murky, lined with smooth round pebbles covered in slick algae. Tiny bottom-feeding piscines dart out of my way as I fill my pockets with some of the rocks to weigh me down.

Under the boathouse, the water's only about a meter deep. Grateful for the swimming lessons my older sister Amy gave us when we were kids, I pull myself along the bottom, staying as low as I can. The oblong shape of the boat passes overhead, and then everything brightens as I swim free of the boathouse.

The rest of the lake is choked with the green stalks of lily pads. I chance a return to the surface, just to peek, and find myself in a huge sea of them. It's quite beautiful, but then I notice the claustrophobically low ceiling. Its artificial light glows a reddish-pinkish sunrise color that feels threatening rather than romantic.

In the middle of the lake sits a large island, crowned with a building that resembles a Roman villa. I spot another dock; the magnetic track on the lake floor must propel the boat between the two.

I dive to the bottom again and begin to push through the lily-pad forest. The stalks feel like snakes brushing against my legs. I shudder, but don't pause.

I try to keep my trips to the surface brief and minimal, but it's easy to get turned around down here, and I want to make sure I'm still going in the right direction. There don't seem to be any cambots circling overhead, at least.

As I approach the island, I realize there's a smooth stone wall all the way around, except for—as far as I can see—a single set of stairs leading to the boathouse at the water's edge. It's going to be difficult to climb up any other way.

The lily pads have been trimmed back close to the island. Here, the bottom of the lake is paved not with slimy pebbles, but with gold cobblestones, which must get cleaned regularly for how shiny they are. I hang back in the lilies, aware that my movements will be easier to spot with the brilliant gold as a backdrop below me.

Another tiger-bot waits at the top of the stairs. It hasn't seen me yet, but I doubt it'll go well for me if it does. So I skim through the edge of the lilies, checking for any weakness in the wall—some crumbling area rough enough to give me a handhold or two.

At last, I spot a dark area that, when I investigate, appears to be a sewer hole. The circular outlet is plenty big for me to swim through, and so I kick my way inside, praying that there's a purifying filter between here and the waste receptacles above. And that the tunnel doesn't get any narrower.

My gen-mods came with the perk of good night vision. But one bend in the tunnel and darkness encloses me, deep enough that even my highly sensitive eyes are blinded. This isn't an area meant for people or even bots. My first assessment still stands: it's probably a drain tunnel for purified sewage.

Hopefully purified.

My fingers recoil from the slimy texture of the tunnel wall, but I persevere. At least the tunnel doesn't branch, as far as I can tell. I imagine myself lost in here, swimming in circles for days, and chills ripple down my spine.

I'm so laser-focused on feeling my way along that I almost don't notice when light seeps in again. The tunnel widens into a circular pool, maybe twelve meters across. It's deep—I can't see to the bottom—with light filtering in from a small opening in the ceiling far above. If someone were to look down through that opening, this might look like a well. But it's too wide to be one.

I surface and pull my mask down, squinting first at the opening meters above my head, then at the slick tiled walls. No handholds.

Blast it. So close to finding my way in, but this is a dead end.

I'm contemplating the unpleasant prospect of swimming back out the way I came when I feel a ripple in the water I didn't cause, a stirring of movement that brushes against me, gentle as a lapping wave. My heart begins to pound.

Something is in here with me.

I yank the breather back over my face just in time. The creature catches hold of my ankle and pulls me under.

A person without fancy gen-mod eyes might thrash about in the mostly dark water, unable to see what has them in its clutches. Lucky—or unlucky—me, because I can see enough to get an idea of what I'm dealing with.

A triangular black-scaled head, bigger than my torso. A long snakelike central body with cilia or tentacles emanating from it like an ink spill. I have no idea what planet the Emperor captured this thing from, but it's perfectly evolved for hunting in dark water. Most people would never see it coming before it was already drowning them.

Even I, with my cat eyes and breathing mask, feel a moment of frozen terror. Of *course,* the Emperor keeps a pet monster in his moat. Of *course,* he has a pool where he no doubt feeds it people who've flared him off. And my foolish ass swam right in—no need to force the Emperor to dirty his hands with an execution order.

Then I unfreeze, Clara's voice flashing through my mind. I haven't spoken to her in years, but for some reason my inner voice sounds just like her in this moment.

::Saray, you literally know how to teleport. Don't just fucking wait to die. Do something!::

Oh. Right.

Teleporting doesn't work if I can't picture where I want to go. I have no idea what the inside of the Emperor's villa looks like, so I can't teleport myself out of the hole.

But I can teleport myself to the rim of the hole above and grab on really quick. Which I do, my fingers burning as I hook them over. I should have gone to the gym all those times Destra invited me! She'd laugh at me now as I force myself through the galaxy's most pathetic and desperate pull-up. Why couldn't I have gotten, like, superstrength or telekinesis? Why did it have to be word synesthesia?

Through what I can only assume is pure adrenaline, I get an elbow over the rim of the hole. The rest of my body still dangling, I quickly take stock of my surroundings.

Interestingly, this hole seems to be right in the middle of a fountain. Water spouts over my head in a merry trickle, coming from—oh, classy—a satyr's penis. There are dozens of similar statues in the fountain's tableau, all spouting water from various body parts into a shallow pool that forms the ceiling of the monster's well. I don't see anyone in the room beyond. It's more of a hallway, with arched doorways leading to other rooms. The high ceiling is glass, showing the false red sky above.

Cautiously, I begin dragging myself forward into the bowl of the fountain. It's an ungraceful flail and, unfortunately, not quiet. I freeze again when I hear the sound of heels clicking on the hallway's colorful mosaic tile.

Someone's coming.

I start sliding backward, intending to hide as far into the hole as I can without falling back in, but a familiar voice whisper-shouts, "Don't!"

Awkwardly, because I've got one leg out and one leg in at this point, I turn my head toward the voice.

"Clara?" I say her name out loud in utter relief, but it echoes so loudly, I swallow the rest of my words. Her gen-mod ability is reading thoughts—I don't even need to speak. *::Thank stars you're not hurt!::*

::You shouldn't have come here,:: Clara replies. *::What were you thinking?::*

As soon as I hear her mental voice, it clicks. The warning to teleport away from the monster *did* come from her.

::Well, apparently you've been able to hear me thinking for several minutes at least, so you tell me.::

::Don't be a smartass.:: She folds her arms across her chest as I heave myself the rest of the way out of the hole and duck under peeing satyrs to climb out of the fountain. *::If he finds you here, you'll wish that monster ate you quick.::*

::I'm here to rescue you,:: I tell her. *::Your partner was crying all over me, worried about you. It was kind of awkward.::*

She gives me a sarcastic look. *::Oh, were you planning to teleport me out? Do you think I haven't tried that? The Emperor's been using nightsweet on me. I can't focus for shit.::*

I wince. Nightsweet is a mind-alt, a mild sedative to keep someone compliant. It also prevents dragon-aided teleportation. And unlike dragon-repellent fields, it works on me and my siblings too. Until the nightsweet leaves Clara's system, she can't teleport away.

The drug would explain her slumped shoulders, drooping eyelids, and the way she leans against a marble pillar for support. There are no visible marks on her, but she isn't safe here.

::I can get you out,:: I say.

She gives my dripping, slimy form a once-over. *::Does it involve going back into the tentacle monster pit?::*

::Well...if we don't want to be caught by the tiger-bots...yes.::

::Yeah, no, I'm good. I'll pass.:: Clara waves her hand dismissively.

Frustrated at how casually she seems to be taking this whole thing, I snap, *::Don't you know what the Emperor plans to do with you?::*

She taps her temple. ::*Obviously.*::

::*Because it sure sounded like he wants to use you to transport his army to Halcyon and destroy them. Probably also capture all our siblings so that we can all be his little dragon-human hybrid servants.*::

::*You forgot a forced marriage in there,*:: Clara says. ::*He plans to depose Lady Geneva and make me his lead consort.*::

Horror floods me in cold nauseous waves. ::*Clara, no. You don't know what he does to those women—*::

She taps her temple again. ::*I've had a front row seat for days. He thinks he has the upper hand, but I'd let every sun in the universe burn out before I'd use my powers to his benefit. I have a plan.*::

::*And what happens to that plan if he threatens Director Quell?*::

Her confident expression flickers slightly, but she squares her shoulders. ::*Ro's already gone. E'll be safe.*::

::*No, e isn't.*:: I let her scan my memory of the past few hours. ::*E stayed because e wanted to rescue you.*::

The look of horror is still dawning on her face when we both hear a distant sound, like a door clicking shut. Instantly, Clara grabs my arm and drags me away from the main hallway, into one of the villa's interior rooms.

She pushes me through a door into a lavish bedchamber, frescoed with images of blonde, pale-skinned goddesses that look a lot like Clara, actually. The white bedcovers are rumpled, and next to the door, a guardbot leans against the wall, its eyelights out.

::*Will that thing wake up?*::

She shakes her head. ::*Only if I turn it back on. I figured out how to disable it the first week I was here. It's probably still recording audio, though, so don't say anything aloud yet. Now strip. You're getting puddles everywhere.*::

She digs through the lavish wardrobe of luxurious clothes that I'm guessing aren't hers. Nothing in that closet is practical for sneaking around, but she finds a mostly opaque robe to drape over me while she shoves my clothes into a cleaning press to dry them. Then she collapses on the bed with a groan.

::*Nightsweet's a glitch of a drug. Just walking around tires me out.*::

::*How long until it's out of your system?*:: I ask. Can I afford to wait it out with her?

::*They'll come with my next dose in the morning, around sixth hour. Hopefully the cleaner bots will wipe up your drip trail before then...unless Melanie starts snooping around.*::

::*So she* is *here.*:: Awkwardly holding the front of the robe shut, I flop into one of Clara's plush armchairs.

Clara wrinkles her nose. ::*Another* honored guest. *Staying two doors down from me. She's soooo sure she can bully me, but I've always been able to read her like a book. I know exactly what strings she's been pulling.*::

::*Oh?*::

Smirking, Clara says, ::*She told the Emperor about us, not just as a get-out-of-prison card, but to install one of us in the Queen's seat. She's hoping I'll use my telepathy to subdue the Emperor and take over. With her as the backseat pilot, obviously.*::

::*That's...not good,*:: I say inanely. ::*Why aren't you worried?*::

::*Her whole plan hinges on me doing what she wants. She's so confident I'm scared of her. It's going to come as a shock when I double-cross her after the Emperor kicks it. Which should be happening—*:: She pauses to check her keycuff. ::*—any second now.*::

I gasp. ::*Geneva!*::

In the chaos with the fountain and the monster, I'd forgotten that Geneva was supposed to come rescue Clara ahead of me. Only now do I realize how badly this has all gone off the rails. Geneva must've decided that, if she's already going to burn everything down to rescue Clara, she might as well also complete her original mission and take the Emperor out.

But if she does, she'll never escape the villa alive.

::Exactly. I can hear her working up to do the deed,:: Clara says. *::She got here just before you. Which is why you really should get out of here now before shit hits the vents.::* She collects my black ensemble, still warm from the cleaning press, and hands it back to me so that I can get dressed.

I scramble into my leggings. *::Tell me where they are.::*

::Saray, don't be ridiculous. You are NOT going in there to interfere. Let her try to kill him. If she succeeds, it's a win-win for us.::

::And if she fails, she dies! I'm not standing by and letting her make Miles an orphan.::

::Look on the bright side. She might make herself a single mother.::

::With a huge target painted on her back? Forget it.:: I focus my mind, catching Clara's golden eyes and holding them with mine. I almost never use this power on people I like...but this is an emergency. "Tell me where Geneva is," I say aloud.

She winces, but it tumbles out of her mouth anyway. "His bedchamber. Dungeon. Whatever. It's downstairs. There are guardbots all up and down the hall. You'll never make it."

::Not,:: I say, *::if I teleport.::*

I don't have a visual focus to get me into the Emperor's chamber. But using a familiar person as a focus can also work. I think of Geneva, blocking out all other thoughts until her face is all I can see.

"Saray," Clara sighs, defeated. "You blasted *fool*."

And I'm gone.

Chapter 22

ENTERTAINMENT SECTOR, THE IMPERIAL MOON PALACE

JED

Simon's eyebrows get the most intriguing little wrinkle between them when he's focusing hard on something. It's a treat getting to watch him work. I just wish I knew how to help. I feel pathetically superfluous right now. At least I'm not the only one. Quell is over in the corner of Simon's apartment, wringing eir hands. Simon's the only one of us with the tools to do anything. I watch his eyes flit back and forth across the holo display as he scans multiple cambot feeds at once, searching for any sign of Prince Miles.

Quell purposely avoided cams when e packed an unconscious Alan Lake into a crate with the prince. But there's near-constant cambot surveillance in the docking area, particularly in cargo. Simon has been tracking groups of Authorities searching the area, trying to pinpoint the moment where Alan was found. There's a lot of footage to go through; the Authorities have been swarming the docks for the past several days, cracking open crates and rummaging through the contents.

"Ah!" Simon exclaims, pausing the vid. He rewinds and pauses, zooming in on one particular crate at the back of the room. The lid is cracked open just a little. As he runs the footage back slowly, he points out the moment the lid pops up, a flash of fingers skimming the rim before pulling it back down.

I move to stand at Simon's shoulder. "Play the vid back."

Quell scoots closer, too. We both watch the scene play out with jaws hanging open: the crate flies open and Alan Lake stumbles out, tipping the crate on its side.

He tries to run, but he's not fast enough. He's limping and stumbling, which I can't blame him for, after being sedated and crammed into a packing crate for more than a day. The Authorities tackle him to the ground, magcuffing him and hauling him away at gunpoint. About fifteen minutes later, they return and search the crate he was in but come up empty.

"No, that's not right," Quell protests. "Miles should have been in there. I definitely put them in the same one. I swear, I—"

Simon rewinds the recording and pauses on the moment Alan tipped the crate onto its side. It fell facing away from the cambot, making it impossible to see inside, but as Alan sprints in the opposite direction, I catch a tiny flash of color in the crack between two crates.

"Did he distract the Authorities and tell the kid to hide?" I scratch the stubble on my chin. "Why would he do that? He has to know he's the one the Authorities want. They'd just take Miles back to his ma, right?"

Quell winces. "Alan never saw my real face. I doubt he knows what's going on. He might think he and the kid are being targeted in some kind of political assassination."

"But Miles saw Alan's face," Simon points out. "As you were kidnapping him."

A stricken look dawns on Quell's face.

"Every royal kid practices kidnapping drills," continues Simon. "If you have a chance to get away from your captor, you run and hide until a safe person comes to get you. That must be what happened. Alan was disoriented and tried to run. Miles took the chance to get away from him."

Simon examines the vid, frame by frame, inching through the minutes with slow deliberation. He pauses on a cleanerbot whirring its way along the bare concrete floor. It's a larger one, with wide attachments made for floor polishing. Maybe just wide enough for a child to cling to its side, sheltering him from the cambots' view, until...

"There," Simon murmurs, pausing on a brief flash of movement in the bot's shadow. It's blurry, but for a second, there's a clear outline of a child's shape darting onto the cargo carousel, crouching behind a crate as the conveyor belt carries it through the scanner into a tunnel. "Oh, kid, I hope you know what you're doing."

I lean forward. "Where does that belt lead?"

Simon switches to a view of the hangar, where the cargo belt dumps crates and luggage onto the waiting platforms of loader-bots. As we watch, a bot scans a crate, then wheels toward the ship where it belongs. It rolls up the ramp and deposits its burden into the cargo hold. Another bot has already taken its place at the end of the belt, waiting for the next crate.

"Did he get in one of the boxes?" Quell's watching intently. "Stars only know where he'll end up if he..."

Simon slows down the footage, watching each crate very carefully. "None of them look tampered with. It'd take more than a five-year-old's strength to pry up one of these lids. Wait—hold on—" He zooms in on a medium-sized hovertrunk. "Am I seeing things, or did that just wobble a bit?"

"He got in someone's trunk?" I laugh. "Smart kid!"

Quell shakes eir head. "Who even knows where that ship was going, or who was on it? The prince might be in even more danger now."

"Yeah, he might," Simon admits. His eyes follow the trunk as a loader bot carries it to a hangar. "I can find out the name and registration of the ship that was parked during this time stamp. But they're almost certainly long gone."

"I'll go after him," Quell offers. "It's my fault all this happened. The least I owe is to get him to safety. Run the search. I'll go now."

"Miles will be trained not to trust anyone he doesn't recognize as a caretaker," Simon warns.

"No problem. I'll just bring my makeup bag," says Quell. "Dress up as the nanny, maybe. I haven't played a woman character in some time. Could be fun."

Simon looks like he wants to protest, but swallows his words and lets out a sigh. "If it gets Miles to safety, then sure."

Quell pauses on eir way out the door. "If you see Clara before I do...tell her I'll be back for her."

Simon nods. I check my keycuff. Time is ticking, both for the prince and for Saray.

"Hurry up, Lady," I mutter under my breath.

Chapter 23

EMPEROR'S VILLA, THE IMPERIAL MOON PALACE

SARAY

Teleporting is an imprecise art. When I use a person as a focus, I'm liable to materialize so close that I startle them half to death.

When I pull myself out of the between-space and into the physical world, I land hidden behind a decorative pillar, an arm's length away from Geneva.

I hold my breath as I take in my surroundings in one adrenaline-sped heartbeat. The intricately carved pillars ring the spacious, circular room, which has no windows and only one set of doors. There's a huge four-poster bed, its covers rumpled and strewn with pillows. It's wide enough to fit half a dozen wives, though Geneva's never given any hint that the Emperor calls more than one of them at a time to attend him.

The Emperor has Geneva backed up against the other side of the pillar I hide behind. I can hear her breathing hard. They're not speaking, but the silence is tense, as if they've just been arguing. I shrink into myself, hardly daring to move as I listen to the Emperor's deceptively gentle, deep voice taunting her.

"I'm half suspicious *you* arranged to make the child disappear," he says. "All those times you begged me to send him away... It offends me that you don't trust my court, darling."

Her voice, when she speaks, is so low and demure I barely recognize it. "Your Majesty knows the danger he faces."

"Of course. I faced it myself when I was only a little older than Miles. My petal, if Miles is as strong as his father, he won't succumb to some ill-conceived attack. He will fight his way back to us and take his place in line to the throne."

Geneva mumbles something.

"What was that, my darling?"

"He is *five*." Now I can hear the steel in her voice she's been softening for him.

The Emperor hisses and steps back, but Geneva follows him with a soft swish of her robe. I hear the dull sound of flesh meeting flesh and chance a peek. She's gone after him with a long, sharp hairpin. He's blocking her with his forearm, but she managed to scratch a long line down his bare chest.

Here in his inner sanctum, the Emperor wears only a simple black robe and loose trousers. His hair is down, mussed, and his eyes are wild as he blocks Geneva's lightning-quick slashes. I never imagined she'd been trained as a fighter—but of course the Emperor would be. He had to, in order to kill all of his own siblings to attain the throne. As is tradition.

"You'll regret this, glitch," he grits out. His voice sends creepflesh up my arms. There's no passion behind it, no wronged affection; he doesn't even seem surprised at her sudden shift. I wonder how many of his wives have already tried to assassinate him.

I clench my fingers over the silver keycuff at my wrist, imagining Lady Haneul in Geneva's place.

Haneul didn't make it.

I have to make sure Geneva does.

Geneva keeps up the onslaught, literally fighting for her life. If she doesn't kill him now, she'll be cut down the instant he regains the upper hand.

Part of my brain urges me to jump between them, but I hold myself back. I have no weapon, no fighting skill—I'd get killed immediately. If only I'd spent more time practicing my mind-bending abilities! Back in Haven, my siblings often shared techniques with each other. It was Clara who helped teach me to manipulate minds, but I've only ever managed to use my skills to compel people to tell the truth, not to put down their weapons.

Geneva is gaining the upper hand. Slashes on the Emperor's face and arms show that she's scoring strikes. His expression has gone from smug to furious.

"Guards!" he chokes out.

The pillar I'm leaning against shudders. I stagger back and stand, jaw agape, as it opens to reveal a guardbot standing inside. It's marble-white, sculpted like an ancient nude statue, but the laser pistol in its hand is perfectly modern—and perfectly capable of riddling people with holes.

All across the room, every pillar is issuing forth statuesque guardbots. They aim their blasters at the grappling couple, but none of them are firing. They've been given orders not to harm the Emperor, I realize, and Geneva is too close to him for a clear shot.

That gives me mere moments to act.

I click a button on Haneul's keycuff, activating an anti-surveillance virus that Simon downloaded onto it in case I needed to disable a cambot. When the bots' eyes go dim, I let out a relieved breath. I wasn't totally sure that the pulse would work on guardbots, but their eye sensors have to work something like a cambot's, don't they?

"Shoot her!" the Emperor yells.

The guardbots lift their weapons obediently, but without sight, they can't aim properly. Shots fly in every direction. I throw myself to the ground.

The Emperor and Geneva are full-on wrestling now, each trying to shove the other into the path of one of the shots. Geneva barely dodges a blast that singes a chunk of hair off—I watch the severed strands drift to the ground. She still has the hairpin in her hand, but the Emperor has hold of her wrist, preventing her from using it. Fighting against his grip—they seem equally matched for strength—she pushes his wrist higher, gasping out a laugh of triumph when a stray shot catches him in the elbow. He curses, his grip weakening just enough for Geneva to wrench free...

And stab her hairpin through his throat.

Relief and fear wash over me in a visceral wave. *She did it. She actually did it.*

The bots are still firing. We have to get out of here.

But Geneva pauses a moment too long, staring at his face as he chokes on his own blood, and a blast catches her in the back of the head.

No!

I bite back a scream as she falls into her husband's embrace.

I lunge forward, dragging her body away from the Emperor's. I refuse to leave her to his mercy, even in death. Draping her arms around my shoulders and supporting her lolling head, I think of Simon and close my eyes to teleport.

Chapter 24

ENTERTAINMENT SECTOR, THE IMPERIAL MOON PALACE

JED

Turns out Simon is one of those people who gets nervous when he doesn't have anything to do with his hands. Now that Quell's gone after the kid, he's starting to jitter.

We can't contact Saray, whose own keycuff is sitting on one of his storage trunks. Pinging his mother's old cuff, he says, would set off all kinds of security alerts. Until Saray returns—*if* she does—we'll be in the dark.

Simon, in the meantime, paces.

"You're going to wear a hole in the floor," I finally say, keeping my tone mild.

Simon scrubs a hand across his face and then flops onto the couch next to me. "Sorry. I can't stop thinking about that poor kid. He's probably so scared. And Saray..." He checks the time on his keycuff. "Don't you think she should have teleported back by now?"

"It's only been an hour. Maybe the Emperor had her sister hidden really well." Tentatively, my heart thumping, I rest my arm along the back of the couch, watching to see if he'll move away. "She'll be fine."

"Better planned assaults on the Emperor's sanctum have ended in death for the assassin," says Simon darkly. "Ask me how I know."

It hits me then. *His mother*. I only knew she was dead—I didn't ask *how*. "I'm sorry."

He sighs and leans into my side. I give up the pretense that I was just stretching my arm and curve my hand around his shoulder.

"Want to talk about it?" I ask.

He lets out a breath. A long silence, then... "She was so kind. Mom. She was soft-hearted and gentle. Too good for this moon."

I nod, waiting.

"The way the Emperor treated her, she didn't have the strength to stand up to him." He dabs the corner of his eye with the collar of his tunic, and I pretend not to notice. "It sent her into a deep depression. She tried to—there were a few hospitalizations. Maybe she thought she would hurt herself so that he couldn't anymore."

Fuck. There've always been rumors, but...

"One night she...well, I found out later she mixed poison into her lipstick. It was intended for the Emperor, but the toxin began to affect her before she could deliver the kiss of death. They called it suicide publicly—didn't want to spread the idea that the Emperor could be attacked that way." He closes his eyes tight, as if to avoid the mental image. "She left me to his mercy. I was only nineteen. The Authorities tortured me for days before they accepted that I had no part in the plot. I think they would have arranged an 'accident' for me if I hadn't disappeared first."

"Stars, Simon." I reach out, ghosting my fingers over the back of his hand where it rests on his knee. His eyes snap to me, his lips parting as if he's about to say something. But he doesn't.

He simply turns his hand palm up and lets his fingers interplay with mine, not quite committing to a clasp of hands, but not rejecting it, either.

"It's in the past," he says softly.

"But it's not." My eyes go to his face, while his stay on our hands. "It's happening all over again, with Geneva and Miles. That's what's bothering you, isn't it? You're afraid that Miles will pay the price if Geneva defies the Emperor. Saray, too."

He nods, lips pressing together. "I...yeah."

"It's going to be fine." I link our hands together and squeeze. "Saray's going to be all right. She's—"

That's when Saray appears from nowhere in the middle of the carpet, supporting a limp form covered in blood.

Both of us scramble to our feet. "That's Geneva!" Simon gasps.

The Emperor's consort is bleeding profusely from a shot to the back of the head, and I can't imagine she has more than a few minutes to live. But if we call emergency medical, they'll alert the Authorities—the ones who very likely just gave her that wound.

"Help her!" Saray sobs. "She killed him, but the guardbots..."

I'm already stripping off my robe, pulling the cloth tight against the back of Geneva's head. Blood soaks straight through.

"Shit." Simon's gone pale. "How is she even still alive?" His fingers are already at his wrist, dialing a call code on his keycuff.

"Don't call the Authorities!" Saray shouts.

"I'm not," Simon snaps back. "I'm calling Dr. Valik."

Thank stars the surgeon is Halcyonite. They're at Simon's door in under a minute, murmuring thanks to the dragon who teleported them.

When Simon opens the door and lets them in, I do a double take. They look like...well, like Imperial nobility. Their long blond hair is half-up, crowned with a glittery headdress. They wear a lovely magenta robe with a feminine floaty train, but masculine boxy sleeves.

Dr. Valik's sharp eyes assess the scene in an instant. Tossing their robe aside and hiking up their slinky skirt, they say, "How long ago did this happen?"

"Around five minutes?" Saray guesses.

"I'm going to need to transport her to an operating room." Dr. Valik sees our faces and hastens to add, "Discretion is paramount, but I don't have the tools or the sterile environment to save her life in this room. Understand?"

Saray looks at Simon. "Do we trust them?"

Simon nods without hesitation. "Dr. Valik is one of ours," he says. By which I guess he means rebels in general, because I doubt this surgeon is a Greenjacket. "Doctor, do what you need to do."

Dr. Valik nods, then cradles Geneva's head in one hand and places their other on her arm. A shimmering dragon appears to wind around them—they must have asked it to wait—and the two of them vanish.

Apparently, dragons will make exceptions about teleporting injured people when their lives are at stake.

The three of us are left in a room splattered with more blood than a crime scene holo-drama. Dr. Valik's magenta robe slides silkily to the floor from the chair where they tossed it.

For a long minute, none of us says anything. Saray lurches to the washroom and starts scrubbing her hands, soap foaming pink. Simon summons his cleaner bot from its charging port and sets it to work on the mess, then silently goes to his garment chest and brings Saray a change of clothes.

After she comes out of the washroom, clean but still pale and shaking, I can't bear to wait any longer. "What happened?" I burst out.

Saray collapses onto the couch next to me. Simon skirts the cleaner bot to sit on her other side, putting an arm around her. His hand brushes my shoulder, and I lean in, discovering that I need comfort, too.

The story doesn't make a lot of sense as it pours out of her. Something about a sea monster, finding Clara, the Emperor's villa, and realizing Geneva was about to carry out the assassination...

"She killed him before I could stop her," Saray whispers, her breath coming almost too fast to speak. "And in the same moment, the guardbots shot her."

"So the Emperor is dead?" I hardly dare to hope it's true. The Greenjackets have been fighting to get an assassin close enough to the old bastard for decades. Could it finally, *finally* be over?

"I...I think so." Saray shudders. "Unless they're able to revive him. She stabbed him through the throat. He wasn't dead yet when I teleported away...but it was bad."

"Shit." That's not what I wanted to hear. I want to be a thousand percent certain that man is never opening his eyes again. I understand why Saray prioritized saving Geneva, but if it'd been me, I would have stabbed him a few more times. "Simon, what's on the newsies?"

Simon's already pulling on his control gauntlet as he wakes up his wallscreen. "They won't announce anything so soon," he warns. "The whole council has to decide the best phrasing, plus they have to have a successor lined up."

"Shit," Saray echoes.

"What?"

"If the Emperor dies, there's a power vacuum. The Imperial princexes are about to go into a frenzy of killing each other for the throne." She stands up, wobbles, and collapses back down between us. "We need to find Prince Miles. Geneva would want him to be protected."

"Quell went after him about half an hour ago," says Simon. "We think he stowed away on a ship bound for Monroe."

Saray's golden eyes fill with tears. "He's all Geneva has. If she dies...I owe it to her to keep him safe."

"Think for a second," I urge her. "You just said that this power vacuum is going to trigger a Moon Palace-centered civil war. Do you think it's safe to go looking for him? Especially as a witness to the murder of Emperor Soren? The guardbots saw you, didn't they? For all you know, they have orders to kill you on sight."

"I put out their sensors before any of them saw."

Simon clears his throat. "I could try to hack the guardbots' orders, but I can't do anything about human Authorities."

I round on him. "You have to be careful, too. Or have you forgotten you're still technically in the line of succession?"

Simon makes a face like I just shoved a lemon between his teeth. "That's my past. I'm nobody now."

"Your DNA link to the Emperor says otherwise. You can't do anything to expose yourself right now," I insist. "If any of your siblings recognize you, they won't hesitate."

"You're not his dad," Saray cuts in, cold and sharp as a knife. "Why do you care what we do? You, of all of us, should be celebrating right now. The Greenjackets just got what they wanted—a dead Emperor and destabilized Moon Palace politics. Why don't you just run back to your team and take potshots at the remaining heirs?"

I recoil. After all this, she still thinks I'm some cold-blooded assassin? *Blast me. Maybe I was right about this glitch.* She only sees people as transactions or political agendas. Never as friends. "Excuse me for giving a shit! How dare I not want to see you both get killed?" I shoot to my feet and stride to the door. "My mistake. Next time, I won't bother."

"Jed, wait!" Simon calls, taking a few steps after me.

Part of me longs to stay and hear him out, but my anger propels me out the door instead and slams it shut behind me.

Chapter 25

ENTERTAINMENT SECTOR, THE IMPERIAL MOON PALACE

SARAY

"You shouldn't have said that stuff to him." Simon stares at the closed door longingly.

For some reason, that stokes my urge to be cruel. "Why not? It's true. He got what he wanted."

Simon sees right through me. "You're lashing out because you're scared," he says firmly. "But don't punish people for caring, Saray."

I shoot to my feet, ignoring the wobble in my knees this time. "I won't, then. You don't need to worry about me anymore. I've always done better on my own."

I hear him sigh as I stalk out, the door slamming for a second time. I'm relieved to find that Jed is already gone, the hallway empty. I close my eyes and focus on the storage locker in the docking area where I stored my stuff.

The reason I stayed was to help Geneva. She's beyond my help now, her life in someone else's hands. It's time for me to accept my exile. I'll find Miles once I get to Monroe, and the two of us will find somewhere to hide while we wait out the oncoming war.

The lightweight dark of the between-space is a relief. The stimulant I patched a few hours ago is starting to wear off, and exhaustion is setting in.

The material world hits me like a ton of bricks when I land in the storage room, startling the hell out of a cleaner bot.

As I stride down the line of lockers, heading for the luggage carousel, I notice the cambots turning away from my approach. *Simon*. I'm equal parts annoyed and grateful that, even after me storming out like a giant glitch, he's still helping me.

Unfortunately, the lack of cambots lowers my guard. As I turn the corner, heading for the main cargo sorting area, I find three Authorities blocking my path.

"Saray Lake," one of them says, "you're wanted for questioning."

"Your General already talked to me," I protest. "I have nothing else to say."

The Authority points a stunner at me. "Oh, I think you do. This isn't about kidnapping anymore, Miz Lake. This is high treason."

They know.

I try to teleport, but the stunner shoots faster. My limbs seizing in agony, I collapse to the floor.

Chapter 26

IN TRANSIT

MILES

The air inside the trunk is getting hot. He's lying on a folded nest of someone's clothes. It's not too uncomfy, but he's worried about being able to breathe.

When it stops bumping around, he pushes the lid up and peeks out. He's in a small room with lots of other crates and trunks. It's a good thing they didn't put anything on top of his trunk, or he'd be stuck in it. He climbs out. It's been stacked on top of a crate. He has to scoot to the edge of the crate and lower his feet as far as he can before jumping the rest of the way down.

The ship lurches under him. Crates shift as the vessel accelerates. They're taking off now.

Miles hopes that means he's finally escaped the kidnapper who was in the box with him when he woke up. He'd kind of thought that Megs or his mother would come get him by now. He did exactly what they prepared him to do if he was ever kidnapped: get free and hide. Except he's realizing that he forgot the last, most important part. He's supposed to stay still in the safe hiding place until someone comes and gets him. Getting into a trunk that was about to be loaded on a ship was a mistake. Now he's going somewhere far away. He's safe, but will they be able to find him?

He wishes he had a keycuff so he could call Megs or his mother, but Megs always said he couldn't get his own tech until he was at least ten years old.

The ship pauses its acceleration, and then suddenly everything goes dark. Miles panics, reaching out to hang onto something, but his body seems to also have gone missing in the dark. He tries to scream, but nothing comes out.

Then he senses a curious presence probing inside his mind. *::You're not supposed to be here,::* it says. Not quite in words, but he understands.

::S-sorry...::

He senses that the other mind is amused more than angry. *::You are an Imperial Prince. You are in danger,::* it says. A statement, not a question.

::Um...yes. I think so.::

::Do not be afraid. I will guide you to safety.::

::Oh! Thanks! Um, who are you?::

::I am what your people call a dragon.::

The lights come back on all of a sudden, and Miles's arms and legs come back too. He falls onto his backside with a sudden bump, tears welling in his eyes as he breathes hard. But he doesn't scream. He wipes the tears on his sleeve.

"I think we just teleported," he says aloud.

::Correct.::

He jumps. The dragon is still here, even though it's invisible.

::In the corner of the cargo bay, there is a pile of old blankets and netting that the crew use to secure fragile crates. Go hide under there. Try to stay still. I will tell you when it's safe to get off the ship.::

"Thank you," Miles says to the air.

The dragon doesn't respond, but Miles senses it's still around some-where, unseen.

Watching.

Chapter 27

IN TRANSIT

RODAN

"Yes, I think my trunk was loaded onto this ship by mistake." I lean closer to the customs bot's platform, showing the name of the ship on my tablet screen. "Can you put me in touch with the pilot so I can reclaim it?"

The bot's eyes swirl as it calculates its answer. Finally, it says, "Flight number 7526-P departed two hours ago. Destination: Clooney Spaceport, Monroe. Please provide your call code, and we will connect you with the ship."

"You know what? Never mind," I say. "New transaction. I would like to hire a taxi ship to Clooney Spaceport."

"Former transaction canceled," the bot says obediently. "When would you like to depart?"

"As soon as possible."

"Scan your keycuff here to pay and receive your ticket. Your flight departs in ten minutes. Have a nice day!"

Five minutes of sprinting across the docks later, I stride up the ramp of a small passenger vessel. The pilot checks my keycuff to validate my ticket, then asks if I have any luggage.

"It's already on Monroe," I lie. All I had time to grab after donning my hasty disguise was the satchel slung over my shoulder. It contains just my makeup case, a couple of wigs, and some costume essentials. Hopefully, I'll be back on the Moon Palace before I have a chance to regret not bringing a change of unders.

The pilot shows me to the passenger bay, advises me to strap in, and then begins powering up the ship to take off.

Teleportation has always made me a bit uncomfortable. There's a reason I barely left Monroe until I was offered the Moon Palace job. I breathe deeply as the ship's anchors disengage, bracing for the moment that the pilot calls a dragon to yank us into the nowhere-space between body and soul.

Even when I'm expecting it, it still takes me unaware. That sudden weightlessness of being without a body, without senses, just a mind floating in nothingness... I try to take deep breaths, but I have no lungs. As always, I'm strongly reminded that dragon-'porting is most likely what it will feel like to be dead.

As always, I experience a moment of fear that I'm *already* dead.

And then the world is back, the ship's lights dim and yellow above me, the faint musty smell of the seat hitting my nostrils too strongly after a moment of absence. I dig my nails into the armrest and take more deep breaths, grateful to have lungs again.

The taxi pilot swoops in for a landing, and that's that. The upside of teleportation: a trip across half a star system took barely ten minutes.

Clooney Spaceport is a lot bigger than the Moon Palace docking area; wandering around looking for the ship that carries Miles might take all day. Enterprising bot-builders have capitalized on this problem by providing little hovercarts to carry people to their connecting flights. I flag one down, pay its fee, and key in the flight number I'm looking for.

As it whizzes across smooth concrete, ships of various sizes and shapes flashing by, I consider how to approach the pilot. *Hi, I think you took my luggage by mistake?* No, they'll have records that show the trunk belonged on the ship. Possibly someone will have already claimed it and gone on their way.

Briefly, I consider telling them the truth—that there's a stowaway prince in mortal danger. Then I laugh to myself. *Yeah, right. Terrible idea.*

The hovercart slows and stops in front of the ship before I've formulated a solid plan. *Right. Improv it is, then.* I step down from the vehicle and approach the ship. It's almost finished unloading—I can see into the nearly-empty cargo bay.

A hauler bot is doing most of the work, but there's a woman in a smart black jumpsuit overseeing the process. I stride toward her, calling, "Hey, there—"

Just as she turns to look at me, a small figure in a maroon robe sprints down the ramp. He darts past the hauler bot and runs straight for me, skidding to a halt by grabbing the side of my leg.

"Megs," he sobs. "You came! I was so scared you wouldn't come."

Prince Miles. I'm relieved that my servant's uniform and hasty makeup transformation were enough to fool him. I doubt it'll be for long, though. The trick will be to get him to safety before he realizes who I am and throws a fit.

The crew member stares at Miles, then glances back to the inside of the cargo bay, clearly questioning how he got in there.

Oh. This, I can work with. I frown and raise my voice in a feminine pitch. "How many times have I told you, sweetie? You don't go running onto other people's ships! I don't care how cool it looks, it's dangerous! That bot could've run you over!"

"I'm sorry," Miles says. He sounds genuinely contrite. I'm not sure a five-year-old is sophisticated enough to know when someone's only *pretending* to be mad.

"This is the last time we take you to the spaceport until you can stick close to me and Mom, understand? We get really worried when we can't see you."

"Uh-huh," the kid mumbles.

I throw a glance back at the crew member, but she's already gone back to directing the bots. Hopefully, by the time she checks any security cam footage and realizes Miles was a stowaway, we'll be long gone.

In a lower voice, I say, "Come on, kid," and guide him toward the hovercart.

He tugs against my hand uncertainly. "You're not Megs. You look like her, but you don't sound like her. And you smell wrong."

I resist the urge to sniff my armpit. It *has* been awhile since I last bathed.

"Just keep walking," I tell him quietly. "No, I'm not Megs, but I'm here to help you."

To my surprise, he doesn't freak out. "The dragon told me to go to you."

"You see? The dragons know what's good for you." It's a total bluff. What the blazes are the dragons doing, getting involved in this? Are they that worried about one little prince?

Then I remember. Miles is the excuse Emperor Soren used to declare war on Halcyon. The dragons probably think that protecting the prince will keep their homeworld safe.

"Where are you gonna take me?" he asks.

It's a fair question. I don't have an apartment on Monroe anymore; I sold it when I got the Pavilion Theater job. The dragons no doubt expect me to bring the kid back to the Emperor and turn myself in for my crimes, exonerating Ambassador Lake. But I'm not fool enough to imagine I'd survive—or that it'd even stop Soren from attacking Halcyon now that he's broadcast his plans.

Plus, if Lady Geneva angers the Emperor by rescuing Clara, she'll want Miles far away from the backlash.

A wall of red catches my eye. A team of five Authorities. They seem to be casually patrolling, but if they see Miles up close, they'll almost certainly recognize him.

"For now," I say, helping him up onto the cart, "I'm going to take you to see a holo." A dark theater is one of the best places I can think of to hide, if only for a couple of hours.

Then maybe I'll try Glenna's original instructions and take the kid to this supposed Waystation café to meet our allied prince.

Chapter 28

JINAN'S SUITE, THE IMPERIAL MOON PALACE

SARAY

I expect to be taken to a prison cell, but instead, the Authorities drag me into a zip-lift headed for Geneva's neighborhood. With my hands magcuffed behind me, I'm helpless to do anything except watch the floor numbers flick by and wonder if the other ladies-in-waiting are getting rounded up, too. It wouldn't be out of the question for Geneva's treason to doom all of her attendants.

But when the Authorities march me off the zip-lift, I realize we're not heading for Geneva's suite. This isn't part of the Imperial wives' wing at all; it's one of the neighboring wings, the one that houses several of the adult princexes.

The Authorities hand me over to a hulking bodyguard at the door, bowing as they're dismissed. The bodyguard unceremoniously throws me over his shoulder, at my protest, and carries me through a hallway eerily similar to Geneva's, dropping me onto a couch in the receiving room.

I struggle upright as I look around. This suite has a very similar layout to Geneva's, but the decor is all different. Where she favors neutral colors, gold accents, and soft lighting, this room's black walls make it seem claustrophobic. The scarlet couch I was dumped on lends the room some color, but the choice of hue feels ominous. Bright overhead lights shine directly above each piece of furniture, lending each chair its own private spotlight. It makes this place feel like an interrogation room, but it's certainly not what I pictured when I imagined the Authorities putting me in prison.

"Welcome, my lady." The sardonic male voice that speaks out of the shadows is one I recognize from newsies and interviews but have assiduously avoided in real life.

Prince Jinan.

The Emperor's heir is a few years older than me at thirty-nine. He wears his smooth, straight hair tied back in a ponytail. His maroon robe frames a black trouser-and-shirt ensemble, deceptively plain compared to outfits I've seen him wear in the past. A gold keycuff and earrings complement the gold liner he's used around his hooded brown eyes. My throat constricts as I recognize the design: the Emperor's signature style.

By wearing it, he's tacitly claiming the throne.

I suppose that shouldn't come as a shock; Prince Jinan has held the title of Crown Prince off and on since his older brother Gunnar was murdered. Popular opinion blames an assassin paid by Jinan for Gunnar's death, though the Emperor accepted his denial with relatively little investigation. In an inheritance war, he's the smart bet to come out on top.

I say nothing, waiting for him to speak so I can taste his intentions. He surely knows I was with Geneva when she killed his father, but what else does he know?

Jinan waves a casual hand at one of the Authorities who brought me here. They jump to angle a shiny, chestnut-brown armchair so that it directly faces the couch on which I lie prone. Jinan drapes himself into it, somehow managing to maintain immaculate posture while moving with casual languor.

"You can speak freely with me," he says at last. "I know everything."

Grass. He believes he's telling the truth.

I laugh. It comes out more like choking. "What percentage of the time does that line convince people to spill their guts?"

Jinan favors me with a vulpine grin. "About fifty-fifty. Works better when they're scared stupid, but I don't have time to torture you properly. Besides—" He looks me up and down. "—I'd rather not damage the goods."

Not a whiff of cinnamon. A chill settles in my bones.

He waves again. One of the Authorities opens his scroll and hands it to Jinan, who selects a vid and puts it in holo mode before pressing play.

The vid is from the point of view of one of the security bots in the Emperor's room. I might have put out their eyes, but the pulse apparently failed to stop them recording holo footage.

My breath comes faster, knowing what I'm about to rewatch, but I can't look away as the scene plays out. Geneva stabs the Emperor, then goes down with a blast to the head.

And then I appear out of hiding to teleport her away.

The scene continues to roll after Geneva and I disappear. The Emperor gurgles on the ground, blood pooling around him. A medic in an Authority uniform arrives shockingly quick—barely two minutes have passed since the stabbing. He works feverishly to stop the bleeding, injecting nanites to repair the damage. But despite his best efforts, the Emperor goes limp, eyes open and staring at the ceiling.

More Authorities pour into the room. General Ajax shoots the medic point-blank in the forehead, killing him instantly, for a crime that I suppose amounts to "treasonously failing to save the Emperor's life." Then he begins barking orders for the Authorities to gather up the Emperor's body, clean the blood away, and pull the security tapes.

The last thing he says before the recording cuts is, "Call Prince Jinan."

I transfer my horrified gaze from the frozen holo figures to Jinan's face, glowing with barely disguised glee. "So he really did die." I had half expected they would revive Emperor Soren and his reign would continue unhindered—except now he would spare no effort trying to kill Geneva and anyone she ever cared about.

The question now is: does Jinan plan to do the same, starting with me?

"Yes, Father is dead," Jinan confirms. "The Authorities are united in support of my rule as the legally recognized successor. All that's left to do is crush any potential opposition, including my siblings and any of Father's wives who plan to make trouble. The council of governors will be interrogated to ascertain their loyalties, of course." He pauses, running a languid finger along his jawline. "And then there's the problem of what to do with you."

I bite back a suggestion on what he can do with himself.

He rolls up the scroll. "I had the pleasure of making your sister's acquaintance last week. Lovely girl. Pretty *and* smart enough to take the deal Father offered her."

He waits for me to ask what deal Clara got offered. I make him wait, wishing I could spit out the cloying taste of his smug attitude. He's so sure he's won that I'm starting to fear he's right.

"Since you asked so nicely," he says finally, "I'll tell you. He let her keep her life in exchange for her total obedience. She was to be his personal weapon—teleporting ships, reading the minds of whoever he asked. His power was set for a meteoric rise above anything his predecessors had ever achieved. All of it was still in the planning stages, of course. He'd barely gotten a chance to announce his first move—subjugating the defiant planet Halcyon—before you came along and helped Geneva end his rule."

That's not exactly how I'd describe what happened. But I let him monologue.

"That's where Father went wrong, you see," Jinan says. "He had *one* Ediya Experiment. He forgot that there are twenty of you."

"Nineteen," I whisper. My brother Raoul's death five years ago still stings, even though he'd misused his power at the end.

"No, no, I'm counting Gaela Ediya's daughter." Jinan lifts his eyes to the ceiling. "What's her name? Amethyst?"

"Amy." Correcting him is a reflex; our older sister hates it when people use the name she was given at birth.

My throat constricts, imagining Jinan with Amy and the rest of my siblings in his clutches. Amy and her wife have *kids*. I forget how old they are—kids aren't really my thing—but they're definitely under ten years old. Is the Emperor counting those children, too? Because they've definitely inherited their mother's gen-mods and abilities. The last time I saw Amy, she was bemoaning the annoyance of a toddler who can teleport.

Most of my siblings choose to live ordinary lives, joining Halcyonite communities to live in peace. It makes me sick to imagine them ripped from their partners, babies, and friends to become weapons for the Emperor.

"Are you going to kill me?" I ask, hearing my voice crack. Hating that I hope the answer is yes. Hating that I know it's not.

Jinan laughs. "If someone dropped a rare jewel into your lap, would you crush it under your foot? Of course not, sweetheart. You'd wear it in your crown." He slides off his chair to kneel in front of me, leaving just enough space between us that I can't kick him in the face. "Saray Lake, you will do me the honor of becoming my first and most honored wife."

He does not phrase it as a question.

My pulse pounds. "I'm not interested in being anyone's wife."

Jinan ignores me. He stands up and dusts off his trousers. "The wedding will be held as soon as possible. A small legal ceremony tonight, with a larger celebration to follow after all my siblings have been eliminated. You'll have to share the ceremony with the handful of Father's wives that I need to remarry for political reasons, but you'll be primary among them. I'll have a few ladies assigned to you as soon as possible so they can begin building your wardrobe. Since you were Geneva's lady, we can skip most of the duty training. I think you'll be well aware of what I expect."

Complete obedience on threat of physical punishment. Sexual submission with the goal of producing healthy heirs. Parading around to every high-profile event to show myself off, using myself as a prop to make my owner—sorry, *husband*—look good.

Oh, yes, I know what Emperor Soren expected of Geneva. And I would rather endure a thousand tortures than similarly debase myself for Jinan.

He blows me a mocking kiss, then sweeps out of the room, leaving the Authorities to manhandle me away. I let them drag me, my mind whirling with half-formed plans.

Jinan may have won this round, but his victories are numbered. He's made a dangerous decision, keeping me close to him.

Because I'll have that many more chances to put a knife in his back.

Chapter 29

ENTERTAINMENT SECTOR, THE IMPERIAL MOON PALACE

JED

Even for the middle of the night, the entertainment district corridors are strangely quiet as I make my way back to the courtesan house. They're not completely empty; people still wander between shops, shooting ranges, and holo theaters with the same carefree abandon. There are just way fewer of them than I'd expect at this time of day.

Even if they're not announcing the Emperor's demise on the public newsies yet, I'd bet my sexy ass that the princexes and some of Soren's wives have already found out. This is the calm before the storm—and the storm is going to be a bloodbath.

The Greenjackets know perfectly well what will happen if a power vacuum opens up. Emperor Soren took power after the (purportedly natural) demise of his mother, Empress Kyra. Kyra's primary consort immediately tried to take over and was assassinated by his own son. Soren then went on to murder his six siblings, as well as Kyra's two other consorts and a good half of Kyra's loyal governing council. Soren's Moon Palace court was decimated to a small core group of people he trusted.

It was effective, too. Despite near-constant threats of assassination and court infighting, Soren's rule lasted over fifty years. The unfortunate reality is that his successful bid for power was relatively bloodless compared to other transitions. A previous version of the Moon Palace was actually blown to pieces—with all of its inhabitants, including the reigning Emperor of the time—about a thousand years ago when an Imperial scion decided he was tired of waiting for the throne.

The Imperial princexes aren't the only ones in danger. Anyone on this moon will be vulnerable until the dust settles.

Including Saray.

Including Simon.

Fuck.

I slip in the back door and clomp down the stairs to the band's basement room. I'm not surprised to find the group huddled around a scroll, watching the newsies in tense silence.

Kyle looks up and sees me first. "Jed, thank stars!" he gasps. "Where've you been? There's a rumor going around that the Emperor's dead."

"He is."

They all stare at me. Then Andi arches an eyebrow and says, "I repeat Kyle's question: where the blazes were you? And how do you know?"

I join their circle and quickly catch them up on the night's events. When I'm done, there's a beat of silence, and then everyone starts talking at once.

Forrest: "We have to contact Greenjacket HQ immediately."

Andi: "This is what we've been waiting for. The Empire is destabilized. We need to take advantage of this opportunity and destroy it for good."

Kyle: "I need to go to Miri!"

That last one stops me short. "What does your girlfriend have to do with any of this, Kyle?"

He gives me an incredulous look. "She's an Ediya Experiment like Saray. If Melanie Ediya is out of prison, she and all her siblings are in danger now."

He's right. According to Saray, Melanie's plan was to install one of the Experiments as a figurehead she can manipulate. I doubt that plan has changed with Soren's demise.

A lead weight hits the pit of my stomach. *Saray's in danger. And I just left.*

I'm such a glitch. She might compartmentalize her feelings to a fault, but that doesn't make it fine for me to withdraw the help I offered. She needs it more than ever.

I think I owe her an apology.

"We'll get a message to Miri as soon as we're out of here," Andi assures Kyle. "She can contact the rest of her siblings and warn them. Our priority has to be dismantling the Empire so they don't have a chance to start a war."

She breaks from the circle and grabs her travel pack. Her screened-off corner of the sleeping area is strewn with discarded items of clothing, which she starts picking up and stuffing into the bag.

"What are you waiting for?" she calls over her shoulder. "Get packing. We need to leave immediately if we're going to get back to HQ in time."

Kyle, Forrest, and Nigel all jump to start packing, too. I just stand there, paralyzed by a sudden conviction.

I can't leave. Not yet.

"Come the fuck on, Jed." Andi pauses in the middle of stuffing a handful of glittery costume jewelry she's pulling out of her mattress lining into her bag. "I know you've had a rough night, but you can sleep on the ship."

"I...I'm not going."

The whole band stops to stare at me. "You're not serious," Forrest says loudly. "Did you not hear the part where this place is going to turn into a war zone? We aren't armed anywhere near well enough for that."

I swallow against the dryness in my mouth. "I know."

We came here equipped with poison, bombs, and tiny personal hand-guns that could be concealed in pockets. Not the kind of firepower it'll take to go against the Authorities—and certainly not enough to make a dent in the fratricide frenzy that's about to go down.

"Look," I say, scrambling for a way to explain my decision logically, "you need a guy on the streets. Someone to report what's happening while you're gone. I'll be the guy. The bird in the mine, or whatever."

Forrest blinks. "You do realize that saying comes from an antiquated practice of using an animal's death to gauge air toxicity? You're volunteering to be a *dead bird*."

Squaring my shoulders, I say, "I'm prepared to take that risk."

"What if we aren't?" Kyle challenges. "Just 'cause you weren't part of our old Knight team doesn't mean we're happy to sacrifice you. You're our comrade now, like it or not."

I sigh. "Right, fine, you got me. I'm not sacrificing myself out of the goodness of my heart. I've gotten really blazing invested with Saray and her shit. Also, I think I'm falling in love with Simon, and I'm not fucking leaving him to go down with this toxic waste dump of a moon all alone. Those two need my help, and instead I stormed off like a jackass. So I'm staying to help them—and maybe you, too, by extension." I wave my hands at them in a shooing motion. "Get back to packing. I give it a couple hours before they shut down the docks, if they haven't already, so you gotta get out while you can."

Kyle holds out his hand to Nigel. "Pay up."

"Nuh-uh. The bet was how long it'd take them to get together," Nigel says. "Jed didn't say they're a couple yet."

I glare at them. "Did you even hear the rest of what I said?"

Andi drops her pack and strides across the room to wrap me in a hug. I tense, patting the top of her blue hair. She's not usually this affectionate. Most of the time, she punches people to show her love.

"Jedrek Blaze," she says, pulling away to tilt her head back and meet my eyes, "you are not fucking allowed to die. Got it?"

"Gonna give staying alive my best shot," I promise her. "Go! Pack!"

As I race back to Simon's apartment, I'm praying to deities I don't believe in that he and Saray haven't disappeared already. If they've given up on me and gone into hiding together, I'll...

Well, I'll feel like a fool, for starters. I also might be a tad jealous. Two hot people hanging out without me, probably talking about what a dumbass I am. Maybe kissing about it? *Ugh. Stop it, brain. I do not need to be a weird combo of angry and horny right now.*

I skid to a halt in front of his door and tap my keycuff to request entry. The few seconds of waiting before the door opens feel like an eternity.

I blow out a relieved breath when the door cracks and Simon peers out at me. As he stands aside to let me in, I realize he's alone in the apartment. Saray's gone, and the place looks torn apart: trunks open, items crammed in. His wallscreen is dismantled, the storage drive ripped out of the wall and loose wires dangling. The screen itself is rolled into an iridescent cylinder, lying on the floor between a crate of spare bot parts and a pile of femme clothing. His Princex Somin disguises, if I had to guess.

"You're leaving," I realize aloud, unable to hide the disappointment in my voice. *Why am I not glad? I wanted him safe, didn't I?*

Simon gives me an exasperated look. "Of course I'm leaving. Why aren't you?"

"The rest of the band is on their way out." I pause. "I decided...someone needed to stay. To report as events unfold."

"That's very noble of you," says Simon dryly. "But if you have a death wish, jumping out an airlock is quicker and less painful."

"It's not a death wish. It's...what I needed to do." I take a step closer. "I'm sorry I yelled at you and Saray."

Simon's throat moves as he swallows. "I get it. She was being reckless. It scared you. Scared me, too."

"Fuck, all of this scares me." I run a hand across my face. "I guess not enough, or I'd be on that ship with my band. But I couldn't do it because..."

"Because you give a shit," Simon whispers. "I know."

The eye contact is heating my blood, even though this is the galaxy's worst timing. I flick my gaze around his room instead. "Saray left?"

"She stormed off, too. I lost track of her somewhere in the docks. I was trying to turn the cambots away to give her safe passage, but my link got disrupted. It's a long shot for the Authorities to get a trace on me, but I don't want to risk it. I need to disappear for a while."

"Oh. Good." There's a sick feeling in my gut. "I was going to suggest the same thing, given your...past. And the fact that Saray used your mom's keycuff to break into the Emperor's sanctum. Getting out of here might be for the best." *I'll just...fucking miss you.*

"Oh, I'm not leaving the Moon Palace," says Simon. "Whoever takes Emperor Soren's place is bound to be worse than him. There are, believe it or not, innocent people on this moon. I'm staying as long as I can to fight for a good outcome for them."

My insides feel like they're melting. Fuck, I'm so gone on this guy. "Simon," I croak, "you're a better person than I'll ever be."

The corner of his mouth quirks up. "Didn't you just say you were going down with this ship to send your team intel? That sounds pretty blazing brave to me."

"Yeah, I said that, but I lied," I burst out. "I'm mostly staying for you."

The amusement in his eyes sharpens into something wild and hopeful. He takes a step closer.

"A-and Saray," I hasten to add. "And Miles, and—"

Simon's hand cups my cheek. "Jed."

"What?"

"Stop talking."

His mouth slants across mine, and fuck, I think I'm going to die. Nobody can survive their blood boiling in their veins, their heart pounding like it'll explode, every nerve ending as sensitive as a lit fuse.

When we come up for air, I'm flushed and panting, one hand in his hair and the other on his ass. I move both hands to the small of his back, but that doesn't feel any less perilous. His body stays pressed to mine. I can feel a tremble in his fingers as his thumb traces my stubbled jawline.

"Whoa," I breathe, rather impressed with myself for making a sound that resembles an actual word.

He smirks. "That's been a long time coming."

"I...uh...you too?"

"Why the blazes do you think I risked my life to go to your concerts in person?" Simon's eyes crinkle with laughter. "Your stage persona was the sexiest thing I'd ever seen in my life. Until I started getting to know your *offstage* personality."

"And then you wanted to punch me?"

"And then I wanted to..." Simon kisses me again, soft and lingering. I momentarily forget how lungs are supposed to function. "You're ruining me, Jed. I don't let *anyone* get close. It's safer that way. But you wormed your way in, and now...I'm afraid we're running out of time."

I kiss him again, once, twice. I back him up to the sofa and press him down into it. It's like our bodies are magnetized—I can't stop touching him. Even when he arches against me with a gasp, not of pleasure but of pain.

He reaches behind his shoulder blades and pulls out a wallscreen control gauntlet. "These things don't look sharp, but *ow*."

The sight of the gauntlet is something of a wakeup call. *Right. He's in the middle of packing up to vanish because he's in very real danger.* I help him sit up, unable to peel myself off his lap. "Do you have somewhere safe to go?"

He nods. "I know a few places I won't be discovered."

"Then let me help you. Let me come with you." I rake my fingers through his hair, combing out the tangles I put there. "You're not getting rid of me after this."

"I should tell you to leave." His tone is regretful. "But blast it, I can't."

Part Five

DAYFIVE

Year 3750 DE, Week 45

Chapter 30

JINAN'S SUITE, THE IMPERIAL MOON PALACE

SARAY

Jinan's suite is little more than a prison cell, but at least it's a luxurious one. Similar to Geneva's in size, it contains a sitting room, attendants' quarters, a kitchen, and the bedroom to which I'm confined. It's fully furnished, including scents, soaps, and cosmetics in the washroom, and a walk-in wardrobe with a stunning array of women's garments. I hesitate to ask where it all came from. Most likely, it belonged to one of his sisters—and a princess would never give away her wardrobe unless it was over her dead body.

Jinan instructed the Authorities guarding me that I was to be given nightsweet every six hours. The drug keeps me sleepy and disoriented, but worse, it makes me incapable of teleportation, just like Clara. And the guards aren't shy about forcing it down my throat if I refuse to eat.

They've even disabled the taps on the washroom's enormous bathing pool, to stop me from drowning myself, I guess. An unnecessary gesture. I fully plan to survive this ordeal. I haven't figured out how yet, but I'm far from giving up.

I allow myself to doze in bed for much of the day. The rest is much needed; I haven't had a decent night's sleep in days. With the nightsweet in my system, looking for an escape route will only exhaust what little energy I have left. When lucid, my brain is constantly churning out scenarios, deciding how best to turn this situation to my advantage.

How can Clara stand it? I hope she escaped in the confusion after Emperor Soren's death and is far away by now. And yet, selfishly, I wish she was here. With both of our skills combined, maybe we could overpower Jinan.

Back in our Haven days, I admired and slightly feared what my sister was capable of. My passive skill had always come to me naturally, but I struggled to actively use my extra-sensory abilities to affect others the way Clara could.

Altering someone's mind, going further than simply forcing a confession, always made me uneasy. There's no clear-cut line between using it for good and causing harm. It's no wonder the dragons don't like us, if we're capable of such power with no checks in place to stop us from abusing it.

But it's life or death now. If I can control Jinan's perception of me, I might survive this. I'll worry about the morality of my actions later.

That's what Clara would tell me to do.

Eventually, the Authorities return. "The Emperor commands you to prepare for your wedding," barks the leader, then shoves four women through the door. "He gifts you these ladies-in-waiting to help you."

With a shock, I realize that the ladies are Geneva's: Pearl, Kina, Yumiko, and Nuala. With unkempt hair, wrinkled garments, and smeared makeup, they look as if they've spent time in a prison cell—a not-so-luxurious one. It didn't occur to me before that they could've easily been executed as co-conspirators in a regicide. They must have begged for their lives very convincingly.

As the Authorities slam the door shut behind them, the four ladies stare at me with expressions ranging from confusion to loathing.

"What did you do?" Nuala's voice is low and strongly flavored with citrus fury.

The drug slows my tongue. Explaining everything is impossible, even if I trusted them enough. "I tried to save Her Grace's life," is what tumbles out.

Nuala sucks air through her teeth. "But you allowed her to commit treason?"

I snort. "It's not like she asked me for permission."

"Well, now we're *your* ladies," Pearl jumps in. "So please give us the courtesy of a warning before doing anything that endangers our lives." Her words taste just as citrus-sharp as Nuala's, but with an aftertaste of vanilla sweetness that I identify as pity.

Normally, I'd chafe at someone feeling sorry for me, but in this vulnerable state, a scrap of sympathy feels like a lifeline.

"You should clean yourselves up first," I tell them, falling back onto my pillows. "I'm in no hurry. Make His Highness wait."

Pearl and Kina look at each other. "His Highness is soon to be crowned our new Emperor," Kina says. "Defying him won't end well for you."

I spread out my arms. "Does it look like it's currently going well for me? Go. Get clean. I know you're desperate to." I've never seen Kina with a single hair out of place, and Pearl always said she'd rather die than be seen with smudged eyeliner.

Three of them bolt for the washroom without another word. Only Yumiko stays behind, perching on the edge of my bed. She takes my arm and lifts my sleeve, moving my unresisting limb back and forth as she examines my skin. I realize she's checking for bruises, like she used to with Geneva.

"You don't have to do that," I mutter. "He didn't hurt me. Yet."

"Would you admit it if he had?" Yumiko says softly. "Geneva was a proud woman, too. It's hard to face physical vulnerability when you have a strong spirit."

Pressure builds in my sinuses, but I blink the tears away. "I'm glad he didn't kill you," I say.

Retroactive guilt eats me up. My worries were only ever for Geneva; I'd failed to imagine what the Emperor might do to the household of a traitor. The ladies' lives hang by a thread right now. Any misstep I make could be punished with their deaths, and I think Jinan guessed, rightly, that he can use that to control me.

"I am thankful to be alive," Yumiko says cautiously. "But we knew the risks of serving an Imperial lady from the start. Her favor was our favor, just as her disgrace is ours." She pauses. "Her Grace cared too much, not only about us, but about her son. It kept her frozen. Don't fall into the same trap."

The washroom door opens again, scented steam billowing out. Nuala, naked except for a towel slung across her shoulders, calls, "Miko, don't you want a shower?"

Yumiko scurries away, shooting me an apologetic look over her shoulder. I get it. She can't repeat what she just said in front of the other three. They'd urge me to do the opposite—sacrifice myself to save their skins.

I don't know if I can make any promises either way. But I do know this: the new Emperor isn't going to keep his throne, or me, for very long. I just have to wait for him to get careless.

The ladies may be angry at me, but they're still experts at their jobs. When they turn me to face the mirror, I almost don't recognize myself—and I'm no stranger to fashionable formal dress.

The outfit consists of an enormous gold multilayered skirt, studded with diamonds. Instead of a bodice, Kina apologetically hooked me into a jeweled bikini top, which weighs twice as much as my actual breasts and is the opposite of comfortable. ("Jinan asked for this style," Kina explained.

"It's very 3004, but I suppose he wants to make a statement.") Twinkling body chains lace across my belly and drip down my bare shoulders. I look like a walking advertisement for a diamond mine, but I feel like a prisoner.

Over the ensemble, a filmy, translucent golden veil covers my abundant bare skin in place of a robe. Fastened to the tiara pinned into my hair, the veil cocoons me like a personal force shield. If only it was as impenetrable as one. Every time I move and the chains shift against my skin, I shudder, imagining Jinan's hands in their place.

That is *not happening*. I'll claw his eyes out with my lacquered nails first.

The ladies, dressed in Imperial scarlet and black, follow me two by two as a team of Authorities lead me to the zip-lift. Yumiko dutifully and apologetically dosed me with nightsweet just before we left—but I think she may have given me a half dose. I'm able to focus a little better than I was a few hours ago. It's not enough to return my teleportation ability, but at least I can stay conscious for the torment I'm about to undergo.

The zip-lift drops us in the lobby of the Moon Palace's throne room. I've attended numerous events here as part of Geneva's retinue. A peek through the open door shows me rows of chairs—half as many as usual—already occupied. At the far end of the room is an elevated dais, on which rests an upright sarcophagus carved with Soren's visage in lifelike detail.

The audience seems to consist mainly of newsie reporters—their cambots hovering attentively above their heads—and a selection of Governing Council members. My heart sinks, even though I know it's foolish to expect any friendly faces.

"I thought you said to prepare for a wedding," I hiss to the Authority holding my right arm. "This looks like a funeral."

I take a step closer, trying to get a better look, but he yanks me away and leads me down a side hallway. I'm pushed into a waiting room full of women—my lips curl in disgust at Jinan deciding to segregate the guests by gender—and deposited on an ornate sky-blue fainting couch at the front

of the room. My attendants are sent to wait at the back of the room with
a handful of other ladies.

I crane my neck to watch them go, wondering why they're forcing the
attendants to stand. Is there not enough space?

Then details start to filter through my drugged brain. Jewels glitter on
every woman seated behind me. They're dressed nearly as lavishly as I am,
but none look happy or excited.

I recognize Lady Clematis, Princess Iris's mother, tears leaking silently
down her pale face. Lady Penelope, another of Emperor Soren's wives,
shivers in the transparent gown I doubt she chose to wear, her nipples
clearly visible through wispy fabric.

Stars. This room holds every currently-living Imperial consort, minus
Geneva. Plus a handful of faces I don't recognize, and one that I regret
recognizing as soon as I lay eyes on her.

Clara.

She catches my glance and nods, letting me know she's listening.

::I thought you escaped!::

Her mental voice is rueful. *::The Authorities aren't as stupid as they look.
They caught me before I even made it out of Soren's villa. Pretty sure Melanie
Ediya tipped them off—curse her.::*

::I assume Jinan monologued at you, too?::

Even though I've turned to face forward, deliberately not looking at her,
I can *hear* her eyeroll. *::Enough for me to get the gist. He's coming for our
siblings, blah blah, wants to rule everyone, blah blah.::*

::So we agree he has to die.::

::Wish it was as easy as agreeing,:: Clara says. *::I'm guessing he dosed you
with nightsweet, too? So we can't teleport, and I can barely think hard enough
to mess with someone's mind.::*

::Me, too,:: I reply, *::but I think one of my ladies is sympathetic and gave
me a low dose. Clara, I need your help.::*

I let her see the plan I've been roughly formulating, the outline of it still fuzzy. Everything rides on the two of us being able to manipulate Jinan not just to tell the truth, but to believe a lie.

::*I'll resend you my memories of how it feels to do it,*:: Clara says, ::*but you've got to break through your mental blocks yourself.*::

I close my eyes, pretending to be dizzy—actually, it doesn't take much pretending—and let Clara's memories of using her power overtake my thoughts. She does it so naturally, it's hard to pinpoint *how*. But it's inextricably connected to the way she passively perceives thoughts, the same way the scent of food triggers a hunger to eat. I just have to bridge that gap between hunger and reaching out to bring a bite to my mouth.

"Lady Saray."

My eyes fly open. I sway, catching myself on the arm of the couch, as I look up into the eyes of the Authority General. His flinty gaze reminds me that it's barely been two days since he questioned me as a suspect in a kidnapping. And he has most definitely not forgotten.

"It's time," he says, offering a gentlemanlike hand to lift me to my feet.

The illusion is shattered, though, by the cruel strength of his grip.

Chapter 31

BOT CHARGING STATION, THE IMPERIAL MOON PALACE

JED

When Simon said he knew a place to hide, I expected an apartment in another sector. Instead, we end up squatting in a bot recharging station that's only accessible to humans through an emergency hatch in the ceiling.

Our refuge resembles a dimly lit, long, narrow closet. Along the walls, cubicles of varying sizes—some ceiling height, some tiny and stacked on top of each other—wait empty for bots to return and plug themselves in. Only a handful of them are currently occupied with dormant mechanical figures flashing their slow yellow charging lights. At the far end, a door slides up and down whenever it senses a bot approaching, allowing them entrance to and egress from the network of bot tunnels.

Simon explained that these tunnels lace through the entire Moon Palace complex, hidden hatches allowing cleaner bots to pop up, scrub an area, and leave unobtrusively. Some larger tunnels allow hauler bots to deliver supplies or remove garbage. Those tunnels are big enough for humans to walk through, but "Don't try it" was Simon's recommendation. "Too easy to get run over."

My surprise notwithstanding, bringing us here is actually genius. Apparently, humans almost never enter the bot areas, and only a handful of maintenance techs have the access codes to get in. There are no security cams in here, and even the cambots stop recording once they enter the tunnels.

As soon as we climbed through the hatch, Simon stacked his crates of belongings in a corner of the largest charging cubicle, then pulled out his tablet and diverted a cleaner bot to scour the place because it smelled faintly of stale garbage. Now that the bot has finished freshening up and scooted back to its charging port, Simon opens one of his trunks and begins making up two piles of blankets for us.

"I have a stupid question," I say, warily eyeing the bot access door as it swishes open to allow another cleaner bot to trundle in. "What if we fall asleep and a bot decides it wants this charging port? Will we get run over?"

He laughs. "No. I overrode this cubicle's signal—it's marked as occupied right now."

"Oh. Smart."

Stars, Simon really makes me feel like a quarkbrain sometimes. Not that he intends to. He's just so blazing clever and so quick with machines. What do I know how to do? Play guitar. Shake ass. Point gun and shoot. And he's a star-blasted *prince* on top of it all.

A prince who works to help and protect the less fortunate.

Fuck. I'm not used to crushing this hard on someone who's so stratospherically out of my league.

I'm also more than a little nervous (and turned on) by the fact that we're alone in a closet. It's full of sleeping robots, which wouldn't be my first pick for a date, but now that we're here, am I weird for thinking it's kind of cozy?

Simon's mind is elsewhere, though. He's establishing a secure, hidden connection to keep tabs on what's going on above our heads.

"Oh, shit," he says suddenly. "There's a live stream going. Just started half an hour ago. Newsies are saying that Emperor Jinan is holding a funeral, a coronation, and a...wedding?"

"Is he marrying all of Soren's wives?" I scoot closer as Simon taps into the stream. "Hey, would that mean he's his siblings' stepdaddy now?"

Simon makes a face. "Gross. Thank stars he can't marry *my* mother."

The holo stream, captured from a bot hovering above the audience, flickers to life in miniature, projected above Simon's tablet. Prince Jinan—*Emperor* Jinan, now, I suppose—has just been crowned by General Ajax. He turns to face the audience.

"I am honored," he says, his voice echoing tinnily through the speakers, "to carry on my father's illustrious legacy. My commitment is to bring stability and prosperity to you, the people of this galaxy." He pauses. "Rest assured, there will be vengeance for my father's untimely death. Any traitors who wish ill to the crown will be swiftly dealt with. But there is time for that later. For now, I hope you will join me in rejoicing as I introduce you to the women who will stand at my side in this new era of peace."

The doors at the far end of the room slide open. Flowers rain from the ceiling as a woman steps through, dripping head to toe in jewels.

I draw in a sharp breath. "Simon, is that—"

He nods grimly. "It's Saray."

Chapter 32

THRONE ROOM, THE IMPERIAL MOON PALACE

SARAY

G eneral Ajax tucks my hand through the crook of his arm, holding it firm there, and marches me down the hall to yet another entrance. This time, it's a dramatic double-door entry through a vaulted arch.

As I step through, petals drift down from above, littering my path and getting caught in my veil. Music swells. The guests stand, turning to look at me with awed gasps. I barely glance at them. My vision tunnels. *Just get through this moment.*

The General all but drags me up the aisle, passing my hand to Jinan, who waits next to an enormous Imperial flag that's been draped over his father's sarcophagus, hiding it from view. His gold robe shimmers with embroidered dragons stitched with scales made of rubies and black diamonds. His sunburst-shaped crown is as tall as my forearm and has to be excruciatingly heavy. If he weren't an evil fucking glitch, he'd be the image of a dashing handsome prince from a sentimental holo-drama. I'm sure there are thousands of gullible people watching this on the newsies right now and swooning.

Jinan's fingers close around mine as tight as a hunter's trap. He leads me up to the stage, centering us beneath the flag. Twin columns twined with blood-red flowers frame us as he turns to face the audience.

"As your new Galactic Emperor," he says, voice magnified to echo around the room, "I hereby take Saray Lake to be my first consort."

That's all he needs to say. Thanks to Emperor Soren, may he rest in torment, the law doesn't require my consent. It doesn't matter if I accept Jinan. He has the right to claim me regardless.

The audience cheers and chants—I'm almost certain there are cues coming through their audio earrings. "Long live Emperor Jinan! Long life and fruitful union!"

Fruitful? Blazing fuck, Jinan's got some nerve. I almost laugh, imagining his face when I tell him I had myself medically sterilized years ago. But no, I'm not going to volunteer that information. He's not getting anywhere near my defunct childbearing equipment, anyway.

Jinan escorts me to one of two identical thrones set at the back of the stage, one on either side of the flag-draped coffin. I'll have a nice clear view of him marrying my next twenty-odd sister wives. *Charming.*

Thankful not to be the center of attention anymore but still uncomfortable at the thought of so many eyes on me, I settle in for the rest of the show.

It's Clara they bring out next. She keeps her chin held high, even though her knees wobble above her heeled slippers. Jinan has her draped in diamonds, too: a minidress that looks to be made entirely of gemstone fringe, with a train of iridescent feathers from some alien bird that didn't deserve to die for this. Her ice-blond hair is crowned with a silver veil and a tiara only slightly less gaudy than mine.

Her wedding to Jinan is just as brief. She endures it with glassy eyes, swaying ever so slightly. I hope the entire galaxy notices and gossips about how Jinan can't control a woman without drugging her.

Then again, he'd probably send assassins after anyone who does.

Jinan escorts Clara to the throne next to mine. I catch a whiff of her perfume as she sits, but I carefully don't look at her. I'm not giving Jinan any ideas about using the two of us against each other.

I expect Emperor Soren's wives to be trotted out next, but instead, the double doors open, and a horribly familiar figure enters. Melanie Ediya walks alone down the aisle, wearing a white robe much more substantial than ours. She's not bedecked in jewels, but the robe is delicately embroidered in gold phoenixes to match the shimmering gold sheath dress she wears underneath. A simple circlet of gold cuts across her forehead. Unbelievably, she's wearing gold eyeliner to match Jinan's. The Emperor's design.

::*Ew,*:: Clara says in my head. ::*He's marrying Dr. Ediya, too? That feels kind of incestuous, doesn't it?*::

I meet my sister's eyes for a brief moment. Her makeup isn't in the Imperial style, and neither is mine. Soren never allowed his wives to wear the same designs—it would have marked them as his equal.

Cold sweat prickles on my neck, sending a shiver through me. ::*I don't think that's what's happening.*::

Melanie steps up to Jinan and then kneels before him. He takes her hand and presses his forehead to her fingers.

Then he says, in ringing tones, "This woman created and raised my two beautiful wives. She is, in a sense, my vow-mother. In the absence of a parental advisor, and to fill the void left by the passing of my father, Emperor Soren, and my beloved mother, Lady Rita, I wish to cement this bond legally. I hereby adopt Lady Melanie Ediya as Queen Mother."

Luckily, I'm the only one who hears Clara's mental shriek of outrage. ::*What the blazes? Can he even do that?*::

::*At the moment, he can do whatever he wants,*:: I reply grimly. ::*Count your blessings. At least she's not our sister wife.*::

::*This is worse,*:: Clara moans. ::*She outranks us.*::

::Doesn't matter.:: I turn my eyes straight ahead, letting them slide right by Melanie as, smirking, she moves to stand between Clara's throne and mine. From the audience's perspective, she's framed perfectly underneath the flag. *::We're not going to let them win.::*

::I wish I had your optimism.::

::It's not optimism,:: I say. *::It's determination. Fueled by spite.::*

Clara has to cough to cover a snicker.

The Authorities signal the audience. I watch, confused, as the reporters in the back row begin to shut down their cambots. The hovering spheres sink slowly into their owners' hands, leaving only the palace's own security cams. I glance at Clara, lifting an eyebrow. *::What about the rest of the wives?::*

But after the cams are packed away, no one stands to go. They remain in their seats, expectant.

So it's the public broadcast that's over. Not the private spectacle.

General Ajax guides the first of Emperor Soren's former wives through the double doors. I'm still struggling to remember her name when Jinan leads her up to the dais and announces, "For the crime of loyalty to a dead regime, I hereby sentence Lady Victoria to death."

She doesn't even have time to finish her startled gasp before General Ajax blasts her between the eyes.

A scream tears out of me. I clap a hand over my mouth, afraid I've drawn too much attention, but the crowd mirrors my horrified outburst. Clara stares dully, fingers white against the armrest of her throne. Stars—she knew he intended to do this and was powerless to stop it.

::All the women in that room?:: I ask her, my stomach rolling.

::They could be pregnant with rival heirs.::

::He said he would have to marry some of them for political reasons...::

Clara shakes her head, ever so slightly. *::He considered it, but decided he'd rather send a message that this is a new regime. All alliances will have to be remade.::*

::Fuck.:: I close my eyes as the Authorities drag away Lady Victoria's body, just in time to lead out the next woman. The puddle of blood waits with Jinan between the floral pillars. *::It's us, then. Just us.::*

::Looks like it.:: Clara sends me a mental image of a hand squeeze. I wish I could reach out and take her hand for real, but her throne is placed too far, and Melanie stands in the gap between us.

::We'll fucking get him,:: I say.

And it's those words we pass back and forth for the next bloody hour, sick and flinching as the Emperor sentences wives and their bodies fall to the floor.

::We'll fucking get him.::

::We'll fucking get him.::

Chapter 33

BOT CHARGING STATION, THE IMPERIAL MOON PALACE

JED

Simon and I are glued to the screen, unable to do anything but watch the shipwreck of a "wedding" unfold in front of us.

"You said this is live?" I choke out. "To the whole galaxy?"

"Not anymore. This is an internal security vid. The newsies were instructed to turn off their cams after Dr. Ediya's coronation."

"We have to stop him." I lunge forward, intending to head for the exit hatch, but Simon pulls me back.

"With what army?" he asks softly. "That bastard Jinan wouldn't be doing all this if he didn't already have the Authorities lining up to defend him. The General himself is the one doing the killing."

I slump back, defeated. "Then what's the point? He already had all those women under his thumb."

Simon shakes his head. "It seems like a warning to me. This is for the Moon Palace elite. A show of strength to dissuade anyone from challenging him."

I turn my gaze away as another of Soren's wives is shot dead. "At least he spared Saray and her sister."

"I don't know if that's a blessing," Simon mumbles. "If he'll do this in public, what is he capable of doing in private?"

My stomach churns. "We have to rescue them, then."

"Stop him from doing any more damage," Simon agrees. "That's a two-birds, one-stone goal. The question is, how? If he had the Authority General ready to place the crown on his head, we're going to have to take out the entire Imperial Authority force before we'll have a chance at him. Tricking the sensors with Mom's keycuff won't work again."

"We can't do it by ourselves," I say. "Simon...can you get me a secure connection to the Greenjackets? I need to alert my team to what's happening." I pause, then add, "Also, dig up any dirt you have on General Ajax. He might be Jinan's right hand, but everyone has a weak point. Even him. Probably."

Simon's mouth twists in a half-smile. "That's a start." He minimizes the horrific live vid and opens a new window on his scroll. "Tell me your team's call code, and I'll get a message through."

Chapter 34

JINAN'S SUITE, THE IMPERIAL MOON PALACE

SARAY

I don't remember being escorted back to my new suite/prison. Everything started blurring after around the sixth execution.

When I come back to awareness, I'm in the new bedchamber, and Pearl is gently peeling bejeweled garments off of my unresisting form. Kina takes each diamond-studded piece and tenderly hangs them in my wardrobe, no doubt planning to clean and preserve them to be shown in a museum or something. She's oddly sentimental about things like that, considering she rarely gets mushy about anything else.

"Did you see?" I murmur through numb lips. "Did they show you the feed?"

"Of the wedding, Your Grace?" The title sounds like it sticks in Pearl's throat. "We ladies weren't allowed to watch. They shuffled us off in groups right after the weddings started." She shrugs. "It's fine. We'll view the recording after you're prepared for bed."

"Don't," I say sharply.

Pearl's exquisitely penciled eyebrows fly up. "Whyever not, Your Grace?"

"And stop fucking calling me that," I add.

"We have to, Your Grace," Yumiko says quietly. Her voice drops to a whisper. "His Majesty, your husband, is more than likely listening to every word we say. If we disrespect his new bride..."

That wretched asshole. Of course he would bug my gilded prison. It's a measure of how addled I am that I hadn't already realized it.

Softening my tone, I say, "Don't watch past the first two weddings. You won't like what you see."

Nuala says dryly, "Your Grace, you do realize that makes us want to watch it all the more?"

"Do what you will, then. But don't say I didn't warn you."

They all share a look of dark resolve. My heart twists because I recognize that defiance—not long ago, I would have been part of it. If Geneva had said the exact thing to me that I just said to them, I'd have ignored her.

Stars. If Geneva lives, I'm going to owe her several apologies.

"Your Grace, Jinan sent word that you're expected in his private quarters tonight," says Yumiko, her voice shaking. "Do you want anything to prepare? A bath? Anti-anxiety patches? Sleepy tea? Or..."

Or something stronger? is the unspoken end to that sentence. Geneva usually made do with only gentle mind-alts—we all admired her resilience for that. It wasn't uncommon for Emperor Soren's other wives to dose themselves with more dangerous and experimental options. Some allow out-of-body experiences, hallucinations, or complete numbing of all pain, physical and emotional. Then there are patches that turn pain to pleasure or boost the sex drive so high that rational reactions quiet to a whisper. Several of them aren't strictly legal due to hideous side effects, but for an Emperor's wife, nothing is impossible to acquire.

I won't lie and say it's not tempting. There is a part of me that wants to give up and float away on a cloud of chemicals, blissfully unaware of what's happening to me. The nightsweet suppresses the fighter in me who would normally shout down any thoughts of cowardice. After that horrific "wedding," my inner warrior has lost some of her control over my brain.

But she's still there in the back corner, knives in her hands and a mouth full of flames, screaming at me not to take this shit lying down. And I know she's the one I have to listen to.

"Nothing," I tell her. "You've already given me enough."

I hope she'll understand what I mean—the reduction in my dose of nightsweet is what I need. The ability to face Jinan with a clear head and at least partial control of my powers.

Yumiko gives me a bow and a very faint smile. "Yes, Your Grace. I recommend getting some rest before you go."

I think she's trying to tell me to sleep off the nightsweet even further before the Emperor calls me in to claim his wedding night. I climb into the soft, luxurious embrace of the new bed, doubting I'll be able to drift off without bloody nightmares jolting me awake.

But I close my eyes nonetheless.

Chapter 35

BOT CHARGING STATION, THE IMPERIAL MOON PALACE

JED

Once we make the connection to my former team, it doesn't take long to explain what happened. The silence as they process the horror of it stretches out much longer.

Kyle—I guess he's Leo again, after leaving the Moon Palace—is the first to speak, his holo-projected face distorting into a grimace. "Looks like Jinan is setting up to be just as bad as, if not worse than, his dear old pa."

"I could have told you that," Andi, now Natalia, butts in. She's redyed her hair, stripping out the blue for her favored orange-red. It's a few shades darker than mine now.

"I doubt anyone's surprised," I reply. "The question is, how does this affect your plans? Jinan's managed to get the Authorities lined up behind him a lot faster than I expected. He'll be preparing for challenges from the other princexes. We might have already missed our attack window."

"I don't think so," says Forrest/Derek. "I'm sure he'd like us to *think* he's already cemented his rule, but new regimes are always shaky at the start. All it takes is one show of strength, one good bribe, one close-enough assassination attempt for his supporters to wonder if they're backing the right side. Then we rain down fire and drive those wedges deeper until he cracks."

I scratch my chin. I haven't had a chance to cleanse or shave in over a day. "Have you talked to the Greenjacket leaders? I know their plan has always been to kill the Emperor, but they never got super specific with what they planned to do after that. Are we talking about installing a replacement ruler? A ruling council? Disbanding the entire system and letting anarchy take over?"

Natalia snorts. "As if anarchy would last long. There are far too many assholes who want to be in charge."

Derek shakes his head. "The plan has always been to return sovereignty to individual planets to elect their own rulers. Removing the Moon Palace elites will only be the first step. We'll have to assist hundreds of worlds in removing the Authorities and Imperial-appointed governors. Not to mention setting up democratic elections all over the galaxy. It won't happen instantly. But it can't happen at all if we don't quickly and decisively take power out of the wrong hands."

"Right. So. Plan for doing that?" I pointedly raise an eyebrow. "Please don't say their plan is 'show up and start blasting.'"

"Actually," says Leo, "that might be where you come in. You staying behind kind of opens up an opportunity for us."

"Yeah? Like what?"

"They're talking about getting someone into the Authority headquarters to use their system. It's the only outgoing broadcast that's not heavily censored. We'll blast information to the galaxy about what's going on and how they can help," Derek says. "The common people are already overwhelmingly on our side. The only place where the Empire has majority support is Monroe. Well, maybe a handful of other wealthy worlds. Everywhere else, the governors and Authorities are hated. We send out a call to action—boom, we've got an army."

"Of farmers and miners? You gonna have them attack the Authorities with a harvester bot?"

"That's only step one," Derek says. "Step two is infiltrating the Imperial banking system on Monroe and redistributing the wealth those elites are hoarding."

Natalia rubs her hands together. "I like this part. Stealing from the rich and giving to the poor."

"Pirate." Leo nudges her jokingly.

"Yeah, well, who do you think came up with the idea? General Royal used to be a—"

Derek raises his voice to drown them out. "It won't just be money and jewels. Codes to weapons lockers and starships will be handed over to people who can use them to aid the revolution. Plus, once the Authorities realize that they aren't getting paid anymore...well, it'll be a test of how strong their loyalties really are. Especially since they recruit heavily from poorer planets."

I nod, mulling it over. "It's not a bad plan, but it'll depend on whoever you get to infiltrate those places. They're gonna have to be good."

"Yeah, they are." Leo gives me a pointed look.

"Me? Fuck no! I can't hack into anyone's systems to save my life."

Then I remember the man who's been sitting to my right, silent, listening to the whole conversation without comment. As soon as my head turns to meet his gaze, he nods. "I'm in."

"Simon, it's too dangerous," I protest. "They can't ask you to—"

"That's why I'm offering." Simon looks into the holo-capture. "It's the chance I've been waiting for since my mother died. Now that Soren is finally dead, I have to see it through to the end."

"If anyone can do it, it's you," Leo says with a smile.

Derek looks down, typing on a keycuff. "Simon, I'm sending you a package of files containing the propaganda blitz we want to send out as soon as possible." His green eyes come up to connect with the holo-capture once more. "But don't take unnecessary risks. We need you alive."

Which is about as close as Derek ever comes to saying something mushy.

"I'll get it done," says Simon, with a haphazard salute. "And I think I have a suggestion for your bank infiltrator, too. I've been working on reestablishing contact with em. I'll send you eir call code so you can reach out personally."

"Knew we could count on you, Simon." Natalia blows him a kiss through the screen. I squash the knee-jerk protective reaction it sparks. *He's mine.*

As soon as the holo-capture closes, I take him by the shoulders. "You can't do this by yourself."

"Of course not." Simon smiles. "You're going to help me, aren't you?"

He leans in and presses a kiss to my stubbly cheek, and I'm suddenly knee-weakeningly, pants-shittingly afraid.

Because for the first time since joining the Greenjackets, I have something personal to lose.

Chapter 36

THE WAYSTATION

RODAN

I wish Glenna had explained more clearly that Grandma & Grandma's Waystation Café is a pirate den. Taking a kid here—a very publicly kidnapped child that *the Emperor himself declared war over*—was a mistake.

The pie's delicious, though.

Miles keeps asking when he can go home and see his mother. I haven't shown him the news. Nor am I going to. My obligation to this child doesn't extend to explaining to him that his mama just killed his daddy and is probably also dead. I just want to get him somewhere safe so I can go back to the Moon Palace and get Clara out of there.

The serving bot didn't react at all when I told it that I was a friend of Prince, like Glenna instructed me. So, as Miles digs into his cherry pie with enthusiasm, I sidle up to the kitchen window on the pretext of grabbing more napkins and whisper the code phrase to one of the cooks.

"Prince, huh?" the guy says, leaning as close as he can get across the prep table. "I can get a message to 'im. Long as he recognizes *your* name. Which is?"

"Director Rodan Quell. Glenna sent me."

"Don't know no Glenna. Don't know you either." The cook looks me up and down. "You look awful rich for this place. Listen, if the Authorities sent you to trap our buddy Prince, don't bother. Us all will fight for 'im. He done a lot of good for the Waystation, and for the owners o' this place, too."

I hold up my hands in a surrendering gesture. "We have a common enemy. The Authorities have my partner captive. I'm just trying to get the kid safe."

I get a narrow-eyed stare, then the cook nods. "Hang tight, then. Coffee's on the house while you wait."

The serving bot brings me a loaner tablet with some kids' games pre-loaded onto it. I nearly kiss it on its angular metal cheek; keeping a five-year-old busy enough not to ask questions or make a scene is an uphill battle. He napped in the starship on our way here, but I'm pretty sure the kid hasn't properly slept in a couple of days.

That makes two of us.

Hours of nursing lukewarm coffee later, I'm startled by a hand slapping down on my table. I look up and meet the twinkling brown eyes of a short, muscular man in his forties, wearing his hair in a maroon fauxhawk. He's got all kinds of piercings in his ears, lips, and eyebrows. Neon tattoos peek out of his collar and jumpsuit sleeves.

"Hey, there! Mind if I join you?"

I cast a pointed look at the rest of the diner, which is mostly empty.

The man sticks his hand out toward me. "Name's Prince DeSanto. Heard you might be lookin' for me."

"DeSanto? I've never heard of you before." I scoot over to let him sit, though. "Which royal consort was your mother?"

DeSanto throws back his head and laughs. "Guess Glenna didn't tell you much when she told you to find me, huh? My *given name* is Prince. I'm about as royal as that coffee cup."

Oh. I feel blood rush to my cheeks. It's not often I'm caught off guard like this. "I'm Director Rodan Quell, e/em. The kid is...well, let's just say he's a bit *more* royal than the coffee cup."

Prince nods. "I've been following the news. The hat is a nice touch, but it won't fool anybody if they're lookin' hard."

I'd bought a knit cap from a Monroe street vendor and made Miles wear it pulled as low on his forehead as possible. I'd also bundled away his fine robe and put him in a brightly colored souvenir shirt that says, *"Diamond Drop Fountain!"* in excitable magenta lettering across an artist's rendering of said attraction. He looks ridiculous, but at least nobody gave him a second glance when we stood in the ticket line for our taxi ride here.

"Well?" I mutter. "Glenna said you could get us to safety. She was talking about my partner when she made the offer, but unfortunately, Clara's a *guest* of the Emperor now. Or *was,* when he was alive. I don't know what's happening now."

"According to the latest live broadcast, she just got married to Emperor Jinan."

A sick weight thuds into the pit of my stomach. "Well, that won't last."

"I imagine you're right," Prince says seriously. "I hope, for your sake and hers, that it ends with her head still on her shoulders."

"And his off." I all but whisper that bit. Even in anti-Imperial circles, speaking treason aloud isn't a great idea.

"Anyway," says Prince, a little too loudly, "I'm happy to take the kid to safety. Can either take him to my home planet, Halcyon—he'll get looked after by the Devotes of a Refuge there—"

"Not ideal," I interject. "The late Emperor was already looking for excuses to start a war on Halcyon. They won't want to be found in possession of his best excuse."

"Fair." Prince nods. "Then, plan B, I'll take him to Susannah. Friend of mine has a bunch of foster kids. She's great with 'em. He'll fit right in." He taps a finger on the table. "You planning on hiding out with him?"

I shake my head in a quick jerk. "Not while Clara's in the Emperor's clutches."

"Excellent," says Prince. "In that case, once we have the boy stowed somewhere safe, I have a proposition for you. A few of us are planning the heist of the century, with the hopes of taking the Emperor and all his loyalists down."

My blood surges in my veins. It's fear—I'm not a confrontationalist by nature—but it's also excitement. Purpose. Since Clara was taken, I've been feeling helpless to the point of despair. Being given a chance to take action feels like a lifeline.

I glance over my shoulder. We've been speaking quietly, but this café isn't completely empty. "You got a ship?"

"Thought you'd never ask. Come on." Prince reaches across and taps Miles's tablet screen to turn it off. The boy makes a sound of protest, which falters when an iridescent shimmer appears in the air next to Prince's shoulder.

"Fairy says ze really wants to talk to you," Prince tells Miles, gesturing to the dragon. "Says you've been making friends with a dragon companion of your own. Come on, now. You want another slice of pie to go?"

Miles nods enthusiastically.

Chapter 37

EMPEROR'S VILLA, THE IMPERIAL MOON PALACE

SARAY

Entering the Emperor's villa through the intended path feels like a dream—no, an exquisite nightmare.

As soon as I step out of the zip-lift, the tiger-bot guard bounds forward to bow low at my feet. "Welcome, Your Grace," it says. "This way."

It ushers me into one of the flat, barge-like boats, which holds remarkably steady as I step down. I sink down among plush cushions and brace one hand beside me as, with a slight jerk, the boat begins to propel itself forward. Some mechanism beneath the surface pulls me along, inexorably drifting toward whatever fate awaits me.

How many women have drifted through this lily-choked moat before me? Did their hearts pound with joy and hope...or with dread? I hold my spine straight, determined to be brave in their honor. If only there was some sound other than lapping water and distant calls of captive birds to drown out the pounding of my heart.

A shiver crawls down my spine. I'm psyching myself out, I know, but it's hard not to think about the horrors this place has seen. Even trailing my hand along the surface of the water reminds me that Soren kept a hungry pet in the depths. This may look like an idyllic garden, but every part of it is a death trap.

The boat glides into the dock on the other side of the moat. Another tiger-shaped robot stands up from its resting pose and bows as I lift my diaphanous skirt to step out onto the smooth boards.

Kina and Pearl swore they were given exacting instructions for how to dress me tonight, but I still feel like this outfit is their revenge for my perceived crimes. The scanty "undergarments" are more body jewelry than anything else. They're certainly not intended to cover anything. My chest is adorned with delicate chains dripping jeweled pendants. They decorated my nether regions with rhinestones pasted directly onto the skin, which I can't recommend for a comfortable walking or sitting experience. The texture of the chains and gems sliding across my skin brings to mind a snake's cool slither, causing creepflesh to erupt across my arms.

Over all of it, an iridescent fabric floats around my body like the barely-visible shimmer of a dragon. If only dragons could help me here. I can still feel the low-grade nausea of the dragon-repulsing device, preventing dragons from teleporting in or out.

Jinan has just married—and effectively caged—the only two people on this moon who could have circumvented that.

I can't wait to make him regret it.

The tiger-bot leads me along a winding uphill path through an exquisitely tended garden that's almost eerie in its perfection: exact spacing between bushes, not a weed or stray tendril to be seen. It's nature as seen by bots, because of course Soren would never have allowed any human gardener to breach his sanctum. It strikes me that this secret, privileged oasis is safe, but also incredibly lonely. I *almost* understand the impulse to collect brides like art pieces, to have an endless array of company to choose from.

But Soren was incapable of treating any of them with the kindness and respect that could have made them true, loving partners. And so he doomed himself to a worse loneliness.

The late Emperor did too many horrible things for me to pity him. I hope the misery haunted him until the day his favorite consort stabbed him through the throat.

The villa's entrance looms before me, an arched open doorway framed by obnoxiously ornate classical pillars and a pair of lion statues flying the Imperial flag from poles clamped between their carved teeth. The tiger stops before the entrance, and its indoor counterpart takes over: an enormous serpent that coils down from a ceiling beam, its dry voice hissing, "His Majesty will see you now."

Its sinuous length brushes against my ankle, bringing on another shiver as it leads me down a hallway, past the fountain that I now know hides the sea monster's feeding hole. I cast out my mental awareness, trying to sense Clara nearby, but Jinan must have stashed her somewhere else. I won't have her support tonight. Only my own wits.

The robotic snake leads me down a staircase and a long, maroon-carpeted hallway. It rears up and taps an entry request button with its flared snout, then retreats. I look over my shoulder to find that the serpent has coiled at the base of the staircase, blocking my exit in case I try to run.

The door before me slides open.

Whatever happens, I am strong enough to survive it. I have the power to take control of the situation. I am afraid, but I am not helpless.

I take a breath and imagine my exhale is fire.

In three steps, I'm inside the beast's lair.

The circular, pillared room is exactly as I remember it from a few days ago. Walking in from the door instead of teleporting, I get the chance to assess it as it's meant to be seen. The pillars frame the luxurious four-poster bed against the opposite wall. The hanging tapestries create curving, organic shapes that are meant to suggest sensuality, but the dark Imperial colors project male power—and, to my eyes, danger.

Jinan is seated on the foot of the bed, one leg casually up, the other dangling. He's barefoot, dressed in tan trousers and a black tunic, his robe discarded on the bed next to him. His eyes glitter triumphantly as he allows them to roam over my body.

I force myself to bow. "Your Majesty."

He slides off the edge of the bed, stalking toward me with movements that put me in mind of the tiger-bot. "Happy wedding night," he murmurs, reaching for my face. I can't hide my flinch as he strokes my cheek, but that only makes his grin widen. "Have you dreamt of this moment since you were a girl?"

"No," I say truthfully.

Marriage never featured in my dreams for my life, regardless of the hypothetical spouse's gender. I intend to be solely responsible for my own future. This sham of a wedding has not dimmed that resolve.

He laughs. "I suppose not. Few women dare to imagine they will be chosen by an Emperor."

Oh, I've imagined it. In my worst nightmares. I flash him a simpering, falsely shy smile.

"How was the wedding?" Jinan goes on, happy to monologue as usual. "Did you like it?"

I let fear touch my expression. "It was..." My voice falters, smooth words failing me. I know he'll enjoy seeing he's cowed me—it was his goal all along, no doubt. But I don't have to fake my horror at the event.

"I created every detail with you in mind, my sweet." His fingers slide under my chin, forcing me to meet his gaze. "Every. Detail."

It's a physical effort not to let him see the hate blazing in my expression. *Fear. Show him fear instead. He believes fear is weakness.*

"Your ladies have nearly redeemed themselves of their connection to a traitor," he goes on, letting his eyes slide down my body once more. "You looked radiant at our wedding, and tonight, you are delectable."

It would be bad if I vomited on him, right? Yeah. It would be bad.

His fingers begin sliding the barely-there robe off my shoulder. I hold still and let him undress me. Looking for the right moment, I reach out with my mind, probing his consciousness, waiting for a weak moment to strike.

"The perfect bride." He smirks, as if he can see through my mask, and leans forward to claim my mouth with his own.

There it is. My moment.

As power-stoked, victorious lust rips through his mind, I strike just as Clara taught me.

::You can make people tell you truths,:: Clara had whispered in my head during that endless bloody wedding. *::Now make him believe your lies.::*

I worm my way into Jinan's memories and begin to plant new ones, cinnamon-flavored and hideous. I fast-forward our night in his head: he kisses me, he puts his hands all over me, he throws me down and does his worst to me. I make him believe it's happening, that it's already happened.

A warm wet spot spreads across the front of his trousers. I have to stop myself from gagging as his lips continue to move passionately over mine. Without breaking the kiss, I push him back onto the bed and curl us together, as if the two of us are enjoying a blissful post-coital snuggle.

I don't let go of his mind yet. I continue to sow suggestions—feelings more than memories. *::You've subdued her to a shell of herself. She'll never dare to defy you again. She believes she's in love with you and will use her powers only in your service.::*

I lie there, so tense I'm shaking, as he snores lightly. And when I'm certain he's slipping deeper into sleep, I rise and put my robe back on. I've survived the first night.

But how much longer can I keep this up?

Chapter 38

ENTERTAINMENT SECTOR, THE IMPERIAL MOON PALACE

JED

To break into the Authorities' broadcast center, we're going to need more than the access clearance, which Simon hacked into their system to grant us.

We're also going to need to look the part.

We debate how to acquire Authority uniforms. I'm for luring two of them into a closet, conking them on the head, and stealing their clothes. For some reason, Simon thinks that's a bad idea.

"Well, do you have a better one?"

"The theater," says Simon. "Surely their costume department has a few Authority uniforms."

"Yeah, but Quell's gone. How do we get in?"

"Everywhere has bot tunnel access." With a few quick taps, he's pulled up a map on his tablet. "And the Pavilion needs cleanup even more frequently than most places. Do you know how many people throw their snacks all over the floor during performances?"

I make a face. Why are the richest people in the galaxy incapable of cleaning up after themselves? "Is it safe to go through those tunnels? You said we might get run over."

"It's not safe, necessarily," Simon admits, "but I can time our entry to avoid bots." When I give him a skeptical look, he says, "It's safer than trying to capture a couple of live Authorities and hoping they don't shoot us."

Ugh, fine. Smart guy's got a point.

The journey from our hiding spot to the Pavilion theater is shorter than I thought I would be. Despite it feeling like a whole other world down in the bot tunnels, we technically never left the entertainment sector. Traversing the twisty labyrinth takes us only about thirty minutes—just a bit more than if we walked from Simon's apartment to the Pavilion up topside.

When we emerge into the theater, it's mostly empty, but there are still a few actors running through rehearsals and stagehands working on setup. We retrace our previous path to Quell's office. I may have been a glitch to that annoying little monkeybot when it tried to give us a tour, but it did helpfully point out prop storage for us.

The storage room itself is organized by performance, not by type of prop. We waste at least half an hour sifting through the various wardrobes and trying to remember if this or that play had modern Authorities in it. Finally, we find red jackets in the wardrobe for a contemporary play called *Meet Me at the Spaceport*. It's set about twenty years ago, but the uniforms haven't changed too much since then.

"The two Authority characters in that play are supposed to be muscle-bound quarkbrains." Simon pulls out the jackets, holding one up to my chest and wincing. "We're going to need some padding."

Once we're done digging through the costumes, our next hurdle is makeup. Simon protests that he's nowhere near Quell's mastery, but by the time he's done with me, my nose has a previously-broken lump in it. He padded out my cheeks to hide my jawline, combed brown-tinted gel through my hair, and built out my brow ridge to give me a permanent glower. I look ten years older, twenty pounds heavier, and a lot less pretty-boy rockstar.

Simon put himself in a blond wig and did a bunch of similar witchcraft to his own face. Our own parents wouldn't recognize us, which I guess is kind of the point.

I stare at myself in the mirror on the back of the wardrobe door, poking at my fake brown sideburns and grimacing. Against my teammates' urging, I didn't dye my hair when we took on our fake Moon Palace identities. Every time I look in a mirror, the ginger connects me to my pa, who was a proud natural redhead. It reminds me what I'm fighting for: a world where little farm lads don't lose their kind, gentle, stubbornly brave fathers when the Authorities decide they want to own the land he'd given the sweat of his brow to farm.

"It'll wash out," Simon tells me gently.

I turn to face him. "I know. It's just...weird, not looking like myself."

"Tell me about it," says Simon, his tone dry, and I remember guiltily that he spends a fair amount of time in disguise.

"I'm just being a baby," I mutter.

Simon leans in to kiss my cheek. "You're still Jed, even if you don't look like a rockstar."

My mouth is dry. I swallow hard, pulse pounding in my neck. "Simon...I want you to know my real name. Just in case...in case this goes sideways."

Simon opens his mouth to protest, then stops himself and nods. "Tell me."

I lean so close to his ear that my lips brush the outer shell, sending a shiver through him. "Jaired Lachlann," I whisper. Then, pulling away enough to meet his eyes, "I was a farmer on Ceres. The Authorities rolled in to take our farmland and indentured my entire family. Pa fought back and got himself killed. I ran and linked up with the Greenjackets." I swallow. "My ma and sisters are still there, as far as I know. If I die...someone should tell them."

Simon nods once, solemnly, squeezing my hand.

"You can keep calling me Jed," I say. "I just wanted someone to know the real me. Before..."

"We're not going to get killed," Simon murmurs, low and fierce. "I won't let it happen. Because I want to meet your ma and sisters, Jaired Lachlann. I want to be the one who tells them they're finally free."

It's impossible not to kiss him when he says things like that, in a fervent tone that makes me believe it might be possible.

Chapter 39

THE PLANET SUSANNAH

RODAN

Prince's friend, the foster mom on Susannah, is a girl in her late twenties with brown hair pinned around her head in a braid crown. My jaw drops when I recognize her gen-modded yellow eyes. She's one of Clara's siblings. Miri, I think her name is.

She crouches down to talk to Miles, her soft voice low and soothing, and Miles immediately clings to her with adoring eyes. I don't think he ever liked me much, which is fair, I guess. I *did* kidnap him.

"The Authorities can't know he's here," Prince warns Miri.

"They won't," Miri promises. "Susannah's barely on their radar, except for when we owe them taxes. But if a patrol comes through, we all know what to do."

I suppose she's used to hiding from them herself. I bow my thanks to her, and Prince and I head back to his ship.

"All right," I say, once the doors close. "Tell me about this heist."

*T**he planet Monroe***

When we touch down on Monroe, Prince makes a quick call inviting someone aboard. Shortly after, the ramp lowers and a team of four stride up: a man with a bit of blond stubble on his chin and head; a woman with short, fiery orange hair; a Paotherrian man with smudgy gray fur; and another man whose black hair falls to his shoulders.

"Leo, Natalia, Chaz, Derek!" Prince greets the four of them enthusiastically. "How long has it been?"

"We were undercover for over a year," says Derek.

"I watched every recording I could find of your concerts. You were absolutely ace!" Prince flashes an approving hand sign. "Natalia, if you ever get tired of being a soldier, you've got a real future as a lounge singer."

She makes a face. "And have everybody following me around wherever I go? Absolutely not. The sooner people forget about Tarantula, the better."

Then it clicks why these people look vaguely familiar. They're Jedrek Blaze's band members. They've changed their hair styles and switched to nondescript green jumpsuits, but it's definitely them.

"You're telling me I'm running this long shot of a heist with a bunch of rockstars?" I complain.

Natalia gives me a side-eye glare. "You're telling us we're running it with a washed-up theater director?" she mocks. "We aren't going to get very far if you want to waste time on doubting us."

"All right, children, play nice," says Prince. "Quell has generously offered to help with the disguise and role-play aspects of this job. We don't have a ton of time before Simon and Jed get the broadcast out, and we're gonna need to have our part done before then."

I sigh, cracking my knuckles. "Then let's get to work."

Part Six

DAYSIX

Year 3750 DE, Week 45

Chapter 40

JINAN'S SUITE, THE IMPERIAL MOON PALACE

SARAY

The knock on my bedroom door wakes me before I'm willing. I didn't dare leave the Emperor's villa until it was nearly morning, and I couldn't lower my guard for a single moment in that hellish, palatial room. After the ladies had tended to me upon my return, I instructed them not to wake me until afternoon unless it was an emergency.

An emergency meaning Jinan's at the door, wanting more of what he thinks he got.

Scrubbing my burning, sleep-crusted eyes, I call, "Who is it?"

"It's Kina, my lady."

"Come in, Kina."

The wardrobe designer enters, wringing her hands in front of her. "You have a visitor, Your Grace."

"His Majesty?" I ask, too sharply.

She shakes her head. "An older woman. She claims to be your mother."

Ever so briefly, my stomach leaps. *Adina?* But there's no way Glenna would send my mother here. Not now, when all of our lives hang by a thread.

And then I understand who waits behind the door, and my gut goes from featherlight to iron-weighted.

"Help me dress," I tell Kina.

I'd already feverishly bathed the night before, washing away every trace of Jinan's scent and the touch of his hands. I don't bother with my hair, letting it hang loose at my back. But I'll be blasted if I meet the most dangerous woman on this moon wearing my nightrobe.

Kina chooses a high-necked red sheath, deliberately mirroring Jinan's Imperial colors. The robe she drapes over it is delicate, see-through gold lace. The new Emperor may have been dressing his wives in insubstantial fabrics to humiliate us, she murmurs quietly, but she can turn it into such a fad that every woman in the galaxy will want their robes translucent and their clothing made of diamond fringe.

With my shoulders thrown back, I emerge into the sitting room to meet Melanie Ediya.

She's drinking tea on the sofa, swathed in a black silk robe with delicate gold embroidery. A tiara in the shape of a sunburst sits atop her braided silver hair. It looks like a miniature version of the one Jinan wore at our "wedding."

My "mother," she calls herself. I think of her as the scientist who gen-modded me as an embryo before placing me in an incubator machine to be birthed and raised by robots. Nothing even remotely resembling a parent.

"Congratulations on your marriage," she says, raising her teacup with pinkie finger out.

"Congratulations on your takeover of the Empire," I respond, sinking into an armchair that faces her at an angle.

My ladies all suddenly find an excuse to be somewhere else. They file out, but I notice they leave the door open a crack. *Ah, eavesdropping, the time-honored lady-in-waiting pastime.*

"I don't know what you mean," Melanie says smoothly. "I merely assisted in the transition. I certainly couldn't have foreseen Soren's tragic early demise. To tell you the truth, it was highly inconvenient."

"You seem to have come out on top." I dig my nails into the fabric of the chair arm. "Impressive, to have gone from a high-security prison to a throne in, what, a matter of weeks?"

"Well, that's the thing about prison, dear," says Melanie, her lips curving into a smirk. "One has a *lot* of time to make plans."

"What do you actually want, Dr. Ediya?" I ask. "Did you come here just to gloat?"

Melanie sets down her teacup and saucer on the sofa cushion next to her. It wobbles alarmingly, but I don't give a shit if the furniture gets stained in my gilded cell. "Mainly I'm here to assess your potential use," she says bluntly.

For a moment I'm back in that gray-walled nightmare of a space station where the Drs. Ediya raised us. Blood draws, "lessons" meant only to test our abilities, siblings we vaguely remembered who had disappeared for "assessments" and never come back. The unspoken pressure to be extraordinary—*or else*. Melanie only ever cared about us as tools.

And that, I now realize, became the benchmark by which I measured myself: how useful I was to everyone around me. A dutiful agent of Haven. A daughter who could protect her adopted father. A loyal lady-in-waiting.

But Melanie's conditioning only goes so far. I'd rather die than serve a man who will use my power to destroy planets.

"And?" I indicate my body with an open palm. "What do you think? He's made me into a nice little ornament. Am I useful yet?"

She shakes her head. "Looking pretty is the least of your uses, Saray. Your tests back on Arrow Station indicated that you can taste a lie on someone's words. That ability may pale in comparison to Clara's mind-reading, but when Clara gets sent out on war missions, you'll be Jinan's right hand. His little spy in the court, whispering to him which courtier is feigning devotion." Melanie smiles. "Did you wonder why I instructed Soren to take Clara and not you, when I knew full well you were both residents of the Moon Palace? That's why. You were kept in reserve until Clara was needed elsewhere." She wrinkles her nose. "It's inconvenient that you caught on and inserted yourself before you were needed. But we can still use you."

I bite my tongue against the impulse to say, "What makes you think I'll help you?"

But she sees the narrowing of my eyes and grins wider. "You think you're going to resist, that you'll work against Jinan instead of doing his bidding. But you're wrong, Saray. Because we still have your adoptive father, alive, if not unscathed. And the second I have the slightest notion you're disobeying Jinan's orders, I'll make sure he's killed."

My heart twists painfully. I'm relieved that Alan's still alive.

But they're going to make me wish he was dead.

Chapter 41

HEPBURN CITY, MONROE

RODAN

I stride toward the front steps of the Monroe Galactic Bank, sinking further into character with every step. I am Lord O'Rourke, planetary governor and holder of one of the bank's largest accounts. I've so fully transformed my features that even O'Rourke's own daughter might kiss me hello—if she weren't too busy dating a butterfly-hybrid from one of O'Rourke's vassal planets, much to his dismay. Though the alliance is proving lucrative, meaning he's forced to hold his tongue. At least, so say the gossip sites.

I have come to the bank today to be an asshole.

The doors swish open to allow me in. A cleanerbot scurries forward to mop up the snow my boots are tracking in. I ignore it, facing the tellerbot wheeling toward me to take my name and identification.

"Haven't got it," I say casually. "Blasted keycuff stopped working this morning. Never mind that—you know who I am. You can scan my face, can't you?"

Now we'll see how good my makeup skills *really* are.

I deliberately blink at the last minute as the bot's scanning light runs down my front. The one thing it's almost impossible to fake is a retinal scan; the contacts I'm wearing to match Lord O'Rourke's green eyes won't fool the machine.

The rest, though...

"Identity: Lord Governor Brian O'Rourke. 95% match." The bot's sensors turn green. "How can Monroe Galactic Bank help you today, my lord?"

"You can explain to me why I found a transaction on my account this morning that I never authorized." I make as if to instinctively show them my keycuff, then hiss with annoyance and go for my tablet instead.

The Greenjackets have been working on the plans for this job for a long time, creating convincing fakes of account statements and even building a whole series of false identities for the infiltrators.

But stealing a governor's identity wasn't part of their original plan—it was my brainchild. While the rockstar team breaks into the server vaults under the guise of maintenance workers, I'm more than just their makeup artist. I'm the diversion.

I flash the fake account statement at the bot but don't allow it to linger long enough to scan. "You see this mess? I'm not dealing with bots or bean counters for something this serious. Let me see the bank manager," I demand. "And make it quick! I don't have all day!"

"Right away, my lord." The bot whirs away.

Already, several other patrons and bank staff are staring at me. I straighten my robes and huff through my nose, keeping my chin high.

The bank manager is a petite woman with a round face and curly gray hair. She's maybe a decade older than me. "Come on into my office, Lord O'Rourke. Let's look at your accounts. Do you have your keycuff today for identification?"

I huff again, acting offended that she would ask, and give her the story about the keycuff breaking. "The bot just scanned me to verify ID. Can't you do that, too?"

"Scan you?" The manager gives me an amused smile.

"*With your eyes*. It's obviously me."

"It's bank policy that we verify keycuff ID every time you come in," she says, overly patient. At my scowl, however, she backtracks. "However, if your keycuff is out of commission, you can answer some security questions."

"Is this really necessary?" I grumble. "I'm in a hurry."

"Unfortunately, yes, Lord O'Rourke."

"*Fine.* Go ahead."

She calls up the governor's account on the holo display on her desk and turns it toward me.

<What was your daughter's first word?>

<What was your childhood pet spiderbunny's name?>

<What famous person are you descended from?>

I have to hide a smile at the first one. *"Dada"* is the clear answer, otherwise a guy like Lord O'Rourke would never have remembered it. I type it in, and the question glows green.

I have absolutely no idea about the other two. I did a fair amount of research on the governor as I was preparing to borrow his identity, but I focused on his mannerisms, gait, and expressions. Not fun facts about his childhood.

Time for the distraction.

I pretend I've just heard a notification alert from my scroll and unroll it, reading the "message." Then I look up at the bank manager, letting outrage contort my features. "My secretary just told me my entire bank account has been drained! What's going on here, Miz—?" Fuck, I'm probably supposed to know her name, if Governor O'Rourke does. I scan for a name tag and find one on the edge of the desk. *Amity Chen.* "Miz Chen, is this the best account security this bank has to offer?"

"My lord, just hold on a second. We will figure this out." As I had hoped, Miz Chen bypasses the other two security questions and dives straight into the governor's account. "It's showing me here that your account has had no excessive withdrawals in the past few days."

"Well, it's showing my secretary something different!" I yell.

A tap at the door. Miz Chen cracks it and says, "I'm sorry, Bobbi, I'm busy right—"

"Some contractors downstairs are here for maintenance, Miz Chen, and security wanted to check with you before they let them in."

"What the fuck is taking so long?" Governor O'Rourke's raspy voice is really starting to wreak havoc on my throat. I'm going to need to steam my vocal cords after this.

"Yes, yes," says Miz Chen distractedly, waving off the security person just as I had hoped she would. She closes the door and faces me. "I'm sure we can figure this out, Lord O'Rourke. Now, I'm going to need you to stop yelling at me and sit down. Then we'll get your secretary on a vid-call and find out—"

I don't let her finish. I sit down on her side of the desk and begin tapping through the innards of Governor O'Rourke's account. I keep my face arranged in a furious scowl, mainly to cover my actual shock at the number of zeroes at the end of his balance. This man truly *deserves* to get his money stolen.

"My lord, I'm so sorry, but you can't do that," the bank manager says, tugging at my shoulder. "I must ask you to step away, please. Only bank personnel are authorized to—"

"It's my money!" I shout. "You're not going to let me see *my own money*?"

On and on we go, me acting belligerent and ass-headed, stringing out every interaction as long as I can push it.

I have to give Miz Chen credit—she does a wonderful job of standing up to me and attempting to deescalate the situation. If the fate of the galaxy didn't depend on me continuing to yell at her, I'd have felt too bad to keep it up. But I'm a professional. I'll never be the first one to break character.

It's a grueling twenty minutes before, with a huge rush of relief, I watch the zeroes on Lord O'Rourke's account flicker and shrink. They've left him enough for a man to retire comfortably, but nowhere near the embarrassment of wealth he had amassed through exploiting the planets he was appointed to control.

"Aha! You see! Look!" I scream. "It's just like I said! Someone's draining my account!"

Miz Chen goes pale and begins tapping madly at her screen, trying to trace the origin of the theft. She'll find, eventually, that it's a virus that Greenjacket techies wrote to infect the entire system, setting a maximum balance for each account. Any excess will be skimmed off and dumped into a dummy account, which some other team is waiting to empty. They'll divert the funds to various planetary rebellion groups for purchasing weapons, medical supplies, and starships.

It's decades of Greenjacket dreams come true in a single second. The rich have lost the power of their credits, and the common people are arming themselves to take back the power of their own governance.

But I can't stay here long enough for her to realize that.

"If you aren't going to help me, I'll find someone who will!" I bellow, stomping out of her office into the hallway.

As I fastwalk away, I nearly bump into three more bank employees sprinting for their manager's office. Apparently, a couple of other patrons have already noticed the reduction in their accounts. Call alerts ring shrilly in the distance.

"Hold him!" Miz Chen bursts out of her office, pointing at me. "He messed with my system. He did something to it! Arrest Governor O'Rourke!"

I stumble into a jog. Running away isn't part of my usual job description. When I want to appear physically fit, I pull out a fake muscle suit from costume storage.

An intrepid banker tackles me around the waist, sending us both sprawling.

"Unhand me at once!" I squawk. "I'm the victim here!"

Someone's already calling the Authorities. Shit. This isn't looking good for me. But if they're blaming Governor O'Rourke for the heist, that means they won't be chasing the team of rockstar Greenjackets downstairs—at least, not yet.

Clara, I think, wondering if she can read my thoughts this far away. *Sorry I couldn't make it back. I hope you make that shithead prince regret marrying you.*

I hope you know this sacrifice is for you.

Chapter 42

AUTHORITY HEADQUARTERS, THE IMPERIAL MOON PALACE

JED

"This sounded like a good idea in theory," I whisper to Simon, "but now that we're here, I think I'm going to piss my pants."

"Just pretend you're on stage," Simon hisses back. "It's all about confidence. Authorities walk through the world knowing they have all the power. When you're on stage, don't you feel the same?"

That's...actually pretty helpful. Except I'm going to have to tone down Jedrek Blaze's rockstar brand of confidence, which involves a lot of hip thrusting.

I square up my shoulders and wait for Simon to key in the access code that will take the zip-lift to the headquarters of the Imperial Authorities.

Simon's makeup is scarily convincing. He didn't even do much, just gave himself a stubbly shadow of a beard and used some kind of weird putty to reshape his nose. The costume is doing most of the work. I've only ever seen Simon either in casual, rumpled plain clothing. The red jacket, filled out by the costuming sorcery of a padded undershirt, looks completely alien on him. When I saw *myself* in the mirror, I nearly tried to shoot my reflection. I have to avoid looking at Simon completely, merely focusing on his voice as we walk together, or the sight of a stranger next to me gives me the skin crawlies.

The zip-lift dings. The doors open. Simon gives my hand one last furtive squeeze before we disembark, holding ourselves with the unbending posture and stick-up-our-ass facial expressions that seem standard issue for soldiers.

No one gives either of us a second glance. There are dozens of other soldiers milling around in the atrium, some of them chatting as they finish their shifts, some in freshly clean-pressed uniforms and smelling strongly of hair pomade about to start patrol.

I let Simon take the lead. He showed me the layout of this place before we came, but I don't have it memorized like he does. All I know is, barracks are a level down, while the Authority General offices and communication tower are close to the moon's surface. The higher up we go, the more restricted the area. We're putting a lot of faith in the high-level clearance IDs that Simon faked.

There are huge, square zip-lifts internal to the Authority sector, designed to carry upwards of twenty people at a time. Simon avoids these and goes for the emergency staircase, remarking to me in a not-very-quiet aside that he needs to work on his leg muscles.

I hold in my laugh until the stairwell door closes behind us. "Really? That was your excuse?"

Simon shushes me. "Stairwell's not private, and it echoes," he whispers against my ear. I shiver at the sensation of his breath.

We stay in character for the whole climb up (six floors! It's a good thing I work out) even though we see no one. "Staying in character" mainly consists of silence, plus me resisting the urge to push Simon against the banister and make out with him until we both forget we're actively committing treason. I keep my hand near the uniform's utility belt, ready for a quick blaster draw if anyone looks at us the wrong way. But nobody does.

It's strange, watching the redjackets going about their daily lives. Without the context of the murders and tortures they've committed, it's too easy to see them as guys doing a job. In another life, they could be my comrades. Half of them probably come from dirt-poor colony planets like I did. Maybe this job was the best option they had.

Stars, look at me. When I started this mission, I'd have punched anyone in the face who suggested I'd fall for a prince and then start feeling bad for the Authorities. Yet here I am.

Simon points at the door ahead to indicate we're on the right level. I let him scan his keycuff to open it with his fake ID, then match his stride as he walks confidently down the hallway. We pass several offices with the names and rank symbols of high-level officers affixed to the doors. *Don't notice us,* I pray. This is where it could all fall apart. How many soldiers are allowed regular access to this area? Not many, and I'm willing to bet there are security officers who know every one of them by name. If anyone happens to be reviewing cambot footage in real time, we're screwed.

The transmission room is ID-locked, too, but that doesn't stop Simon and the all-level clearance he's given his false identity. The door slides open before us, revealing a room full of wallscreens and a single enormous databank in the middle of the room.

This one databank holds every scrap of information ever uploaded to the galactic uniweb, updated hourly. Syncship pilots teleport between inhabited planets and the uniweb's Monroe hub, syncing each ultra-wealthy planet with the newest information every hour. Poorer planets are synced once a day, though less populous worlds sometimes go weeks or months without regular updates. But syncship trips between Monroe and the Moon Palace are scheduled every ten minutes, keeping the Imperial seat and its most loyal, wealthiest vassal as intimately connected as possible.

Inconveniently for our purposes, the room is full of people. There are four techies in red jumpsuits—not quite Authorities, but certainly on the same payroll—using control gauntlets to swipe through holoscreens.

I don't know much about this stuff, but someone probably has to run checks with every new update to make sure there's no corrupted files or viruses that will bring down the entire uniweb.

They're going to be a problem.

The fifth person in the room has the access badge of a syncship pilot pinned to her chest. She's a woman with bright-white hair in shoulder-length braids, wearing a gray maintenance worker's jumpsuit that doesn't do her pale complexion any favors. She sits cross-legged in one of the techies' desk chairs, playing a game on her scroll while she waits for the sync to finish. As Simon and I watch from the doorway, one of them approaches her to hand over a box with a handle sticking out of the top, about the same size as a thick briefcase. She signs <*Thank you,*> unfolds herself from the chair, and heads for the door, brushing past us with the data box clutched tight to her chest.

As she exits, the techies notice us. I watch an expression of alarm flash over one man's features before he arranges his face into a pleasant interrogative. "Yes, sir? Did you need something?"

They're just regular guys doing their job. I feel bad for what I have to do next...which is zap them with my stunner in quick sequence, then tie up their unconscious bodies.

I still do it, though.

By the time I'm done, Simon's already stolen one of their control gauntlets and has his hands all up in their holo-screen. "Shutting down the surveillance," he narrates as I finish binding the last techie and run over to lock the door.

"Fuck." I survey the unconscious bodies strewn across the floor. "If we get caught, they're not going to shoot to stun."

"Which is why we aren't going to get caught." Simon tears his eyes from the screen to wrinkle his nose at me. "Here. Watch this screen."

He's set me up with the hallway cambot feed. I can't keep my knee from bouncing as I settle into a chair, eyes glued to the surveillance footage.

I keep glancing at his deft fingers in the gauntlet, now interfacing his own tablet memory with the already-compiling data for the next syncship driver.

The memory chip slides out of the machine, and he immediately slots it into a protective case just like the one the last pilot took.

I jump at motion in my periphery. "Someone's coming!" They're dressed in pilot gray, thank stars, not Authority red.

"Right on time." Simon closes up the case and strides for the door. As soon as the pilot reaches to tap their identification on the door, he slides it open and yells, "You're late!"

The pilot glances at their keycuff, startled. "But the time I've got says..."

"Make sure you sync properly next time," Simon snaps. "Here. We expected you five minutes ago. Don't hit the next pilot on your way out of the hangar."

He shoves the case into the pilot's chest—the next load of synced data with our message lurking inside—and slams the sliding door shut in the startled man's face.

"Do you think he bought it?" he whispers with a guilty giggle.

I check the cambot feed. "Uh, he's running like there's a swarm of biting flies after him, so...seems like it."

Simon collapses into a wheelie chair, laughing. "If he's rushing, hopefully he won't notice if anything else is off. We did it, Jed!"

"We still have to get out of here before our message hits the rest of the uniweb. Or before there's a shift change and the night crew arrives to find their colleagues passed out on the floor."

"Details." Simon waves his hand. "If we disappear into the bot tunnels again, they'll be five steps behind us. It'll buy me time to figure out how we're going to spring Saray from whatever prison Jinan has her in."

He checks the cambots one last time before sliding the door open and looking both ways down the hall. He doesn't quite run, but his pace is brisk, and I have to lengthen my strides to keep up.

As soon as the door to the zip-lift closes behind us, we collapse into the seats. A relieved laugh bubbles up my throat. "I can't believe we got away with that," I whisper.

"Not to brag, but you're with an expert." Simon's eyes twinkle as he secures his safety strap.

The zip-lift jolts, rocketing us toward the docks. I reach out for his hand and squeeze it hard as the acceleration presses us back into the seat.

"This'll drop us off in a corridor a few levels down," Simon tells me. "There's a tunnel entrance barely ten meters from the lift. We're almost home free..."

But we haven't gotten ten steps out of the zip-lift before a line of Authorities step in front of us, aiming blasters at our faces.

"Whoa, hang on," I bluster. "What's happening? We're all on the same side here."

The Authority in front sneers, "*Are* we?" Then he gestures to his buddies.

A blaster digs into my temple as two Authorities magcuff my hands. Neither Simon nor I say a word. Anything we say will incriminate us, and our silence is damning enough.

We got our message out to the galaxy, at least. Hopefully the bank job went better than ours. I have to believe it did, that we all made a difference, that the revolution has started in earnest.

Because I don't think we're getting out of this alive.

Chapter 43

THE IMPERIAL MOON PALACE

Saray

"Your Grace." It's Yumiko, bowing at my bedroom door. "Emperor Jinan is here to see you."

I push myself upright from where I've been sprawled on the bed, trying to think of a way to get Alan out of prison. "Here?" In my apartment?

"Yes, Your Grace."

Blast it. I fix my robes and pull in a deep breath before gliding into the sitting room to meet my husband.

He lounges on the sofa with bodyguards standing at attention on either side, smiling at me in a languorous, satisfied sort of way.

I want to punch his lights out. Instead, I bow and say, "What would you have me do, Your Majesty?"

"Excellent question." He stands and takes both of my hands, bringing my fingers to his lips. "My spies tell me that a handful of my remaining siblings have formed an alliance against me. I need you to infiltrate their gathering, learn their plan, and report back to me this afternoon."

He taps his keycuff against mine, transferring an address. I stare at it, fighting the urge to laugh. Did Jinan marry me or recruit me as an Authority? I guess I'm his chief spymaster now.

"Yes, Your Majesty." I bow again, waiting with my eyes lowered for him to make the next move.

"Good girl." He pats my shoulder almost affectionately. I hate having to act like a dog with my tail between my legs, the bite and snarl whipped out of me.

Just as I think he's about to leave, he tips up my chin for a long, slow kiss. "I very much enjoyed our time together last night," he whispers against my cheek.

I hold very still.

"Much more to come," he whispers in my ear, the heat of his breath snaking down my neck.

It takes all my effort not to flinch.

He finally releases me, gesturing to his bodyguards to clear the hall for his exit. "I've taken the liberty of linking our devices," he says casually over his shoulder. "It'll be like you're reporting to me in real time."

"Perfect, Your Majesty," I say to his retreating back.

Thanks for warning me you'll be spying.

After Jinan leaves, a very polite argument ensues about whether I should be allowed to go on this "errand" for the Emperor alone. The ladies-in-waiting think I should take at least two bodyguards. Since these would be Imperial Authorities, I argue that would defeat the purpose. If they let me in at all, getting the princexes to trust me with their brother's army at my back would be impossible.

"If you go without any backup, they'll tear you apart," Nuala says. "Or try to hold you for ransom."

"Aww, Nuala, I didn't know you cared."

She gets a look on her face like she's smelled something bad. "Hating you and wanting you dead are two very different things."

"Glad to hear it." I fold my arms. "I can handle myself, ladies. Send me with a guardbot if you must, but I think it'll work better if I can pretend

I—" I pitch my voice in a breathy damsel-in-distress imitation—"*barely escaped with my life!*"

"And if it backfires?" Pearl demands.

I shrug. "Then I'm dead or kidnapped." I don't say it out loud, knowing Jinan's listening, but I let my face say it for me: *How much worse could it be, compared to this?*

"Glitch, what do you think happens to *us* if you die?"

That gives me pause. These women's lives now depend on my good behavior. "I'll do my best not to die, then." When that's met with several choked exclamations of outrage, I add, "Ladies, please trust that I know what I'm doing. His Majesty didn't assign me this task for no reason. He gains nothing from my death—but everything from my success."

I haven't entirely convinced them. The final compromise is that a guard-bot will follow me to the location and wait outside, ready to be activated by a single shouted word should I require backup. As with most compromises, I'm just as unhappy with it as my ladies are. But it gets them off my back.

The information Jinan transferred to my keycuff includes a copied formal invitation to the gathering. In true Imperial royalty fashion, their meeting of sedition is a masquerade party. The masks, I'm guessing, are a practicality—no one wants to wear their own face when plotting treason and probably regicide.

Normally, the ritual of makeup, hair, and wardrobe is comforting—part of the rhythm of life in the Imperial court. But now, as Pearl paints my face and Kina affixes gems and feathers to a mask, the pampering merely heightens my anxiety. I have to keep reminding myself that all of this is another form of deception, another way to manipulate people's thoughts and feelings about me. It's a disguise, intended not to conceal my identity, but to highlight only the parts I want people to see.

I only wish it didn't take blazing *hours* to put on.

At last, they release me—hair done, makeup set firmly enough to wear a mask over it without smearing. Kina drapes a robe around my shoulders, a silvery piece she took from Geneva's abandoned closet. "Aligning you with the late Emperor's murderer is a gamble," she told me in an undertone, "but I think they might see it as rebellious."

The Authorities clear the hallway for my exit, but once I step onto the zip-pod, it's just me and the expressionless guardbot. Once again, I'm alone, in control of my own fate. Or as much as I can be under the circumstances.

The greatest victory is that Yumiko skipped my dose of nightsweet entirely this morning. With some sleight of hand, she'd pretended to prepare the drug, but what she handed me to drink was sugar water. For the first time in days, I feel fully conscious and alive.

I'm also vaguely nauseous and sweaty-palmed. Playing both sides is a dangerous game, and the stakes couldn't be higher.

The ballroom they've chosen for this gathering is familiar—it's not far from Geneva's old suite, in fact. With the demise of Emperor Soren's wives and the abscondment of most of his children, this sector is a ghost town. Lights have been dimmed and atmo controls turned down to minimum, leaving the hallways a cold, dark shell of their pristine glory only a week ago.

I assume the choice of location was an attempt at misdirection. They thought no one would expect them to hang out in a dark, freezing room. But it's so predictable that I almost feel sorry for them. This is what people always do on fictionalized royal-intrigue holo-dramas. The only thing they could do that's more obvious is to disguise themselves as servants.

Tucking the cloak closer around me, I disembark from the zip-lift and motion for my guardbot to wait in an unobtrusive alcove. It's not the only guardbot here; as I approach the ballroom doors, I catch a glint of several others in the shadows. Nobody came here expecting to be safe.

Inside, the room is lit with a ring of lamps that project the hologram illusion of torches. There's no other decorations, refreshments, or servants—uncharacteristic for a royal masquerade. Soft music fills the air, but it seems to be coming from portable speakers.

There are maybe fifteen to twenty people in this enormous room, making it feel ludicrously large. They're huddled together inside the circle of lamps, a few of them speaking in low tones. Most of them stand awkwardly in silence. If they were trying to make this an enjoyable party, they've failed miserably.

But it still tops the list of best-dressed attempts at treason.

I approach the group, expecting to be challenged, but aside from a few polite greetings, they all but ignore me. No one's recognized me, then. *Good.*

I scan the dimly lit, masked figures and make a small game of guessing who they are. The woman in blue is almost certainly Princess Iris. Across the room, the man with the wolf mask—Prince Ervin, I'd bet.

Some of their number aren't even princexes. I recognize a lady-in-waiting, Aimee, who served one of Soren's dead wives. I had assumed Jinan executed their ladies after he cleaned house on the princexes' mothers, so I'm impressed that one of them—at least—managed to escape.

The conversation is muted, and much of it escapes me, but what words I do catch are flavored strong chocolate-orange. Fear and anger. Unsurprising, and easy to work with.

"Do you think the Authorities can be won from Jinan's side?" I ask a masked guest at random, hoping their reply will help me guess their identity—or at least give me an "in" to the conversation. Nobody seems to want to speak first in this room, perhaps for fear of reprisal.

"If he has access to the Imperial purse, he owns them," the princex responds bitterly. "Entirely mercenary, our army. No sense of loyalty, no morals."

Their companion snorts. "That's rich, coming from you, K—uh, *you*."

Aha. I think I've found myself in a conversation with Princex Kivan and their partner, Lady Janae. Kivan is only around nineteen, a newcomer to the playing field of royal politics. I don't know them well, but neither do they know me. That's a good start.

"Sounds like we need to cut the Imperial purse, then," says another bystander.

It's an older woman, and at first, I scramble to place her as one of the consorts. But she's not a deceased wife, she's a cousin. Lady Dreena was Soren's niece, a sweet-cheeked toddler at the time he took the throne. She was one of the few relations he allowed to live, and for that reason, she stayed utterly loyal to him. I can't count the times I've seen her on the newsies, gushing about His Majesty's endless mercy and goodwill, about how much he cares for his subjects. I could never tell if she actually believed it or if it was the price she paid to keep her life. In person, her flavors were always muddled with the sickly-sweet taste of artificial bliss, although she hid the symptoms of addiction well.

Dreena's words taste sober today, citrus with fury. Maybe she truly did love her Uncle Soren...or she resents his death pulling the rug of luxurious servitude from under her.

"Near impossible," Lady Janae says, with a tinge of jasmine despair. "One would have to cut off all communication with the Monroe banks for long enough that his personal funds run out. And there hasn't been a communications disruption longer than a single day since the Moon Palace was reconstructed. No, the only way to cut him off is for someone else to be recognized as the legal heir."

"Jinan was the Crown Prince when Soren died," I muse aloud. "According to succession law, his claim is the strongest. But Soren's own succession law states that any other blood heirs to the throne must declare their loyalty and renounce their claim before Jinan's rule is secured—or they must die."

Princex Kivan snorts. "Well, I certainly won't bend the knee, and I'm not going down without a fight."

"If enough of you could band together to challenge him, perhaps you could sway the Authorities to back someone else." I tap my chin, as if I've just thought of this idea. "Or several someones. A council of princexes, representing different sectors of the galaxy." Jinan will be furious at me for saying it, but right now, he can't stop me.

Lady Dreena throws back her head and laughs. "Share power? I'll eat my slippers if a single princex agrees to that without secretly planning to stab the others in the back."

I fold my arms. "You're working together now, aren't you?"

"Working? Who's doing work?" Princex Kivan gestures around the room. "We're here to have a party."

"Ah. Yes. Of course."

I came here assuming that the party was a thinly veiled front for plotting sedition—that was what Jinan seemed to think it was, anyhow—but now I wonder if the Emperor's children truly know how to do anything other than dress up and talk shit about each other.

Enough tiptoeing around.

I draw Lady Dreena aside and reach for her mind, coaxing her to believe I can be trusted. "So, what *is* the plan?" I ask, keeping my tone casual. "Let Jinan murder us all?"

"He can go to town on these little shits," Lady Dreena murmurs. "*I* plan to be the one standing in the ashes when the rest of this place is rubble. That's why I let the Authorities overhear me talking about this little event. Jinan's goons should be here any minute to finish them all off."

I might've slapped my forehead with my palm, if I wasn't wearing a mask. Jinan will be only too happy to oblige, I'm sure, but I'm honestly disappointed in these fools. Part of me had been hoping this *was* an attempted coup, that I could somehow play both sides. But they aren't thinking beyond their own self-interest.

"Legally, you gave up your claim when you were a child," I remind her.

"If I'm the only blood heir left..."

She doesn't get to finish the sentence before a nearly silent laser blast puts a hole in her forehead. I jump back, unable to stifle a scream.

Princex Kivan holds the blaster, a tiny handheld thing easily concealed in a sleeve. "Glitch called the Authorities," they yell. "Scatter!"

The room's dull murmur rises to panicked yells. More blaster shots go off—Kivan wasn't the only one hiding a weapon up their sleeve. I nearly teleport away, then remember I'm supposed to be pretending I can't. Dropping to my knees, I jab the button on my keycuff to summon my guardbot. The dark, cold room is ablaze with blasts now, and there's more than one body joining Dreena's on the floor.

Urgently, I whisper, "Your Majesty, if you were planning on sending Authorities in here, now would be a good time." Then, after ducking another shot, I add, "Make sure they have shields."

Twenty minutes later, with the atmo controls turned back to normal and the room warming to a comfortable temp, Jinan strolls into the ballroom.

The Authorities have already dragged the bodies into a corner and are in the process of zipping them into bags. Jinan stops to look down into the unmasked faces of some dozen of his siblings, plus a handful of their partners and noble hangers-on. Not one attendee of the party survived to tell of it—no one except lucky little me. My guardbot deflected the blasts until the Authorities burst in to surround and shield me while they executed the rest of the attendees.

Jinan's facing away from the General, so I'm the only one who notices when his dispassionate look breaks for a split second into a triumphant little smirk. This couldn't have worked out better for him if he'd planned it himself, the bastard. Despite her best efforts, Dreena died doing one last favor for Soren's son.

Jinan wipes the smug look off his face and turns to me. "Well done, wife," he says in a grand, ringing tone that tells me he wants the Authorities to hear it. "All these traitors slain in one blow. As your first mission, I'd call this a success."

I want to cast up. Instead, from my position in a half-reclining puddle on the floor, I bow. "Thank you, Your Majesty."

He grabs my chin and forces me to look him in the eyes. In a growl meant just for me, he says, "Don't think I didn't hear your little incitement to rebellion when I was listening in. Just for that, your father is losing a finger tonight."

When I gasp, a plea on my lips, he stops me with fingertips laid across them. "Think about how many fingers he has left," he murmurs. "Those are your number of chances before I start carving bigger pieces off." Then he waves at the group of Authorities who are still guarding me. "Take her back to her suite. Get her cleaned up and dressed for a court appearance. I have another matter to attend to this afternoon, and I'd like her to join me."

Another twisted loyalty ceremony? Will he make all his councilors kneel before him and have them shot if they don't bow low enough?

Feeling wrung out and horrified at myself, I allow the guards to lead me away.

Chapter 44

HEPBURN CITY, MONROE

RODAN

Over the course of my life, I've taken great pains to avoid getting on the wrong side of the law. Yet here I sit, cuffed to a chair, awaiting my turn for processing at the Authority station in downtown Hepburn City. My neighbors in this waiting room include an assortment of shoplifters, people coming down from bad hallucinogen trips, and one woman who appears not to be a lawbreaker so much as a sufferer of a contagious pox who broke quarantine. Apparently, they don't care enough about us to quarantine her from this waiting room.

If I live through this, I'd better go get my immunoboosters freshened up.

At this point, I'm feeling pretty good about the fact that I'm alive at all. After the bank staff reported me to the Authorities as a suspect in the hacking of several high-profile accounts, I thought I'd get blasted on the spot. But then the uniweb started blaring that Greenjacket broadcast from every connected device, and they sort of forgot about me.

I didn't hear much of it before they shut it off, but I heard enough of the Authorities' chatter in the hovercar to the station that I can tell it's been effective. They're scrambling to control riots brewing in the streets of every major city on Monroe—of which there are *a lot*. The number of Authorities stationed on this planet isn't enough to handle dozens of simultaneous uprisings.

Especially not once they realize that said uprisings are shockingly well-funded. I smirk to myself. They haven't put two and two together so far. When they do, I'm exed for sure, but I can take some perverse satisfaction in knowing that so are they.

In the meantime, I get to cool my heels in this waiting room. I slump in the chair I'm cuffed to, seeking a comfortable posture that I can nap in.

And that's when Leo Galway, erstwhile rockstar Kyle Cannonball, teleports into the middle of the waiting room.

I struggle upright again, my jaw hanging open. "Leo? What the blazes? How did you do that?"

"With this dragon's help." Leo waves to the iridescent snake-creature as it shimmers into invisibility above his head.

"They mean, how'd you circumvent the dragon-repelling field?" one of the shoplifters yells. "If I knew I could teleport outta here, I'd have said yes when this junkie offered me some of their mind-alts!"

"You can still have 'em," says the blissed individual next to her. "Except they're pretty far up my ass right now, so you'll have to help me get 'em out first."

Leo opens his mouth, then closes it again. "You know what? I'm just going to ignore that. Anyway, we didn't like our chances busting you out of here the normal way, so Prince's dragon told us where the dragon-repelling device was located, and Andi—I mean Natalia—blast, I'm still getting used to not being undercover—anyway, she snuck in to turn it off." He checks his keycuff. "We probably don't have much time before someone figures it out, so let's get you out of those cuffs."

The whole waiting room rises in a clamor of people demanding to be next. Leo frantically shushes them, but not before the noise alerts a guardbot. It whirs through the door, scanning the scene.

Leo sighs, says, "Sorry, bud," and blasts its core processor out.

"You got the release code?" I ask, yanking nervously against the magcuffs. "Because if you were planning to shoot these off me, I'm good, actually. I'll just stay here with my wrists intact."

"Was kinda hoping you could teleport yourself out of them," Leo says. "We didn't get around to stealing any codes. Short on time."

"I'm not exactly in the chillest frame of mind," I mutter, but I close my eyes anyway.

I've called dragons before, but not often. Teleporting is a somewhat off-putting sensation to me. Whenever there's an alternative transportation method, I usually go with that.

"Want some of my ass drugs?" calls the junkie across the waiting room.

I ignore them.

I shut the whole world out and focus on Clara. Only Clara. Not where she is now or the fact that I may well never see her again, but the flashes of our history that bring me joy. Playing improv games over dinner, pretending to be prehistoric humans or spies or forbidden lovers meeting in secret. Quietly reading scripts next to each other in our tiny living space on the Moon Palace. The moment I wake in the morning, listening to her breathing inside the sleep pod with me, holding still so I won't disturb her until she stirs, too.

::Let me out.:: I reach outward with my mind, searching for a dragon willing to listen to me.

A consciousness touches mine, curious but not yet on my side. *::You are imprisoned.::*

Fucking dragons and their ethics. *::Unjustly. Free me, so I can rescue my partner.::*

::Is it not just imprisonment when you have done what they accuse you of?::

I sigh. *::I committed the crime, yes. But the crime itself was justice. It's the law that's unjust.::*

::My kind does not understand the nuances of currency movement that your people value so highly.::

::I'm not going to explain human economics to you. Will you free me or not?::

The dragon is still probing my mind. I hold very still, thinking of nothing.

::You have spent much of your life resenting us.::

::Not resenting,:: I protest. *::Your power over the human race felt unequal, that's all. If you ever chose to sever ties with us, our society would collapse. But if we humans cut dragons out of our lives, you wouldn't even notice.::*

::Untrue. We gain much from our relationship with humans. Knowledge. Growth and advancement that we are no longer capable of. Entertainment. Companionship.::

::But nothing you can't live without.::

::I concede your point.:: The dragon wavers, a tendril of doubt crossing our mental link. *::We want you to prosper. We do not hold you back intentionally. Quite the opposite.::*

::Not intentionally, perhaps. But as long as we rely on you, we will never be pushed to our full potential.::

::Then I suppose I should leave you in these cuffs to find the solution for yourself.::

::Wait—no!::

The dragon's mental presence vibrates with amusement. *::I am—what is the human phrase?—ah, yes. Fucking with you. Open your eyes.::*

As I do so, gravity returns without me ever noticing it was gone. My feet plant firmly on the floor, my wrists freed.

::Thank you!::

::Remember this moment, Rodan Quell,:: says the dragon, *::and know that this is the last time a dragon will ever help you. You believe in standing on your own two feet. Go and do so. Create the justice you yearn for.::*

And it disappears.

I shake myself. "Whew, that was weird."

"Tell me about it," says Leo, looking around the room with a stunned expression.

I follow his gaze and realize that I'm not the only one the dragon freed. Every prisoner in this room, even the ones who were very obviously not in the calm mind-state that dragons prefer, has been teleported free of their bonds.

"Hey, thanks!" the shoplifter calls.

Leo throws her a casual salute. "If you're looking for a way to thank me, go join the revolution happening out front."

There's a stampede for the door. The only person remaining is the woman with the pox, who scratches her arm and says, "I think I'm going to the hospital."

"Good call. C'mon, Quell, time's ticking." Leo grabs my arm and drags me out the door.

Leo's team has already met up with a larger Greenjacket troop. Most of them are out in the streets, recruiting, inciting, and directing the building riots. When we catch up with Leo's teammate, Derek, we find him down an alley monitoring reports trickling in from other planets.

"There's been a mass prison break on Topaz," he says, naming one of the galaxy's worst penal colonies. "Esperanza's factories are empty. The workers are storming the governor's penthouse. And Paotherr..." He grins. "The Authorities surrendered to the resistance already. Apparently, they got freaked out when one of their guys got torn to bits as an example."

His teammate Chaz, the feline-humanoid guy from Paotherr, grins and lets out a yowling cheer.

"Don't get complacent yet," I warn. "Rebuilding is going to be a long haul. People have lived for generations under Soren's laws. It's not going to be easy for everyone to change."

"Maybe not everyone," Leo says, "but the folks at the bottom who've been getting exploited have been dreaming of a fair chance. I can't wait to see what they do with it."

Derek checks his tablet one more time. "Oh, we've got a status report from the General. They're in position to storm the Moon Palace."

"Already?"

"Royal begged some help from Haven, sounds like," Derek says. "Glenna sent over a couple of the Ediya Experiments to help teleport the fleet."

I wince at the thought of Clara's siblings being moved around like chess pieces. "When you say, 'storm the Moon Palace'... Do they have any sort of plan to get innocents to safety?" *And will Clara count as an innocent, if she's now Jinan's wife?*

Leo leans over to look at the message over Derek's shoulder. His already pale face goes a shade whiter. "Uh..."

"Show me that." I snatch the tablet from Derek, who grabs at it with a futile protest.

<*General Royal DeSanto: We cannot afford to hesitate. Assume anyone on the Moon Palace is complicit in Soren's and Jinan's crimes. The first opening you get, blow the entire thing to space dust.*>

My breath comes in short wheezes. "Clara," I gasp out. "And your friend Jed. And Saray and Simon. They're all still up there."

Leo nods, pressing his lips together. "I'll call them. They have to get off that moon *now*."

Part Seven

DAYSEVEN

Year 3750 DE, Week 45

Chapter 45

THE IMPERIAL MOON PALACE

JED

The Moon Palace dungeon is about as unpleasant as I imagined. It's not the dank, moldy cell of a period drama, but as I discover, the Authorities unfortunately do hang people by their wrists from the ceiling sometimes.

Simon and I are at least in the same cell, but that's almost worse. I have to watch his face twist in agony as he tries to keep from groaning in pain at the cuffs digging into his wrist.

"Hey, listen," I say quietly, into the pained silence. "If we don't make it out of this, I want you to know—"

"Don't you fucking dare," Simon grits. "I don't want some mushy confession just because we're dying. Tell me when we're safe or not at all."

"I don't think we're getting that choice." My wrist burns as I twist it against the cuff, still futilely trying to pull them off even though they're far too tight. "And I don't want you to die thinking I was just fucking around because we were in danger for our lives. I've been gone on you for *months*. At first I thought it was just that having you whispering in my earpiece during missions was hot...but it turned into more than that. You're so smart, always one step ahead of the rest of us. And you *care*. Don't think I didn't notice you checking up on the survivors of the concert disaster—I saw their hospital-room feed when you minimized your wallscreen tabs. You helped Saray, even when it put you in danger. Blazes, you even made me feel guilty about being mean to that little monkeybot. What I'm trying to say is, you're a good person, Simon Kim. And I..." I swallow. "I love you for it."

Simon lets out a shaky breath. "Blast it, Jed, you had to go and say it *now*? In a dungeon?"

Half-laughing, half-groaning, I say, "Doesn't make it less true."

"No, but it *hurts*," Simon moans. "I spent so long trying to pretend it was just a silly crush because you were a hot rockstar who was good at flirting. If I'd just invited you over to my apartment sooner, I'd have wasted less time being scared you would hate me for my past. But you accepted me without even blinking. Because you're a good person, too, and *stars*, do I love you." His eyes go glassy with unshed tears. "I spend so much of my time hiding and blending in. You're the only one who ever took the time to *see* me."

"Fuck, I want to hug you so badly." I rattle my chains. "You think those sadists knew this was the only way to keep our hands off each other?"

"Oh, definitely." I can't tell if Simon's crying or laughing, but if he's feeling like I am, there's a good chance it's both at once.

I'd give anything for more time with him. But I don't see how we're getting out of here alive.

The cell door swishes open, and four Authority soldiers pile in, two for each of us. They release my arms, roughly tugging them behind my back before I can shake out the pins-and-needles sensation.

This is it. I can feel it in my gut. I'm about to die.

I always thought I'd be a fighter in a situation like this, kicking and screaming. But a strange calm comes over me instead. I let the Authorities shove me forward, marching me down the hall. I shoot glances behind me; between broad red-jacketed shoulders, I glimpse Simon being similarly propelled forward. I'm more flared off for how they're treating him than for myself.

My brain focuses to a point of total clarity: I'll do anything in my power to make sure Simon lives through this. Even if it means I don't.

There aren't any escape routes in this narrow corridor, however. The place is swarming with Authorities, and all the doors are passcoded. If they're marching us to an incinerator or a tiny room with a firing squad, we're vortexed.

Never thought I'd find myself praying for a public execution, but here I am.

Looks like I'm going to get my wish. The Authorities bundle us into a zip-lift. The two beefy guys on either side of me have fingers like strangle vines—they dig into my arm muscles until I wince.

Just gotta distract them for a second...

Limbs tense, hyperaware of every movement the guards make, I wait for my moment.

But it doesn't come. The zip-lift *dings*, and they pull Simon and me out into a long, vaulted-ceiling hallway lined with Old Earth Roman-classical pillars and frescoes. My lungs have forgotten how to expand. I know this place. There have been countless vids panning down this hallway, probably captured by the same cambots that float over our heads. Through the enormous double-door archway at the end lies the Emperor's throne room, only used on ceremonial occasions. It was last used a day ago, when it was bathed in the blood of Soren's wives.

If there was no escape down in the Authorities' dungeon, there won't be one here. The very walls have guardbots in them. If I tried to run, or to distract them for Simon's sake, I'd be shot before I made it half a step.

The doors open to admit us, revealing the obnoxiously ornate room lined with nobles standing shoulder to shoulder against the walls. On the dais, two figures sit enthroned.

Jinan...and Saray.

I lock eyes with her. She seems physically unharmed, her arms bared in a tight, form-fitting strapless gown with a sheer purple-red cloak draped across her shoulders. The moment she recognizes me, she's unable to control her expression. Her mouth drops open in horror.

My eyes flash to Jinan's face. I catch the way his mouth tilts up just a little. He somehow knows about her connection with Simon and me. I don't know how the fuck he found out, but I'll bet this little show is all for her benefit. He wants her to know that he can, and will, destroy every chance of escape that she has.

The Authorities notice my faltering feet and shove me forward. I'm not allowed to stop until I nearly trip on the stairs to the royal dais. Distantly, I'm aware that the courtier audience is shouting at us—booing and cursing. It rolls right off. Insults from these people may as well be compliments.

What stings is knowing that I'm going to die without being able to protect *two* people I care about.

Jinan raises his hand for silence. "Even the most legitimate reign may begin with some dissent," he announces. "Earlier today, my darling new wife helped me discover and end an attempted insurrection, poorly concocted by my father's children. Those who love peace in this galaxy will be relieved to know they are dead."

I glance over at Simon, wondering if he knew about this "insurrection." I know he's been keeping count of how many of his half-siblings are left since Emperor Soren's demise. Before our little adventure in the Authority Headquarters, the number was down from nearly a hundred living heirs to around fifty. Many of Soren's younger children, easy targets, were executed by the Authorities at the same time as their mothers. Any imprisoned, hospitalized, or otherwise vulnerable princexes were eliminated as well. Only adults and teens quick enough to recognize the danger and take action to protect themselves survive now.

My guess is that Jinan's quelling of the "insurrection" will have cut the remaining number of heirs in half again.

Does Jinan realize that Simon, too, carries the dangerous bloodline of a man royal enough to challenge him?

"Thanks to the quick action of my Authorities, we were able to uncover yet another pair of traitors attempting to hijack our communications room," Jinan announces. "Naturally, their attempt was unsuccessful. Our communications specialists fought valiantly, and the miscreants were apprehended as they fled. Imagine my shock when I recognized one of their faces."

Cambots swivel toward me en masse, no doubt zooming in on my all-too-recognizable face.

"Tarantula's guitarist, Jedrek Blaze, has been a secret traitor all this time," I distantly hear Jinan announcing. "Authorities confirm they've been investigating the band since the destruction of my brother's pod last week. The rest of the members have fled, leaving only Blaze here to do their dirty work."

With every eye in the palace—and soon the galaxy—on me, there's only one thing I can think of to do with all their attention.

I wink and blow them an air kiss.

The Authority holding me growls and slams a fist into my lower back. "Wipe that smirk off. You're not long for this world."

"No, really? I thought Jinan was about to marry me." I don't bother to lower my voice. "Isn't that what he does to his enemies?"

A murmur ripples through the crowd at my words. I lift my head to the dais and meet Saray's eyes. Is it my imagination, or have the corners of her mouth turned up ever so slightly?

If she has to watch me die, I want her to think I'm not afraid.

"Jedrek Blaze and Simon Kim, I sentence you to execution by firing squad," Jinan proclaims. "Kneel before your sovereign."

The Authorities are shoving us down, so we don't have a choice. But I make sure to angle my bow toward Saray, holding eye contact with her.

I'm not sure if even her powers can save us now. But if there's a chance...

Jinan lifts a hand, and the Authorities behind us take aim.

I turn my head so that Simon's face is the last thing I'll see. But he's still staring intently at Saray. Jealousy flashes through me for just a moment, before I realize what he's seeing: Saray is slowly getting to her feet, eyes locked on us.

No, just *above* us.

She's staring at the Authorities standing behind us. And she says, in a low voice that somehow rings just as loud as Jinan's: "Your families at home are watching."

Jinan turns to her, disgust wrinkling his features as he reaches to push her back into her seat. But she's already dodging him, dropping to slide off the dais and walk toward us. She doesn't stop eye contact with the Authorities.

"What does loyalty bring you?" she asks. "Money to send to the families your overlord intends to keep under the boot of poverty? Jinan is weak, scrambling to hold up a legacy that took his father a lifetime to build, and he's slaughtering innocent women and children to do it. All of his power comes from you and your guns. Without it, who is he? Just another princex, like the ones you executed earlier. You've been ordered to kill any of Soren's children on sight, haven't you? The man you see before you is *just another princex*. And he's willing to murder children *just like yours*."

With that line, she drops to her knees before Simon and me, pushing our heads down...

And the Authorities fire.

On Jinan.

The sudden change of target makes some of the shots go wide, but enough of them land. The Emperor crumples, blood pooling on the dais. The crowd erupts in screams and shouting as the Authorities mill about, some looking at their weapons in confusion.

Oh shit. She used her mind-control on them. My breath comes in short gasps as my brain catches up, reeling from how close I came to death.

She saved us.

"Unlock them," Saray commands, eyes above my head. Hands grasp my arm, and with a click, my hands fall free of the constrictive magcuffs.

"Can you two run?" she whispers.

I let out a relieved half-laugh. "Like our lives depends on it."

"Then go *now*."

But we've barely taken one step before the muddled Authorities call, "Hold it! Where are you going, prisoner?"

"They're innocent," Saray tries, but the Authorities are getting wise to her manipulation.

They aim their blasters at us. "Doesn't matter," one of them says. "They still have to stand trial—"

A shudder rocks the ground. The crowd hushes for a moment as everyone quiets to listen for the continued hum of atmo. "What was that?" someone whispers.

Another shudder, this time accompanied by a distant *boom*. Atmo-grav stays on, but everyone's reaching for the emergency breathers we're supposed to keep in our pockets at all times.

I reach for mine automatically as well, then meet Simon's eyes in a panic. They would've been in the pockets of our red Authority jackets—the ones that were stripped from us when we were captured.

If we lose atmo-grav right now, Simon and I are dead.

"Run," Saray says between her teeth. "Now!" She's already moving.

As the ground rocks beneath us with a third explosion, we stumble into a run and sprint out the double doors of the throne room.

"Every zip-pod has an emergency kit!" Saray yells.

Simon veers toward the zip-lift and mashes the call button. The doors open, and we tumble in, scrambling for the kit stashed in the compartment under the seats as the lift doors close behind us.

I've barely got the box open before lights and gravity cut out, leaving us floating inside the dark pod.

I feel around until my fingers hit the hard cylinder of a portable torch-light. I switch it on and distribute masks, breathing a sigh of relief once everyone's head is encased with a thin bubble. Supposedly, these devices will keep us breathing for a couple of hours or so—enough to make our way to one of the emergency shelters, where backup generators will keep us warm until the bots fix the damage to the atmo-grav dome.

But now that we're safe-ish, I say what we're all thinking: "That sounded like a bomb."

"The Greenjackets." Simon taps my wrist, where my keycuff—now that my arms are freed—miraculously still functions. The Authorities took my scroll-tablet, but they didn't waste time hacking my keycuff. The built-in identity protections on personal cuffs are hard to crack, even for Imperial law enforcement. "Are your coms working? See if you can contact your team."

I scoff. "Uniweb will have cut out, too—"

And then I see the latest message notification on my cuff's tiny holo display—sent hours ago, when I was languishing in prison with my wrists bound above my head.

<*Kyle: Jed, you need to get off the Moon Palace NOW. General DeSanto is going to bomb it. He's told the Greenjackets to leave no survivors.*>

Chapter 46

THE IMPERIAL MOON PALACE

SARAY

"Message them back," I urge Jed at once. "See if they can get the fleet to hold their fire."

Jed's fingers fly over the tiny holo display. But as soon as he hits the Send button, we all see the flash of red. The uniweb might have still been up when he received that message, but coms were probably the first thing the Greenjackets took out.

"Blast it," he swears softly. "Simon, how far is it to the docks, if we have to walk there?"

Simon winces. "Through typical routes, at an average pace, assuming no obstacles...about twelve hours."

I roll my eyes. "Did you two forget that I can teleport? Getting to the docks is the easy part. The problem is that none of us own a ship. Any public transport left is going to be swarming with evacuees right now, and half of them will be trying to kill each other, now that Jinan's out of the way."

"Also, if I know the Greenjackets, they'll target the docks first," Jed says grimly. "They wouldn't want any inconvenient nobles escaping to try to reclaim the throne later."

"Saray," Simon asks, "your teleporting doesn't have the same limits as dragon-'porting, does it?"

"It depends." Explaining feels awkward—I haven't had much practice. "I can't teleport us to another planet without a ship, if that's what you're asking. We'd probably die in the void of space." To be honest, I've never tried it, so I could be wrong—but I'm not eager to take that chance. "I'll teleport people who are sick or hurt, though, and I don't require consent. Those are rules the dragons imposed out of concern for the ethics of their relationship with humans, not out of any physical limitations."

"So you could, in theory, 'port us outside the dome?"

I nod. "For all the good it'd do us. We wouldn't suffocate with these breathers on, but we'd freeze to death."

Simon raises a hand. "What if I told you I know where we can find a hidden escape ship?"

Jed raises an eyebrow. "Outside the dome?"

"My mother had it prepped before her attempt on the Emperor's life," Simon explains. "She told me about it because, if she succeeded, she knew I'd be in danger, too. I hid in that cockpit for days after the Authorities tortured me. Long enough for people to think I'd died, too. But I never started it up, because I had nowhere else to go. As far as I know, the ship's still out there, right where she left it."

"How did you get to it, if it's outside the atmo-grav dome?" I ask.

Simon shrugs. "Spacesuit."

"Know where we can get three of those on incredibly short notice?" mutters Jed.

"Actually, yeah," says Simon. "All maintenance closets have a few in storage, just in case all the bots go down and they need to send a mechanic outside the dome."

"And the nearest maintenance closet would be...?"

Simon consults his map. "Uh...as the dragon flies, the closest one is in the next sector over. But..."

I narrow my eyes at him. "But what?"

"That might be where the bombs hit," Simon murmurs. "It's close to Authority headquarters and the communications hub. If I was a Greenjacket, I'd aim for that first."

A sickening thought occurs to me. "The prison. *Alan.*"

Part of me wants to be reassured that Alan's probably fine. But they know better than to lie to me. Simon's face is somber, his voice gentle as he says, "There's nothing we can do for him now, Saray."

There's a beat of silence, in which I curse Jinan's ghost for keeping Alan captive. For good measure, I throw in a mental "fuck you" to the Greenjackets for bombing a moon that's home to plenty of innocent people, none of whom I have the power to save. And finally, I curse myself, for not having made a move to rescue us all sooner.

Which brings me back to cursing Jinan for keeping me under the influence of nightsweet. At least it's out of my system now. Yumiko's final gift to me. And I'm repaying her by letting her die.

I pull in a long breath through my nose. The important thing right now is that, while I still have a heartbeat, I have options. There's two people here that I can still save.

I breathe out.

"We can't just stay in this zip-lift until another bomb drops," I snap. "Grab my hands, both of you. Simon, focus on a maintenance closet—any of them, I don't care which. Jed, try not to think about anything."

Two hands slip into my outstretched palms: Jed's large and callused, Simon's clammy with sweat but with an unexpectedly strong grip.

I breathe deeply again as my eyes close, letting my awareness expand to encompass the two men next to me. I don't often open myself to other people's energy—it can be dangerous, as my sister Miri could attest. Without the ability to shut it off, she found herself meddling with other people's emotions...and sometimes being too easily influenced by them herself.

Luckily, I wasn't cursed with Miri's heightened perception. I have to focus hard to feel other people, and most of the time I don't bother. But to let Simon lead us to the correct location, I need to connect with him on a deeper level than just skin-to-skin contact.

I can't quite read his mind—Clara's skills are still just out of my reach—but his scent memory is more accessible. I smell dust, machine oil, the sharp tang of cleaning chemicals, and the faint, sweaty musk of old fabric as it unfolds after years in storage.

Focusing hard on those cues, and praying that Jed keeps his mind blank, I tug us forward through the black space between.

The experience of teleportation is normally devoid of any external sense. But this time, a sharp, numbing cold stabs at me for an agonizing moment. *Dome breach.* Panic rattles my concentration. Breather masks or no, exposure to the void could freeze us to death.

Senses crush back in on me. Gravity hasn't returned, but the torchlight in Jed's hand illuminates a room full of shelves, weightless objects hanging midair around us. The atmo-grav must be merely damaged, not defunct. In its total absence, the moon's gravity is weak, but things do eventually fall to the ground.

It's blessedly warm in here compared to the bite of the vacuum. I squeeze Jed's and Simon's hands before letting go; they're both responsive, alive, unfrozen. *That was close.*

Simon exhales. "I felt it," he says, his quiet voice loud in the close quarters. "We passed through the void."

"If we hadn't had our masks on, we'd be dead," I say, delayed terror making my voice curt. "Get suited up."

The two of them don't argue. Simon grabs a shelf and pulls himself down the wall hand over hand to a small red-painted locker. "Jed, can you shine the light?" He pulls the locker open and pulls out a neatly folded suit. Then one more. Then—

"That's it." I can hear the panic creeping in. "There're only two."

"Shit." Jed tosses the first suit to me. "Get it on, Saray."

"You first."

"Fuck no. *You* first. You're the one who's teleporting us around—"

"He's right," Simon interjects. "We need Saray to teleport us, and we need me to find our way around. We'll get Jed another suit."

I catch him mouthing, *Sorry, love,* as the two of them make eye contact. Jed reaches out to squeeze Simon's hand.

Seems Jed finally pulled his head out of his ass.

Maybe I'm supposed to be jealous, but when I examine my feelings, all I find is happiness. Romance isn't for me—I've always known that. But I think there's room in my life for affection and friendship, more so than I ever allowed myself to believe. After all they've done for me this horrible chaotic week, there's no denying that Simon and Jed have become my true friends. I care about them. I want them to be happy.

And that starts with keeping them alive.

I start pulling the suit on. My dress bunches up, so I pull it over my head and fling it away. They could already see half my tits anyway—why not the whole show? *Curse Jinan and the degrading outfits he put me in. I hope he's reborn as a slug on a desert planet.*

"Tell me there's another maintenance closet close by," I spit out as I shove my arms into the sleeves. "I don't want to risk teleporting us through a vacuum again. Not without Jed suited up."

"I think I can find one—"

Simon cuts off as the room shakes around us, the shelves rattling against the wall.

"We're gonna need to make it quick," I say.

"Th-there's a bot tunnel at the back of this room. We can shortcut through there to the next maintenance room." Simon's voice shakes, but he wastes no time batting trash out of the way to clear our path to the access hatch between two shelves. He keys in an access code and dives in first, beckoning us after him.

"Are the bots still active?" Jed calls as he floats through. "Do we need to watch out in case they run us over?"

"Most likely, they're in emergency shutdown," Simon responds. "All but the maintenance bots. They'll be working on fixing the atmo-grav."

"*Most likely,*" I repeat under my breath.

With the spacesuit on, I'm sweating, although I can see by Jed's shiver that it's cold in this tunnel. The suit restricts my movements, making me clumsy as I grab handhold after handhold to propel myself along the tunnel. Simon takes the lead, Jed in the middle, and me at the rear.

I swallow the urge to ask how far we have left to go.

It's probably fifteen minutes total we're crawling through those tunnels. We don't run into any bots, but two more explosions shake the ground badly enough that I'm worried these tunnels could collapse on us. By the time we reach an access door that leads to another supply room, my suit is humid with sweat and my breath is coming in quick pants.

Simon keys in the access code and hisses when it flashes red at him. "Atmo breach in this sector," he says. "It won't let me through for safety reasons."

"I'll go then." It's easy enough to teleport a few meters through a single wall, grab a suit, and teleport back. Especially if the space is nearly identical to the closet we just visited.

"Careful—" Jed says, but I'm already disappearing.

Now that I know what I'm looking for, finding the suit barely takes a minute. I grab the extra one in the locker, too, just in case. Then I close my eyes to teleport back into the bot tunnel and—

::*Saray?*::

That's Clara's voice.

::*Saray, can you hear me?*::

::*I hear you. Where are you?*:: I try to follow the sense of her mind, but she doesn't feel close.

::*I'm in the villa,*:: Clara says. ::*The zip-pods are all down. I've still got nightsweet in my system, so I can't teleport. Coms are down, and I can't reach anyone else. What's happening? Are we under attack?*::

::*Yeah, we are. Jinan's dead, and the Greenjackets are blowing this place up.*:: Blast it, I can't just leave her. But we've got precious little time left. ::*Hang tight, Clara. I'm on my way.*::

I teleport back into the bot tunnel and hand Jed the suit. "Get it on," I say shortly. "I'll drop you two at the ship. My sister is trapped in the Emperor's villa, and I need to go get her."

Jed shakes his head as he stuffs his legs into the suit. "Saray, there's no time."

"I can't just leave her." I'm already abandoning Dad and the ladies-in-waiting. If I have to condemn my sister, too...hear her screams in my head...

"Then we're coming with you," says Simon, with a decisive air. "We all get out together. Or not at all."

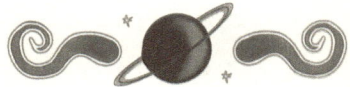

N ow that I've been to the Emperor's villa twice, it's easy to teleport there. I think that horrific, beautiful place will be burned into my brain for the rest of my (potentially very short) life.

We land on the villa-side dock, right next to the furry heap that is the guardian tiger-bot. It's powered down, an uncanny mix of dead and asleep. The moat sloshes against the dock, agitated and choppy. The fancy cushioned boat lists to one side, water slopping into it. The false sky above our heads glows that ominous red.

Simon is breathing hard, eyes darting here and there as he takes in the landscape. I remember with a hard pit in my stomach that this is where his mother died.

"Are those *people?*" Jed points out onto the water.

"Might be the Emperor's sea monster," I say automatically.

Then I take a good look at where he's pointing. There *are* dozens of heads bobbing in the water, struggling toward land. They're getting tossed around in the rough waves as they push a hoverslab across the water in front of them.

"I'm sorry, the Emperor's *what?*"

I guess that detail got lost in the chaos. "Never mind, but don't go in the water."

Simon shades his eyes against the false sky. "Is the color off in here, or are those red jackets?"

I squint. Shit, he's right. Those are Authority coats. What the blazes are they doing in here? This area should be off-limits to them unless Jinan himself calls for...

Uh-oh. *The hoverslab.* I can't make out details of the person lying on it, but if the Authorities managed to get Jinan some medical assistance in time to save him, we're vortexed.

Even more so than we already were.

"Let's get out of here," I urge. ::*Clara? Where are you?*::

::*Coming.*:: Along with her mental voice, I get a quick flash of her surroundings. She's rushing through the gardens in the dim emergency lighting. I start climbing the hill and catch sight of her pale head of hair approaching.

She crashes into me, throwing her arms around my neck. "Thank stars," she gasps. "I thought I was going to die down here."

I'm not in the mood for hugging it out. "You still might, if we don't hurry." I shove the suit at her. "Put this on. There've been a bunch of dome breaches."

Clara hikes up the slinky nightgown Jinan had her wearing and starts to pull the suit on. She zips it up over her chest and begins to activate her breather mask, when suddenly, she freezes.

"What?" I ask, dread coiling inside me.

"Melanie's down here," Clara whispers. "And Saray...she's not alone."

"Then we have to go before—"

"No. Saray. She has your dad."

The bottom drops out of my gut. "Alan," I whisper. I gave up on him once. I can't do it again. "Where are they?"

Clara turns toward the villa. I follow her gaze and watch as Dr. Melanie Ediya emerges from the pillar-flanked entrance, holding the muzzle of a blaster pressed to the side of my adoptive father's head.

I take off running toward them, but skid to a halt when Melanie clicks the power switch on the blaster. It powers on with a faint whine.

"That's close enough," she says, poisonously sweet. "Be a good girl, and I won't have to hurt him."

Seething, I show her my hands. "What do you think you're doing, Dr. Ediya? In a couple of hours, this moon is going to be an asteroid belt around Satang. We have to get out of here."

"That's right," says Melanie. "And if you behave yourself, I might let you come with me."

"Fine. I'll bite. What does 'behaving myself' entail?"

"You were very disobedient earlier." Melanie clicks her tongue. "Tricking the guards into shooting their sovereign—oh, yes, I was watching. Your father lost a whole hand for that." She nudges Alan. "Show her."

Slowly, he lifts his left arm, displaying the bandaged wrist ending in a stump. I swallow a wave of nausea. He's missing his spex, and dark circles underline his eyes. He's pale as a corpse. But he still meets my eyes, bleary though his vision must be, and sets his mouth in a defiant line. I can almost hear what he'd say: *Don't worry about me. You can't let her win.*

"Lucky for you, Jinan was only injured," says Melanie. "Now, here's what's going to happen. There's an escape ship hidden below this villa, a last resort for an imperiled Emperor. You are going to help me get His Majesty into it, then you and Clara will teleport us to safety, where we can regroup and wait for the Emperor's recovery."

I tear my eyes from Alan to glance over my shoulder at the Authorities in the water. They're close to shore now, still pushing Jinan along on his hoverslab. Jed and Simon have both picked up oars from the boat, preparing to defend us—though I doubt they'll be much help against soldiers with blasters.

"You really want me to help the man who held me captive the last few days, shot a score of women dead in front of me, and took me as his unwilling bride?" I scoff.

Melanie smiles without humor. "I hold your father's life in my trigger finger, girl. I don't think you want to test me." She flicks her gaze to Clara. "And just in case *you* get any ideas, I've been told your partner has been arrested on Monroe. I would hate to have to call for eir execution."

"You can't." Clara's voice wavers. "There's no uniweb connection."

"There doesn't have to be. Monroe Authorities have their orders. If I don't check in by tomorrow, Rodan Quell is to be found dead in eir cell. Tragic. E just couldn't live with eir former girlfriend marrying the Emperor..."

"*Current* partner," Clara says viciously. "I didn't break up with em. And I didn't consent to be married."

"Careful," Melanie singsongs. "Other Imperial brides have lost their heads for saying less."

The ground rattles with another bomb strike, this one closer. The ship under the villa may be our only choice left—I doubt we could get to Simon's mother's ship even if we wanted to.

"What's the point of this?" The fight's beginning to drain out of me. "Why go to such lengths to save some asshole prince? Haven's anti-Imperial. You were, too, once, Dr. Ediya. Wasn't the whole point of your work to evolve humanity beyond violence?"

Melanie laughs. "That's what *Glenna* wanted. I was the only one who saw the true future of our work: the power to take control of this galaxy. Humans with abilities to rival the dragons could quickly become worshiped as gods. You've been wasting your potential, and so have I, withering in prison for half my life. No more. Soren was a tool, and Jinan as his successor takes me one step closer to where I always intended to be. *In charge*." She wrinkles her nose. "So, yes, I'll rescue the asshole prince because he's useful right now. Once the two of you produce heirs, we can get rid of him, and set ourselves up as regents while your children grow…"

::*Stars above*,:: Clara says in my head. ::*She's lost it*.::

::*I can't even get pregnant*.::

::*Neither can I*.::

I nearly laugh out loud. It's honestly not even funny, but…

::*No way I'd subject a child to living in a mind like mine*,:: Clara says. ::*And that's assuming I'd let Jinan near me. Did the wedding-night trick we planned work for you?*::

::*Like a charm*,:: I tell her, barely holding back a smirk. ::*Well? Do we help her, or…?*::

::*I think we have to, for now. But the second she's distracted, we get Alan away from her, and…*::

There's another enormous *boom*. The ground starts to disintegrate under us as the emergency generators powering the sky begin to flicker.

"Time's up," I say grimly. If we don't get off this moon *now*, we're going down with it. "Fine, Dr. Ediya, you win. We're rescuing the Emperor."

And that's when we lose gravity.

Chapter 47

EMPEROR'S VILLA, THE IMPERIAL MOON PALACE

JED

I don't recommend being near a large body of water when the artificial gravity starts glitching.

One moment I'm standing on the dock, holding an oar and getting ready to bash the Authorities swimming toward me. The next moment, my feet leave the ground.

I howl in surprise and nearly shit my pants as the water follows me up. The Authorities scramble to escape the surge of water as it rises out of its moat to form enormous floating spheres. The lucky ones manage to grab the dock pilings, including the Authority General, who's grabbed Jinan's limp, unresisting body by the collar. A few of the less fortunate soldiers get swept up in the rising water, fumbling for their breather masks with panicked eyes as the water carries them away from solid ground.

I can't bring myself to feel bad for them.

Further up the hill, Saray and Clara have managed to grab hold of a tree's branches to anchor themselves down. Melanie Ediya has one of her legs wrapped around a pillar, still threatening Alan with the blaster in her hand.

Simon hooks his oar under the edge of the dock and pulls himself to the ground, grabbing for a handhold. He begins crawling along the ground, hand over hand, propelling himself away from the looming bubbles of water. I copy him, using the oar as a lever to pull myself closer to solid ground.

"The shield isn't going to hold," Simon shouts. He's looking up to the dome above our heads. The image of a false sky is totally gone—the dome is transparent, showing the enormous cracks in the rock that encases this underground room. Explosions batter ever closer.

This villa was built to be the Emperor's emergency bunker in case of attack. It has the strongest technological protections that credits can buy. If those are failing, and the moon is breaking apart around us...

"Get to the villa!" Saray yells.

I crawl through the garden, bush by bush, clinging to grass when that's all I've got. The sensation of "down" no longer being down is messing with my head, making me dizzy and nauseous. I try not to look up—the sight of enormous chunks of moon floating away from the dome will make me want to cast up even more.

Time slows. When every second could be the one when our atmo dome fails, every fumble of my suit-gloved hands feels like a life-ending mistake. But at last, I find myself grabbing onto a pillar framing the villa's doorway. One of the Emperor's powered-down tiger bots drifts nearby, disturbingly still coiled in a cat's sleeping posture.

Simon was waiting just inside the arch for me. He reaches out and catches my hand, the first thing that's made me feel solid since gravity shut off. "We're going to be all right," he says, just for me to hear. "I'll make sure of it."

Saray and Clara both cling to the walls as the roof trembles and begins to buckle overhead. Melanie holds her blaster trained on Saray's father, who's scrabbling with his one remaining hand to push rubble out of a partially blocked doorway, revealing a set of stairs leading downward.

General Ajax and his crew are straggling up the path toward the villa, making better time than I did because they're not suited up. I can tell it's getting cold for them, though. The atmo must be powering down along with the gravity generator. If the dome breaches, they'll have minutes at most.

I was hoping they'd leave Jinan behind as dead weight, but they've still got his limp form in tow. Blast it.

The General doesn't waste any time. Brushing past me, he pushes off from the wall and, shoving Jinan's bandaged body ahead of him, makes for the stairwell Melanie unblocked. The Emperor isn't looking so good—he's a ragdoll in the General's grasp.

General Ajax grips the edge of the fountain, intending on using it as a kickoff point to propel himself into the stairwell. But suddenly, a surge of water bursts out of the top of the fountain, toppling two of the naked satyr statues.

I let out a cry of horror. The water holds an enormous shadowy mass of tentacles.

What was that Saray said about a sea monster?

Ajax pushes away from the fountain but loses his grip on Jinan. The injured Emperor floats almost peacefully, eyes closed, as Soren's pet monster lunges out of the water bubble and pulls him in. The Emperor is enveloped in its inky body in seconds, devoured whole.

The General screams, "Attack it! We need the Emperor's body!"

The soldiers don't seem in a tearing hurry to antagonize that thing. "Just leave him," I hear one of the soldiers mutter. "He's already a goner."

General Ajax is practically foaming at the mouth. "You fools! The escape ship is DNA-passcoded! Without Emperor Soren's bloodline, none of us are going anywhere."

Another shudder. Glass rains down from the shattered ceiling. The Authorities aim their blasters at the monster, but the devices flash warning lights instead of firing.

"Water damage," a soldier spits, tossing the useless blaster aside, where it floats midair.

"We're all going to die!" wails another.

"Get out of my way." Simon pushes off the wall, nudging the General away from the stairwell. "Does the ship actually need blood, or will an ID scan work?"

"What the—" The General glares at him. "Who—?"

"I'm Simon Kim, sixty-seventh son of Emperor Soren," says Simon. "At this point, I might be the last living heir. I'm *definitely* the only one you've got right now." He draws himself as close to upright as anyone can get in zero-grav, puffing out his chest. "I hereby officially claim my blood right to the throne."

Then he adds sardonically, "For whatever good it'll do me before it explodes into stardust," and gestures for us to follow him down the stairwell.

I don't argue. I dive straight down the dark slope after him. Hand over hand, we crawl in pitch darkness. Saray and Clara follow, with General Ajax hard on their heels. Melanie's already far ahead of us.

There's a passcoded door at the bottom of the stairwell, which Simon finds by soundly knocking his head against it. I fumble in the spacesuit's pocket for the torchlight I'd stowed there. Shining the narrow beam of light across the door, I find the sensor and gesture at Simon to scan his cuff.

It flashes red.

Simon curses. "Must be my name change throwing it off. Let me try a bio scan." He strips off the spacesuit's glove and places his hand against the pad. We both hold our breath.

There's a chime, and the door slides open.

"Long live the Emperor," I say softly.

Simon makes a face at me, then gestures for me to follow him through the door.

The escape ship, a cozy, round twenty-seater with state-of-the-art shielding, is powered down like everything else, squatting silently in the dark. The tiny escape room gets uncomfortably crowded as the Authorities join us. The walls rattle with every explosion, bumping us into each other.

The heir apparent to a crumbling Empire lowers the ramp to allow us to board.

I wink at him as I float inside. "Can I have the copilot seat?"

He yanks me in to steal a kiss. "It's yours forever, Jaired."

"Actually," says Melanie, "I believe it's mine."

Ugh. I'd managed to forget about her. Poor Ambassador Lake looks half-dead with exhaustion and pain, but she's still got her blaster to his head.

"Just strap in and sit down," Clara grits out. "Can we please survive first and quibble about the details of who's in charge later?"

"No." And suddenly Melanie drops Alan and turns the gun on...*me*.

Well, shit.

"You'll be doing exactly as I say from now on, *Your Majesty*," she says to Simon, "or your lover dies."

Out of the corner of my eye, I watch Saray lunging for her father to check his condition.

Simon holds his hands up in surrender. "What do you want, then, Dr. Ediya?"

"I want you to activate the ship's controls. Then command Saray and Clara to teleport us out of here."

"No need to threaten us to do that," Saray says.

General Ajax, shockingly, seems to agree. "Dr. Ediya, put down the blaster. We're all trying to survive here."

But Melanie Ediya isn't trying to survive, I think. *She's trying to* win.

Simon straps himself in at the controls, using his handprint to wake the ship. With a flip of a switch, he releases the ship's anchor. Artificial gravity kicks back on. My knees almost buckle when my feet hit the ground.

"Atmo's gone," he reports tersely. "It's now or never. We have to teleport."

Saray, who's just finished helping her dad into a seat, grips his hand and closes her eyes.

Everything goes weightless and dark.

In the nothingness of the between-space, I hear Clara's voice, calm and clear as if she spoke aloud. *::Jed, as soon as the teleport is over, I need you to duck.::*

::Why?::

I guess she'd rather not explain her plan. I hear nothing else.

A heartbeat later, we're back in gravity once more. This time, I let my knees go out and drop to the ground.

Melanie waves her blaster at me, commanding, "Get up," sharply.

"I think I'm injured," I lie, holding my calf. "Can you help me strap into a seat?"

And then Saray teleports again, this time by herself, without pulling the rest of the ship with her. She disappears from next to Alan and materializes directly in front of Melanie, seizing her around the wrist and digging in her nails to force the geneticist to drop her blaster. With her other hand, she grips Melanie's chin and looks straight into her eyes.

"You need rest," she says.

I expect Dr. Ediya to fight back, but she stays frozen, held by Saray's gaze. Then I notice Clara approaching from behind, her eyes closed in concentration, hands outstretched. They're working together.

A chill runs down my arms. I've seen a lot of people do a lot of ethically dubious and outright evil things, but this might be the scariest shit I've ever witnessed.

"You're so, so tired." While Clara's eyes remain closed, Saray's are wide open, holding Melanie in thrall. "This is all so inconvenient. You ought to just give up."

"N...no..." It's weak, but Dr. Ediya is fighting back.

Honestly, having been on the wrong end of Saray's compulsion before, I'm impressed the geneticist can even think straight. But then again, we're talking about the mind who *created* Saray's mind. They can't hold her forever.

Simon stands up from the ship's controls. "Authority General Davan Ajax."

The General looks up, startled. "Yes, Your Majesty?"

"As heir apparent to the Imperial Throne, I command that you arrest Dr. Melanie Ediya for threatening my royal consort." Simon throws his shoulders back. "Take all her weapons and gag her."

There's a tense moment where I'm not sure General Ajax is going to comply. But then he nods and says, "Yes, Your Majesty," and gets out his magcuffs.

Saray and Clara step away from Melanie, both releasing a tense breath in unison.

"Where are we?" Simon asks Saray quietly. "Where did you take us?"

I turn to look out the viewport and instantly recognize the violet gem of a planet below us, encircled by its silver rings.

"Halcyon," I murmur.

At the same time, Saray glances at her father and smiles before answering, "Home."

Chapter 48

HALCYON'S KNIGHT STATION

SARAY

It was a risk bringing Halcyon's worst enemy into its orbit. But for some reason, in the heat of the moment, with the moon I called home vaporizing into an asteroid field around me, my home planet was the only place I could think of to go.

Simon contacts the Knights' space station in orbit. He tells them that we're refugees from the Moon Palace, and they invite us to dock. As Simon steers us toward the station, the rest of us collapse into stunned silence. The magnitude of what we've just been through is starting to hit.

All my clothes are gone, is my embarrassingly shallow first thought. I'd been building that wardrobe since my early twenties—from reworked castoffs given to me by Geneva, to bespoke designer pieces I'd saved up for with credits I earned working in a boutique long before I ever set foot on the Moon Palace. Not to mention the expensive collection of cosmetics and hair products I'd amassed. I'm not terribly attached to any of my other possessions, but the loss of my wardrobe hurts. It feels like starting my life from zero.

Then, as memories dredge up of getting dressed with my fellow ladies, the grief hits. *Nuala. Pearl. Kina. Yumiko.* I can only pray they managed to evacuate—but, knowing how tightly Jinan kept them locked down, I doubt it. None of them deserved this fate.

And Geneva. After Dr. Valik disappeared with her bleeding body, I never had a chance to find out if she lived or died. If she was still on the Moon Palace when it blew, she's gone as well.

Alan reaches for my hand, and I smile at him, fighting back tears at the bruises marring his face. I thought I wasn't going to be able to save him. I suppose I have Melanie to thank for that, if absolutely *nothing* else.

There's a shudder as we maneuver into the Knight station's docking bay. The Authorities around me mutter amongst themselves—I think they've finally realized that the tides have turned against them. They start stripping their red uniform coats off, stuffing them behind the seats.

General Ajax doesn't, though. He holds himself stiff and proud, chin high despite wearing the enemy's colors. And when the Knights board us to check our IDs, he hands over his weapons and submits to being cuffed.

One of his soldiers interjects, "Don't hurt us. We serve the new Emperor now."

This does not relax the Knights. Not until Simon sighs and says, "I think they mean me."

Several Knights transfer their aim from the Authorities to Simon. Jed jumps in front of him, arms out. "Whoa, whoa, whoa. It's not what you think. Simon might be in the line of succession, but he's not interested in taking the throne. Right, Simon?"

"I've spent the last several years working to dismantle the Empire," Simon confirms. "I support the right of every planet to democratically rule itself. If I take the throne, my first and only action will be to sign that into law."

The Knights relax...but only enough to stop pointing their blasters at him. "Cuff him as well," a soldier barks.

"Wait—no!" Jed doesn't have a weapon on him, but he looks ready to start swinging. "Call my friends. Leo Galway, Natalia Lantz, Derek Arbor,

Chaz Rathurr. They used to be Knights. They'll tell you—Simon's been helping us. He's not like the former Emperor at all."

"If that's true, he'll be released shortly," the Knight responds. "We're taking all of you into custody until your identities and intentions can be verified."

"What about the Ambassador?" I interject. "He needs a healer."

The Knight gives Alan an up-and-down glance and winces. "He'll be under guard in the infirmary. We need to investigate his connection to a recent alleged kidnapping."

Well, I guess that's fair. Annoying, though. I put out my wrists for the magcuffs and sigh. Wish they'd let me change out of this bulky spacesuit first. It's chafing my bare skin in all the wrong places.

We don't have to wait around in the Knights' station for too long. Jed's old teammates get word that he survived the explosion and rush to join us, abandoning the rebellion on Monroe.

The only warning we get is the whir of the reinforced prison door unlocking before the room is full of Natalia/Andi's loud presence. She throws her arms around Jed and pounds him on the back, yelling at him not to scare her like that ever again.

Derek/Forrest, Leo/Kyle, and Chaz/Nigel follow her in, crowding the cell. Simon stands shyly back in the corner until Natalia pulls him into a hug, too. I glimpse his wide, startled eyes over her shoulder.

Leo doesn't hug Clara, but he puts his hand on her shoulder and whispers something in her ear that makes her tear up and grin widely at the same time. "Thank you!" she exclaims, flinging her arms around him. Leo makes such a disgusted face that I snort a laugh.

"We thought you guys were exed for sure," Natalia's saying. "How the blazes did you escape at the last minute like that?"

"I'm not entirely sure," is Jed's rueful answer. "It was close. Y'all managed to time your attack to help us escape execution, so, uh, thanks."

"Man, we all but started a coup to hijack the controls and get them to stop shooting," Leo says. "We kept saying one of our own was down there, but General DeSanto was willing to make the sacrifice because our window before the Authorities responded to the threat was so small. He said you'd rather give your life than see the Empire win."

"It worked out in the end," Jed says, patting Leo on the shoulder. "Thanks for caring, though, Kyle."

"Jar!" Derek, Leo, and Natalia chorus in unison. Then the three of them start cracking up laughing. "We're trying to get used to calling each other our real names again, so the Wrong Name Jar's been repurposed."

"Fuck you guys," Jed grumbles, but taps his keycuff to transfer them a credit. "You know, that means you have to start calling me Jaired."

"Come get dinner in the mess hall and we'll practice," says Natalia. "You're released."

Jed takes a step forward, then stops and glances at me and Simon. "How about them?"

"Uh..." Leo scratches the back of his neck awkwardly. "So, they're still working on clearing them. It'll probably be at least a couple more hours..."

"Then I'm staying," Jed says. "Wouldn't mind if you guys brought us dinner, though."

Natalia groans in protest, but Derek nods. He hasn't said much this whole time—not really one for gushy shows of affection, that guy—but now he says, "Proud to have you on our team, Jaired. Loyalty is the mark of a good soldier."

"I think," Jed says, reaching for Simon's hand, "that I might need a break from being a soldier, actually. What do people do when the battle is over, and they just want to rest?"

"Settle down on a farm and raise a family," Leo says, with a wistful note that reminds me that my sister is waiting for him in a farming town on some nowhere planet.

"Go to the fucking beach," Natalia says.

Derek offers, "I might try to get another university degree."

Simon, very quietly, says, "I've always wanted to be a private investigator."

"Maybe," Jed says with a smile, "I'll try out being a rockstar for real."

Derek groans. "You're going to have to find a new band. If I never have to perform again, it'll be too soon."

"If I never have to *hear* you perform again, it'll also be too soon," Natalia snarks.

"Excuse me, Miz Set-the-Keyboard-Synth-to-Autoplay..."

Jed's team disappears out the door, amicably ribbing each other. I force a smile and look away as Jed and Simon share a kiss, wishing I could leave them to their private bubble.

"What are you doing after this, then, Saray?" Simon asks.

I whip my head back around. "Me? I..."

There are two planets left in the universe that I have a reasonable claim to call home. First, there's Halcyon—Alan's home, a peaceful place that will come away relatively untouched by this war. At least ten of my siblings still live quiet lives there, suppressing their gen-mod abilities. And yet, I can't imagine settling back into that world. For a short time, to rest, perhaps. To help my father recover. After that...

The other option is Monroe, and the Haven community.

Monroe will be a dangerous place as the galaxy transitions away from Imperial rule. A planet that was so heavily Empire-loyalist will likely elect a former noble as their new leader, potentially even try to conquer some of the other worlds. If I settle on Monroe, among the very revolutionaries who set this whole thing in motion, I will have to accept that this war isn't over for me. My abilities will continue to be sought after—potentially dangerous to me and anyone I love.

But I can make a difference. I can *help* people.

"I think I'll return to Monroe," I say. After a deep breath, I add, "You know, Hepburn City's a big place. Lots of crime to be investigated. Lots of music venues in need of talent. If...if you two wanted to come with me?"

I'm embarrassingly gratified when both of them break into enormous grins.

Chapter 49

HEPBURN CITY, MONROE TO HALCYON'S KNIGHT STATION

RODAN

When the Moon Palace shatters, I break with it.

The Tarantula team camps out in a subtrain station along with scores of other protesters, waiting for a snowstorm to pass so they can get back to besieging the Authority Headquarters. We watch the Palace break apart on what's supposed to be a live feed, though it lags several minutes behind due to the distance.

"Did they get out?" Chaz asks softly through furred fingers pressed to his mouth. "You did get a message through, before...?"

"I sent the message," Leo says. "I don't know if they got it. General DeSanto will have gone for the Palace's comms first."

No one will have gotten a message to Clara. She's a prisoner, trapped at that whelp Jinan's whim. The best I can hope is that he escaped and took her with him.

No. I can't bring myself to hope that Jinan survived. Even if it means Clara also didn't.

I stare into space, unhearing and unseeing, for what must be hours. All I can think about is her last moments. Whether she was afraid. Whether she was alone. Whether she thought of me. *I'm sorry. I'm sorry. I'm sorry. I never should have left you.*

When I come to, it's because Natalia slaps me. Hard.

I reel back, my arm coming up late to defend myself. "Whoa! Hey!"

"We've been calling your name for several minutes, Quell," she says, folding her arms. "We just got word that Saray, Jed, and Simon escaped the blast with Melanie Ediya and some of the Authorities. And your partner's with them."

I'm so numb, it almost doesn't register. "Don't say things like that," I mumble. "Don't get my hopes up."

"The Chief Knight sent us a list of survivors' names himself. Clara Seranath. That's her name, right?"

My heart tentatively begins to beat again. Then faster, faster. I push myself to my feet, stiff and aching from overexertion. "Take me to her." It comes out a flat monotone, not for lack of emotion behind it. "Take me to her *now.*"

The team is more than willing, though they have to jump through several hoops to get us permission to leave. The Authorities who formerly ran Air Traffic Control have been replaced by Greenjackets, who are being extremely stingy with who's allowed on and off the planet. They're funneling all new arrivals through a stringent vetting process, trying to catch any straggling Imperial loyalists.

Once we finally get the green light to leave, I jitter in my seat the whole flight. We've been given little information about the state our friends are in. I'm praying—for once in my decidedly un-spiritual life—that I'll find Clara alive, well, and unharmed. But watching the palace explode has me fearing the worst.

We get another round of questioning once we dock at the Knights' station. Emperor Soren's declaration of war obviously put them on edge. I can hardly blame them, but it's nearly impossible to sit calmly and cooperate, to let their dragons sift through my mind, when they refuse to answer my questions about Clara in return.

After what feels like an eternity, they release me. The Tarantula team skated right through, the little fuckers. I guess it's because they used to be Knights.

They lead me to their "holding zone," basically a row of prison cells. One cell contains a group of Authorities, missing their jackets but still recognizable by their severe haircuts, tight pants, and glum faces. I flash a rude gesture at the Authority General as I pass.

Melanie Ediya sits in a cell by herself, poised like a queen waiting to receive her court. She has her eyes closed, her hands in her lap. I imagine, after abetting the Emperor in trying to destroy Halcyon, she'll remain imprisoned for the rest of her life. She's lucky the Knights don't believe in execution. I doubt the Greenjackets would've been so considerate.

Finally, we come to a cell that emanates jubilant laughter and chatter from inside. As the Knight unlocks the door for me, a hush falls. The Tarantula team is inside, sharing a meal with Jed, Simon, and Saray. Clara sits against the wall, a bowl of soup cupped in her palm, looking troubled.

When her golden eyes meet mine, my soul lights up.

I hear her voice inside my head, tentative, like she doesn't dare believe I'm real. ::*Ro?*::

::*You're alive,*:: is all I can think to say back.

The soup bowl tips to the floor. She flies across the room to me, flinging her arms around my neck. I lift her up and tuck my chin into the crook of her neck.

"You all are free to go," says the Knight loudly. "The Chief Knight cleared everyone in this cell. If you'd like to follow me to the guest quarters..."

The others file out, leaving Clara and me alone in the cell with the door standing open.

Clara loosens her tight squeeze on me only to reach up and kiss me five times in quick succession, then one long one, her hand cupping my cheek. "They threatened to kill you," she whispers. "I thought I'd never see you again."

"Same here." I comb my fingers through her pale hair. "Is Jinan dead? Because if he isn't, I'll kill him myself."

"Eaten by his own lake monster!" says Clara with some satisfaction. "I hope it hurt. Guess I'm a widow now."

"Not for much longer." I don't have a bond-gift or any speeches prepared, but fuck it. "Will you marry me? I don't want anyone *else* to get there first."

A smile breaks across her face like rosy pink dawn. "Ro..."

"I suppose it's fine if you'd rather wait," I babble. "We haven't really talked about registering our bond officially. But I want you to know that it nearly killed me to hear you were Jinan's wife. I knew then that I'd never get over you."

Her smile fades into a pensive frown. "He wanted magical heirs more than anything. Not that I would have let him touch me. But Ro, is it all right with you if I never want to have children? We've never discussed it because, well, it would take extra effort for the two of us to even try. But I...I just can't put this danger on another human being. I've lived most of my life in fear that someone will use my loved ones against me to force me to hurt people. No one should live like that."

I laugh. "Clara, darling, I don't even *like* children. I'm happy keeping you to myself."

"Then yes," she says, pressing her lips to mine.

I let myself sink into her softness, but only for a moment. When we pull apart, I lean my forehead against hers and say, "I don't know where we're going to live. The Moon Palace blew up with all our things on it. Hepburn City is probably on fire by now."

Clara nods slowly. "We could go back to Haven. I know you have a complicated history with them, but I think they mean to work for the common good. Now that the Empire is in shambles, they'll be helping people rebuild from the ground up. We could be a part of that."

I shudder. "I'm sorry, love, but I don't think I could do that, even for you. I've stared down the barrel of mortality a few too many times this week. I just want to find somewhere to hide until things blow over."

She nods solemnly. "I feel the same way," she says, to my relief. "It may be selfish, but...when I was the Emperor's 'guest,' I saw so much darkness and cruelty and despair in people's heads. I can't bear to be around more of it. I need rest." She gestures at the station around us. "Halcyon is my home planet, you know. I grew up in a community here. We could stay here as long as you want."

"The dragons don't exactly like me. In fact, they swore never to help me again." That'll be a long story for later. "Do you think they'll let me stay?"

"Yes," says Clara without hesitation. "I know you've done bad things in the past, Ro, but it's your intent for the future that counts. Do you plan to hurt anyone?"

I think of Prince Miles and Alan Lake. The guilt that wracked me after what I did to them, and the horrible consequences I never intended. And before that, my involvement with Melanie Ediya and Clara's brother Raoul, a situation that could have destroyed the life of this woman I care for so deeply.

"Never again," I vow. No more plotting and scheming. "I just want to live in peace."

"Well, there you have it, then." Clara smiles.

"Maybe...after a few months of rest, we'll feel ready to help." I hear the uncertainty as I'm saying it. I want to believe I'm not just running away, that someday I can begin to make amends for my past mistakes. But I don't think I have any more bank heists or kidnappings left in me.

Clara puts her hand to my cheek. "There are all kinds of ways to help in dark times. Being on the front lines is only one of them. Ro, you've always excelled at making art that reminds people how to laugh and cry and love against all odds. I'd argue that's one of the most lasting ways to transform the world around you. You don't have to force yourself to be a fighter if you aren't one. The galaxy has need of bards, too."

"And of wizards." I laugh, kissing her forehead.

She smiles. "Saray and I aren't the last of our kind, you know. I have a dozen siblings down there on Halcyon. I bet I even have a handful of niblings by now. Someone needs to teach those kids to control their powers as they grow into them. They need to know the stories of what we've been through. I want them to know their own strength, so they won't ever be coerced into using their abilities as a tool for harm."

"I can't think of a better teacher than you," I tell her.

Her grin turns cheeky. "I can think of one."

"Oh, stop—"

She giggles. "But I'm serious, Ro. You're the master storyteller I learned from. I want you to help me tell this one, over and over again, until the lesson is learned."

"And what lesson is that?"

There's pain in her golden eyes as she says, "No one should ever hold absolute power over another's life, or body, or mind."

One Week Later

DAYONE

Year 3750 DE, Week 47

Chapter 50

HEPBURN CITY, MONROE TO HAVEN SETTLEMENT

SARAY

T he home I left on Monroe is well and truly gone.

After the Knights released Jed, Simon, and me, we returned with Jed's band to the front lines of the Hepburn City uprising. Haven had already moved from its old community building, leaving the place bare and empty, but it was stunning how much else changed around it in just one week.

The bustling city of my memory had locked down, rich families hiding in houses ringed with security bots for fear of insurgents encroaching to claim their land and imprison them as Imperial loyalists.

When I lived in Hepburn City, it was all but a crime to be seen without full makeup and a designer robe. Now, the only people who roam the streets freely are dressed in simple tunics, the "peasant" clothing of farmers or miners. At first, I thought the poorer classes must have risen up and killed all the wealthy people who live here. Then I looked closer and recognized the face of a famous actor under a ragged hood or a popular singer wearing trousers with holes. This is simply a new fashion trend, brought on by sheer desperation as the former privileged class scrambles to telegraph that they are no threat.

My first thought was, *Pearl would be simultaneously horrified and impressed*. And then came the pang of loss. Pearl and Kina will never get the chance to design miner-core fashion. They'll also never be able to loudly bemoan their hatred of this trend.

Peace will be a long time coming, both for the city I love, and for my own soul.

So when I receive a message from Glenna Ediya inviting me to Haven's new colony, I accept with relief. Maybe my family and friends there will provide some guidance for weathering this chaos.

The agent Glenna sends to guide us to Haven's new home is none other than my little sister. Miri arrives at Clooney Spaceport in the passenger seat of Leo's shuttle, a vessel which is technically for Greenjacket business. His team chose to pretend they didn't know that he'd deserted and flown to Susannah to see Miri as soon as the rest of us were relatively safe.

The two of them are as pink-cheeked as teenagers, holding hands as they disembark to greet me. Miri squeezes me with one arm while her other hand remains entwined in her partner's. "I'm so glad you're safe! News was spotty on Susannah, but we heard about the Moon Palace, and...well, when Leo told me you made it, I was so relieved I almost cried."

"Almost?" Leo teases.

"Hush, you." She sticks out her tongue. "Come on, Saray. There's someone on board who wants to say hi."

I climb up the ramp and peer into the shuttle's passenger bay. Perched in one of the seats, playing with a wooden puzzle toy, is Prince Miles, alive and well.

Until this very moment, I didn't realize how much anxiety I'd been holding for him. It releases in a rush, and...ah, shit, now it's my turn to cry with relief.

Pressing my hand to my mouth, I gulp back sobs as my shoulders shake. Miri finally disengages from Leo to rub my back. The strong rush of emotion fades into manageable joy and relief at seeing Miles safe. I let out a shaky breath, using my sleeve to dab under my eyes.

"Nice trick," I murmur. If it was anyone else, I might believe she just has a really calming touch—but it's my sister. An Ediya Experiment. I know better than to underestimate us.

Miri smiles. "It comes in handy when I work shifts at the healing center. Easier to set a broken arm when the patient isn't hyperventilating."

After a calming breath or three, I approach Miles and kneel next to his seat. "Hey, kid. Remember me?"

When he looks up from his toy, I get to watch his whole face light up. "Saray!" he exclaims. "You're back! Are you going to take me home to Mama?"

My heart breaks all over again.

Miri steps in and says, "Yes, Miles, today you get to see Mama."

I look at her, eyebrows raised. *Is she pacifying the kid or...?*

"Strap in," she tells me. "It's easier to let you go see for yourself."

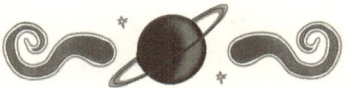

Haven's new settlement is on a planet called Eden.

"There it is," Leo calls, but even as I peer out the viewport, I don't see the dome until we're nearly on top of it. The force-shield camouflages the buildings underneath, tricking the eye into seeing just another swath of jungle.

I gaze in awe at the vibrant landscape as we swoop closer. "How has the Empire not claimed this planet? Are all the trees poisonous?"

"Actually, they did," says Miri. "Centuries back, there was a human settlement here. Their terraforming efforts went awry, and the ecosystem collapsed. Everything died. Eden was categorized as a dead planet and abandoned. If you check the Imperial records on the uniweb, it still says that."

"But it all grew back in the end."

Miri nods. "No one knows how, but isn't that amazing? Life always finds a way."

The dome opens to let us land. As soon as the camouflaging effect is gone, the settlement comes into view. There are several small houses and long compound buildings with solar roofs, with more in progress nearby. The exposed bones of the houses show that the walls are made of a lattice of branches covered in mud.

We land in a grassy field next to a small fleet of starships, mostly two- to four-seaters. Compared to the Knights or the Greenjackets, Haven doesn't look much like a rebel organization. Thinking back to Glenna's many rants about her philosophy when I lived with them, I wonder if they ever really were. All that scheming, mad science, and secret infiltrating to bring down the Emperor...and it was for what? Not to take the Emperor's place.

It was for this. For freedom.

A small group gathers to greet us when we step off the ship. At the forefront are the rest of my Ediya Experiment siblings associated with Haven: Rosa, Harris, Ian, Fatima, and Talia. We're only missing Clara and our late brother Raoul.

Miles clings shyly to Miri, searching the crowd with wide eyes. I don't notice Geneva among them, though.

There's a round of hugging, which I reluctantly participate in before asking, "Did you all hear from Clara?"

"Oh, yes, she contacted us days ago." The voice belongs to Glenna Ediya. She sweeps in, regal even in her old age, which she refuses to have artificially reversed, and envelops me in a floral-scented hug. "I am so thankful the two of you were able to help each other survive. It sounds as though you've been through the vortex together."

I'm surprised by a sudden flash of anger at Glenna's words. She's the one who sent me there, after all. She knew full well that I might not make it back.

I swallow it, though, because I agreed to go with the same knowledge. And I made it out, didn't I? I wouldn't change anything I did, even though...well, I wish I could have saved more people, that's all.

"I have plenty of stories, that's for sure," I say dryly. "Is Adina here? Seems pretty quiet."

"Actually, we had a heads up you might be coming for a visit, or we wouldn't be here either," says my sister Rosa. "Glenna's had us out in the field on a bunch of different planets—educating people, distributing aid, helping plan elections, all sorts of stuff. Haven's been building up to this moment for a lifetime. This is our home base, but we're not gonna hole up here to sit out the war."

I nod approvingly. I should have known my siblings and the peaceful rebellion built around them wouldn't be idle during this crisis.

"Come," says Glenna. "Adina is in the healing center. She has something she wants to tell you. Bring the boy."

I take Miles's hand and follow Glenna toward one of the compound buildings. It's been five years since I've seen my biological mother's face or heard her voice. Hearing Alan relay messages between us just wasn't the same.

Glenna pushes through the beaded curtain into the compound's main entrance and leads us down the corridor to a side room. She taps on the door. "Adina," she calls in a soft voice, like she's trying not to wake a sleeping child. "Saray and Miles are here."

"Saray!" I hear the exclamation, the rustle of a quick rise, and then footsteps as my mother rushes to greet me. She pushes aside the door and envelopes me in a tight hug.

I swallow hard to keep myself from bursting into tears again. No matter how long it's been, my mother's arms feel like home. I was in my early twenties the first time I met her, but even then, I trusted her instantly—a face that looked so similar to mine.

"Mom." My voice trembles. *Ugh, how embarrassing.* "I made it."

"Of course you did." She kisses my forehead, then both my cheeks. "My brave, strong daughter."

She's tugging my hands, pulling me into the room. It's mud-walled, like the rest of the buildings, but there's a clean smell and a soft rhythmic beep of machinery. I wonder for a second if Alan's made his way here, but my father was recovering in a Refuge on Halcyon when I last saw him. His physical injuries healed quickly, but the mental ones, he said, would take time and counseling.

Glenna falls back, smiling in her enigmatic way.

I squeeze my mother's hand as she leads me forward. "Mom, what—?"

"There's someone who's been wanting to see you."

My heart stops for a moment. I step through the doorframe and see the figure lying on the cot, and the tears I almost shed in my mother's arms break the dam and flood out.

"*Geneva!*"

My lady's head is shaved and swathed in bandages. A floral headwrap makes a cheery attempt at disguising the damage to her skull, but she's clearly very weak. Some of the roundness has sapped from her cheeks, leaving her looking older than I've ever seen her look. But she's alive, eyes open, lucid and smiling as I enter.

Miles shrieks with delight when he sees Geneva and immediately climbs up onto her bed. He lies in the crook of her arm, snuggling with her, as tears run freely down Geneva's face.

"My son," she says, over and over. "My son, my son."

Tears prick my own eyes at the blissful look on both their faces.

"You *lived*. You made it out." That's what I intend to say, but it comes out as a barely coherent wail as I dash forward and fall to my knees at her bedside, grabbing her hand.

"Yes," Geneva murmurs. "I am alive." Her speech sounds a little slurred, unfamiliar in her own mouth.

Adina isn't the only one in the room with her. A blonde femme I vaguely recognize as the doctor who saved her life sits at her side, reading diagnostics on a scroll-tablet as they run a scanning device over her forehead.

"Looking good, Lady Milagro," they say, smiling. "The implant is functioning well with your organic brain, and the nanites should finish the bulk of their repairs in another week or two. Though you should be careful not to do any strenuous activities for another month while the cybernetics fully assimilate in your system."

"Cybernetics?" I turn what has to be an alarmingly wet face to them. "You saved her by making her a cyborg?"

"No one will ever have to know," Dr. Valik says with a wink. "You'd never know *I* have a cyborg brain, would you?"

I gape.

"I had intended to petition the ruling council to revise the laws restricting cybernetic brain enhancements while I was on the Moon Palace." Their lips twist ruefully. "Then somebody got the hilarious idea to blow up the entire council. Now I'll have to start over with a new government."

"After what you've done to save Geneva," Adina says, "Haven will make it our personal project to ensure your lifesaving surgery technique is legalized under new governments." She presses her palms together. "Again, Dr. Valik, we can never thank you enough."

"I was simply in the right place at the right time. As my wife keeps saying, it was fortunate that I needed to take Lady Milagro offworld for proper treatment—otherwise I'd have been on the moon when it blew." Dr. Valik stands up. "The scans look great. I'll leave our patient to rest, but please do call me if anything comes up."

They let themself out, leaving me, Adina, and Miles alone with Geneva.

I wipe my eyes on the bedcover, trying to reclaim control of my emotions. "I'm sorry, my lady," I say, "but I didn't have a chance to save your other ladies-in-waiting. Yumiko, Pearl, Kina, and Nuala are dead."

Geneva's face contorts, like she's relearning how to make the proper expression of sadness. A tear drips down from her eye. "Not your fault," she says haltingly, reaching out to take my hand.

I squeeze back.

Adina perches on the edge of the bed next to Geneva, facing me. "Saray, there's something I have to tell you. I should have said something before you left for the Moon Palace five years ago, but Glenna said it was better to keep the secret. After I almost lost both of you...I think the time has come."

She puts her hand over where Geneva's and mine are clasped. "When I was a young girl—barely nineteen!—I fell in love with the most beautiful girl I've ever seen. She stepped into the food shop where I worked, and I thought I might die if I didn't get her call code. We dated for three months before she told me that she was a gen-mod child, created in a lab. Not because her parents had modded her for good health and beauty, but because a rebel organization needed a beautiful girl as bait for a wicked Emperor. She had been raised with this knowledge, that this was her task. Though she could have refused it—because these rebels were not heartless—she had chosen to go through with it, because she believed she could save many lives. She told me she couldn't be with me, and it broke my heart into pieces."

I look between the two of them, my jaw hanging open. "You two—dated? Before Geneva was married to the Emperor?"

"Not only that." Adina smiles a small, sad smile. "As a parting gift, Geneva gave a sample of her DNA to the Ediyas to create what they said would be a superhuman child to change the next generation of humans.

And I did the same, with the instructions that our DNA only be used to create a child together. A child who would be half of each of us."

My head spins. In a small voice that sounds nothing like my own, I say, "Me?"

Adina and Geneva both nod. Another tear slips out of Geneva's eye.

"During the time she was married to the Emperor, we were completely and totally separated," Adina says. "Glenna forbid me from sending messages to her, in case the Emperor discovered it and executed us both for infidelity. But Geneva couldn't accept that. She asked a certain princex, who was indebted to Geneva for helping them escape their father's wrath, to be our go-between. For years, all Geneva and I had were coded love letters, written on edible paper and slipped into her hand during public appearances."

"Simon," I breathe.

He'd passed one of those messages to Geneva at the concert, before I even knew his name. In the confusion of the last few weeks, I had entirely forgotten that mystery.

"Then, when an opportunity came to send her a lady-in-waiting—someone she could rely on, someone who could assist her in finally freeing herself from that slimy Emperor—I convinced Glenna that it had to be you." She smiles. "It helped that you were naturally suited to the role: fashionable, charming, with an excellent nose for bullshit."

"I had no idea," I stutter.

I knew Geneva was older than she let on, but old enough to be my mother? That means she spent thirty-plus years trapped in the Emperor's clutches. What a horrible exile to undergo for the slightest chance at killing him—only to choke when she had the best chance because of her love for her child.

My hand goes to my mouth. "Does this make Miles my...?"

"Brother," says Geneva, running her fingers through the boy's hair. "Miles, love, did you know Saray is your big sister?"

The kid lifts his head, inspecting me from the safety of his mother's arms. "Oh," he says, then goes back to hugging Geneva.

I chuckle. "He's not going to let you out of his sight ever again."

"Good." Geneva sighs in contentment.

Adina strokes my cheek. "You look rattled, Saray. Talk to me. Is this all too much?"

"No," I say, surprised to find that I mean it.

I used to think I was better off not getting too close to anybody so they couldn't be used to hurt me. But I've realized that the people who bring out my vulnerable side are a strength, not a weakness. They push me to do what feels impossible, in the name of creating a better world for us all.

With my newfound family and friends at my back, the possibilities of the future unfold before me. I am free, entirely my own. No responsibilities, no nobility to tell me what to do. I can do anything I want.

I choose to make them proud.

Three Years Later

DAYSEVEN

YEAR 3753 DE, WEEK 9

Chapter 51

HEPBURN CITY, MONROE

SARAY

This is my favorite part. The part where the vaulted, stained-glass double doors to the courtroom swish open, and I step through, my heeled shoes making dramatic clicks against the tile floor.

I take my time walking to the stand. Let the crowd admire my outfit, which, by the way, looks *fine*: a dramatic, curve-hugging, translucent black robe over a saffron-yellow minidress. My hair is hidden in a matching golden headwrap. As always, I wear a mask to hide my identity. The one I've chosen today is shaped like a fox head.

I don't *have* to make a dramatic entrance—I could just show up at the beginning of the trial and stay for the remainder—but I'm a busy woman. I have about five of these appearances a day, and I still have to make time to do my fashion design homework.

I pause at the head of the aisle, glancing at the defendant to refresh my memory on this case. Ah, right. This is the guy who was accused of consistently underpaying employees while pocketing the difference. I interviewed him last week, despite his defender strongly objecting to it.

"Truthsayer," intones the judgebot, "submit ID for verification." A pair of human judges flank the sharp, rectangular shape of the AI that reviews evidence and rules whether it warrants conviction. I approach and allow the bot to scan my keycuff.

The bot is the only entity in this courtroom who can confirm the Truthsayer's identity. I've taken care to maintain my privacy, especially as word of someone with my abilities got out. I've been all over the newsies. There's even an upcoming holo-drama about me, dramatizing how I've never been wrong about a conviction, even when evidence is lacking.

Lots of people think I'm a false magician who simply reads people well, like the fortune-tellers in their street-fair tents. But the Peacekeeper force, our reformed law enforcement agency, has gone to great lengths to test my skill and confirm its accuracy.

"Verified." The bot emits a warbling tone that I like to interpret as clearing its throat. "What is your recommendation in this case, Truthsayer?"

"I recommend a guilty verdict," I say. The mask distorts my voice as I speak. "In our interview on Week 8, Dayfive..." I spend several minutes laying out every single lie the defendant told me. Out of the corner of my eye, I see him cringing as I speak.

His defender lets her head fall into her hands, groaning audibly.

There was already plenty of evidence to convict the man; he definitely did the crime he's accused of. But his defender was trying to play the "He didn't realize what he was doing" card to get a lighter sentence, which was when the prosecutor called me in. I relish the victory of stopping yet another corrupt person from quietly gaining power through stealing money from people who trust him.

It's not always this easy. Sometimes, people commit crimes for reasons that make me pity them. Even though the fighting has mostly ended on Monroe and a lot of work has gone into redistributing wealth to make sure everyone has enough, there are still people who slip through the cracks. Revenge killings done against former nobility are common.

Politically, the galaxy is far from settled. A handful of princexes have turned up and tried to claim the throne, even though Simon officially ended the Empire's rule three years ago. Planets that were severely exploited by the old regime have sent envoys requesting restitution for their suffering. There's been a long-drawn-out argument over whether the Galactic Bank Heist was repayment enough or whether they deserve more.

General Royal DeSanto, the Greenjacket leader, even appeared on my defendant stand a year ago. After the Moon Palace fell, the man deserted his own army and went back to piracy, claiming he wasn't any good at being a law-abiding citizen. His son gave a passionate defense of him as a hero deserving leniency, but the man who blew up the Moon Palace still did time in the Hepburn City jail for small-time smuggling. Privately, with the deaths of my fellow ladies-in-waiting still heavy on my heart, I thought he deserved worse.

When I'm done giving my speech, the judgebot warbles again. "In light of the evidence and the Truthsayer's testimony, the defendant is sentenced to the following. Loss of leadership position in his workplace. Fine of sixty thousand credits to go toward repayment of the employees' lost wages. And community service of no less than ten hours per week for the next year."

I nod, smiling under my mask. It doesn't bring me any satisfaction to see people locked away in prison. When the Peacekeepers took over from the Authorities, they recalibrated the judgebot to recommend community service over jail time unless the person was a flight risk or danger to society. As a result, we have a lot more people working to clean up the city, feed their neighbors, and assist people in need than Hepburn City has ever seen.

"May I be excused?" I murmur to one of the human judges.

"We're almost wrapped up here, Truthsayer..."

"I know," I say. "It's just that I have a wedding to get to."

Chapter 52

THE PLANET CERES

JED

I'll admit, after the last wedding I witnessed, I wasn't eager to have one of my own. Not that I figured there'd be a ton of murder at mine. But, y'know, shit like that tends to put a guy off the idea in general.

I should've known better than to doubt my ma.

The first thing she did was swear on Pa's grave that it wouldn't remind me one single bit of the Moon Palace. And she's kept her word.

My sisters spent all week doing the hay barn up with streamers and wildflowers. Ma invited half the town and a fiddle quartet. The neighbors all bring a dish to weigh down the long buffet table against the wall. Rich scents of barbecue sauce, cheesy noodles, and tangy salads drift through the clean night air, making my stomach growl.

We decided not to bother with a public bonding ceremony. Simon and I already registered our union months ago in the Hepburn City courthouse, with Saray as our witness. No, Ma makes sure we get straight to the feasting and dancing.

"Those are the fun parts, anyway," she says with a wink.

Simon leans into me and whispers, "Have I mentioned I love your mom?"

Only about a dozen times over the past few weeks we've been visiting. My ma has been pulling out all the stops hosting us, and Simon is drinking it in. I think it's more bittersweet than he's letting on; I've caught him looking wistfully at his mother's archived uniweb profile a few times. But seeing him love my family as hard as they (and I) love him is the best thing that's happened to me since, well, him.

Ma's in heaven, too. She's been after me to come for an extended stay ever since I messaged her to reassure her that I survived the Moon Palace explosion. I did drop by for a few weekends, but it's taken us longer than expected to extricate ourselves from the mire of Hepburn City politics.

Simon's retirement from government work was recent, but it couldn't come quickly enough. In the weeks immediately following the Moon Palace demise, he leveraged his royal blood to hold claim to the throne just long enough to pen a series of decrees. He dismantled the Empire and granted legal authority to elected designates on every planet. He also cut off payroll to any remaining Authorities left fighting for the former Empire. It was kind of funny how quickly their loyalty dried up once they were no longer getting paid.

After that, he spent about a year working with the Greenjackets, cleaning up loose ends. Some of it was tracking down Imperial nobles who escaped the Moon Palace explosion and wanted to set themselves up as the next Emperor. I'd done a bit of the shooting for missions like that. Most of his work, though, went to helping build the technological infrastructure of a new governing system. Secure voting systems. Propaganda education and uniweb info literacy campaigns. He also consulted with the banks to close loopholes that allowed rich citizens to hide credits in tax-free secret accounts.

He pulled so many twelve-hour days that I started to worry he was going to collapse. When he announced that he would retire now that he had confidence the systems he'd helped start could run without him, I wanted to throw him a party.

Instead, I married him so I had an excuse to take him on a honeymoon.

Our first stop was two weeks on Hades' famous black sand beach, swimming in bath-warm waters and drinking too many cocktails. But when I asked him where he wanted to go after that, he said he wanted to spend time here, on my home planet, surrounded by people I love.

"My ma's going to want to throw us a wedding," I said.

Simon smiled. My spotlight-shy, introverted husband said, "I don't mind."

I didn't quite believe him. Until I saw him with my family.

Right now, Simon's pink-cheeked and laughing, dressed in a simple but smart dark-blue tunic and gray trousers. Ma tried to get him to wear one of Pa's special-occasion robes, but Simon refused.

"I don't want to look like a prince today," he said.

And in the best way possible, he doesn't. He looks like the farm boys I watched out of the corner of my eye at parties when I was growing up: handsome, clean, respectful, a little sunburned. Not fashionable or wealthy, but the kind of man I could trust. The kind of man who'd help Ma with the dishes and compliment her cooking before taking me upstairs and blowing my...mind.

Stars, I'm so gone, it's almost embarrassing.

At this moment, he's about to get pulled into a dance with my sisters. He's taken to them immediately—teasing wild-child Jaynie and dry-witted Tenna. It took seeing him with my family to realize something important about the man I love.

Simon didn't hide himself all those years because he disliked attention. He hid because his identity put him in danger. With the weight of the world off his shoulders, he's finally free to enjoy himself.

I didn't think it was possible to love him *even more*.

"Congratulations, Jed!"

I whirl around. "Director Quell! You made it!"

I sent em the invitation on a whim, not expecting the director to answer. We haven't been in regular contact since the fallout of the Moon Palace destruction—last I heard, e had decided to un-retire from the Monroe theater scene.

Clara clings to eir arm, her platinum-blond hair spilling dramatically over one shoulder. The two of them missed the "farm wedding" memo; they're wearing matching pink silk robes, holo-star makeup, and a glitzy assortment of costume jewelry. Ro's shaven head is crowned with a circlet of fake roses.

I plant my hands on my hips, mock-angry. "It's bad manners to outshine the happy couple."

Ro looks uncertain for a half-second, but Clara grins. "Not my fault you wore that old thing," she tosses back, gesturing at my emerald-green jacket.

I tug at my collar. "Had to pay homage to my years of service as a Greenjacket agent."

"Then you should have worn *no* shirt," Clara says, "and a lot more eyeliner."

"Touché."

Ro cuts in on our banter to ask, "Do you play guitar much anymore?"

I shrug. "Off and on."

The funny thing is, even after all I went through as Jedrek Blaze, I still miss the high of a screaming audience hanging on my every note. These days, when I play gigs, they're in smoke-filled public lounges with audiences of less than a hundred. A few people remember me from my rockstar days, but the hype isn't near what it used to be.

"Can you sing?"

"Depends on who you ask," I say wryly.

Saray would say no. She's been sharing a two-bedroom apartment with me and Simon back on Monroe and complains good-naturedly whenever I "caterwaul at all hours of the night." Although Simon swears he's seen her wiping tears when I play a wistful ballad.

Ro taps eir keycuff. "I'm sending you an invitation to audition," e says. "Clara and I have been writing a musical based on the Moon Palace. It's called *BOOM!*. We're looking for cast members."

I can't help but snort a laugh. "Wouldn't that be a little on the nose? Acting myself in a play about stuff that happened to me?"

Clara says, "Trust me, the script's very dramatized. Ro even threw in a romance between you and Saray's character."

I wrinkle my nose. "Seriously?"

"Oh, stop it," Clara says, waving a hand. "It's not *that* far-fetched. I read minds, remember? I know you dated her."

"Yeah, before I thought I had a chance with Simon." I can't help the goofy smile that spreads across my face at the mention of his name. "She's aromantic, anyway. We work better as friends."

"Anyway," says Ro, "I wasn't thinking of auditioning you for Jedrek Blaze. I think you'd make an excellent Emperor Jinan."

A look of horror contorts my face before I can stop it. Then I burst out laughing, surprising all three of us. "He would fuckin' *hate* that."

"We know," says Clara with a wicked grin.

My keycuff *dings* with the received message. I glance over the audition information. I *could* make time for this, actually. My work with the Green-jackets is spotty these days and consists mainly of contract jobs. And it's not like musician gigs grow on trees.

"I'll think about it," I tell Ro. "Thanks for coming, you two."

They drift off to join the dancing. I spot Leo and Miri on the dance floor, giggling at each other as they compete for silliest dance move. Beyond them, the rest of my band are warming the wall and sipping the punch, which Andi—blast it, I mean *Natalia*—spiked. I guess I owe another credit to the jar.

I'm about to go over and tease them about being my backup wedding band when another latecoming group walks in. I grin at the sight of my erstwhile ex and current grouchy roommate, who also decided to ignore the hay-barn dress code and show up in a dress that flows from royal purple at the shoulder to sunset orange at the hem. A gauzy, sparkling cape falls down her back, like the stars coming out at dusk.

Her mothers went the low-key route, however. Both are wearing leggings and wide-sleeved tunics, Geneva in plum and Adina in maroon. Between them, a solemn eight-year-old Miles has his hair combed neat above a plain black shirt and trousers.

"Hey, Miles," Saray says, pointing to me. "Remember Uncle Jed?"

Miles shakes his head uncertainly.

"That's fine. I'm sure his feelings won't be hurt at all." She says the last bit more to tease me than Miles. "Hey, Rockstar. You look happy."

"Hey, Lady." I fold her into a hug. "How was court?"

"Same as ever. The guy got community service."

I nod approvingly. "Your sister Rosa's going to be happy to hear that. She was looking for hospital volunteers. Someone's gotta clean the bedpans."

Saray laughs. "Well, I'm going to go raid the food table. I didn't eat before I left Monroe—I'm *starving*. Come on, Miles, let's go get some cheesy noodles."

Her little brother—and, I realize uncomfortably, my half-brother-in-law—follows her eagerly. Geneva and Adina linger just long enough to each give me a kiss on the cheek and whisper congratulations before they, too, head for the buffet.

I look around for my ma, considering asking her to dance, but abort mission when I see Simon breaking away from the dance floor to run toward me. His eyes are luminous with excitement as he shows me a message on his scroll-tablet.

"Look, Jed! I only put up my ad for private investigative services last week, and it doesn't have my name attached at all. But the uniweb just synced, and I have *two* messages from potential clients!"

I grab him by the shoulders as he all but jumps up and down in front of me. "What'd I tell you, huh? You are the best."

He smacks a kiss onto my cheek, sticky from punch and sweaty from dancing. I hook an arm around his waist and reel him in. "Just promise me you won't do any more twelve-hour days, yeah?"

"I promise I won't let myself get super stressed anymore," he says.

"That's not what I—"

He distracts me with another kiss, this time on the lips. I tug him closer, getting lost in it. I could kiss this man for hours. Three years hasn't been nearly enough time.

"You haven't danced enough tonight," he murmurs against my mouth. "Let's fix that."

A lifetime might just about cover it.

END

*T*hank you for joining me on another *Halcyon Universe* adventure! If you enjoyed this book, please leave a review. Turn the page to subscribe to my newsletter so you can stay updated on future books in the series!

Free short story
with newsletter
signup!

Pirates shouldn't mess with the grandmas who feed them...

Welcome to Grandma Rae and Grandma Toni's cafe, where delicious home-cooked comfort food is served up daily on an asteroid pit stop for long-haul starship pilots. The Waystation's thriving businesses might look like a juicy target for a pirate attack, but watch out! When the grandmas' livelihood is threatened, they won't go down without a fight.

This short story takes place in the Halcyon Universe series after the events of Petrichor Blooms. It can be read standalone.

Sign up for Mindi Briar's newsletter and receive this FREE story in your inbox!

Adrift in Starlight

S tart the Halcyon Universe series from the beginning with cyborg surgeon Tai's story...

When set adrift in the universe, some things are worth holding onto.

Titan Valentino has been offered a job they can't refuse.
Tai, a gender-neutral courtesan, receives a scandalous proposition: seduce an actor's virgin fiancée. The money is enough to pay off Tai's crushing medical debt, a tantalizing prospect.

Too bad Aisha Malik isn't the easy target they expect.
A standoffish historian who hates to be touched, she's laser-focused on her career, and completely unaware that her marriage has been arranged behind her back. This could be the one instance where Tai's charm and charisma fail them.

Then an accidental heist throws them together as partners in crime.
Fleeing from the Authorities, they're dragged into one adventure after another: alien planets, pirate duels, and narrow escapes from the law. As Tai and Aisha open up to each other, deeper feelings kindle between them. But that reward money still hangs over Tai's head. Telling Aisha the truth could ruin everything...

Their freedom, their career, and their blossoming love all hang in the balance. To save one might mean sacrificing the rest.

Available now!

Petrichor Blooms

*U*ncover the origins of the Ediya Experiments...

The hardiest love blooms in the rockiest soil.

Danya Xiang would rather dig potatoes than wield a blaster. Raised as a member of the Greenjacket rebel organization, she's content to stay away from military glory and spend her days in food production—until her soldier twin, Nox, is injured right before a mission. Nox begs Danya to take her place, hoping to use their secret telepathic link to spy through Danya's eyes.

Reluctantly, Danya agrees. But her loyalty to the Greenjackets is stretched to its limits when she's asked to capture university student Amy Ediya, whose mother's valuable genetics research has been missing for a decade. The Greenjackets are convinced that Amy has it hidden.

Danya realizes that, while Amy may not have the research, she's the only one who can find it. The two of them desert the Greenjacket army and Amy's university studies to embark on a quest for Amy's estranged family. As trust grows between them, attraction blooms, too. But that only means they have more to lose when the search draws them into danger.

Available now!

The Invisible Bright

*F*ollow Leo and Miri's courtship in the sequel to Petrichor Blooms...

Can rekindled love survive a plot to destroy the planet?
Miri's secret abilities are ruining her life.

Genetically modified with alien DNA as a child, Miri is now part of a religious order that reveres these very aliens. Her superhuman ability to influence others' emotions often causes chaos. When she's cast out of the Refuge after an emotional misstep, Miri is desperate to suppress powers she never wanted and can't control.

A second chance at love is the last thing Leo wants.

Leo's childhood crush on Miri ended in heartbreak, and now, years later, he's just trying to move on. But when Miri unexpectedly shows up in his hometown, lost and looking for answers, Leo finds it hard to ignore the chemistry still burning between them. She's determined to keep him at arm's length, but their undeniable bond is hard to resist.

Then an impossible murder challenges everything they believe in.

When a shocking crime rocks their peaceful community, Miri and Leo must work together to uncover the truth. As secrets unravel, the investigation pulls them closer and reignites the love they thought was long gone. But Miri's powers have made her a target of dangerous forces that threaten not just their relationship, but the fate of the planet. Trusting the wrong person could mean disaster—both for them and for the world.

Available now!

Coming Soon:

THE BLACK SANDS OF HADES

*S*tay *tuned (via newsletter or Instagram) for more information about my work in progress, a sultry sci-fi beach horror inspired by the Halcyon Universe holodrama "Bikini Vampires of Black Sand Beach."*

Safety Information
(compiled by the Hades Tourism Association
in collaboration with the Hades Ranger Academy)
Thank you for visiting our beautiful planet! We want you to enjoy your stay without accident, injury, or death.
Here are some tips to remember as you vacation on Hades:

1. *The sand remains hot even at night. Prolonged exposure can lead to burns. Protective footwear is recommended while walking on the beach.*

2. *Dawn alarms will sound twice. We recommend that you strive to be underground by the time the first alarm goes off. If you hear the first alarm and you are still aboveground, promptly make your way to approved, climate-controlled underground areas.* ***Do not*** *wait*

until the second dawn alarm.

3. *Do not leave the fenced perimeter of the resort without a certified ranger present.*

4. *Swimming is permitted in designated areas. Do not swim outside of designated areas without a certified ranger present.*

5. *Wildlife attacks are rare, and extremely unlikely within resort boundaries. If the rangers sound an alarm, please exit the water as quickly and calmly as possible and move to a safe location underground until the all-clear is given.*

6. *It is recommended that you keep your suite doors locked and bolted during daylight hours. Hades Resort Co. is not responsible for any thefts or assaults that occur during your stay.*

Acknowledgements

I took my sweet, sweet time drafting *The Taste of Lies*. During the two years that I spent on it, I went through some of the hardest years of my professional career at my day job, I parted ways with my former publisher, and the political climate of my country descended further into madness. In short, I was under a lot of stress and had a lot of simmering rage—of the feminine variety as well as the laboring-under-capitalism variety—and this book ended up being where I put a lot of those feelings. If any part of it resonated with you, I want you to know you're not alone, and we'll get through this together.

My Discordant Owl friends: y'all have been a lifeline. I've learned so much from you, and I don't think I'd have found the courage to self-publish without watching you all absolutely SLAY it first. One of the things I wanted most from a writing career (besides, you know, seeing my books in print) was to find a close community of writers whose work I loved and who I could rely on for mutual support. I couldn't have lucked into a smarter, kinder, or more talented group of humans.

To my editing team: Skye Kilaen, your insight as a beta reader is worth a book's weight in gold. Gabriel Hargrave, thank you for a stellar copyedit and kind words of support. Anyone reading these acknowledgements should go look up both Skye and Gabe's books and read them immediately. I'm grateful to have worked with two such phenomenal authors to polish this book up.

I may never have finished this book without my standing weekend co-working sessions with my friend Chelsea. Some weeks I literally did no other writing than the two hours we spent in a local tea shop, hogging a table on a busy Sunday. Thanks for keeping me accountable!

As always, I have to shout out Joe, my support human through all of the crap I mentioned up there in the first paragraph. You're the reason I continue to believe in the transcendent power of love. (And our fur-children, Comma, Apostrophe, and Nimi, without whom this book would probably have been done sooner.)

Finally, every writer owes a debt to the works that inspire them. As someone who strives to read inclusively, I recommend checking out the following list of M/M romances written by men and transmasc folks.

Adult:

- The Orchid and the Lion by Gabriel Hargrave

- Yours Celestially by Al Hess

- Cat's Got Your Heart by jem zero

- Heir to Thorn and Flame by Ben Alderson

- The Fox and the Dryad by Kellen Graves

Young Adult:

- The Sunbearer Trials by Aiden Thomas

- The Darkness Outside Us by Eliot Schrefer

- Most Ardently by Gabe Cole Novoa

- Teach the Torches to Burn by Caleb Roehrig

- The Extraordinaries by T.J. Klune

About the author

Mindi Briar's favorite book as a child was "Commander Toad in Space," an early sign that she was destined to become a gigantic nerd. She lives in the Seattle area with her husband and three cats, two of whom are named after punctuation marks. She will be your friend if you offer tea, or if you want to talk about Star Wars.

She is the author of the Halcyon Universe sci-fi romance novel series. Her short stories have also appeared in three anthologies, with a fourth releasing soon.

www.ingramcontent.com/pod-product-compliance
Lightning Source LLC
Chambersburg PA
CBHW050008120726
47903CB00006B/1687